The distortion di~~~~~~~~~ as the image cooled, and suddenly the booth contained a woman. A large gold hoop depended from an ear and a brightly colored scarf covered her hair. The medical team scurried forward as the glastic door of the booth slid open. LaMer collapsed through it onto the floor.

Frieda hurried after the medical team. She knelt on the floor and studied LaMer's profile through a gap between two of them. She's beautiful, Frieda thought, skin like a newborn. A medic grasped LaMer's chin and forehead and expertly moved the head to one side. Frieda saw, suddenly, her full face. An empty socket stared accusingly at her and the corner of the mouth under it was drawn up in a sneer.

Frieda tried to stand, but her legs would not hold her. She sat down hard, eyes still on the twisted face. The chatter of the medical team covered her single gasp.

DEUS
EX MACHINA

J. V. Brummels

BANTAM BOOKS
TORONTO · NEW YORK · LONDON · SYDNEY · AUCKLAND

DEUS EX MACHINA
A Bantam Spectra Book / April 1989

ISBN 0-553-27977-7

Published simultaneously in the United States and Canada

Bantam Books are published by Bantam Books, a division
of Bantam Doubleday Dell Publishing Group, Inc. Its trademark, consisting of the words "Bantam Books" and the
portrayal of a rooster, is Registered in U.S. Patent and
Trademark Office and in other countries. Marca Registrada.
Bantam Books, 666 Fifth Avenue, New York, New York 10103.

PRINTED IN THE UNITED STATES OF AMERICA

O   0 9 8 7 6 5 4 3 2 1

for RBR and Cindy,
Josh and Barb,
and for Gilbert Vaughan

Chronology

1945	Old War ends; Cold War begins
1948	Scattered Third World wars
1956	Rock and roll revives the Great Age of Radio
1961	First television president
1965	Cold War ends
1968	The assassinations
1969	Americans walk on the moon
1975	The fall of Saigon
1977	First personal computer marketed
1983	Jesse Blocker marries Willi(??) Jones
1986	End of American space program
1987	The fall
1988	David Jones born
1990	The Sanity Pact signed
1991	America declared "Cable-Ready"
1993	Nine-Nation summit stalemated in ECON–Ø
1994	The Fall
1995	Global Third World wars
1997	First successful transmatation
1999	"New City" Constitution ratified
2000	Worldwide transmission of the Dawn of the New Millenium, a gala celebration of the Union of City-States

Tella,

I've done as you asked. (When haven't I? Allow me this one note of complaint. This Jones of yours is not the easiest background. I had to touch every base in the city to access anything, and moving around in this heat is très difficile.) (Is that why a certain editor hasn't left her office in weeks? Well, it grows worse, madame.)

O-yes-the-clock-is-ticking. The life of Jones: Now resides in that unspellable suburb, in the same house in which he was born. (The packagers will love that.) No record of public schooling. A home-education would not be unusual, given the time-space. Just as likely the records were never posted. A good university education, and slight evidence of his literary presence—an honorable mention in the senior contest.

Considerable number of media fillers pitched and a few produced following graduation. Some remain extant, preserved by a syndicate of ac crits. He has the one good prize to his name and the usual assortment of near-misses. Output has dropped off markedly in recent years, and what was a clear career path has blurred. Maybe he's spent a lot of time on this production.

Now, Tella, here's the dangerous thing: Beyond a small stipend—a pittance, really—for teaching the occasional class through his local Adult Education system, I see no visible means of support. He's not registered with the Guild, and the Monitor shows neither a record of additional income nor allotment status. He's obviously not, living where he does, of independent means. Besides, he was a scholarship student. Anything untoward here might, I fear, negatively impact his standing with the Screening Committee.

Therefore, his nomination is risky.

If you persist (I expect you will), my recommendation (thanks for asking) is that we highlight the accomplishment that this collection represents. Frankly, though what's there is substantial enough to establish credibility, it takes some close familiarity with the field to see it. Not really the kind of research the Screening Committee is likely to want to get grubby doing.

There's more, but equipment is seizing up. I'll keep the references.

Jomo

12:17

The nearest cultural/literary analogue with any Q would be the Utah Lee.

12:18

PART I

1

Record Heat

"Go to hell, little bitch."

If Maybelline had shouted, David wouldn't have bothered. Waiting for the el before work got on everybody's nerves. Trading insults eased the tension. Besides, the crudity of sitters' language was legendary. According to one of David's pet theories, it brought out new customers and kept the old coming back. This time, though, Maybelline's voice had cut the unnatural heat of the evening with a coolness and a certainty that he recognized as dangerous. He left off fiddling with the radio and slid out the Torino's open door.

A meter-high wall of pressed plastic divided the old Kennedy Expressway and the platform of the el and formed a barrier between the suburbs and the New City. Maybelline leaned against it. Ms. Kitty stood upon her toes and arched her neck to glare into the taller prostitute's eyes. Her body quivered with tension, and the line of her jaw was set. The various shades of heavy facepaint, blending in the weird light of sundown, made both faces appear purple with rage. David walked across the wide Expressway to the sitters without any apparent hurry. He pivoted and leaned against the barrier beside Maybelline. Neither woman looked at him. He dropped dark glasses over his eyes. Other scouts and sitters moved away from the scattering of parked cars and took up positions along the barrier. All welcomed the diversion. Many wished to see the competition trimmed. Some hoped for blood.

He watched Ms. Kitty through tinted lenses. If Maybelline made the first move, he doubted he would be fast enough to stop her. "What's the problem?" he asked finally.

Neither gave a sign she'd heard. The moment stretched tauter. When Ms. Kitty blinked, David snaked a hand between the sitters, grasped Ms. Kitty's arm, and turned her away from Maybelline. He draped his arm over her shoulders and walked her back across the Expressway and around the Torino. He opened the passenger's door with his free hand and gave her shoulders an extra squeeze. The tension in her body was all but gone. "Hey," he said, "it's just Maybelline. You know how she can be."

Ms. Kitty turned so that her face was centimeters from his chest. He raised her chin with the crook of his finger. Still she would not meet his eyes. "Hey," he said softly, "I'm your friend. Remember?"

Ms. Kitty shrugged. "She didn't mean anything. She was playing. She called her 'old lady,' like in a joke." Her eyes rose to meet David's.

He smiled. He had tried to stop Ms. Kitty from talking of herself in the third-person, but the habit had proven too strong. It identified her with others her age and distinguished them not only from Insiders but from the older residents of the suburbs as well. David understood that it was a distinction they prized. "Maybelline's touchy about her age," he said, "and maybe it's too hot for a joke." He paused, as if to consider something tangled in her hair. "I'll explain it to her while you do something. Okay?"

Ms. Kitty nodded.

"Find the Blue Baby."

Ms. Kitty's eyes opened wide. "She can sit in front?"

David laughed. Maybelline rode in the front seat, except when they were working. Ms. Kitty sat there, then, but always on some Insider's lap or jammed against the console. "Sure, little sister," David said. "I wouldn't expect you to tune the radio from the backseat." He kissed her on the forehead, lightly, so not to cover his lips with facepaint, and embraced her. He looked across the top of the car to where Maybelline still rested against the barrier. The ring of spectators had disintegrated. He released Ms. Kitty.

"Now, let's see if the Blue Baby's signed on."

Ms. Kitty smiled, nodded, and slid into the seat. She leaned close to the dash to study the radio, selected a knob and twisted it. White noise filled the car, and Ms. Kitty smiled up at David. He smiled back, held up a hand, and rubbed two fingers together. Ms. Kitty turned the knob again and the volume of the static dropped. She chewed a fingernail a moment before selecting another knob. She turned it slowly, her eyes on the red band as it marched through the meaningless numbers of the frequency display.

David reached into the car and turned the visor down. He extracted two cigarettes from the plastic box clipped there. Ms. Kitty looked up from the radio to smile. He returned it and added a wink. When he turned away his face went suddenly blank.

Maybelline took the cigarette he offered, awkwardly, with her left hand. David struck a bookmatch. He nodded to her right hand. It rested near her naked thigh, the palm cupped over the slick surface of the barrier. He lit his cigarette, then Maybelline's, and dropped the match. "You'd have cut that little girl for making a joke?"

Maybelline exhaled a plume of blue smoke. "Maybe."

David let his cigarette dangle from the corner of his mouth. He grasped Maybelline's wrist and twisted her hand around hard. He lifted the razor out of her palm and released her. He moved away along the barrier a step. He looked Inside. The New City lights twinkled in a wide belt that marked efficiency spaces, but the center of the city fell deeper into darkness as he watched. A shift in the breeze wafted smoke into his eyes, and he removed the cigarette from his mouth. He lifted his glasses and examined the razor he held. It was a beautiful antique, brass with ivory inlays polished smooth to the touch and faintly glowing in the failing light. David caught the curved steel tongue in the crook of a finger, and the perfectly balanced blade jumped out as if of its own accord. The razor's edge shone with careful honing. Beautiful, he thought, but difficult to use effectively. Still, he knew Maybelline to be an expert. He rubbed a smoky tear from his eye. Below, the el, its cells sparkling, began to climb toward them.

"Little bitty bitch."

"She's a little girl, a kid," David answered. "There was no reason for you to be hard."

"Yeah, I cut the bitty bitch and the Law comes. Bad for David's business."

"Worse for Ms. Kitty's."

Maybelline's chuckle was forced, thin. David turned and rested the blade against the barrier beside her. She looked at him. "Hard because the bitch's right," she said.

David examined her profile with an experienced eye. Her face was good, though facepaint in the sitters' hallmark pattern—stark, thick, white foundation; scarlet cheeks; blue-and-green splotches around the eyes—obscured age. With the darkness usual for a sitter's business, anyone under twenty-five could pass. When he'd taken her on, years earlier, Maybelline's height had been his one reservation. Perversely, it'd brought premiums from a number of quirky regulars.

Maybelline sighed and settled closer so that her upper arm touched David's. He unsnapped the shoulder bag dangling between them and dropped the razor in. "It's not your age, friend. What you have to look out for is getting hard. You get hard and they won't like you anymore. That's just the way Insiders are. Better to take the face off."

Behind them the el silently slid to a stop. David flicked his cigarette over the curb. Maybelline blinked away a tear forming in the corner of her eye. A muscle spasmed under the facepaint. She jutted her jaw, swallowed once. David's hand shot out, and he grasped her hard by the upper arm. He delicately removed the cigarette from her trembling fingers, took a last hit from it, and dropped the butt between his feet. He leaned over her and whispered, "Won't do to upset Henri's virgin." Cigarette smoke curled around her ear. Maybelline's eyelids fluttered, and the tears began in earnest. "That's right, friend," he said, and the tic subsided. "Just like that." He gripped harder, then let go. He turned and made his way through the other scouts and sitters to the knot of Insiders on the platform. He recognized Henri standing beside a shorter, younger man. His hand shook as he lifted it to wave.

David sat several booths away from Maybelline, Ms. Kitty, and their customers. He concentrated on slurping the last of his butterscotch shake up through a plastic straw. He set the cup on the table but kept his fingers locked around it. He first listened to, then risked a look at, the group. He heard the bass murmur of Henri's voice. He saw the virgin sitting stiffly beside Maybelline. David willed the young man to relax. Henri finished his story, and the women responded with high-pitched giggles. The virgin spoke, and the women's heads pivoted, as if pulled by strings. Henri sat back and casually draped an arm over Ms. Kitty's shoulders. She scooted down the seat nearer him. The virgin's face opened suddenly into a smile that showed no trace of nervousness, and David looked away.

Feldon came out from behind the counter with a damp towel. He marched down the aisle between the booths, his apron flapping across his legs and his eyes straight ahead. When he passed he gave David a wink without averting his attention from something farther on. David returned the wink without looking up.

He concentrated on the empty cup in his hands, the end of the straw jutting up through the plastic top. The patter at the other table had fallen off. His focus narrowed to the white space between two red pinstripes and the tiny dent a tooth had made there. Patience was an indispensible virtue for a scout, he reminded himself. Henri chuckled and the virgin joined in. The sitters giggled.

David's attention to the straw faded. He had nothing to do but wait till the foursome had finished their cheeseburgers and fries. Then, Henri would want to find a genuine suburban liquor store and cruise the streets while they drank. Only afterward would they be ready for the motel.

David stiffened, sure he was being watched. He looked to the other table, but his group was busily chatting. He turned around and jumped at the face there.

His reflection in the plate glass jumped too. David made a weak attempt to laugh at himself but did not succeed. He worked a bandanna out of his jeans pocket and patted his forehead. He'd experienced the feeling of being watched three or four times over as many weeks, but he was far from accustomed to it. He could only guess at the cause. He'd always spent the off-season on what he

considered his real work. This year, though, there'd been
no lull. The winter had been extraordinarily mild, spring
early, and business steady. Perhaps, too, the weather had
simply upset a biological, rather than professional, clock.
Maybelline had proven increasingly difficult, as well.
Maybe she suffered from whatever afflicted David. He
hoped that's all it was. He wiped his palms with the
bandanna. He shook his head to clear it, then listened
attentively to his party.

He could hear Maybelline's voice but not her words.
As he listened the inflection rose, became almost shrill,
then ceased abruptly. David felt the awkward silence. He
stiffened, counted to five. He slid over to the edge of his
bench and started to rise. Ms. Kitty launched into some
of the bubbling nonsense at which she was so adept.
Laughter followed her words. Ms. Kitty's voice tinkled
again, and the volume of the laughter rose. David glanced
at the table. Even the distance and the facepaint didn't
entirely obscure the worry in Maybelline's eyes. Ms.
Kitty—dim, charmed, innocent—rattled on.

When Maybelline spoke again, her voice was as tinny as
a toy trumpet. David cocked an ear and picked out a few
words. He recognized them as part of the past Maybelline
had invented over the years to tell Insiders when they asked,
as they often did. He knew Maybelline's actual biography
to be considerably more varied and interesting than this
match-girl fiction. He also knew that no Insider, old or
young, man or woman, wished to hear it. For them she
needed to be a guileless baby doll nearly two meters
tall. David rubbed his eyes with a thumb and forefinger,
then allowed himself a glance at the men. Their smiles
had become stiff, their eyes stony. He waited for Ms.
Kitty to take up the slack. She wouldn't do it for
Maybelline, David understood, she would do it for him.
Finally, she broke in with a one-liner. The men laughed
politely.

David found that he'd been holding his breath. He
exhaled, then breathed deeply as Ms. Kitty took over,
helped by Henri's easy prompting. The odor of hot grease
from the grills and fryers lifted his spirits a bit. He
thought again of the plan he'd developed. He would ask
Maybelline to be his partner. They would find her a car,
and they would work together to find new sitters. She'd

be one of the few women scouts around. They could change her name, create a persona she'd be more comfortable playing. She could train the new sitters, take care of them. With two cars running on the weekends he would be king of the suburbs.

He crushed the empty cup, the straw, and the plastic lid into a tight little ball. The plan was fantasy. The sitters didn't need much training. After a year or two at the Government Complex middle school, girls took to sitting with a ferocity that frightened David. And David had no reason to believe Maybelline'd get along with new sitters if she couldn't get along with Ms. Kitty. Besides, he didn't want a partner or to be king of the suburbs—he wanted out. He'd talk to Maybelline. Maybe they'd both just quit. He hoped she'd saved some money.

The time was finally right. He rose and made his way to their booth. All four looked up as he approached. The cold remnants of cheeseburgers and a few greasy fries lay scattered among their plastic wrappings on the scarred tabletop. David smiled. "Gentlemen and ladies, may I suggest a nightcap? Perhaps an auto tour? It can be quite stimulating this time of night, though I must warn you there is some small danger."

Henri looked to his friend, who, after a moment's hesitation, nodded. Henri turned to David. "That would be just the thing, David. Thank you for the suggestion."

"Right this way, then." David stepped back and extended an arm as if to guide them to the door and beyond to the parking lot. Both men giggled, and David and the women smiled. Maybelline carefully unfolded her long legs and slid out of the booth last. As the men turned toward the door, David shifted his smile to her. She returned it as she stood. The new man, aping Henri's gallantry to Ms. Kitty, offered her an arm. David allowed his smile to fade, threw down a blue bill for a tip, and followed the others out. Feldon held the door open for all of them. He gave David's arm a pat as he went through. They crossed the parking lot to the Torino. "You folks be sure to come back," Feldon called.

David paused by the car door for a quick, deep breath of warm night air. In the moment he and Maybelline had exchanged smiles he'd been grabbed by a sudden sense of looking into a mirror. Only when he leaned over to look through the car window did he understand. It was more than their false smiles reflecting each other. Deep in Maybelline's eyes he'd seen terror for the second time of the evening. The first had been in the wide eyes of the plate glass face of his own reflection.

2

First Love, True Love

David caught himself at the first sharp touch of the thing
and stifled a curse. He curled his bare foot around it and
brought it, primate-like, up to his hand. He held it close to
his eye, saw it was a broken piece of sidewalk concrete,
and tossed it out into the motel parking lot. It tinked off
the roof of an abandoned Chevrolet. He slipped up to the
door and, avoiding the peephole, placed his ear beside
the numerals tacked there. He heard strange voices, then
orchestral music rose to cover them. Then Ms. Kitty,
surprisingly close, said, "Does he want it there? Or off?"

He heard Henri's slow, relaxed laugh. "Leave it on."

David moved to the window and stepped back. A gap
in the drapes showed a stripe of eerie blue light that, as he
watched, abruptly changed to red. He shifted his line of
sight and located the mirror he was looking for. Reflected
in it were dancing images from the screen mounted on
the opposite wall and Henri sitting on the bed, the skin of
his broad back almost purple in the red light. David
caught a quick, pink glimpse and Ms. Kitty entered the
frame of the mirror. She lowered herself onto Henri's lap,
her back to him, resuming the position they had held for
over an hour in the passenger seat of David's car. David
passed quickly to the next room.

He stood squarely before the window. Only a little
yellow light seeped out along the edges to frame it. The
closed drapes were a bad sign. An Insider visited the
suburbs to shuck his leash and, therefore, needed watching.
This virgin, David felt, needed it more than most. He had
pulled too often and too hard on the bottle they'd passed
while cruising. Once, in the rearview mirror, David had

13

watched the virgin recoil at Maybelline's touch. For the rest of the drive Maybelline's knees were jammed into the back of David's seat.

David moved to the door and placed an ear there. He heard nothing, another bad sign. Henri and Ms. Kitty, piled together in the Torino's bucket seat, had laughed and talked easily, had fallen quickly into the relationship both, for different reasons, desired. But then, David thought, neither of them were virgins.

David started at Maybelline's disembodied voice from beyond the thin door. "Let me turn out the lights, Jorge. We'll open the drapes a bit to let the moon and the stars in. I much prefer natural light to artificial, don't you?"

Jorge's response was a faint, "No." David found himself suddenly angry with Maybelline. The old Maybelline would have found a pet name for a customer rather than speak his own, especially in such flawless accents. The old Maybelline would have used the third-person and anything else that would have diminished her in Jorge's eyes. Just as suddenly, the closed drapes were nothing to him but the natural reaction of a nervous virgin. Jorge said something abrupt and muffled, as if he spoke to the floor.

"No, look all you want." Maybelline's tone told David she did not mean at her. A customer happy with simply looking would have been a relief. "But it's all there," Maybelline continued. "It's in order."

David could see the print in his mind's eye: the thick, document-weight paper; the Government Complex logo; the neat column of "negatives" opposite syphillus-R, AIDS, hepatitus-B, the rest. This time he could make out Jorge's faint words. "Yes, it appears to be."

Maybelline spoke again, farther away now from David and closer, he hoped, to Jorge. "Is it something about me that you don't like? I really want you to like me. I like you."

Again Jorge's response was muffled.

"Let me help you," Maybelline said. And, after a moment, "Isn't that better? We can be free here."

"Yes. Yes, that's a little better," Jorge said clearly and gave a long, grateful sigh.

David walked quickly across the parking lot to the Torino. He reached through the open window and found

the box on the visor. He lit a cigarette, coughed quietly.
His aching muscles began to relax. He reached in again
and flicked the ignition key one notch. The radio came on
clear and quiet. The Blue Baby was playing rock and roll.
He rested his back against the car. He felt chilled, and he
realized that his shirt along his sides was soaked with
sweat. He looked up into the sky and shivered.

The horn of a quarter moon rested atop the unlit
Motel–12 sign. Stars shone brightly above it but were
obscured by the dome of diffused New City lights closer
to the horizon. Although the sun had set hours before,
the western sky still showed streaks of turquoise. David
studied the odd flickers of color for some minutes. He
wondered if there was a thunderstorm Out There. He
shrugged. The Blue Baby would announce the weather
during a break in the music. The Blue Baby would know
if rain was coming. He looked around the sky and counted
the red lights of fifteen microwave towers at varying
distances and in different directions. He saw the lazy W
of Cassiopeia, gazed at it as he would a friend he'd not
seen for a very long time.

One of the stars in the constellation moved. David
stared, his mouth open, as the star cut a straight course to
the west. Finally, it melted into the lingering sundown.
Slow freight, he thought. Only what was bulky and needed
in no particular hurry was shipped by plane anymore. He
slid into the driver's seat of the Torino, switched on the
dome light, and pulled a thick, ancient notebook out from
beneath the seat. He pulled a writer out of the spiral
binding and flipped the book open. Yellowed pages, covered with notations, flipped out from under his thumb.
He found a blank sheet, balanced the book on his knee,
and readied the writer above it. The Blue Baby announced another song, a group he recognized from the
musicology courses of his university days, and he paused
to listen.

David's hand was still poised above the blank sheet
well after the song was over. The problem was obvious to
him. He had an image—the figure of death cruising
suburban streets looking for one particular Insider who'd
stayed too long out of the New City—but it seemed better
suited, to David, for a short than a pome. Nobody watched
shorts anymore, although a few professors still read them.

The form required too much attention span. Maybe he could force his idea into the shape of a pome. He jotted a line down.

It wasn't any good. He shoved the notebook beneath the seat and reached behind him. He groped around until he came up with the neck of a bottle. He held it up to the light. It still held a swallow or two. He uncapped the bottle and passed it under his nose. His nostrils crinkled. Beneath the fragrance additive of synthetic scotch he detected another odor. Not gasoline, but something akin to it.

He followed the sense memory back. Soon after the Fall. Another dome of light, this one over polished wood. His mother's table. Three or four vague figures lay upon a white-and-green dinner plate. A bell, a man. A word from childhood floated free and rose to consciousness. "Cookies," he said aloud.

David sniffed the bottle again. There had been plenty of gasoline, of course, millions of gallons in the refinery tanks in the skirts, but kerosene had been scarce. People had rationed what little they happened to possess or come by. When the solar generators of the New City began to supply power to the suburbs, the carefully hoarded kerosene became, like gasoline, practically worthless. He threw the bottle out the window. It broke on the street with a crash. Worthless, he thought, except to Harv's Liquor Mart.

The Blue Baby gave the news and weather: a transmatter's death; Gross Urban Product had posted a healthy, moderate rise in the last quarter; local economy had risen similarly. Tomorrow would be unseasonably warm with no chance of precipitation.

A car pulled into the far end of the parking lot and stopped before the last room. Someone, a teenage boy by the self-conscious look of his strut, got out and went to the door. It swung open, and a girl stood there framed in light. David saw dishwater-blond hair and guessed her at Ms. Kitty's age. A long rooster tail of hair arched from the boy's scalp. It bobbed and glinted red when he spoke. The boy entered and closed the door behind him. The Blue Baby cued up more rock and roll.

David felt drowsy. He took a perfunctory look at the motel. No light showed around the door or window of

Maybelline's room. All appeared normal. He lolled his head back against the seat. He began to dream.

"She said her good-bye before." Lu twirled a slow finger into her hair.

Nicky spoke as if to the doorjamb. "He come this far to see her again. He's all packed. T Stone's waiting at the place." He nodded his head, and the rooster tail bobbed toward the car behind him.

"Come in," the girl said and backed away from the door. When he followed she turned around, walked to the bed and sat down. She watched him come toward her in the mirror. She hoped he would look into the mirror so their eyes could meet, but he kept his face to the ragged carpet.

"He'll come back. She knows he will."

"Maybe he won't be able to come back."

"He'll come back. For her."

"No one ever comes back. For nothing."

He reached out and placed a hand on her shoulder. "He will," he promised again.

Lu fought the urge to rub her cheek against the back of his hand. She shrugged the hand from her shoulder instead.

Nicky turned away, raised his hands to the blank screen on the wall. "T Stone says because it's not hard like here. When they see how it's not hard the people never come back."

"T Stone says, T Stone says, but T Stone don't know." Lu watched in the mirror as he ran a hand over his rooster tail. When he began to turn to her she dropped her eyes.

"T Stone knows. T Stone's friend who's his brother went Out There. He said if he didn't come back that meant to follow." Nicky spoke more quietly. "He said if it was hard he'd come back. Why wouldn't he come back?"

Lu considered a minute. "Maybe the dogs ate him."

Nicky laughed, stepped between Lu and the mirror and dropped to one knee. "He had the gun. Besides, the dogs are here. Out There, there ain't nothing but sleep under the stars at night, wake up in the morning light, or anytime, and pick breakfast off the trees. It's like a greenhouse except it's big as the world. T Stone's friend who's his brother said so." He traced the slim scar over her eye and across her cheek with his finger. "Doesn't she see?"

When she didn't answer, Nicky said, "He got this for her." He produced a candy bar from his breast pocket. He rested it across his open palm. "Take it," he said.

Lu picked up the candy by the ends of its paper wrapper, held it to her nose, and smelled it. Saliva filled her mouth and tears began to run down her cheeks. She dropped her face into his still open hand and kissed his palm. He pulled the hand away and used it to stroke her hair.

"They could housestead," she said.

"And eat what?"

"They give the people seeds."

Nicky locked his eyes on hers and shook his head. "It's all Out There already."

"They could go Inside."

"And have the laugh of them?"

"They could go to the Complex. They could learn how to make no one have the laugh of them."

Nicky tensed. "Be fish-people? Dress in coveralls?"

"At least they'd eat."

He gently took the candy bar from her hands, slipped the brown paper sleeve off and unfolded the white wrapper. He broke off a bit and held it up. Lu opened her mouth like a hungry nestling.

Lu's nervous system responded before she'd even swallowed the morsel. More tears formed and coursed down her cheeks. The hollow in her belly became a lightness, and the muscles of her legs and arms began to thrum. Nicky fed her piece after tiny piece. She caught some spittle that had dribbled through her lips with her finger. She licked the finger. He held the last piece for her, but she took his hand and guided the chocolate to his mouth. He closed his eyes with pleasure. She opened her blouse and peeled the tear-wet cloth from her skin. She encircled Nicky's head with her arms and pulled him down till his cheek lay upon her shoulder. She lifted her chin, and Nicky nuzzled into her neck.

He pulled away to look at her. He asked, "Nicky'll be Lu's only boy?"

She smiled weakly and nodded once. "Sh-h," she said, a finger across his lips.

his chest. He kept an eye on the two men. He added the pressure of his hand over hers against the flow of blood. His nostrils flared with the smell of it.

"You mean this?" Jorge asked.

Henri took it. "Yes, cousin. You know what this is?"

Jorge shook his head. David both wondered where Ms. Kitty was and hoped she would stay out of the way.

"This is a razor for shaving whiskers from a long time ago. You shouldn't use it to hurt people." Henri drew the edge between his fingers and David watched his eyes widen at the blood there. Maybelline made a choking noise deep in her throat. He grabbed for the wastebasket behind him and guided Maybelline's face toward it with his other arm. The first of the vomit missed and was absorbed by the thick cotton of David's shirt. Jorge watched them, as if puzzled by their presence. Only when David moved Maybelline's face onto his shoulder did his attention return to Henri.

The razor had disappeared, someplace into Henri's disheveled coveralls, David assumed. "Come," Henri said. "Let's clean you up and dress you. Where are your clothes?"

All three men looked about the room. David discovered them in a pile within arm's reach. They were of the usual sort Insider's wore to the suburbs, syn-fab reproductions of denim, wool, and leather in a single piece. David recoiled at the idea of touching the syn-fab, the unnatural feel of its recombinant structure. Henri bent down and picked the coveralls up. As he rose they exchanged glances. Henri's eyes showed panic that belied his casual manner. He gently guided Jorge to the washroom.

David pulled a case off its pillow, wadded it up and placed it under Maybelline's hand. He took a quick look at her face. Her eyes were open but unfocused. Her nostrils flared with quick, shallow breaths. He heard Jorge wheedling, like a child who didn't wish to bathe, over the sound of running water. David took two deep breaths, got his bloody hand under Maybelline's knees, and rose with her.

Ms. Kitty stood outside the room. She had not thought to dress. "What happened?" she asked.

"That crazy virgin cut her with her own razor," he

huffed. "Go ahead and open the door." He nodded in the direction of the car.

Ms. Kitty ran across the parking lot, then stood, absurdly, beside the open door until David reached it. He lowered Maybelline into the seat as gently as he could and belted her into place. He picked up her free hand and set it in her lap. He slammed the door. Ms. Kitty looked up to him. "Stay here," he said, "and stay away from that crazy motherfucker."

"Which one?" she asked.

He strode around the car. "The ones who cut are crazy." He dropped in behind the wheel and turned the ignition. The engine roared. He pulled the headlights on and slammed the gearshift into low. He glimpsed a young face peering at him from the dark door of the last room as they accelerated around the corner of the motel and out into the street. He shifted once and then again when the car straightened out and once again as he raced down the street toward the Government Complex. Maybelline began to retch again, but he kept both hands on the wheel. The Blue Baby played rock and roll. When he risked a glance at the dash he saw the speedometer needle quivering against the far peg.

3

Red Sun Rising

It rose like the giant it was, preceded by waves of blue heat, then lurching powerfully above the far line of the planet. David lowered his dark glasses against it. His face and naked chest soaked in its heat. He squinted into its center. Some dream from the night before lingered on the dark side of his memory. Now it receded farther from the light.

"I've never seen it look like that before, so blue before dawn, so red at its core."

David looked to Henri. They were parked at the terminal, awaiting the first el of the morning. "It looks different here than Inside."

"Still..." Henri's thought trailed off.

Still, David finished, the sunrise had been spectacular. A trivial observation, he decided, with Maybelline stitched together, lying drugged in the hospital ward of the Government Complex. The radio played static. He shut it off. "Must be a lot of dust in the air."

"Or smoke," Henri suggested. "Maybe everything Out There is burning. Grass fires?"

David ignored the question and adjusted the rearview mirror. Jorge slept in the backseat, curled next to Ms. Kitty. Her cheek rested on the arm she had around his shoulders, and she snored very quietly. Except for her facepaint and his thin beard, they could have been five-year-olds worn out from a grand adventure. "Not your cousin."

Henri pursed his lips. "No," he said, "more a client."

David looked at him. "Client?"

Henri shrugged, "Patient, then."

From the driver's seat David could see far down into the New City. He watched through the glare of the climbing sun for the el. It was his turn to shrug.

"You're not surprised?"

"Too tired. Besides, it makes sense. A dozen trips here, always with a different guy. Therapy?"

"Yes."

"Well, Doc, you screwed up this time."

"Apparently. Still, a very telling incident."

David shot him a look.

Henri gestured with an empty hand. "Do you understand why sitters of short stature are the norm?"

David looked away, then back. "Let's hear it, Doc."

Henri stretched as far as possible in the cramped vehicle. "Well, there is what I consider to be the more obvious reason: the customer has the simple superiority of mass, and though no man or woman would, in proper society, admit to a desire for physical advantage, it is still a deep-seated drive." Henri warmed to his subject. "What is even less popular, though more powerful, is the pedophiliac element. You know the term?"

David nodded.

"I take it you don't find this line of intellectual inquiry repugnant. The subject is abhorrent to most people, even many of my theoretically enlightened colleagues."

David continued to gaze at Henri through dark lenses.

"I suppose that neither supposition presents a novel explanation to one in your particular line of work, though of course some of the vocabulary I use to talk of them is, I imagine, foreign. My work, by the way, deals mostly with the obverse of this phenomenon. I specialize in cases, most often males, where development has been arrested in the adolescence. Often this is a product of sexual confusion stemming from repressed feelings toward an authority figure, most often the patient's mother."

A guffaw escaped David, and Henri's expression changed.

"I suppose this is awfully abstract," he said.

"No, no, it's not that." David waved Henri's words away with a tired hand. "I just thought the neo-Freudian was extinct."

Henri smiled grimly. "Almost," he said, then added, "You're an educated person."

David shrugged.

"Then you can surely see the efficacy of the arrested adolescent confronting his fears in the form of a mother figure."

David guffawed again.

"The location of the wound? That must be significant."

David quickly sobered. "Doc, he cut her when she caught him going through her things. He turned, swinging from the shoulder, and that's where the razor caught her. If she'd been 'of short stature,' he'd of cut her throat."

"You see, though, don't you?" Henri persisted. "Going through her private things constituted an attempt to understand his mother. That the mother-figure would have a weapon, well, in his state of mind you can understand how threatening that would appear."

"Get out, Doc."

"Excuse me?"

"Another time, another place. Now get out."

Henri did as he was told. David climbed out and reached into the back. He had a sleeping Jorge by the front of his coveralls, the greasy feel of the syn-fab making his hand itch. He heaved once, and the man came out of the backseat, his eyelids fluttering open. David dragged him to the curb and leaned him against it. "Next time," he said into the man's awakening face, "I will kill you." He left him standing there stock-still and wide awake. He waved in Henri's direction. "Don't come back, Doc."

Henri protested. "But the el isn't here yet."

David stopped before he got into the Torino. "It'll get here." He hesitated to think something over, then said, "You people preach deference and good grace. When it makes you crazy you come out here to blow it off. If you want us to exorcise your demons you need to be better prepared for the consequences."

"Then why didn't you call the Law? You could have called from the motel, they'd have sent a rescue unit and someone would have arrested Jorge."

"Rescue units don't run in the suburbs, Doc, and the Law stays in its cruisers." David nodded toward Jorge, still standing in the position he'd left him. "What will you do with him?"

Henri shrugged. "Continue therapy."

David slipped in behind the wheel, called through the

open window, "What I said, Doc." He started the engine,
pulled out of his parking spot, started down the Expressway. He patted his pockets for the money and Maybelline's
razor. He adjusted the rearview mirror. Ms. Kitty stretched
in the backseat. "Good morning, little sister," he called.

"Where are they going?" she asked between yawns.

"Back Inside."

"No. David and her."

"I'm going home to get a fresh shirt. You're going to
the Complex. When Maybelline wakes up you call me."

"Does she have to?" Ms. Kitty whined.

"Maybelline would do it for you. Remember that."
They left the Expressway, took the shortcut through the
cemetery. The graves triggered something, and parts of
the previous night's dream came back. His mother had
played a role, but he couldn't say what. And someone
else he knew but couldn't name. He saw movement far off
among the stones. He slowed the car and pointed. "Look."

Ms. Kitty made a sound of disgust. "Dogs," she said.

David hurried on. "Be careful," he warned. "They
must be awful hungry to come out during the day."

Ms. Kitty made the noise again.

David stopped the car in the parking lot of the Government Complex. Ms. Kitty got out and walked to the hospital
entrance like the sulky child she was. She turned at the
door, hoping for a last-minute reprieve. David drove away.

He had driven the route so many times that it had
become automatic. He passed by deserted stores and
through clots of abandoned office buildings. He turned
onto Pine Heights Road without taking any conscious
note of where he was. An empty mall slipped by on his
right. While his hands and eyes and feet drove the vehicle, his tired brain pieced together the dream. His mother's presence unified the scattered images: her face, far
away and fading; her voice, the words unclear but
disconcerting. Since her death, her visits to his dreams
had invariably comforted David. Until this time. And
there had been someone else—not his father, he felt fairly
sure. Perhaps his mother spoke to him of someone. Yes,
that seemed right. But who?

He pulled into the drive. He did not bother with the
garage and entered the house through the front door. A
big, old, black dog, excited as a puppy, greeted him by

bounding around the room. David rubbed his head and neck, then opened the door for him. Recalling the dogs in the cemetery, he called, "Don't go too far, Felix."

He sat at the dining room table, the one the whiskey had reminded him of. The kerosene lamp, unused for years, sat before him. He fished the previous night's receipts out of his pocket and made four equal piles. He pushed Ms. Kitty's pile to one side, Maybelline's to the other. The two in the middle were, according to custom, his and the car's. He stacked them atop Maybelline's.

The dream fretted him like a puppy worrying a bone. Of whom had his mother spoken? Someone from long ago, an old friend. Of his mother's? Of his? David sighed. *That's easy,* he thought, *how many friends do I have?* Red sunlight streamed through the window. He rose to close the drapes.

Frieda took small bites of the wafer she'd gotten from the vending machine and chewed slowly to make it last longer. When she was finished she carefully gathered the crumbs from the desk before the console into one palm and dropped them in the wastebasket by her feet. She drummed her fingers on the desktop and looked around. Before her was a keyboard, and to her left and right carefully labeled clusters of digital read-outs. More read-outs marched slowly up the main screen resting on the console. Mounted high on the far wall were more screens, each labeled for a different New City. Lined along all four walls were banks of electronic equipment. Red, blue, green, and yellow lights ran up and down in sequence. Occasionally the values of the red numbers on the display changed. A tingle of panic started up Frieda's spine, and very suddenly she was overwhelmed by the complexity of transmatation. She argued with herself for reassurance. She had been thoroughly schooled in the principles behind the equipment. She knew the exact function of the components. She understood how each contributed to the whole. She rested a hand on the red button of the console. Besides, help was very close.

As soon as her anxiety passed, Frieda was again bored. She stared at the empty transmatation booth in the center of the room. She had spent four years preparing herself to do what she was now doing. In only her second

shift, she had developed doubts. The routine and isola-
tion were stultifying. She wondered how her friends from
university felt about their new jobs. She missed the
society of classes, of study sessions, of weekend parties.

She had an idea. She would send her mother an
old-fashioned letter for her birthday. The quaintness and
ingenuity of the idea excited her. She scrubbed the screen
of its routine read-outs and typed

5:32

Dear Mother,

Happy Birthday! I can imagine your surprise. A letter!

How are you? I am fine. I wish I could be with you but I can't.
Because of the job which is not all it's promoed to be, frankly. My
shift supervisor is a grump. But I can hear you say it's too early to
judge. As the new woman on the block I have the worst shift.
Here, PDT, the sun is just coming up, I know, tho I can't see it
down here where I am. By now you've been up with the time
difference and all for a while. Me, I've been up all nite on this shift
and still have two hours to go. Not much happens, tho in a half
hour a transmatter comes in from London. That is something, isn't
it? One moment there, and the next here. Really the same moment.

Well, Happy Birthday again! I hope you like the letter.

Your loving daughter,
Frieda

P.S. Love to Daddy!

5:49

Frieda read through the letter, thought that it was fine.
She punched a button and the printer began its steady
swish. She couldn't send it from the center, of course.
She'd transcribe it on her own screen—brand-new, a
graduation gift from her parents—and send it when she
got home. She tore the print off its roll and placed it near
her on the desk. She told the screen to return to its
normal function and glanced at the read-outs as they
came back up. She settled back in her chair. She kept her
eyes on the screen. Her eyelids began to flutter, and she

dozed off before one particular read-out, outlined in green and pulsing brightly, rolled onto the screen.

Frieda came wide awake to the sound of a klaxon. She sat stiffly in her chair, recognized immediately where she was, saw the London screen flash on above the empty transmatation booth, and panicked. Her stomach heaved, and the effort to keep the wafer she'd eaten down caused sweat to break out over her body. A man stared at her from the London screen. She overcame the urge to run.

"What?" she asked. "What did you say?"

"Do you have reception, L.A.? Has she been delivered?"

The booth was empty. Frieda shook her head.

London said, "We have not received the automatic signal. Are you prepared to acknowledge receipt now?"

Frieda felt torn between the frantic klaxon and London's professional, cool voice. "No," she said finally. "No, we don't have delivery." With monumental effort she turned her mind from what London must think of her. The first step of the procedure had swum into her brain. She doubted the necessity of it for less than a second. She brought her fist down on the red button. She thought to say, "Hold, London."

The read-outs on the screen before her dissolved, and the image of the shift supervisor coalesced. "Status?"

Frieda took a deep breath. "Incomplete reception."

"Incomplete?"

"No," Frieda corrected, "no reception at all."

The skin around Dr. Lester's eyes tightened. "I'll be right down," she said.

Frieda turned to the other screen. "Do you show anything on your end, London?"

He shook his head. "We're all clear here."

"Please hold, London." She went unself-consciously to the next step. She punched in the code she'd been given at the start of the shift. The program didn't take. She tried again, pressing each key very deliberately. The screen before her split. She had the book in front of her.

She began the first of the procedures detailed there. Read-outs ran quickly up the right side of the screen while the book on the left remained stationary. She sensed Dr. Lester behind her. The last read-out disappeared.

"Okay," Dr. Lester said, "follow the book till you find it."

Frieda went to the next procedure, watched it run. Again, nothing stuck on the right side of the screen. "Don't stop," Dr. Lester said. Frieda went on, slowly, her fingers becoming sticks of wood, in her mouth the taste of copper. The atmosphere of the center had become stifling. She paused once to rub the sweat from her brow with the back of a hand. Dr. Lester spoke over Frieda's shoulder to London.

"You show nothing on your end?"

London looked up and straight out from the screen. "Say again, L.A.?"

Dr. Lester reached across Frieda and pressed a button. The klaxon ceased abruptly. "You see nothing, London?"

"All clear here, L.A."

"How many times?"

"Just completing the run-through."

"Full check prior to transmat?"

"Of course, L.A."

Frieda cringed but kept her fingers beating against the keyboard.

Dr. Lester drummed her fingers on the desk, a single, short series of four taps.

"Do you wish me to commence a re-search?" London asked.

"Yes," Dr. Lester said, then, quickly, "No, London. I'm releasing our book to you. Begin with zed." She held down two buttons simultaneously.

"Yes, ma'am, we've got it."

Dr. Lester punched the red button. A face replaced half the book. "Medical." She cut off communication without waiting for a reply. The rest of the book reappeared.

"What the hell's going on?" Dr. Lester said to herself. She continued more loudly. "You know Bankok lost one yesterday, don't you?"

Frieda shook her head and kept typing. She had not seen the media before coming to work, and no one had mentioned anything when she checked in.

Dr. Lester looked up. "Who do we have, London?"

London glanced up briefly, then looked again to his keyboard. "LaMer," he said.

"Jesus," Dr. Lester said.

Frieda could not make her fingers work. She knew with absolute certainty how she would always be known in her chosen profession: as the transmat tech who'd lost LaMer.

"Keep going," Dr. Lester said, "keep going."

Frieda depressed one key, then a second, then a third. Her fingers gained some strength, some speed.

"It's in there," Dr. Lester whispered, "it has to be in there." She shifted her attention to London. "What was she doing coming through unannounced? During graveyard?"

London didn't look up. "I don't know. Her passport was marked diplomatic. We received her yesterday. Twelve hours later we sent her. The 1-As don't tell us much." He shot a look across the screen. "Maybe they tell you, but they don't tell us."

Dr. Lester ignored the remark. "Time elapsed?" she said into Frieda's ear.

Frieda quickly depressed the key with her little finger. The screen read "00:20:16."

"If we don't terminate the event in the next few minutes," Dr. Lester announced to both Frieda and London, "I'm putting more help on line."

Frieda sat back with a ragged sigh. She lifted her hands in a gesture of helplessness. "I'm through, " she said. "London has the last procedure."

"London?" Dr. Lester said.

"Working," came the response.

"Break it down, then," Dr. Lester said to Frieda. "You take the sub-books on the odd-numbered procedures."

"Nothing," London said.

"Sub-books. Even-numbered procedures."

"Yes, ma'am." London went back to work.

Dr. Lester desperately wanted thirty uninterrupted seconds in which to think. She moved behind Frieda and began to massage the younger woman's shoulders. She willed the tension up into her hands. Finally, some of the muscles stretched and softened beneath her fingers. All right, she thought, enough thinking. She'd bring two more techs on line to help with the sub-books. She'd ask London to move the beam to a different station, Mexico City, if he could. Failing that, she'd try to have the orbit pulled into an ellipse to maximize the time away from the sun.

"What happened? In Bankok?" Frieda asked. Her fingers drummed against the keyboard.

"Technical delay. Then the usual."

"Sunspot interference?"

"That's the usual."

Frieda steeled herself. "What duration?"

Dr. Lester's hands rested lightly on Frieda's shoulders. "Twelve minutes."

Frieda's vision swam as her eyes welled up. She told herself that she would not engage in self-pity, and the thought made her feel melodramatically noble, which in turn brought her closer to tears. She blinked and almost missed it.

"There it is!" She turned in her chair and was surprised to see the medical team waiting patiently by the door. "We found it!" she said to no one in particular.

Dr. Lester leaned over, and Frieda turned again to face the screen. "Okay," the older woman said, "that's the element, and there's the back-up. Lay it in." She looked up. "London, we've located a malfunction and we are by-passing it now. Please continue with your procedures. Finish the odds when you've completed the evens. We don't know that it's a single malfunction."

"Yes, ma'am," London said.

"It's laid in, ma'am."

"London, we're going to attempt to take delivery." Dr. Lester poised a finger over a button, hesitated. "You," she said to Frieda, "get your finger out there." Frieda obeyed. "Press the damn thing," Dr. Lester said, and Frieda did.

Someplace deep in the transparent emptiness of the transmatation booth a faint, reddish glow appeared. "We got her," Dr. Lester said. "Put some power to it." Frieda tapped in a code and the glow grew stronger. Tiny, fiery dots, strung together in a line, began to circle slowly within the glow. "Come on, baby," Dr. Lester said. She reached her hands, palms up, toward the booth. "Come on," she said again, curling her fingers slowly. The string of dots increased in velocity, struck the glastic sides of the booth and spiraled away. The glow intensified till Frieda's eyes ached with it. The dots sped around the interior of the booth, lost their individuality, became, instead, bands of pulsing light. Here and there the bands crossed each other and, touching, adhered. In a few moments they had formed a spiderweb of light around a burning core. In another, the figure of a woman had become visible. She appeared as one who had caught fire or as if she had walked into the sun and was now exiting the other side. Bubbles, large and small, formed and burst, pocking the torso. Light ran like liquid to fill the craters. Limbs took on definition. The face took on its features. The mouth opened in a silent scream. The distortion disappeared as the image cooled, and suddenly the booth contained a woman. A large gold hoop depended from an ear and a brightly colored scarf covered her hair. The medical team scurried forward as the glastic door of the booth slid open. LaMer collapsed through it onto the floor.

Frieda hurried after the medical team. She knelt on the floor and studied LaMer's profile through a gap between two of them. She's beautiful, Frieda thought, skin like a newborn. A medic grabbed LaMer's chin and forehead and expertly moved the head to one side. Frieda saw, suddenly, her full face. An empty socket stared accusingly at her, and the corner of the mouth under it was drawn up in a sneer. Frieda tried to stand, but her legs would not hold her. She sat down hard, eyes still on the twisted face. The chatter of the medical team covered her single gasp.

"That's old, isn't it?"

"Yeah, it looks like."

"Check."

"It looks old."

"Check. You can't know for sure in a transmatation trauma. Remember that. What's obviously new is new; what's obviously old might be new too."

"My god, the leg."

"Cut away the cloth."

"Oxygen. Brain damage?"

"The trauma's on the leg. Maybe that's all."

"Maybe the eye."

"Good sign. The leg. Far from the brain."

"Check the eye."

"Hey you!"

Frieda had fallen a long way into the empty socket, and the man had to call again. She looked up into his stare. "Call up her medical file. I want to know if it shows her missing an eye. And anything else. Get me a print. Now."

She was back in under two minutes. The man snatched the print from her trembling fingers.

"Yeah. Old," he said. "Different accident. Long damn file." He tossed the print to one side.

LaMer's head began to wobble from side to side. "How long?" she mumbled.

"What's she want?" someone asked.

"Doesn't matter. Extract as much of that cloth from the wound as you can."

"It's recombined with the flesh."

"Work on it. Leave the recombinant matter for later."

"How long?" LaMer asked again.

Frieda went to the console and called up a response. She returned and knelt in a space between the team members. "Forty-four and thirteen," she whispered into LaMer's ear.

"Respiration, pressure okay. Look, I don't think we've got any internal problems."

"Damn, I think we're going to lose the leg."

"Forget the leg! We'll settle that later."

LaMer pulled the corners of her mouth up in a tired smile. "Thanks, little sister," she whispered.

"Okay, stable for the time being. Brain damage?"

"She's talking."

"What?"

"She spoke. A couple of times."

"Good." Someone pushed Frieda back. "Excuse me," he said. The man who had asked for the print addressed LaMer. "Ms. LaMer," he said, "can you hear me?"

LaMer made no response.

The man tried again. "It's very important that you acknowledge if you can hear me."

Still LaMer lay quiet.

"Ms. LaMer, I'm a medical doctor. I want to help you. Can you hear me?" The man nearly shouted.

The whole team fell silent, awaited a response.

LaMer's single eyelid flickered open. The eye stared out. It seemed hardly more cognizant of the world than the empty socket.

"Shit-eater," she said.

"What was that?" someone down the line asked.

The man at LaMer's head turned. "She called me a shit-eater. Get her on the stretcher. We're taking her out."

"Little sister?" LaMer said. Frieda moved into the spot the doctor had just vacated. LaMer's eye had closed.

"Yes?" Frieda said.

"Is David here?" LaMer asked.

Frieda looked up at the team. "Are any of you David?" she asked. One or two shook their heads, and then the team lifted LaMer to the stretcher. Frieda leaned down to her. "I don't think so," she said.

"Funny," LaMer said, and then the team was carrying her across the room. The door slid open, and they were gone.

Frieda found herself kneeling on the floor, the room suddenly still. Dr. Lester stood behind the console.

"Delivery acknowledged," she said. Frieda looked over just in time to see the London screen go blank. She stared at the darkness until she felt Dr. Lester's presence behind her. She picked herself up and turned to the older woman.

"Take us off the line," she said. "I'll get someone down with a new element."

Frieda nodded.

"Finish your shift, put your report together, and don't forget to send this." She held Frieda's letter out to her. "Your mother will appreciate the effort you put into it."

Frieda carefully folded the print in half. "Thank you," she said. Dr. Lester turned and began to walk away.

"Ma'am," Frieda called.

Dr. Lester hesitated. "What is it?"

"Was it my fault?"

Dr. Lester shrugged, then faced her. "If the element went out prior to transmatation and if the malfunction appeared among the read-outs and if you missed it, then it's your fault. We don't know, and there is no way to find out." She paused. "Is that what you wanted to know?"

"Yes, ma'am," Frieda said, "something like that."

She held the letter in her hands and watched the older woman leave. She stood there alone, missing her mother terribly.

4

Adult Education

David sat in the hall outside the hospital ward, a folder of prints across his knees. Occasionally, a nurse walked by and they exchanged smiles. David's was nervous and false. He disliked the Government Complex as much as most suburbanites, and he hated the hospital ward. He'd been hospitalized only once, and that was as a child and in a different place. Still, he'd seen a man die there.

David shifted the folder on his lap. There had been nuns there. He wondered, absently, if his parents had been Catholic. Probably it had been the only hospital operating in the suburbs during the Fall. When the Government Complex had been built, the old hospital had been abandoned. David had seen it recently, windows broken, grounds untended, when an errand had taken him far out in the skirts. He never saw a nun anymore. The orders had ceased to exist years ago.

David sighed and gave in to the memories. He'd found a dog in the garage. It'd devoured the scrap of sandwich David offered it. When he pulled his hand away the dog, starving, had gone after that. David had tried to run, and the dog, panicked, had shaken him so hard that both bones of his forearm snapped. His screams brought his parents running into the garage. David could not recall, if he ever knew, what had happened to the dog. Perhaps it had run away; perhaps his father had killed it while his mother held him, crying and screaming in terror and surprise.

For a while he'd been in a room with an infant. The baby, apparently strapped into its crib with tubes and wires, had never cried, had never awakened. The days were long and still. In time they moved him. They gave him a reason he didn't believe even at the time. Two men, one old, one the age of his father, were in the new room. They chewed tobacco and spat into tin cans. They told stories and gossiped. They talked in strange accents about things he could not grasp. Brown spittle sometimes ran down the old man's chin. The days passed quicker with them.

The nurse passed again and smiled, but David did not notice. He had suddenly realized that his adult room-mates had not been from the suburbs. They had come from farther out, beyond the skirts even, from what people now called, if they spoke of it at all, Out There. The tobacco-chewers, drawn by the need for medical care, must have been among the last to come in.

The old man had had a leg amputated. The day he was supposed to leave he had dressed in a starched white shirt crossed in back by dark suspenders. The empty pants leg of his black trousers was pinned up to the knee. A hat made of white straw rested on his pillow. He stood on his one leg and clutched the frame of the bed to balance himself. A nun passing in the hall leaned through the open door and said to him, "Don't you think you'd better rest?"

The old man had hopped along the edge of his bed, got his hat, and put it on. He looked at the nun and smiled. He fell to the floor. The nun had tried to get a basin to him, but the old man's vomit had already pooled on the floor. He collapsed into it, then rolled to his side, the white shirt stained. He spasmed once or twice, then his body quivered, and he was dead. Nuns ran this way and that, a doctor came in, some men with a gurney. David had seen it all from the perch of his high bed. He'd had a toy car in his good hand, and he had been running it up and down the cast of his broken arm.

Later a young nun had come to sit beside his bed. It was night past the tall windows, and the room was only dimly lit. The younger man rested silently or slept, his bed in shadows. The young nun had had a sweetheart who'd gone away, she said. She had cried and cried, no matter what anyone said or did to comfort her. A pool of tears

formed at her feet, and the pool became a lake, and still
she cried. Soon the lake could hold no more and her tears
began to flow together to make a stream. Only when the
stream had swollen with her tears to become the Missou-
ri River did her crying stop.

A door to the ward opened. A nurse, different from
the one who had patrolled the hall, looked out. "You can
come in now," she said.

He held his folder at his side and walked past the
nurses' station and down a long aisle. Here and there
a patient looked up. Others moaned in pain or a night-
mare. He found a chair and dragged it over. "Hi," he
said.

Maybelline's face, the paint scrubbed off, showed some
color and her smile was only a little tired. She nodded to
his folder. "Class today?"

"Last meeting of the quarter."

"Start another soon?"

"Not till fall. Credit hour production's too low."

"Oh." David looked at her more closely. Without the
facepaint she seemed a different person. He supposed
that, in a way, she was.

"You look really good."

"Thanks."

"How bad is it?"

She started to shrug, but she stopped the motion with
a grimace. "Not bad," she said instead. "Food's the worst."

"I suppose."

"It's mostly protein, the green stuff. They dress it up a
little, but that's what it is."

"You need to rest."

"Well, I'll do that at home."

David and Ms. Kitty had cleaned up Maybelline's
room. Still he could not imagine her returning to it.
"We'll find you another place."

"No, it's okay. The screen's there for company. I'm
used to it."

"Why don't you come to my place? I've got a screen."

"No thanks, David. You need your time." Her gaze had
become dreamy, and he wondered how heavily sedated
she was. "I'll be all right."

"I replaced the doorjamb," David said. "It's not very
pretty but it'll work."

Maybelline nodded, then said, "It's today, David. They're letting me go today."

David was startled. "Four days isn't very long," he said. "It's not long enough."

"They need the bed."

"I'll pick you up after class."

"Did you know Ms. Kitty has a new boy?"

"She told me."

"I'm going to meet him. They're coming to get me in a little while. He has a car."

"Will it run?"

Maybelline allowed herself a careful laugh. "Ms. Kitty says it will." Her expression became somber. "Look," she said after a moment, "I'm taking the face off. I couldn't do it anymore, even without the scar."

David nodded.

"It's the acting, mostly. It's always being the person, the thing, they want. I'm tired of taking cues, going on stage three nights a week. I can't be everybody's sister and middle-school sweetheart and butch buddy anymore."

David found a package of tissues on the stand by the bed and handed her one. She blew her nose.

"You know the worst of it?" she asked. He shook his head. "The worst of it is that it makes me happy if I can really help, really be what they need."

"Job satisfaction," David said.

"What?"

"Nothing."

"It's just that I'm scared there's no me left. I've got to find that out." She sniffled.

"What will you do?"

She shifted her gaze to the foot of the bed. "I'm making some plans."

"Inside?"

She shook her head. "I don't want to be somebody's domestic. Too much like sitting."

"There are other things."

"Maybe," she said and looked up at him suddenly. "I don't blame you, David."

"Do you have any money?"

She nodded. "Some."

David took a wad of blue bills out of his pocket and held it out to her. She made no move to take it. He placed

it on her smock near her folded hands. "There's a little
extra there. Henri wanted to make things right."

Maybelline gave a short, humorless laugh.

"Call if you need anything. Anything, understand?"

Maybelline nodded.

He rose to leave. She said his name.

"Give it to me. I want it."

He thought about lying to her, telling her that in the
confusion he'd lost track of it. Instead, he reached into
his pocket, brought out the razor and held it out to her.
She snatched it away from him and expertly palmed it.
She glanced around the ward to see if anyone had noticed
the transaction, then slipped the razor under her pillow.

"Thanks, David. For that."

He shrugged, turned and walked out of the ward. It
was her razor, he thought, to do with what she wished.
He had been wrong to think of not returning it.

"B-b-b-but wh-wh-wh-at if no one c-c-cares?" The
class waited with varying degrees of patience for Carly to
stammer out his question.

David, to whom it had been addressed, lifted his open
palms from the table and looked to the others.

Mad Tom found a dirty, ragged fingernail to study
while his foot continued a manic tapping. JoyCee, though,
did not avert her eyes, even the centimeter her chin brace
allowed.

"It's a question," she huffed, "of audience."

David pretended to consider her words before speaking. "Fair enough, I think, but can you say more about
that."

"If someone doesn't care, she can't be your audience.
If no one cares, your only audience is yourself. So,
finally, it doesn't make any difference." The fine wires in
JoyCee's eyelids trailed back across her temples and into
her hairline. She blinked and half-blinked a short, complex code. The atrophied fist of her right hand rose from
the armrest of her chair; the index finger extended to
point. "Did I do that for me?" Her breath caught in her
throat. She got it back under control with an effort of will.
"Or for an audience? Does it matter?"

"Th-then it's imp-p-portant to c-c-care yourself, at
l-l-least."

When neither JoyCee nor Mad Tom responded, David rested his elbows on the table. "Well, you can't expect anyone else to if you don't. And if you don't it shows."

"And it's important to do what you care about most, because there's not enough time to do it all." Recalling the position of her hand, JoyCee blinked it back to the armrest before going on. "And what the person who's making the pome cares about probably isn't going to be what anyone else cares about." She took a long, ragged breath. "So there goes the whole concept of audience." She blinked and the chin brace turned her face to David.

"Sometimes others care. We're all people." He ended the thought abruptly. He had been ready to repeat what he often said to classes, that all people experience pain and joy, when he realized that, at least in the physical sense, JoyCee could not feel. He wondered if the memory of pain remained fresh for her or if it had faded irretrievably away. "Sometimes," he said finally, "what we and others care about coincide in ways both parties recognize."

Mad Tom jumped to his feet, knocking his chair over, and threw his arms out. "Who cares?" he shouted. He pointed to each of them in turn.

"Him!"

Carly's lower lip quivered.

"Her!"

JoyCee blinked until her chair turned to Mad Tom.

"Him!"

David maintained a steady gaze.

Mad Tom began to pace about the room frantically, gesturing first with one arm, then the other. "They don't care! Even for each other! Or Mad Tom! Not for what his prints say! Not for what goes in and comes out of his student union coin-in-the-slot console! Not for what comes from here!" He slapped his forehead so hard Carly flinched. "Or here!" he thumped his chest with his fist.

David held up a finger. "Speak it, Mad Tom, speak it."

"Sp-sp-speak it-t-t," Carly echoed, spraying a fine mist of saliva on the last word.

"The pome, Mad Tom." JoyCee said softly and clearly. "Speak it."

"Mad Tom don't-don't stut-stut-stutter in the wind like him!" he began. "Mad Tom ain't her, two eyes a machine's onliest read-out!" He paced so quickly and

turned so often that his long, limp hair fluttered in the
still room. Drops of sweat bounced from his face and
jiggled to the floor. "And he ain't him there, drawing the
government pay each month-day! And sitting his blue
women for the Insider meantimes." He thumped his
chest again. "No, he's Mad Tom, blue as money himself
but he ain't owned; spit from his mama like dishwater
and bad rubbish the day after the Fall, dropped like a hot
potato on far-out, baking skirt streets, left to toddle on
down if the dogs ain't ate him yet."

Mad Tom caught a leg on his overturned chair. He
broke his fall with both hands and pushed himself up
immediately. He kicked the chair savagely, and it scooted
away a couple meters. He fell into a crouch and showed
them his open palms. "Mad Tom's up like toast and still
rising! He's past the puny grasp of the Law, and the Insider
ain't counted high enough to number his onliest face.
Mad Tom's standing way top of the Expressway"—he
grabbed the flesh of his forearm with the other hand and
squeezed—"ninety kilos of unpattied hamburger for the
Quick-Stop grill, sizzling and having the laugh of them,
only, and only one other thing"—he pulled the hand
away and they saw the blood where his ragged nails had
broken skin—"the high-card ace satan-god they thought
they'd orbited into the skirts of space. This he says in the
face of him and him and her, and him and her that might
listen later." With that Mad Tom dropped his arms to his
sides and his chin to his chest. The room was still again.

JoyCee blinked in a complicated rhythm. Her withered
fists rose from the armrests. The fingers peeled away from
the palms, and the fists opened like twin buds. She
clapped her hands together with firm, exaggerated blinks
that pulled her cheeks and brows close and made a sound
like the snapping of dry twigs. Carly rose and straightened Mad Tom's chair. Mad Tom kicked behind him,
caught the seat of the chair with his heel, and knocked it
over again. Carly stood back and clapped.

JoyCee turned to David. "He thought about the assignment," she huffed, "about finding that which is truly
him. Do you think you can help him get it produced?"

Mad Tom's head snapped up in attention, and the two
stopped their applause.

"Y-y-es," Carly seconded. "C-c-can you help h-h-him?"

David kept his eyes on Mad Tom. "We haven't even critiqued it yet."

"But isn't it he? Doesn't it show us who Mad Tom is?"

"It's the b-b-b-best thing he's d-d-d-done."

"Do you want a critique, Mad Tom?" David asked.

Mad Tom glared at David, his nostrils flaring. His sweat carried a faint odor of nicotine.

"It's promising," David admitted, "but I think that if Mad Tom shows us the print it'll differ from what he spoke. Some of the spoken is better, probably, than the hard copy. The trick is to take the best and make it a uniform piece."

"You c-c-could do it, c-c-couldn't you, M-m-mad T-tom?"

"And maybe then it would be expanded. As it is it's a little short for a media filler, which is the market he'd have to pitch it to."

"He could build a quarter hour around it," JoyCee said with great deliberation. "Use it as the centerpiece."

"Until he has the rest of the material he can't tell where this pome belongs. Anyway, without other credentials, it'd be almost impossible to get someone to produce it."

"Y-y-you c-c-could h-h-help h-h-him." Carly's face reddened with effort.

"I have a hard enough time getting my own work produced." David turned his eyes from Mad Tom's smoldering stare to JoyCee's intent gaze.

"He could if he wanted!" Mad Tom shouted. "He could! He could! He could!" With that he picked up his chair and smashed it down on the table. The furniture, molded out of miraclastic, did not even bend, much less splinter. Mad Tom brought the chair around for a second try. JoyCee blinked herself backward.

Mad Tom brought the chair down again and again, each collision resulting in no more than the loud *clack!* peculiar to miraclastic. The table sat so squarely and solidly that even the folder of prints before David did no more than bounce a centimeter. Mad Tom flung the chair into a corner. He began to drag his ragged nails across his chest again and again. David waited for the chance to distract him.

Soon, Mad Tom had reduced the front of his shirt to rags. Long, shallow lacerations ran across his naked chest.

Winded, he looked around. David held up his index finger. Mad Tom shook his head violently and bellowed, "No!" He turned and ran to the wall and crashed into it. He fell backward, then stood and repeated the action. The third time, instead of falling, he reeled back across the room. The table caught him groin-high, and the upper half of his body collapsed across it. He grasped the edge on each side of David and pulled the table slowly over upon himself. The folder of prints slid to the floor.

David studied the young man's face, the thin beard wound into stringy braids, the patches of acne-studded skin. Mad Tom's sawing breath was the only sound. David reached out to lift the table, and Mad Tom flinched as from a blow. He squirreled his legs from beneath the table and got to his knees. He spied the prints and gathered them up, stood, and wobbled backward through the open door. They could hear him bouncing off the walls as he reeled down the hall.

Carly and JoyCee gazed into thin air without comment. Finally, David said, "I think it's time for our break."

JoyCee lowered her eyelids. The blue fingertips of one wizened hand came up to cover her pursed lips.

JoyCee and David sat in the empty classroom like two more pieces of scattered furniture. They did not speak, nor did they move beyond the small, inconsequential shiftings of David's hands. The class, like all studio classes, ran several hours on the one day of the week it met, and it was David's practice to provide his students a lengthy break. In previous quarters he had become accustomed to thinking of these quiet times in the deserted classroom as his own. He had been disconcerted, early in the term, when he realized that he would have company in the person of JoyCee.

Whatever JoyCee's physical needs might be, they were taken care of by some machinery behind the shield of her chair. Only JayCee's head, adult in size, and her shoulders and arms, those of a young girl though devoid of any vitality, showed above it. At first he had ignored her handicaps, imagining that she would prefer that. He had tried to make idle conversation to fill the time till the others—there had been several more students then— returned. Soon, he realized that to respond cost her dearly, and that she preferred to sit quietly. He then began to use the time to look over the prints he always carried with him, finding her unwavering gaze only slightly unnerving. Finally, he understood that meeting her eyes for some few uninterrupted minutes constituted some substantial pleasure for her. He doubted she had many others.

He was surprised then to see, a little while after Carly had slipped away after Mad Tom, deep in JoyCee's eyes some hint that he'd come to recognize.

"It has life and movement."

"Yes," he answered, "that's true."

"It would make all the difference in his life."

"I'm not sure of that. Most often, it doesn't."

"Still, Mad Tom needs something."

"I'm not sure I can give him what you want."

"Or me?"

JoyCee's pomes were often superbly finished and occasionally elegant, but David was not sure that she was speaking of her work.

"I'll give you the best advice I can," he said.

"Please."

"You read too much."

She flinched, and her hands fluttered toward her face for a moment before dropping back to the armrests.

"Too much of the wrong stuff."

"Explain, please."

"Your work is full of what's secondhand. Your reading is very current, and you've absorbed too much of the work of others who also read each other too much. That what others write should color your attempts is natural and good, but we need to expand the source of your influences."

"I see."

"A merging of styles into a distinct and personal voice speaking of a particular subject will mark the work as uniquely yours."

"But my life does not allow me a subject."

"It must."

"No. Nothing ever happens to me, you see. I read the media to know of the lives of others."

"That is what a reader does. A writer writes of her

own life, often covering it with several levels of disguise, for others to read."

He continued "I gave the assignment with you in mind. You need to isolate that which is you. Your work often speaks like something done by an Insider, and I believe that wrong for one whose experience is so terribly different."

She blinked a code. A hand rose and a curled index finger touched her temple. "There is only this."

"There is this," he said, waving his hands before him. "The air and the light that colors it. There is a place, whether a luxury suite at an Inside hotel or a room in a motel out in the skirts, walls, a bed—"

"I do not require a bed," JoyCee interrupted. "That comfort I can never enjoy."

David studied her unwavering stare. Her eyes were an ordinary shade of blue, common in the suburbs. Still, some vitality burned there.

"There is no love in my life, other than what my mother calls love, which is really only duty. Even very recently I thought that it might still be possible for me to find someone to whom I could give myself, at least that which is left of me." JoyCee had never laughed in David's presence and could not, he presumed. The certain lift of her upper lip that he understood to show her humor— invariably dark—appeared. "Such giving, I believe, would be a gift to myself as well. I have thought of you often, David—" Desperation in her eyes forced him to drop his gaze. He watched, instead, her mouth labor as she spoke— "in those times that pass, for me, as sleep, and in those reveries that are, for me, dreams."

Words flew into David's mind, flocked to make the beginnings of statements, fluttered, and disappeared. JoyCee's hands lay upon the armrests, blue and motionless as stillborn things. Finally, he settled on "I'm sorry."

Carly burst into the room. "H-h-h-h-h-he's h-he's—"

David looked into the young man's red and anxious face. "He's what, Carly?"

"In the w-w-w-w-washr-r-r-room."

"Mad Tom?"

"Y-y-y-yes, and h-h-h-he's g-g-got h-h-h-hostages."

David rubbed his eyes with a thumb and forefinger.

"I'm coming," he said before he looked up. "Get the Law."

Carly raced from the room. David looked to JoyCee. Her head in its braces was as unnaturally erect as always. The shield before her was slick with tears. Her eyelids fluttered in her weeping, each blink causing her hands to open and close on fistfuls of empty air.

5

End of the Quarter

David walked quickly down the deserted hall past the vending machines. He entered the alcove that led into the washroom and the door. It was locked. He knocked gently.

"Mad Tom? This is David."

The door muffled Mad Tom's reply. "What does he want?"

"I want to help. What is it you want?"

"He wants some respect. R-e-s-p-e-c-t."

"You have my respect. Let me in so we can talk?"

"They are talking."

"Why don't you let the hostages out?"

"Hostages?"

"Hostages. Carly said you had hostages."

"He does," Mad Tom said after a long pause, "and he's going to tear them up and flush them down the convenience."

Giddiness, from confusion or fear, expanded like a bubble in David's chest. "Let me speak to them," he said.

"He tried that before."

"Let them speak to me, then, Mad Tom."

"They've got nothing new to say."

"I can't respect you if you won't let them talk."

"Okay."

"Okay what?"

The Law entered the alcove, trailed by Carly.

"He's Mad Tom up like toast and still browning..." Mad Tom chanted through the door.

"You're the distressed party?" The Law was dressed in khaki and held a nightstick. "What's the situation here?"

"One of my students has locked himself in."

48

The Law rapped loudly on the door with his stick, then shouted, "Come out of there this instant!"

David, Carly, and the Law listened. Mad Tom continued to chant, but the words weren't intelligible. He had either dropped his voice or moved farther from the door. The Law looked at David. "Well?" he asked.

"Well what?"

"What's he saying?"

David shrugged.

"H-h-he's s-saying—" They looked at Carly who paused to concentrate. "'Bl-bl-blue like Ins-si-d-der m-m-oney.'"

The Law cocked his head like a robin looking for a worm, then rapped again. "I mean it!" he looked at Carly. "What's his name?"

"Mad Tom," David said.

"I mean it, Mr. Mad Tom!" the Law shouted at the door.

The convenience flushed. Carly's face blanched.

"The hostages!" Carly said clearly and incredulously. "This is a hostage situation?"

David shrugged. "That's what they say."

"Why didn't you tell me?"

"You didn't ask."

The Law placed a hand on a jutting hip and rolled his eyes to the ceiling. "I distinctly asked, 'What's the situation here?' I always ask, 'What's the situation here?' First step in the procedure's 'What's the situation here?'"

"H-h-hostage?"

"That's better," the Law said. He turned back to the door. "You in there! Mr. Mad Tom! Release those hostages at once or I will have no alternative but to ticket you!"

The convenience flushed again.

"The h-hostages!" Carly moaned. "He's fl-flushing them!"

The Law turned to David as if for translation. David shrugged, "Mad Tom said he was going to tear them into little pieces and flush them down the convenience."

The Law studied the back, then the palm of his own hand. "But how would that be possible without surgical instruments? Is this Mad Tom an especially strong fellow?"

"V-v-very strong!"

The Law awaited David's confirmation.

David nodded. "Yes, he's strong."

The Law dropped into quiet thought. The conve-

nience flushed periodically. Finally, he spoke. "This Mad
Tom business...the name suggests a possible imbalance.
What do you know of its origin? Did he select it himself?"

The Law looked at David, and David turned to Carly.
"H-his f-father g-gave it to h-him."

"Probably not a significant factor then," the Law mused.
He turned back to the door and rapped again.

"What!" Mad Tom screamed.

"Tell him to let the hostages come out," said the Law.

David called through the door, "Mad Tom, the Law
says you have to let the hostages go."

"Tell him if they are harmed he'll be in big trouble."

"Look," David began, "I don't think you understand—"

"Tell him! We've no time to waste."

"Mad Tom," David said, "the Law says that if any
harm comes to the pomes you'll be in big trouble."

"Pomes?" the Law said.

"Pomes and shorts. Prints. For the class. He's got the
other students' work in there too."

"So it's not so much a hostage situation as theft?"

"Well, they're just prints. I mean, the students can
always make other copies."

This time the Law turned to Carly to explain David's
words. Carly flushed crimson, and he was too flustered to
attempt to speak.

"Hm-m," the Law said. "Verify this hostage thing, will
you?" he asked David.

David knocked lightly. "Mad Tom, do you have the
prints in there?"

"Not anymore," Mad Tom said.

The Law pulled himself up straight and said, as if
personally affronted, "Well!" He considered a moment.
"Tell him he has until the count of five to come out."

"Are you sure—" David asked.

"Go ahead. I am the Law."

"Mad Tom, the Law says you have to the count of five
to come out."

There was no answer.

"One!" the Law said.

"Are you sure—" David tried again.

"Two!"

"—that he's breaking the law?"

"Three!"

"I mean, everybody locks the washroom door."

"Four!" The Law paused. "That's true, isn't it?"

David nodded his head. "I do. Often, anyway."

"Hm," the Law said. He turned his back to the door and spoke in a low voice. "Between you and me, most of this stuff that gets on the media ought to be flushed down the convenience anyway."

A little square box clipped to the Law's belt buzzed. He flipped a switch on it. "Got to go," he explained, "another emergency." With that, the Law strode off. Carly and David craned their necks around the alcove wall and watched his stiff back until he turned a corner.

"W-w-we c-c-can't just l-l-leave him in there."

David sat against the alcove wall, his face cupped in his palms. He had never known Carly to be so determined. An hour had passed since the Law'd left. Mad Tom had occasionally spoken, usually bits and pieces of his pomes, but he'd given no sign he intended to ever leave the washroom. Other than turning away a few people who wished to use the convenience, David's only break in the monotony had been when he'd checked on JoyCee. The classroom had been empty, the furniture back in neat order. As he stood in the door, a maintenance officer came up behind him.

"You stop those people from doing that."

"Did you see a young woman in here? In a wheelchair?"

She wagged a finger up into his face. "You stop that. We expect the rooms to be kept neat." She turned on her heel and left him standing there with his mouth open.

"W-w-well?" Carly asked.

David stood. "I'll call a friend who might be able to help. You"—he threw his hands up—"do what you can."

David walked down the hall, past the vending machines and deserted classrooms, to where the pay-consoles were kept. Ranks of them, deserted now that the quarter was over, stretched across the open bay. He sat down at the nearest one, pushed his Card through the slot, and studied the list of functions that appeared on the screen.

He selected "Call." He couldn't remember Preach's number, so he typed in his name instead. The screen commanded that he make a note of the number.

Preach's face appeared on the screen at once.

"Why, bless me, it's my old friend." Preach's eyes burned a little unnaturally, and his cheeks and nose seemed flushed, even over the fuzzy pay screen.

"I hope it's not too late, Preach."

"Ah no, Davy. Just beginning my evening communion."

"I'm sorry to interrupt you."

Preach waved a large, golden cup before the screen. A little liquid, red as his nose, splashed out. "Not at all, Davy. Always glad to see an old friend. Friendship's a sacrament, too, you know."

"It's good to see you, too, Preach, but this isn't a social call. I've got a problem here, down at the Complex."

Preach was suddenly solicitous. "Ah, Davy," he said, "if it's a matter of bail, I'll have to check the poor box."

"No, it's not money," David hurried to explain. "It's not even me, really, but I think you might be able to help."

Preach leaned into the screen and he turned his head so that he presented David a large ear. "A friend, then?"

"Actually, a student."

Preach gave a puzzled look, then brightened. "Yes, that's right, Davy. And how is the teaching going? The whole congregation is so proud of you, you know."

David had never known Preach to have a congregation. Apparently, Preach had been communing for some time.

"Mad Tom, the student, locked himself in the public washroom down here—"

"Mad Tom? I knew a Long Tom once, and there was Mad Betty. You remember her, Davy? Wandered the streets after the Fall? Always talking to herself about mutual funds and CDs? You'd have thought she lost her children."

"Anyway Preach, he's locked himself in the washroom—"

"The washroom, you say?" Preach smiled hugely, then shook with quiet laughter. "All those people standing in line, hopping up and down." He giggled.

"Well, the place is pretty much deserted right now."

"Did I ever tell you about the controversy we had when we first went to heterosex washrooms? You'd have thought occupying the same convenience constituted fornication. The things some people get confused." He laughed uproariously. "I suppose," he said between guffaws, "that the case *could* be built for simultaneous occupation."

David smiled in spite of himself. When Preach had settled into shaking his head and clearing his throat he said, "Preach, one of Mad Tom's classmates is here and is desperate to get him out. I guess I'd feel better, too, if I knew Mad Tom wasn't going to spend the summer there."

"Say no more, Davy. Just let me saddle up the Yamaha."

"Maybe I should come get you."

"No need, Davy, it usually starts on the second or third kick. That friend of yours is a genius with engines."

"McGee."

"Yes, that's the fellow. Well Davy, I'll be right—where did you say you were?"

"The Complex. Adult Education."

"Twenty minutes." Preach was communing as he hung up.

"Perhaps you know of me." Preach sat on the floor of the darkened alcove, a small bag, it's leather ancient and cracked, and his helmet before him. He spoke conversationally, as if no door separated him from Mad Tom. "They call me Preach, and I am the last person of the cloth in the surburbs. I was ordained before the Fall, and my flock are the lost and lonely of this decay. Speak to me, Mad Tom."

"The black shirt and round collar? He lives in what some call church and works the skirts for ones who don't home up early enough? The ceremony man? The old one?"

"That is I." Carly sat nearby, too tired to be excited by Preach's presence. "Now tell me your name."

"He's Mad Tom, bluest of the blue people, caught this side of the curb and happy here."

"Tell me more."

"He's done for and done in and doing to others."

"A rule man, then."

"He has his rules, though none else does."

"Others do, Mad Tom. Tell me yours."

David relaxed. Preach's reputation in the suburbs made him out to be a bogeyman, but David'd never known anyone to withstand his charm upon speaking with him.

Mad Tom ground to a halt.

"Mad Tom," Preach said, "we're having a discussion of what, in the learned traditions, is called theology."

"Theology," Mad Tom repeated.

"I find your theology and mine are one theology."

"One," Mad Tom said

"Open the door, Mad Tom, it is time to affirm theology." With that he lifted a deep, wide cup from his black bag. Even in the dim light of the alcove its golden finish glowed. Preach then brought forth a square, squat jar, an antique of real glass, filled with dark liquid. Only after he'd placed candles on the floor and lit them did he fill the chalice. He placed it near the door.

"Open your nostrils, Mad Tom, if not the door," Preach said. "In the learned traditions theology is celebrated in this way." Carly stared, wide-eyed, at the candle flames' reflection dancing on the surface of the cup, spellbound in the dark fragrance filling the alcove.

The door opened with a creak. Mad Tom appeared centimeter by centimeter. When the door was wide enough he pushed himself, still sitting, though with only a little awkwardness. The door creaked closed behind him.

"Welcome, Mad Tom," Preach said. "You come to complete our circle." He handed him the chalice.

"What is it?" Mad Tom asked.

"It is wine."

Mad Tom drank. He closed his eyes, and a smile, the first David had ever seen there, appeared on his lips.

Preach took the chalice from Mad Tom and offered it to Carly. He drank eagerly, then coughed a little of the wine back out between his clenched teeth. Preach wiped his chin and the hand he'd used to cover his mouth with a clean white cloth from the bag. He patted Carly's back. "It takes a little time to go from water to wine," he said.

"Who did that?" David asked. He took the chalice from Preach's hands. "Turned water to wine?" The wine glazed his tongue and trickled down his throat like sunshine.

Preach took a long drink, then smacked his lips. "Ah," he said, then passed the chalice to Mad Tom.

Mad Tom looked down into it and studied the reflection of the flames. His nostrils flared. After he drank he held the chalice back to Preach. Preach motioned it away with two fingers. "Take and drink," he said to Carly.

After what seemed like a very long time, Preach said, "I don't remember, Davy. Who do you think?"

David took another drink. The glow had spread deep into his belly, and his head was fuzzy as if he'd spent a long day in the hot sun. He handed the chalice to Preach.

"Abraham Lincoln? Ghandi?" Preach suggested.

David shook his head slowly. "Ghandi maybe. Abraham Lincoln was political. How about plain Abraham? Or was he the one who discovered it."

"I used to know all that stuff. Lord, but that was a long time ago."

After a while Preach said, "No, Moses discovered wine. No, not Moses. The other one."

"Noah," David offered.

"Yes, that's the one. Rotten grapes." He looked to Mad Tom and Carly. "Fruit of a kind you don't see anymore. Anyway, being of an experimental frame of mind or, more likely very hungry, he gave it a try. Apparently, he liked it, for in no time at all he was rolling on the floor, naked and singing. One of his sons stumbled in and found the scene so funny he laughed out loud. After the old man passed out, his other sons came in and covered him up. Noah woke up the next morning a lot worse for wear, I guess, and with a real grudge for the one who laughed."

Mad Tom and Carly giggled at the story.

"No, he was so angry he punished him—sent him away or something like that." Carly fell quiet. Mad Tom's face showed some somber, distant recognition.

"He's my favorite—the one who laughed," Preach sighed.

"This is not synthetic," David said after a pause.

"Now Davy, don't ask. It's a gift from the powers."

"Privileged information. A matter of confession?"

"Precisely."

Preach filled the chalice a third time. David saw him size up the other two. "There are other sacraments—"

"Excuse me." David rose, but the others hardly noticed his leaving.

He walked down the hall to the nearest exit. He stood in the empty parking lot and took two deep breaths. The spring air was flavored with wine. David had partaken in many of Preach's sacraments. His favorite was poker, though he regularly watched his money disappear into the open maw of Preach's poor box. The old man's smile beneath his green eyeshade was far from holy. No, Preach could play cards with the devil himself.

He saw no trace of the Law. He walked to the Torino and reached in through the open window.

"David?"

He jumped in surprise. He breathed deeply to steady himself and bent down to look in the window at Ms. Kitty. Even in the evening light the tracks of earlier tears were visible on her unpainted face. He got a cigarette from behind the visor, lit it, and tossed the match away.

"Go ahead," he said.

"She checked like David called and said to do."

"And?"

Ms. Kitty's voice broke. "She's dead. She did it herself!"

David smoked quietly while Ms. Kitty sobbed.

"She's sorry," Ms. Kitty squeaked through her tears.

"Sorry?"

"She sat in the front seat without his permission."

The cigarette burned his fingers, and he tossed it away. He got into the car, reached over, and hugged Ms. Kitty. "I'll take you home," he said, "and have a look." He started the car, awkwardly, one arm still around her heaving shoulders. He'd call Preach in the morning. At the moment the old one had his hands full with the living.

6

Sunday Drivers

McGee drove like the serious gearhead he was, hands on the wheel at two and ten o'clock, back stiff, eyes bearing down on the street ahead. He avoided potholes with a quick twist of the wheel that caused the tires to squeal. That he did not discriminate between the left and right lanes meant little in the suburbs. David slumped against the right-hand door, watching McGee's profile through dark glasses.

"Hot," he suggested by way of conversation.

"Too hot, too early." McGee did not take his eyes from the street. "At least, the humidity's not bad."

David gave the radio dial a spin. The cab filled with white noise. "I wish the Blue Baby'd work days." He turned the radio off.

"You want me to sing?" McGee asked.

"No, just concentrate on your driving. Where are we, anyway?"

McGee frowned. "Broadhurst and Benson."

"Bookstore's open on Sunday."

"All that dust makes me sneeze. Besides, I asked them to find the rest of the *Groos* for me five years ago. Guess how many they've come up with? *Nada*."

The bookstore's selection of classics had been decimated in its first few years of operation, and almost nothing from the New City producers found its way to the suburbs. The shelves were filled with stacks of agricultural bulletins, economic reports, and math texts from before the Fall. "It's all media these days," David said.

"I heard reading's optional for the primaries."

"Really?"

McGee risked a glance at him. "I thought you knew all that stuff. You're a teacher, after all."

"Different level. Besides, I'm just a part-time assistant instructor. They don't tell me much."

"Do you think it's true, though, about the reading?"

Ahead some small children were tunneling under a sidewalk. One looked up from the hole to watch the pickup pass. He had a muddy table knife in his hand. "The world keeps changing," David said.

"The good things have gone to hell," McGee intoned.

David laughed. "You're a romantic, McGee."

"Damn straight," he said, then suddenly added, "Hey, you see a collar?"

A lone dog was crossing the street ahead, his head down and his gait wobbly. David decided on the truth. "Nope."

McGee pressed the accelerator, and the extra barrels of the pickup's carburetor kicked in. The mufflers reverberated with the power of the pickup's oversized engine.

The dog continued its meandering. It looked up only in the moment before impact. It made three thumps as it rolled and bounced beneath the high-clearance vehicle. McGee took the pickup through a long, slow, sliding 180-degree turn. The big engine idled. "Do you think we got it?" McGee asked.

"Yeah, I think we got it." McGee's eagerness to kill ferals was one thing David did not understand or like in his friend.

McGee took his foot off the brake. The pickup began to crawl toward the dog.

They stopped ten meters from the carcass. "I think it was sick," McGee said, "moving like that and all alone."

"Sick, maybe old. It looked more starved than most."

"Those are the worst," McGee said. After a second he asked, "You don't want the ears, do you?"

"Hell, no." People still collected them for the bounty they could get at the Government Complex. David had done so as a boy, always careful to hide the evidence from his parents. Now, the idea of cutting through the hard cartilage while stripping the ear away nauseated him.

"Me, either," McGee said. "Let those kids have them."

The children who'd been digging in the dirt had run

up to watch. They stood on the sidewalk. The biggest had
an open Barlow knife in her hand.

"Hell, yes," David said. "Go up there and turn left."

"Whatever you say, boss," McGee joked. He'd killed
the dog almost by reflex, but now he seemed as eager as
David to leave the scene.

After they turned the corner, McGee asked, "Where're
we going, anyway?"

"Just a drive-by. Go right on Morningside."

They passed an abandoned school. Symbols and signs,
spray-painted in red on the pale brick, covered much of
the older, written graffiti.

"Was it pretty bad?" McGee asked tentatively.

"Bad enough," David said. He rubbed his eyes against
the image of Maybelline sitting erect against the head-
board of the bed. Still he saw her, eyes lifeless as lint, the
long cut like a second smile across her throat. "There was
an awful lot of blood," he said.

"You know why?" McGee asked.

The sweat under David's arms began to run down his
sides. "No," he said. "I talked to her earlier in the day.
She wasn't great, but I thought she'd ride it out. She
always came back after this sort of thing before."

"Sometimes it's just an impulse. If you can live with it
for a minute, it passes, and then you're all right." The
conviction with which McGee spoke suggested a private
familiarity with the impulse.

"The smell of it was the worst."

"People get old, scared. They don't know what they're
going to do."

"She was younger than either of us."

McGee shrugged. "She was a sitter."

"Everybody's scared," David said.

"Hell," McGee said, "people don't need a reason,
especially in this heat. There's Preach."

The old man stood beside his church with a spade
and a watering can.

"Do you want to stop?" McGee asked.

"Like I said, just a drive-by. I'll see him later." He
waved as they passed.

When the pickup disappeared around the corner of the
block, Preach dropped his hand and returned to his spading.

A voice in his mind, distant and neutral, spoke. *It's late for marigolds.*

They might grow here, in the shadow of the church, Preach thought. *With lots of care.*

Lilies of the field, the voice said.

Preach was used to voices in his head. He chopped at the spaded-up clods a while before answering. *When did I last hear that?*

Seminary? the voice said. *Before the Fall, anyway.*

That used to mean something different. It had to do with sin.

Your life was devoted to the concept of sin.

I must have been very bored, to worry so much about wrong and right.

Nobody talks much about wrong and right anymore. Not out in the skirts. Maybe Insiders do. The clods were reduced to gravel. Insiders were as distant to him as the young seminarian had been.

Preach spread water on the bed, then dropped to his knees. He worked the moisture into the soil with his fingers. He tore open a plastic package marked with a Government Complex logo. He scattered the seeds freely over the earth and sprinkled dirt over them. After he had watered the plot again he found his knees had locked.

Old bones, the voice said.

Preach grasped the spade for support and hauled himself up hand over hand, along the handle. He breathed great, ragged lungfuls of sun-heated air, and gazed out over the deserted neighborhood. The church's shadow fell halfway across the overgrown and garbage-strewn lawn. The roof, except for the longer shadow of the steeple, separated dark and light in a single razor-straight line. The farthest shadow—the cross's slender darkness—appeared to buckle in waves of heat.

McGee honked the horn again. David looked around the refinery field, past the huge tanks, their white paint grimy and rust streaked. Nothing moved.

The pickup sat between the pump and a tiny shack. Both were on skids, and the pump was connected by a thick hose to the nearest tank. "Well," he said.

"Well," McGee answered, "I've got to pee. Have her fill it up—if she shows." He handed the bottle to David and got out of the cab. He disappeared behind the tank, his fly already half-undone.

David took a pull from the bottle and shuddered when the synthetic gin hit his stomach. He puckered his mouth at the metallic taste. Despite the heat, he longed for some of Preach's dark and heavy communion wine. Better yet, he thought, something cold. A vision of Maybelline's icy body lying in the vault at the Government Complex hit him with sickening suddenness.

"You okay, mister?"

Rusty stared in the driver's-side window, slowly wiping her hands on a greasy rag. Thick red hair bushed out from beneath her undersized grease-black cap.

"Yeah." He got his voice under control. "Fill it up."

David watched in the side mirror as she unscrewed the cap to the tank and inserted the nozzle. She met his gaze. "Windows?"

He nodded.

She got a bucket from beside the pump and a short stepladder from the shed. She climbed up and began to slosh water on the windshield with a sopping rag.

David remembered Rusty as a girl in long, baggy coveralls working next to her father. The coveralls had shrunk and shrunk as Rusty had grown. They had become so ragged that, finally, she had torn off the legs and arms, and inexpertly sewn patches covered much of the torso. Old-fashioned diaper pins stretched across the broken front zipper, and greasy skin showed in the gaps between them. For all that, she remained an enigma. David wasn't even sure of her name. It might have been stitched on the coveralls before she got them.

"You call this service?" McGee stood by his door.

"Yes, sir," Rusty said. She moved the stepladder around and mounted it in front of him.

"What's that? Some kind of joke?" McGee pointed to faded, amateur lettering high on one of the farther tanks. It read OPEN 24 HOURS 7 DAYS/WEEK.

"We're open, sir."

"We had to wait for half an hour."

"Can't get good help, sir." Rusty leaned far over to rub a spot. Her rag squeaked against it. She finished, stepped off the ladder, and faced McGee. "Check under the hood, sir?"

"You know better than that," McGee said.

Rusty came around, removed the nozzle from the tank, and screwed the cap back on while McGee counted out some bills.

She held her hand out for them. "Thank you, sir, I'll get your change."

"Keep it."

"Thank you, sir. Come again." Rusty disappeared into the shack. McGee gave a low whistle before climbing back into the cab. He started the pickup and drove away, shaking his head. "Why does she always do that?" he wondered.

"Do what?"

"Ask to look under the hood."

"Maybe she's trying to be helpful." They passed through the gate in the chain link fence surrounding the refinery field. McGee hung a left and accelerated with a squeal of tires and a full-throated roar from the mufflers.

"She knows who I am. Nobody touches my engine but me."

"You afraid she'll find out you're a quart low?"

"I've never been a quart low in my life," McGee said without humor.

They approached a windowless, concrete-block building. Letters on one side read ACME. The rest of the sign had weathered to obscurity. "Do you have any idea what goes on in there?" David asked.

"Where?"

"There." Two teenagers stood in the sun by the single door. One quickly hid a cigarette in his cupped hand.

"No," McGee said, "I don't."

"Kids are always hanging around."

"Kids hang around. It's what they do."

"Hit the Alley, will you?"

"Hand over the bottle." After a long swallow and a grimace, McGee returned to Rusty. "Why doesn't she get some new coveralls? Those are going to shake off sometime."

"You're just worried you won't be there to see it."

McGee said nothing.

He tried again. "Maybe she won't wear syn-fab."

McGee wasn't listening. "I've been in there a thousand times," he said, "and it's just 'sir' this and 'sir' that."

They crested a hill. Fast Food Alley lay below them.

"She's the same with everybody. I've never met anyone who claimed to know her. Personally, I mean."

"She could make a bundle on all that gas. I don't know why she doesn't charge more."

"Probably doesn't want trouble. If it's cheap enough, she doesn't have to worry about people trying to steal it."

"Hell, that's what her old man did, just set up shop after the Fall like he owned it."

They neared an abandoned K-Mart. "Pull in here."

David wondered if McGee had heard, but at the last second he pulled into the parking lot by the Burger Barn.

"I'll be right back. You want anything?"

"Sure," McGee said without looking from the windshield. "Just leave the bottle."

"You've got it there between your legs."

"Okay," McGee said. He was rubbing his chin and watching with great interest something David couldn't see.

David was the only customer. He sat in a booth and nodded to the little girl who stood behind a cash register. She disappeared behind the grill and fryers.

Feldon came over and dropped a plastic case on the table. David threw down some blue bills, picked up the case and rose.

"Missed you last night," Feldon called to his back.

McGee still gazed, moon-eyed, through the windshield. David got a cigarette out of the case.

"You know," McGee said, "I've got some old coveralls at the shop, if some stray didn't eat them. I'll bet they're not syn-fab, but I don't suppose they've got the right name on them."

"Dogs won't eat them unless they're syn-fab. And she could sew the old name patch onto new coveralls, if she could sew."

McGee turned to him. "Really?"

"Sure." David took a deep hit from the cigarette. "It'd be a nice gift."

"What?"

"Gift. Present, whatever."

"Whatever," McGee repeated dreamily.

Blue cigarette smoke curled out the window and vanished into the bright day. "Take me home," David said. "It's time I get ready."

The funeral took place at dusk in the cemetery at the foot of the Kennedy Expressway. Preach and David were there as were Mad Tom and Carly. Preach had suggested his two novices as grave diggers. "They need the money, Davy," Preach had argued. "Poverty is an unnecessary vow when it is a fact of life." Ms. Kitty did not come, but even four was a larger than normal turn-out for a suburban funeral.

Preach stood beside the mound of earth, leaning on a spade for support, and David stood a meter away. At his feet lay the small, neat bundle the clerk at the Government Complex had called personal effects. The two younger men sat on the ground a little way off, looking very serious in their black robes and facepaint. It was a first for both of them. Death was common enough in the suburbs, funerals hit-or-miss affairs.

A long, quiet time passed. "Ashes to ashes," Preach said finally. He waved an arm as if to take in all of the cemetery. "I've preached more funerals than I can count, boys, and I've said that at every one of them."

He picked up a clod of dirt. "Dust to dust. I've said that, too, though now I've forgotten why."

After a moment he went on. "I've forgotten almost everything I've ever known, but I can walk down these rows and tell you something, some one thing at least, about everyone I've buried. That's what I need to be able to do for the *salvation of my soul*, whatever that means.

"An old man wonders, sometimes, what has happened to all the people. He looks around and sees only children, and the children are already dying.

"Ashes. Sure, that's from desire, isn't it? That in us that burns hottest. We're all, for a little while, the flame begat in the heat of a woman and a man who, at least for that moment, open themselves each to the other. There are twin miracles for you—trust and love.

"Dust? The clay around here is too hard for dust." He dropped the clod back onto the mound. It rolled to a stop. "Only at the end of the long, dry summers do we have much dust. That's when the wind gathers it up. And 'sometimes we see the wind whirling down the street, don't we? Carrying the dust and trash of the skirts? Maybe that's us, ground down to powder and mixed in with garbage from the streets.

"Maybe life's a wind that carries us for a while, until it blows itself out and we settle back to earth."

The sun had nearly set. Drying facepaint had pulled David's skin taut. Peace was falling with the sun.

"What things will I remember about Maybelline? That a terrible thing happened and that her life did not carry her far enough? Perhaps. That on the day I buried her I planted flowers? Maybe." He paused and considered. "I think this: when the wind whirls up the streets in the heat of the summer, its arms full of dust, I will remember to remember Maybelline."

Preach bowed his head. A rough, clunking engine idled down the street that cut through the cemetery. David smiled to himself. Ms. Kitty had come at least that far. In the twilight David picked up a clod of dirt from the mound and stepped to the open grave. Maybelline's body, wrapped in an old bedspread he'd found in his house, was a long, light presence in the shadow. He put the clod in one palm and placed his other hand over it. He rubbed his hands together, and a trickle of dust sprinkled down on Maybelline. He turned away.

Carly and Mad Tom stood. Preach signaled them, and they each approached the grave. Carly grabbed the spade and dribbled dirt into the grave. Mad Tom took his turn.

The night went suddenly electric. The world and the weather held their breaths. From out of the cloudless evening sky came an explosion sharper than a gunshot, more attenuated than the longest roll of thunder. Carly, his eyes still on the body of Maybelline in her grave, clapped his hands over his ears against the sound. David fought the urge to do the same. The ground beneath moved as if the earth were only a child's top wobbling on its axis. A wind like a great breath lay the long grass of the cemetery down and tugged at the men's clothes. The night was suddenly washed in red light. Men and tombstones, back-lit, threw shadows long and thin as blades. Mad Tom pivoted to the west, dropped the spade he held and covered his mouth against the scream within him. David met Preach's eyes and knew that he, too, had yet to look to the source of light and wind. Something, an aged resolution, showed in his eyes, and, slowly, Preach turned to the west.

The old man gasped and fell to his knees. David moved his tongue in a mouth gone dry. He held a flat hand over his eyes against the light, then, and turned as if drawn. Beyond the skirts, at some distance far, far Out There, red flame like a hand reached higher and higher, making the sky black against its brilliance. David felt the burn of it on his upturned face.

"Sweet Jesus," Preach called above the wind, and David looked down at him. Preach blinked behind the fingers he'd spread to block the light, and tears ran down his cheeks. "They've called her home," he gasped and, choking, fell prostrate toward the fire.

7

Supreme Headquarters

Yellow light flowed across the large redwood deck, through the double patio doors and flooded the main floor of the newly designated Supreme Headquarters. The Commodore sat on a high stool at the kitchen counter facing the rising sun. His cotton bathrobe, stiff from having been air dried over the railing of the deck the day before, hung low on his shoulders, the knot at his waist working loose. He stared intently at an assortment of jars, small hand tools, and eccentrically shaped pre-Fall plastic and metallic components spread before him. Slowly he raised a screwdriver and then, just as slowly, set it back down. Several still, silent minutes passed. Then, with sudden alacrity, he picked up two of the plastic pieces and snapped them together. He swept others to the side, pulled an old-fashioned white electrical cord from the oversized pocket of his robe, ran his hand up it till he found the end. He stripped insulation from the cord with a knife from the counter. He curled the exposed copper fibers around the terminals soldered to a metal sheet and tightened down the pair of small screws with the screwdriver. He snapped the sheet into place beneath the joined plastic parts. He found the largest component—a metal base with a plastic arm—and joined it to the conglomeration he had just concocted with a satisfying snap. He placed a number of screws in their appropriate holes and turned them home.

The Commodore plugged the pronged end of the cord into an outlet on the counter. "Do we have electrical to the house circuits?" he called. The thing sat silent before him. He studied it for a moment, then carefully moved a toggle switch to one side. There was an immediate dry chortling by way of response.

"We have electrical!"

The Commodore uncapped one of the jars and emptied it through a grate at the top of the contraption, and it gurgled its thanks. Liquid began to drain onto the metallic element with a hiss. He crinkled his nose at the odor. He found a handled jar and put it beneath the stream. When the stream stopped he poured the contents of the jar back through the grate. Only then did he look up.

She stood at attention, a dark silhouette against the streaming sunlight, a shadow in the glare of the pine-paneled room. Behind her and beyond the deck, hills furred with evergreens stretched away for kilometers.

"Relax, Major." When she did not, he used his left hand, since his right was around the handle of the jar, to return her salute. "At ease."

"Permission to speak freely, sir."

"Certainly." Again liquid dribbled into the jar.

"What is that—fragrance, sir?"

"Vinegar, Major Korsikahv. Come here and take a look."

The Major marched over and leaned close.

She studied a small, plastic logo. "Mr. Coffee?"

"Exactly."

"Would the Commodore enlighten the Major on a point?"

"I'll try."

"What is 'Mr. Coffee'?"

"It's a machine for making coffee."

"Does the Commodore require a machine for making coffee? The Major understands that Supreme Headquarters is hot-water-capable, and the stores contain a supply of powder."

"Blech-ch."

"Or organic beans, then, if the Commodore prefers."

"Oh, the Supreme Head certainly prefers beans, Major. The Supreme Head has already hand-ground a supply."

"Yes sir, but what does vinegar have to do with it?"

"Call me Mike. I can't let anyone call me Commodore, much less the other, before I have my coffee."

"Is that an order, sir?"

The Commodore sighed. "I don't give orders, Major."

"But, sir, you must!" The Major, startled, dropped her line of sight and noticed, for the first time, his robe. "Sorry, sir. I didn't realize you were out of uniform."

"Major, I don't wear a uniform."

"I only meant, sir—"

"Major, I never dress before coffee."

"Yes, sir."

"I never wear a uniform."

"Yes, sir."

"And I never give orders."

"Yes, sir."

"Is that clear?"

"Yes, sir."

"Now lighten up, at ease. Smoke 'em if you got 'em."

"Sir!" she said, scandalized.

"Mighty fine with that first cup of coffee."

"Sir!" she repeated.

"Relax, Major. Just kidding. A joke? Humor?"

"If the Commodore's sure?"

He dismissed the idea of lecturing her on the traditional irreverence of American humor. He had already shocked her more than he'd intended, and a reference to nationalism would constitute a breach of decorum, one the Major might not choose to forgive. That both the First Secretary of the New Cities and the Supreme Head of the Combined Services were, ancestrally, Americans made the subject additionally sensitive. His predecessor had expressed it in the most cynical, and succinct, terms he'd ever heard, when she said that continued American domination of the New Cities did not rest comfortably on the necks of the more recalcitrant cultures.

Hot vinegar streamed into the jar. He knew, too, of the theory that the Fall and, by extension, the Third World Wars were the results of American socioeconomic engineering gone awry. He did not know whether it was true, but he assumed that many who harbored strong nationalistic loyalties believed it. The military attracted people with deep cultural memories. He himself was one. The Major might be another. Any truly erratic behavior on his part could one day be used against him. He sighed, despite himself. Nationalism aside, there was still personal ambition—no one rose to her rank without it. He poured the vinegar down the sink. He would watch her closely.

The faucet gasped, then ran enough rusty water for him to rinse the handled jar. He stared at his hand.

"Pot!" he cried.

"Sir?"

"Coffee *pot*! That's what they called it. Pot."

"Yes, sir."

The Commodore shambled over to a cupboard. The door opened with a creak. He extracted a stack of ancient papers. The top one crumbled in his hand. He placed the second in a plastic basket. He opened a jar, held it to his nose, and smiled at the dark, real coffee aroma. He offered the jar to the Major, who declined with a shake of her head. He sighed, scooped coffee into the basket and slid it into place. He poured bottled water in and sat back.

"Sit down, Major. You must be tired—transmatting out of New Moscow yesterday, riding in a lorry half the night."

"I enjoy transmatting, sir."

"Sit down, anyway."

She took the stool opposite him.

"Let's talk for a minute, officer to officer."

"Yes, sir."

"What do you know of me?"

"Only what I've heard, sir."

"And what have you heard?'

"The Commodore is reputed to be extremely able and"— she hesitated—"eccentric, if you pardon me saying so."

"I don't find the description offensive, Major."

"Very good, sir."

"Major, we're going to be working together for a long time. I want you to speak your mind."

The coffee bubbled into the pot. The aroma began to drive away the vinegar smell. "Why here, sir?"

"You mean a sailor this far from the sea?"

"No, sir." She allowed herself a tight smile. "I mean, wouldn't N.D.C. have been more convenient? And safer?"

"We're out here, Major, because it's time we looked around. Convenience?" He nodded to the console behind her. "That machine over there makes it all terribly convenient. Safe? The most dangerous thing we've run into in fifty kilometers of unexplored Out There is a cow. By the way, how was the bovine detail progressing when you came in?"

She smiled again. "With considerable difficulty, sir."

"We're going farther," he said, "if we have the time."

"If, sir?"

"When, Major. We'll stay put for a time. Maybe we'll use some of these trees to make a sailing ship."

"You're a romantic!" Startled by her own words, she added, "Sir."

"So are you, Major. What other reason is there for joining up? What else is on your mind?"

"Why make coffee the hard way?"

"Just warming up for the bigger stuff." He stuck his thumb over his shoulder at the array of appliances built into and resting upon the kitchen cabinets.

The Commodore poured out the coffee. He pushed a mug over to the Major and sipped his own. "Well?" he asked.

"Delicious," she said.

"I'd hoped for real milk in my real coffee. I think we'll just keep Mr. Coffee to ourselves, Major, till the grunts locate the appropriate end of that cow."

"Maybe she's not giving milk right now, sir?"

"She has a young one—a calf. It's not, ah, weaned."

"Yes sir, that makes sense."

"The world makes sense, Major, though the circumstances of an era dictate what's sensible. New Cities are all identical because the planners of each resolved identical problems with identical technologies. People lived Out There for generations, because it made sense to them. Maybe if we adopt their perspective it'll make sense again. Cows give milk. That's a detail in a hundred storybooks and fairy tales, as well as a fact of mammalian biology. And it makes sense. A Mr. Coffee was a complicated way of making coffee for a generation of people who loved complication."

"And good coffee," the Major said.

He refilled both mugs. "Now that we've had our first cup, we can talk business—Old Trace called last night."

"Pardon me, sir?"

"Tracy. Our boss." She nearly saluted. "At ease."

"Yes, sir."

"I understand you observed the phenomenon firsthand."

"Yes sir."

"Describe it, please."

"The Commodore certainly must have seen it."

"The Commodore did. Describe it anyway."

"An exceedingly bright light of reddish tint, in the apparent form of a flame, emanating from the horizon."

"Do you care to speculate as to the source?"

"A natural phenomenon, such as volcanic eruption, or something left from before the Fall—the explosion of oil tanks, perhaps, or even nuclear weapons, detonated by eroding ignition systems, a lightning strike, or even by some band of revolutionaries attempting to continue the Third World wars by bringing such a weapon to a New City. They didn't know what they were doing—*Bang!* They're vaporized."

"Any other ideas, Major?"

She smiled.

"Go ahead," he said.

"Well, my driver thought that you had blown this place up with what she called your fiddling."

The Commodore tightened the knot of his robe with a jerk. "Fiddling?"

"Yes, sir, fiddling."

"Is she on the milk detail?"

"She was holding a rather soiled tail when I came in."

"Good." He appeared satisfied. "As you might imagine, the First Secretary has given us the job of checking out the sorts of possibilities you've mentioned."

"Yes, sir, that's very gratifying, sir."

"Somebody's got to do it, Major."

"Yes, sir."

"And it's a waste of time."

"Sir?"

"The reports from two dozen New Cities are identical."

"The Major fails to see the Commodore's point, sir."

"Same magnitude and same time—right after sundown. A single event at a single locus would have been perceived to be of different magnitudes, proportionate to distance, and at different times, according to zone. Savvy?"

"Pardon, sir?"

"Understand?"

"Yes, sir. Sir, does the First Secretary concur?"

"She does now. After I explained it to her."

"Oh. What would the Commodore like me to do?"

"Return to your quarters and get on your console. Order the Air Force, whatever planes are air-worthy, up for reconaissance. You don't mind giving orders, do you?"

"No, but, sir, you said it didn't have a single locus."

"Maybe I'm wrong. Get on the line to the civilian freighters, ask them to keep an eye open." He reached down beside his stool and brought up an ancient toaster in the grip of a single, large hand. "Maybe it's a number of very similar and somehow associated phenomena."

"Warnings? Set off equidistant from selected New Cities?"

The Commodore picked up a screwdriver and held it poised over the toaster. "Warning, sure," he said as much to himself as the Major. He sharpened his attention. "Set off? I believe that a paranoid response, Major. There aren't enough revolutionaries left in this tetrasphere to man the kind of facilities necessary. Even if they worked together, which would be an historical first. You might call up the file and try some triangulations, that sort of thing. I dumped all the information under 'Rescue Effort.'"

"Why that name, sir?"

"No reason."

"If the world makes sense, there has to be a reason." He smiled to the toaster.

"Might I ask what the Commodore will be doing?"

"Working on this toaster."

"Yes, sir." The Major rose and saluted.

The Commodore waved the screwdriver in return. The Major pivoted and marched across the room.

"Major?"

She turned. "Yes, sir?"

"Come back in a couple hours and we'll talk some more." He had already removed the base from the toaster. "We'll have coffee and toast. You bring the milk."

"Of course, sir."

The Commodore worked steadily for some time. He dismantled the toaster and cleaned the elements and contacts of corrosion with a small brush. The room fell into shadow as the sun rose above the lintel of the patio

doors. He looked up only once, when he heard a cow
bellow. A calf bleated in response from a different direction. He reassembled the components and plugged in the
toaster. The elements within grew warm, then red-hot.

He rose and walked down the hall. He climbed out of
the bathrobe and into a shirt and shorts. He padded
barefoot to the console. He finished buttoning his shirt
while he tapped in brief responses to a long series of
security questions. The image of the First Secretary
appeared.

"What'd they say?" the Commodore asked.

"You have a reluctant consensus, Mike."

"Do they have any other explanations?"

"Nothing worth repeating."

"Identical minds."

"You've made your point. How do you want the tran-
scripts routed and classified?" She raised a writer.

"1-A."

"Mike, the media will want access."

"Classification of your file is a political decision."

"All right. What file?"

"Rescue Effort. And Trace, that file is 1-A."

The First Secretary's brows arched high. "Aren't you
being a little too security conscious? And what does that
mean, 'Rescue Effort'?"

"Just a label. And Trace, I want all the information
you've got on long-range transmatation."

"What do you mean, long range?"

"Long range."

"Mike, there are banks full of information on long-
range transmatation. Twenty-five years' worth."

"I want the status of any experimental or theoretical
procedure to protect the transmat beam from sunspots."

"Bankok and L.A.? Those were equipment failures."

"I wasn't thinking of them."

"Are you going to tell me what you are thinking of?"

"I'm bored. I need something to work on."

The two of them sat facing each other. The First
Secretary, starched and pressed, her cheeks and eyes
subtly highlighted by a subdued shade of facepaint, em-
bodied efficiency and charm. The Commodore reached
up to scratch his chest and found that he had buttoned
his shirt through the wrong holes.

Finally, he spoke. "I think we're only seeing the phenomenon for a moment, but that it's there all the time."

"Don't you think we'd have detected it before?"

"Nobody's been looking. It increased in intensity until it became obvious. Soon, it'll be more obvious."

The light in First Secretary Tracy's eyes became fierce. "What are you suggesting?"

"I'm suggesting we begin work on interstellar transmatation and that we figure out some system for selecting who gets off the planet first." He paused to swallow. "And I'm suggesting that if we're going to have anymore conversations like this you authorize a higher security code. I don't want the Assistant Deputy Chief Theorist at Solar Voltics calling up this conversation."

"You're crazy."

"That's why I want the code. I don't want everybody to know I'm crazy."

"1-A then."

"For now. Something higher as soon as we can."

"There is nothing higher."

"Invent something."

"Everybody already knows you're crazy."

"Humor me."

"I already humor you."

"What if I'm right?"

The First Secretary tapped her writer in a gesture of impatience. "What if you're wrong?"

"Fire me."

"You've only been in the job a month."

"I'll resign."

She nodded at the inescapable conclusion. "Yes, you will." She continued more loudly. "I'll authorize the funds as pure science with the possible benefit of increased protection of our transmatters. I'll hold on the new code, though. It will be impossible to explain it if anyone finds out." She reached high on her keyboard, preparing to terminate the conversation. "I hope you're wrong as a person can be."

"So do I."

"Good-bye, Mike."

The screen went blank. The Commodore sighed. He used his shirttail to wipe the sweat from his face. He straightened the buttons with shaking hands.

Later, when the Major came in with a jar of warm milk, she found he'd taken apart an electric can opener. He was honing its tiny wheel with something that looked to be a piece of stone.

8

Seeds

When Cari returned to her place Lu looked both ways down the line. Her visor and the tool man stood upon separate stepladders, busy with the broken chain. In the hooded eyes of the others in the circle at her station, she saw tacit consent.

Once hidden by the curtains of the convenience alcove she hooked her knife and whetstone to her belt and found a cigarette and matches in her pocket. Blood had soaked through the cloth of her smock into the paper. She rubbed a thumb over the stain, found it dry and stuck the cigarette between her lips. She lit it, inhaled deeply, smothered a cough with her free hand, and sat down on the convenience.

Her tired muscles relaxed with a shudder so violent the ash shook from her cigarette. Her vision seemed to unhinge, and the textured surface of the curtain swam out of focus. She wondered how much of the shift remained. She wondered how long she could live the way she was living. As long as she needs to, she thought, as long as it takes him to get back. She wondered how long he'd been gone.

Lu's vision cleared. Nicky had been sure he'd return. She'd never believed he would. It was more likely, she decided, that Nicky was right. In the times when she didn't know what to do, Nicky'd always an idea. She stubbed the cigarette out on the floor and dropped the tiny butt into her pocket. She tried to remember the promises she'd made to Nicky. No more sitting, she thought. That was one of them. That was why she was here.

Lu walked back out on line. The visor and the tool man, still busy with the chain, did not look down. Warren left as soon as she had unhooked her knife. Carcasses hung at intervals down the line. They came from a place no one spoke of, already decapitated, emptied out inside and their skins stripped off. They arrived in the backs of pickups as blacplastic-covered mounds. They hung in the big freezer that each shift emptied out a little more. Then the pickups returned with more. Lu studied the nearest carcass and wondered what it had looked like when alive. More like a dog than a person, she observed, not for the first time.

Lu's job was to make the correct cuts on the bottom leg on her side of the line. It was easier than Cari's job—she stood on a ladder to cut the thicker, top leg—or Warren's—after the cuts were made, he wrenched and twisted each leg from its socket. A conveyor ran parallel to the line and carried the flesh they sliced and yanked away. Now it ran empty, and far down the line the grinders whined in hunger.

Lu hated the greasy feel, like icy syn-fab, of the carcass. When she'd started the job she sometimes hadn't held the leg steady enough. Her knife work had been clumsy, too, and the cuts sometimes shallow or far from the joint. That made Warren's work very hard. He would use the leg like a club, once he had it free, to hit her. After she learned to duck the blows, he held her head with one hand and shoved her face into the meat. He let go only after the cold blood and fat covered her from forehead to chin. Some of it got into her mouth. The thought of it now made her spit onto the floor. Soon, she had learned to hold the leg and to make her cuts precisely.

The visor climbed down and swung her arm over her head. The chain started up again, and the carcass in front of Lu shuddered away. She reached out her free hand, caught the next leg, and made her cuts. She turned. Warren was back to take the leg. He pushed up once, hard, then swung it down and to each side. The joint popped out and he tossed the leg onto the conveyer. He smiled at Lu.

"He almost didn't make it," he said over the machinery noise.

Lu grabbed the next leg. She was glad he'd made it.

She made her cuts. He had taught her her job—she
grabbed the next leg—and without her job she would
have to sit or starve. She made her cuts. Not to starve—
she grabbed the next leg—was another promise to Nicky.
She made her cuts.

Lu felt in the pocket of her bloody smock, for her
day's pay—two blue bills and a dozen cigarettes—and
looked down the street past the squat refinery tanks. She
blinked in the bright afternoon sun, then looked around
her. It was against the regs for the help to hitch this close,
but she was in a hurry. A car sped toward her. She held a
cigarette above her head. The driver hardly glanced in her
direction.

Lu began a brisk march down the street. Walking, she
studied the fresh cut, thin and precise, among the net of
scars on the back of her hand until her vision swam in
the heat. When she looked over her shoulder at the sound
of another car, the muscles of her neck and cutting arm
felt as if they would tear free of her body.

She again extended the cigarette. When the driver
didn't look at her, she walked on.

Some noise or a movement caught in the corner of her
eye caused her to look down a side street. In the waves of
heat rising off the asphalt she couldn't be sure she saw
anything. She rubbed her eyes, and sweat from her fingers made them sting. She blinked the tears away. The
blood and fat on her smock had begun to turn rancid in
the heat. She looked again. Two blocks away a lone dog
sat on its haunches, outlined against the weathered sid-
ing of a house. She knew running might bring the dog
after her. She knew others might be nearby. What breeze
there was blew from the dog to her. She moved her
cigarettes into the red purse on her wrist and the bills
into a back pocket of her shorts. She shucked the smock
and balled it up tightly. She weighed the price of a new
smock against the danger. Finally, she walked slowly
across the wide street and up the porch steps of an
abandoned house. The dog hadn't moved. She stuffed the
smock into the rusty mailbox and walked away, glancing
back once to be sure of finding the house again.

When the next car came along, she did not hesitate to
double her offer. The driver braked with a squeal of metal

on metal from the front wheels. Lu ran to the door, opened it, and jumped in. She handed the cigarettes over.

The driver looked at her from behind dark lenses, took the cigarettes, lit one, and slipped the other into a plastic box banded to his visor. "Fares are going up," she said.

"Like a balloon." The driver took his foot off the brake and the car began to roll forward. He accelerated.

Lu ran a hand over the dash. "His is a nice car."

He smiled under his glasses. "Where's she going?"

"The Complex."

The smile faded. "He ain't going that far. He'll take you down the Alley."

Lu frowned, her compliment wasted. "Two cigarettes is worth the Complex," she argued.

"Not to him it ain't."

"Then give her back."

The driver smiled a different way. Half the cigarette he smoked was gone. "Take back," he said.

Lu settled against the door, her fists on her lap. In a while the driver tossed the butt out his open window. "She looking for work?"

"No, she already got work."

"Then her scout should take her to the Complex."

"She doesn't have a scout."

"Pretty girl could make a lot."

"She promised not to."

The driver snorted. "Promises ain't hard to bust."

They rode in silence except for the irregular squeak of the front wheels.

"It so happens he's got an opening."

"Take her to the Complex?"

"Sure. What's her name?"

"Cari," she said.

"He's Tommy Gunn."

Tommy Gunn parked at the far end of the Complex lot, and Lu got out. "She'll be right back," she said through the window.

Tommy Gunn nodded without looking up from the radio he was tuning across a band of static.

She walked across the hot asphalt and up the steps. She held the door open and looked back. Tommy Gunn had his head back and his face up as if sleeping or listening to music. Lu doubted he'd follow her in, and if he waited, she would find another way out.

Lu stood perfectly still to avoid the aches the smallest change in attitude caused. She gripped a fistful of prints in one hand. The other had started to bleed again, and she pressed it to her side. The woman at the desk lifted red-rimmed eyes. "Yes?"

"She'd like, she'd like—" Lu stammered. She held out the prints. The red purse dangled from her wrist.

The woman took the prints and scanned several. "Housestead?" she asked without looking up.

"Yes," Lu squeezed out. "And seeds!" she blurted.

"The seeds go with the housestead. Sit down."

Lu sat beside the desk. None of the other women and men behind desks she had talked to over the last three hours had offered her a chair. She hoped that meant she was close.

The woman looked up from the prints. "Look, it's nearly the end of the day. I'll give you a pass. You'll be first in the morning."

"She can't. She has her work."

"Housesteads aren't for people who are gainfully employed." She held the prints back to Lu.

Lu looked at the woman's tired eyes without flinching. The thought that her visor might find out she had said something about work scared her as badly as not having a housestead. "She means in her friend's garden. Her friend is teaching her so she can know how to in her own housestead."

"That's not work then."

"Oh."

The woman put the prints on her desk and glanced at her wrist. "Okay, we just might get it done. Let's get started." She tapped a few keys on the console beside her. "Name?"

"Lu."

"Is that a name you've chosen?"

"No." Lu'd found, after only a few days of toying with each of them, that she had liked none of her inventions.

"Full name then?'

"What?"

"Pay attention. Full name?"

"Louisa Mae Carlton." A memory grew with each, equally weighted syllable.

"And that's a given name?"

Lu nodded. The bench had been dark blue and warm with sunshine. The park had been deserted. Her mother had said it to her again and again and again.

"Present address?"

"Nowhere."

"N/A then."

"Birth date?" Her mother's face came very near.

"Birth date?" The face was no older than Lu's.

The woman turned to her. "Honey, you have to be sixteen to qualify. That means you'd have to have been born before today's date in ought-five. Do you understand?"

Lu nodded. "Fifteen October twenty-ought-four."

"Yes, then," the woman grimaced and entered the information. "Do you have the filing fee?"

Lu dug the two bills out of her back pocket and pushed them across the desk.

"You cut yourself," the woman observed.

Lu pulled the hand back as if bitten. The woman clipped the bills to one of the prints and tapped a key.

"Living relatives?"

"N/A," Lu said.

"You learn fast, honey. Mother's name, if deceased?"

Lu shrugged. "Mom."

The woman rubbed her eyes. "Mom Carlton, then. Do you have an ID number?"

"N/A," Lu said.

"Or access to a screen? And a route number?"

"N/A."

"If there's no mailbox, you should get one."

"Where?"

"I'm not telling you to do this. You understand?"

Lou nodded.

"I imagine there are plenty of unused ones handy that no one would miss. Theoretically, you'll receive a Card and some documents at your new address in a few weeks, if you have a mailbox. Memorize the number and keep the Card. If you can establish credit you can use it to make purchases."

"Purchases?"

"Buy things. But you have to make an arrangement with a bank first."

"Oh."

"It's not so bad, no worse than this. Once you have a permanent address you'll get an allotment. The bank'll let you use the Card till each month's allotment is used up."

"Bank?"

"You have to go Inside. That's where the Banks are."

Lu shook her head. "N/A," she said.

The woman smiled. "You might change your mind later. It'll take time for the Card to come, anyway."

"Just the housestead. And the seeds."

"Okay." She rubbed her eyes again. "Do you have a particular place in mind?"

"N/A."

The woman tapped a few more keys then sat back. "It's posted." The screen flickered. "And accepted." She hit a button, and the printer whirred. She tore off a few centimeters of paper and handed it to Lu. "This is your new address. Congratulations."

Lu studied the print.

"Can you read?"

"Addresses."

"Do you know the street?"

"N/A."

The woman found a map among the prints. She studied it for a minute before marking a spot with a writer. "Here it is." She handed it to Lu. "Can you find it?"

Lu looked at the X. She nodded. "Yes."

"Good." The woman dug through the prints again, found a small booklet and scribbled something in it. She tore out the top sheet and handed it to Lu. "Take this back down the hall. Take the first right. There'll be a row of cubicles there. Go to the one marked A."

"Her seeds."

"Yes, this is for the seeds." The woman glanced at her wrist. "If it's too late, you can pick them up tomorrow."

"Yes." Lu rose to go.

"Good luck," the woman said, but Lu was already gone.

Cubicle A, and all the others, were empty. Lu pondered

for only a moment before turning back down the hall. She found the room she wanted, opened the door and went in.

The empty washroom was lit by failing sunlight through a frosted window. She raised it a couple centimeters and looked out. The twilit parking lot was empty. She closed the window, entered the single stall and sat down on the convenience. She alternately studied the print and the hand that held it until it became too dark to see the address on one or the scars on the other. She put the print in her purse, then, and slumped down farther and farther. In a while there was a far off sound like thunder. The frosted windowpane pulsed red and purple but Lu was already asleep.

9

State of the Union of City-States

David stopped dead in the hall. What he heard from the bedroom screen was not the movie he'd just called up on the study console. He knew every line of the dialogue by heart. Besides, he had asked for the standard delay. He glanced at the screen as he entered, then walked to the nightstand. He got a cigarette and an ashtray from a drawer.

Ms. Kitty lay on her stomach on the bed, surrounded by a square of midmorning light from the bay window. She gazed dreamily at the brightly colored, glossy squares of a magazine, her chin in her cupped hand. She did not look up.

He lit the cigarette and dropped the match in the ashtray. "What's Ms. First Secretary talking about?" he asked.

"David, what does this say?"

He turned. "What?"

"This." Ms. Kitty rolled onto one hip and pointed. David's gaze followed the curve of her waist up to her shoulder. "This, David," she giggled. She held a finger on the big, block letters beneath a square.

"'Parlor.' It's a kind of living room."

She rolled back on her stomach. "Why don't they just say 'living room'?"

"'Parlor's' fashionable again."

He sat at the foot of the bed. Ms. Kitty bent her knees so that her feet hovered near his ear. They crossed and uncrossed as she turned the pages of the magazine.

"Have you been listening to this?"

"Hm?" she said.

"Have you been listening to Tracy?"

"Her? No, she's been reading."

"It's important." He stubbed out the cigarette and reached for the control. He turned the volume up.

"That's it!"

The Commodore sat at the kitchen counter, his head in a nearly empty metal box. When he responded his voice echoed large and hollow. "That's what, Major?"

"She's gone public."

He pulled his head out, found a red-coated wire and looped its naked end over a terminal within the box. He kept his eyes on his work. "She is public, Major. That's the nature of politicians." He carefully tightened a screw.

"No, sir, I mean she announced the Rescue Effort."

"'Announced,' Major?"

"Well, sir, she said that if the situation did not stabilize, the government would mount a rescue effort."

"Did she mention details?"

"No, sir, not yet anyway."

"What's she talking about now?"

"I can switch it to American and turn it up, sir."

"I'd much rather you didn't, Major." The screwdriver slipped and gouged a thin line in the box's plastic veneer.

"She's enumerating the theoretical explanations. She's on flora fires now."

The Commodore worked quietly. First Secretary Tracy's voice droned, like the buzz of an insect, beneath a covering Russian translation.

"Sir, she mentioned it again," the Major called.

"What did she say, exactly?" The Commodore snipped some frayed wire from an electrical lead.

"It would translate something like, 'once we find the source or the cause, and if it continues to accumulate in intensity and we can't find a method to diminish it, we will develop a means or instrumentation to provide for the safety of everyone.' More or less, sir."

"That's fine, Major," the Commodore said into the box.

"What's that, sir?"

"That's fine." He attached the lead to a terminal, put the screwdriver down and looked across the counter. "As long as she doesn't mention the military or the Screening

Committee or get us tied into it in a way the media can figure out. Let's pray she doesn't mention us by name."

The Major's face briefly showed disappointment. She rose from her chair and walked across Supreme Headquarters to the kitchen counter.

"Mike, what is this thing you're working on?"

The Commodore smiled broadly. "A microwave oven. They were very proud of their microwaves. Every family had one."

"Do you want some of this coffee?"

He glanced at the half-full pot and stuck his head back in the box. "Sure." What he said next was muffled.

"What did you say?"

"You don't wear a pacemaker, do you?"

"What's that?"

He brought his head back out. "Got me." He looked into the mug she handed him. "I saw a sign once in a museum warning people with pacemakers. Get the milk, will you?"

The Major went to the refrigerator. "Do you want the thick stuff on top?"

"Go ahead."

She poured a dollop into her mug, then did the same for the Commodore's. The refrigerator began to hum.

"I'd feel better if I knew what a pacemaker was."

"How's that, Major?"

"Well, then I'd be sure if I had one or not." She sat down to listen to the rest of the First Secretary's speech.

Mad Tom's voice, then Carly's stammer, wafted through the open window of the rectory. Preach paused to see if his intervention was necessary, but the argument was replaced by the solid and steady *thwap* of horsehide against leather. In another moment they were calling "Way to go!" and "P-p-p-pep-p-per 'er in there!" Preach smiled at the myriad of sacraments, then frowned, wondering where the parish's bats had gotten to. He returned his attention to the screen.

In a while he spoke. "Heavens, she makes it sound as if careful planning will forestall Armageddon." Then, after a lapse of several minutes, "Says you, Ms. Tracy-First-Secretary-lady." Finally, he asked the screen, "Are you ready for Judgment Day?"

"Why, I believe so," he answered himself.

"Are you prepared to meet your maker?" he asked.

He sighed and dropped his needle. It hung by a black thread from the shoulder seam of the cassock bunched in his lap. His bright plaid shorts and white thighs contrasted dramatically with it. It was ancient, one of his from seminary, the shorts nearly as old. The cassock would do nicely for Carly, Preach thought.

"But are you prepared to meet your maker?" he asked more insistently.

He joined his hands over the cassock and shook them up and down heartily. "Actually, we're already on good terms."

Lu stood in a bright square of sunlight against the brick wall of Edie's Bar and Grill. A woman, muscular and broad shouldered, walked down the sidewalk. When she put her hand on the doorknob, Lu brought five cigarettes out of her red purse with a flourish. The woman considered them, then found a blue bill in a deep pocket of her plastic-spattered dungarees. Lu handed over the cigarettes. Without further ceremony, the woman entered Edie's. Lu followed.

She stood in the stale gin smell for the time it took her eyes to adjust to the darkness. Someone was talking from the screen in the corner. Something sizzled on the grill. She sat down on a stool and pushed the bill across.

"Food," Lu said.

Edie struggled to turn her attention from the screen. "Huh?" she asked.

A man in white coveralls made a noise of exasperation and stode from the door to the screen. He looked left, right, and above the screen, then made the noise again. "Where could it have gone to?" he said aloud. He heard a rustling behind him and turned. LaMer lay against her pillows, one arm extended, the control in her wobbling fist.

"Is this what you're looking for?" she asked.

"Oh, Ms. LaMer, you're—awake."

LaMer dropped her arm to the bed. "God, I didn't know which was the screen, and neither one of you would change channels." She pointed to the image of First Secretary Tracy. "That one would flicker a bit."

"She's on all the channels. They've pre-empted everything. And I don't think you ought to watch it."

"You're real, aren't you? You're not just a dream?"

"No, I assure you, Ms. LaMer, that I am quite real."

"You could be just saying that."

He held out his open palm. "The control, please?"

"Not till I get this sorted out."

He put his hands on his hips. "Would you like to see your doctor?"

LaMer looked at the hand that held the control, then to its empty neighbor. She shrugged. "Beats me."

There was a moment when she realized the nurse was gone. When it passed, she again attempted to change channels. Then she understood that someone was addressing her.

"Ms. LaMer?" a voice repeated monotonously.

She realized that First Secretary Tracy was talking to her. She kept her eyes closed. *Fuck her,* LaMer thought. *Let her find her own damn bed.*

First Secretary Tracy instructed the nurse to sit in a chair until relieved. If the patient regained consciousness he was to immediately beep First Secretary Tracy, who would be making her rounds.

Great, LaMer thought, *now I've got the movies confused.* She wanted to switch one off, but could not lift the hand with the control. When she again opened her eyes, though, it had worked itself out: the First Secretary had retreated to the smaller of the two screens, and the nurse was walking across the larger.

"Don't do that," LaMer instructed.

He turned quickly. LaMer had a clear image of him standing against the glass wall, outlined in bright sunlight, his hand upon a cord.

"The sun's moved around. I should pull the drapes."

LaMer closed her eyes. "Leave them be," she said.

It was all perfectly clear to LaMer. They had fallen into a fairy tale, and a monster was going to eat them all up. She wanted to get up and spit in its eye, as her mother had instructed her. *Now there was a tough cookie,* LaMer thought, and a very scary fairy tale. The four of them had left home far behind, and the magic place was still far away. Her big brother's face was scared, but her mother's face was smooth and round and unafraid. They walked night after night. The moon was friendly but sometimes went on vacation, and sometimes the clouds wanted to shut it up. Everyday was a new place and her father's low voice saying *stay down* and *keep an eye out the window*. She pretended sleep while her parents whispered the names of monsters—*road blocks, work gangs, murder, rape, starve*. Then they spoke the name of the magic place—*New City*.

And, after a terrible time, they arrived. Night and day, LaMer raced with her new friends through the alleys and streets, around the construction sites, over to the barrier. When hunger struck, they ate what they found. The adults were very busy building, building, building, but always looking Out There, waiting to see who or what approached. By then it was only her mother. *Now there was a tough cookie.* She ran, she hid, she played until she knew every niche and hole of the growing New City. She led her friends on expeditions that lasted several days. She showed them where it was warm and dry to sleep and the quickest way from here to there. The adults who knew her from the early days would stop what they were doing to talk a moment or two. They called her Scout—it had meant something different in those days—and the Indian, and the new people, those who had been coming in every day of her life in the New City, knew her by those names as well.

She grew and the space within the barriers shrunk so that, finally, it threatened to choke her. She began to wander alone near the barrier, hiding from everyone, capable of disappearing for days. Her thoughts turned again and again to Out There, where her father and brother remained. Her mother had told her to never go beyond the barrier, and she obeyed. Soon, though, it became clear to her that they intended her to spend her entire life in a circumscribed place of building, building, bulding.

She had asked her mother once shortly before she began university. It was a rare night together in the space they had been assigned. She had thought of the question, then waited until the right moment. "Could he still be alive? Joshua?" she asked. Slowly, her mother shook her head, ever so slowly, her eyes focused more on that distance Out There than upon the slices of apple on the table before her.

LaMer had accepted that. Her brother was dead. Her mother believed it, and she believed her mother. Joshua was dead. Of course, she knew for sure about her father. She had seen it happen. Her mother had tried to push her head down, had tried to cover her completely with her own body in the dusty backseat of the abandoned car, but she had peeked through the hole where the door should have been. She had seen the other men holding him, but the one she had watched was the one who held the pistol. That man said something, and LaMer's father spit in his eye, a motion of the neck and shoulders like the quick, unleashed S of a snake striking. And then her father was dead, shot in the face even as he tried to summon more spit. Even as a little girl, she understood that no one could put the pieces back together again. It was all perfectly clear.

LaMer sat up in bed and the control clattered to the floor. She got her hands behind her for support and fought dizziness by making of her eyes the tightest of slits. She gulped air through flared nostrils and open mouth.

"Doctor! Doctor!"

Arms embraced her, attempted to force her back. She steeled herself, would not yield.

"Ms. LaMer, you've had a terrible ordeal. You must rest."

LaMer responded with equal emphasis on each word. "Get your damn hands off me."

Suddenly, she was free. She saw them standing a meter away and allowed herself to fall back onto her pillows.

"We thought you were undergoing cardiac arrest," the woman said.

LaMer listened to the blood pumping rhythmically through her ears. "I'm fine," she said. She looked to the nurse. "How long?"

"Thirty-three days," the doctor responded.

"L.A.?"

The nurse nodded.

"Ms. LaMer, you've experienced considerable physical trauma," the doctor began.

"What is it this time?"

The doctor considered for only a second before she responded. "The lower leg. We saved the knee."

LaMer pulled herself back up, grasped the sheet in one hand and snapped it away.

The blue smock crossed her thigh in a straight line. Below her thigh was the knee. The bandages and the sheet were so nearly the same color that, at first, she didn't see the stump. Finally, she made out a dozen centimeters of loose dressing. Beyond that, there was only the sheet.

"What's she going on about?" LaMer nodded toward First Secretary Tracy on the screen.

"She's just finishing up," the nurse offered.

"Some kind of unexplained solar activity," the doctor said. "Now, lie back down, please."

"What kind of solar activity?"

"Sunspots. Something like that. Now, please lie back before we have to put you in restraints."

LaMer prepared to spit in her eye, but some part of her brain had recorded Tracy's words, and they came swimming back to her. She lay back to consider them. The doctor and the nurse were speaking to her, covering her again with the sheet. She attempted to kick it off, but the stump rose and dropped ineffectually. She studied the spot. It was all perfectly clear.

The loss of the leg bothered her only a little. She had come to believe, while at university, that choosing a life meant choosing a death as well. LaMer smiled. She and her roommate had made that a creed at the tail end of a night of drinking. The sun had been coming up when they came upon that truth. Still, it was perfectly clear that the trouble was serious.

"Get me a new leg," she said.

"We will, we will," the doctor assured her.

"Now."

"We'll start physical therapy in a day or two."

"Today." LaMer looked around her. Sunlight bathed the room. "And get me my clothes."

Ms. Kitty flipped over the last page of her magazine, rolled over, and sat beside David. She put her arms around his neck. "Is that the movie?" she asked.

"What?" David said.

"Is that the movie?"

"Yes. It just started."

"What did that lady want?"

David didn't answer. Ms. Kitty carefully removed the ashtray from his lap and set it upon the floor. She again loosely embraced David, this time draping a leg over his lap. She kissed his ear.

"David—"

"Hm?"

"He's not mad, is he?"

"Mad?" He turned to face her.

"Because she wants to work for her boy instead of him."

He shook his head. "No, no," he said. "That's fine."

"She'll miss David."

"I'll miss you, too."

She scooted in closer, and her hold tightened. He put his open hand against the smooth skin of her back. He began to kiss her, then stopped. "What's his name?"

"She told you," she said and kissed him.

Her lips were soft, and her open mouth wet, warm and dark. Kissing her made him feel safe.

He pulled back.

"Amos Dandy, but maybe he'll choose another one."

David nodded.

"They don't want to talk about it now," she said.

"No, they don't." David pulled her close with a surge of strength he could hardly control.

PART II

10

A Toss of the Coin

Tella-Dotun glanced, bleary-eyed, at her wrist and sighed. She found the control on the arm of the couch and pressed a button. Floor-to-ceiling drapes rolled silently back on invisible tracks. Beyond the glass wall lay a high, thin overcast. She succeeded in stretching some of the kinks from her neck and back, then gathered four sets of prints from the floor and carried them to her desk. She quickly stacked and stowed the prints, books, and media recordings already there and tossed a double handful of waste into a stylish, miraclastic recepticle. She paused to examine the desktop. The four sets she had carried from the couch lay in a neat row. Satisfied, she walked to the washroom, one hand unzipping yesterday's coveralls, the other covering a yawn.

Needles of water pelted her skin. Tella-Dotun pushed the shower cap higher on her forehead and shut her eyes against the spray. She could not, for the moment, remember when she'd last been home. Not since the week of the First Secretary's announcement, she decided. She ran a synthetic sponge over her legs and arms and surprised herself by wishing for someone to go home to. She grasped the shower nozzle with both hands and hung on weakly. "Let's not start that first thing in the morning," she said, rinsed her mouth, and spat toward the drain between her feet. She turned and let the spray work at the tension in her neck. A series of faces appeared before her mind's eye. She arched her neck, and the hollow roar of water striking her cap drove out the regrets, large and small, each face represented.

Toweled dry, Tella-Dotun picked up her watch from

the back of the convenience and checked the time. The
quick shower had gained her a little time. She turned to
her reflection in the mirror. Her body did not interest her,
and she gave it only a perfunctory glance. Her face,
though, fascinated her. Finding her eyes a little red, she
reached for and applied drops. She blinked the excess
away and went on to examine the forehead, cheeks, the
line of her jaw. The skin around her eyes remained
smooth as when she was a girl. She studied each profile
for a long minute in her peripheral vision. She reached
for her facepaint and brushes. She rubbed the bristles of
one vigorously into the yellow and held it to the corner of
her eye. She paused, as if to say good-bye to the face only
she was allowed to see.

The butterflies were nearly complete when Tella-Dotun
heard a vague noise that might have been the outer office
door opening. She reached over with her free hand and
locked the washroom door. She knew Jomo's sexual orientation to be much more clearly defined than her own—
given the smallest opportunity he talked endlessly about
his love life—and she knew that he would not approach
her in that way. Still, there was the constant, implicit
offer of a cloyingly intimate friendship in his demeanor,
and she took every possible step to discourage him. Soon
she heard the unmistakable sounds of Jomo sorting and
printing the day's mail. She returned to her facepaint.

Her grandmother, filled with the old ways, had spent
hours each day all through Tella-Dotun's twelfth year
experimenting with the design. Once she had settled on
the pattern and colors Tella-Dotun still chose to wear, the
old woman had wished to tattoo the design. Only the
strenuous vigilance of Tella-Dotun's parents had prevented
her from using the needles. Though the act of applying
facepaint kept Tella-Dotun in touch with her childhood,
and though she enjoyed the ritual as much as any part of
her day, she sometimes wished the old woman would
have had her way. Her stamp upon the girl would have
been absolute and permanent, then, in a world that had,
during Tella-Dotun's life, changed until it was nearly a
new one altogether.

Tella-Dotun lay down her brush and studied the effect.
The entirety of her face was covered, though much of it in
a shade that only heightened her natural skin tone. The

twin butterflies sparkled as she fluttered her eyelids. She
molded her lips into a smile while her eyes soberly
judged the result. It was as devastatingly brilliant as she
knew it would be. She reached into the little closet and
found coveralls freshly wrapped in the cleaner's blacplastic.

"Make all the recommendations you want," Jomo was
saying. "They didn't say that you couldn't."

Tella-Dotun sat back and turned the fountain pen
around in her hands. A famous writer had given it to her
when she was very young, and she had become addicted
to handling it during moments of stress. She set it down.

"That's just a way of ducking responsibility and quite
probably would end as a disservice to everyone we
produce."

"You'll have to explain that." Jomo crossed his arms.

"If I go into the meeting with our whole list, our
colleagues will counter with their entire lists. If I insist,
so will they. Inevitably, then, the combined lists will be
forwarded without deletion to the Screening Committee.
The Screening Committee can't approve everyone, so it
ends up making the decisions that we should have,
though of course without our expertise. Worse, the Committee looks at our lists, where every writer appears equal
to all others, throws up its collective hands in frustration
and assigns very high numbers to them all, effectively
dismissing them. Would you like that, Jomo?"

"Well, suggest several. I mean, it's like you were
playing God or something. Why go in with just one?"

"Because I will argue for the shortest possible list to
ensure that those we nominate stand the best chance of
receiving low numbers. I can't, then, make the case that
this division deserves what would quite rightly appear to
be disproportionate representation. The media specialists
would have a field day."

"Oh, who cares what they say?"

"Jomo, I know it's convenient to dismiss them, but
those people resent our very presence. And don't bother
to remark on my stature in the field. That counts for very
little, compared to the rather meager profit we show and
the rather extensive resources devoted to our produc-
tions. It is a business, after all."

"I would have said it was art," Jomo said petulantly.

"Yes, of course. The aesthetic high ground is always the easiest to defend."

Jomo reached out and touched a finger to each of the four sets of prints. "Eeny, meeny, miny, mo—"

Tella-Dotun slapped his hand away. "This is not a game!" she cried.

Jomo cradled the hand against his chest and made a sound as if something had caught in his throat. His eyes brimmed with tears.

For half a minute, while Jomo's whimpers grew in volume and rapidity, Tella-Dotun sat immobile, further remonstrations racing neck and neck through her mind with apologies. She had never struck a human being before, yet Jomo had become, of late, maddening. His attempts to insinuate himself into a personal relationship were unwelcome, but she recognized how difficult she had always made it for those who wished to be her friend. He copied her manner and affected her mannerisms, but that was an indication of his admiration of her. He occasionally questioned her judgment in a brazen way she found presumptuous in one so inexperienced, but she recognized her own youthful iconoclasm in his ambition. He was young, but it was quite possible that the sun would erase that advantage.

"You must forgive me, Jomo. I am terribly sorry," she said, her words crisp and her tone correct.

"Do you want me to leave?"

"No, I want you to help me make this decision." Jomo wiped a finger under his nose and sniffed. His teary eyes had still not met Tella-Dotun's calculating gaze.

"As succinctly as possible, tell me what you think of this." She held a finger on one of the sets of prints.

Jomo cocked his head to look at the title print. He sniffed again before he spoke. "I think she's wonderful, as you know. A little difficult, perhaps, but more's the pleasure for the practiced reader. Squarely in the literary tradition back to the Fall and before. World-class."

Tella-Dotun moved her finger. "What about this one?"

Jomo hesitated.

"Tell me what you really think, not what you think you're supposed to think."

"I think he's an overblown, boring old windbag."

Tella-Dotun allowed him a smile. She dropped the prints in the trash recepticle at her knees. "I agree."

Jomo gave her a look of immense gratitude.

"This one," Tella-Dotun directed.

"It's very odd and old-fashioned. There are some interesting things, but I don't think people would much care."

"That sounds like a marketing concern."

"I don't mean consumers. Ac crits and—you know—people who've devoted their lives to knowing."

Tella-Dotun rested her finger on the last set.

"Technically superb. Limited in range and a little repetitive. Sometimes precious. Still, an amazing stylist."

Tella-Dotun folded her hands. "How do we proceed?"

Jomo sniffed. "One observation?"

"Go ahead."

"Our loyalty should be to those we have already produced. Now isn't the time to be working with a newcomer."

"Perhaps you're right." Tella-Dotun picked up the middle set and put it aside. She looked up.

Jomo looked back and forth between the two remaining sets. Finally, he faced Tella-Dotun and shrugged.

"Yes," she sighed, "me, too."

"Toss a coin?" He flinched as she looked at him.

But she was not angry. "Maybe that's what it's come to." She passed her fountain pen from hand to hand. "One more time," she said abruptly. "Just the negatives." She pointed with the pen.

"Old-hat, stilted. Academic."

She tapped the set on her right.

"Never makes me laugh. Never makes me cry."

Tella-Dotun nodded. "Again, but now the positives."

"A life, a personal struggle, beautifully translated."

The pen made a barely audible tap.

"Wonderfully made."

She plopped the third set back down between the others.

"I'm not convinced he knows his technique."

"And?"

Jomo shrugged. "It made me laugh."

"Oh," Tella-Dotun said. "It made me cry."

"It's very foreign."

"Yes, it's so distant in place, almost in time. It kept reminding me of things I couldn't quite name."

"Yes, but it's so personal. Or something."

"Or something. I know what you mean."

"Still..." Jomo said.

"Yes, of course." She removed the set with a sigh.

Each studied the two remaining title prints. Finally, Jomo spoke. "Do you mind if we talk a while? Just talk?"

"No," she lied. She glanced at her wrist. "Do you know what the single most influential technology is?"

Jomo nodded to the console beside her. "That thing."

"Try again."

"The holographs?"

"No."

"Video? Transmatation?"

"No."

He held his open palms up. "Well, what is the single most influential technology, dear?"

Tella-Dotun arrested a blink at the last word, then let it go. "This," she said and held up her wrist. "The smallest machine, and it controls our lives to a greater extent than the rest put together."

Jomo gave an appreciative laugh.

"I've got about ten minutes," Tella-Dotun said. "What did you want to talk about?"

"Anything. You. What it was like in the early days."

"You mean, how was Gutenberg at cocktail parties?"

Jomo flushed red. "I'm sorry. I didn't mean that."

Tella-Dotun knew that Jomo considered her a conduit back into a grand tradition. At his age her passion had been very similar. "It was about as you've heard, I imagine. The most common misconception is that everything was wiped out. In fact, almost everything remained intact—the books, the technologies, and the media. What we did lose, however, were the writers themselves."

"Killed?"

"Writers fared no worse in that way than the general population, I suppose. But a new world calls for a new literature. I doubt you would recognize five names from the list of those deemed important prior to the Fall."

Jomo considered his next question while Tella-Dotun considered him. "Is it true that you started with a copier?" he asked finally.

Tella-Dotun smiled. "Until the toner ran out."

"The what?"

"Fluid that enabled the machine to make copies."

"How did you find the people to produce?"

"When the old socioeconomic order went, it took the established arts with it. New artists were sucked in to fill the vacuum. There was an embarrassment of riches, really. Earlier, I asked you about technology. Technology has more to do with the size of the audience one can reach than any other facet of production." She picked up the fountain pen. "Back then, we had people standing on a platform in the street, sometimes with construction going on all around them, and speaking to whomever would listen. There, the platform was the technology."

A flicker of Jomo's eyes told her that her last point had not registered. "Yes, but what were they like?"

"They were people. They were hungry to speak. Sometimes they didn't even know what it was they needed to say, they just had to do it. I was hungry to help people speak." The melodrama of her phrase suddenly embarrassed her. "Don't ask me why."

Jomo put on his impish look, an expression Tella-Dotun especially despised. "Then why not?"

"Because I'm not sure myself. It had to do with youth and politics and living beyond ourselves."

"Immortality?"

Tella-Dotun shook her head. "Maybe for some, but I don't think for most. We wanted to live for something other than ourselves, some grander purpose. We considered doing otherwise very selfish."

"You succeeded. You made all this." He waved his hand to indicate the New City skyline beyond the glass wall.

"It was not a material endeavor," she said dryly.

Jomo hurried to explain. "I meant that a whole new world has been built by the energies of a generation."

Tella-Dotun made no response.

"I think I'm envious. My generation can't do what yours did. We haven't the opportunity. And it appears we never will. Is that a terrible thing to say?"

Tella-Dotun looked at the two sets of prints before her and considered, very briefly, asking Jomo to make the choice. "No, I don't find it terrible, but you ought to be more optimistic. A month from now it well may again be business as usual."

"But that's just it. If it all goes back to business as usual, my opportunity to do something significant will pass. My life will just be another ho-hum existence."

Tella-Dotun weighed her answer. "I predict," she said finally, "a long life of considerable influence for you."

Jomo smiled in great relief.

Tella-Dotun held up her wrist. "I have a decision to make, Jomo, and I need some time alone to make it."

"Would you like me to leave you a coin?"

Tella-Dotun shook her head. She did not return his conspiratorial smile, however. Jomo rose and walked, almost on tiptoe, out of the office.

Tella-Dotun pulled herself away from the reveries that had trapped her. She checked her wrist and looked again at the two sets of prints before her. She opened a drawer and pulled out a small jar. She shook some powder from it into her cup, then got hot water from the washroom tap. She stared absently at her desktop while she sipped coffee. When the cup was nearly empty she picked up her fountain pen and began to pass it from one trembling hand to the other. She used a tissue to dab the moisture from her hairline. Soon, a series of shudders took her and she hunched her shoulders to stop them. After they had passed, she lay her head down between the prints.

The numbers upon her wrist changed with maddening regularity. Jomo's questioning had started her thinking along lines she would have rather avoided. What the media had dubbed a golden era in production had been reworked and reported so many times that Tella-Dotun sometimes found she doubted her own memories. During the occasional interviews she granted to the media or graduate students, she was often asked a certain question. Tella-Dotun's invariable response was that she considered her present the most significant time of her life. It was a convenient and politic lie. The truth was that the last two decades were mere shadows of a past life. Both the drama of the time and the youthful energies that had fed it were gone. Though still young, she felt herself ancient, an archaeological relic.

The numerals of her watch transformed themselves

into letters and the letters formed the names of those she had known. Some had been famous, many nearly so, or well known within a certain circle. They had become rich or they'd never been able to keep their Cards current. Some had retired, some had gone insane or had always been so. They had died or disappeared, sometimes out of choice, sometimes simply lost in a shift of fashion. She alone had survived. She could find no pattern or reason to any of it, and what she had accounted her great good luck now seemed a curse.

The doubt grew and spread. Soon, the confidence that had carried her through the entirety of her adult life had rotted away. She could not make the decision required of her. She felt an unaccustomed sympathy for Jomo and his needs. He and his generation should face this crisis, she thought. A sudden recognition of irony pulled her lips up over her brilliant teeth in a bitter smile. For all purposes to which she cared to devote it, her life had ended when she was little older than he.

The watch buzzed. She straightened in her chair and used another tissue. She stacked the two sets of prints and, as an afterthought, placed the third atop them.

11

Liberty

The Commodore shambled among the hurrying nurses and quick-stepping doctors in the wide corridor. The presence of so many bustling people after much time spent virtually alone disoriented him slightly, and he consciously exaggerated that condition in his walk. He paused now and again to peer through open doors or check a room number against the brief print he held in his hand. His dark coveralls and shaggy hair among the crisp, white uniforms of the medical staff lent him the appearance of a slow-witted bear loose among chickens. He stopped to read the print again, but it fluttered, like a white feather, from his hands to the carpet between his feet.

"May I help you?"

He straightened and held the print out to a man in white coveralls. "Ah—" he said.

The man removed a hand from one hip, took the print and glanced at it. "Who are you looking for?"

The Commodore gestured vaguely toward the nurse's hand. "Ah—" he repeated.

"Yes, but the name? I want to check that you have the right room."

The Commodore reached out suddenly, and the nurse jumped back in fright. When the nurse had steadied himself, the Commodore tried again, this time with great deliberation. He slowly took the print from the nurse's hand and unfolded it. "Ah—" he said again.

The nurse read the name there. "You're not media, are you? The media aren't allowed."

The Commodore pulled his slack-jawed expression together long enough to mumble, "No."

The nurse seemed unconvinced, but pointed down the hall. "Third door down. Rooms are numbered in order, you see."

The Commodore smiled with an excess of gratitude and nodded his head slowly, like an alien visitor just learning the language. "Thank you," he said and held his hand out.

The nurse dropped the print into his big, open palm. The Commodore walked around him and down the hall, studying the door to each room, right or left, as he passed.

The nurse called from behind him. "Wait a minute."

The Commodore stopped in midstep, and the nurse strode around to face him.

"You're not family, are you?"

The Commodore shook his head vigorously.

"I'm afraid I'll have to see some identification."

The Commodore made a show of patting his coveralls. He pulled his Card from his hip pocket and held it out.

The nurse snatched it away with a quick sigh of exasperation. The Commodore watched with great and private glee as the nurse's face reorganized itself in recognition.

"Oh. I—" He handed the Card back. "Right this way."

The nurse knocked on a door. "Visitor!" he called.

A heavy thud answered from the other side, and the nurse stepped back. He smiled nervously at the Commodore, then explained, "She's a little frustrated with her physical therapy." He turned the knob. "My heavens! She's locked the door!" He looked at the Commodore and elaborated. "That's completely against policy."

The Commodore spoke, his tone mild. "Then why put locks on the doors?"

"Well..." he trailed off. "I don't know."

The Commodore smiled without showing his teeth and politely insinuated himself between the nurse and the door. "It's alright," he said soothingly, then spoke in a louder voice through the door, "Are you decent?" There was no answer. He swung his shoulders away and back on the base of his spine, like an inverted pendulum and, with the same enigmatic smile, smashed the door from its hinges.

The Commodore went sailing through the frame, fell

and slid along the suddenly prostrate door. He rolled once into a sitting position, smiled back into the horrified face of the nurse, then turned his attention to the patient.

LaMer looked down at him from the bed, a quizzical expression on her face.

"Visitor!" the Commodore said, a little breathless.

"Get me my leg, will you? It's under the door there."

The Commodore looked at the nurse. "She's been having delusions of one kind or another ever since she regained consciousness," the nurse explained.

The Commodore arched an eyebrow in LaMer's direction. She smiled sweetly. "Under the door," she repeated.

The Commodore rose, grasped one corner of the door and flipped it over as if turning a page. On the carpet lay a glastic rod three centimeters in diameter and half a meter in length. A complicated-looking harness was attached to one end. The Commodore tossed it toward the bed.

LaMer snatched it out of the air. She slid her hand down its length and began to pound the end into her open palm. "I intend to use this on your square-rigged head."

"Belay that, mate."

"I'm not your mate and never was."

"Ah, there's a pity."

LaMer tossed the leg in the air. It turned twice, the harness trailing, and she caught it again. "How are you doing, Mike?"

"Still have all my parts," he said.

"That's not what I heard."

"You want proof?" He cupped a hand over his crotch.

LaMer chuckled. She turned her attention to the broken door frame. "Dismissed," she said to the nurse.

He shook himself to life. "Ms. LaMer—" he began.

"Scat!" she said, and the nurse disappeared. "Toady bugger," she said to the Commodore.

He pulled over one of the twin visitors' chairs, sat, stretched out his legs, and put his feet on the bed. "See," he pointed, "two good legs."

LaMer arched the eyebrow over her single eye. "Two, anyway. What brings you here, Mike?"

He clasped his hands behind his head. "Come to pay my respects to what's left of you, mate."

"I told you about that 'mate' business."

"Aye, but all things change." He unclasped his hands and held them before his face as if they were strangers. "What do you have to play with?" he asked them.

"The color box needs a tune-up," LaMer said.

The Commodore craned his neck to see behind him, then rose and went to the screen. "Turn it on," he said.

"Aye, aye." LaMer punched the control and the image of a media caster filled the screen.

"He does look a little green."

"Maybe it's the news," LaMer suggested.

The Commodore chuckled, then gave the top of the screen an experimental tap. "It's none too good."

"Gunboat Mike gets his ultimate command just in time"—LaMer waved her hands like a magician producing a white rabbit—"for the end of time."

"A minor, personal irony. I dwell on it not at all."

"Not more than twenty-three hours a day."

He spoke in mock indignation. "But I get more done in that last hour than any atom-scrambled, light-speed freak does in a week." He walked to the bed and took the control from her. "I just can't get over it," he said, looking at her with an appraising eye. "What are they doing? Using the parts to build a new model?"

"Broke the mold a long time ago. Besides, it's just a minor, personal inconvenience."

The Commodore, nodding his head, returned to the screen with the control. He flipped channels, then searched his pockets. He used a screwdriver to pry the receiver panel off the screen. He began to twist and depress the knobs and buttons there with the subtlety and finesse of a cellist. He spoke without looking away from the innards of the screen. "Do you even know how many this makes?"

"Many what?"

"Traumas, partial receptions, whatever you call them."

"I used to, but"—she raised the stump of her leg—"I was keeping count on my toes."

"What'd they do with it, anyway?"

LaMer shrugged. "Reconstituted as protein and shipped to the suburbs, for all I know."

The Commodore shot her a look. "I had protein for breakfast," he said. "How's that?"

"Better, much better. Mike, you're a genius, an anomaly of Academy training."

"I know." He returned to his seat. "Ever a sign of brain or neurological dysfunction?"

LaMer's single eye focused on one of his. "The tests are incomplete on the last one, but my skull's pretty thick." She considered him. "You know all this anyway. I'll bet a bottle of rum you've got everything about me on a neatly folded print in one of those pockets."

He smiled, then reached over and took the prosthetic leg from her hands. The knotted and twisted harness dangled before his eyes. "Yes," he said, "I do."

"So," she asked, "what have you got to work with?"

"Not much, I'm afraid. Maybe enough, though. Just maybe." He reached into the web of harness and spread his fingers. "Why no family, LaMer?"

"People die."

"I mean one of your own."

"Why no family, Mike? One of your own?"

"Oh, I had a sweetheart in every port. I couldn't make up my mind, so they made up theirs." He hooked a last finger over a line in the lattice of the harness so the web was spread over one hand like a cat's cradle. He held the leg itself in the other. As he pulled his arms apart, the harness trailed out neatly, the twists and knots gone. "Awful lot of straps," he said.

"Just like lacing up a shoe, they tell me."

"Why keep going back? Why not give up transmatting?"

"Death wish."

The Commodore chortled, then brought a scrolled silver flask out of a back pocket. He handed it over.

LaMer uncapped it and sniffed. "Aye, bless you, Mike." She took a slug.

"Be careful, mate. That's the genuine one-fifty-one."

LaMer swallowed, then gave him a withering look through her squinting eye.

"Sorry," he said. She handed the flask back. He tipped it to her and said, "Skoal!" before drinking. He returned it, the rum still in his mouth.

"Ah-h!" he said after he'd swallowed. He reached into another pocket and brought out a lock-blade knife. He held it and the leg up to her. "Do you mind?"

"I'll just hang onto this till you're done." She took another drink. "Now," she said, "tell me what you got."

"I got"—he watched a thin sliver of glastic curl up ahead of his blade—"the Old Woman's data banks."

"So?"

He held the blade like a writer, point to the leg. "So she thought about a lot of things she never had time or resources to work on."

LaMer took a swig. "They never appreciated her."

The Commodore shook his head in sympathy. "Neither side." He scratched a thin line in the leg. "I've got this team going through them." He looked up. "Hotshot Major in charge of the team. She loves anything to do with the Old Woman more than she loves to give orders, and she loves giving orders." He gouged the line deeper. "Already, she's found dozens of references to an insulating layer." He nodded to LaMer's stump. "No more interference."

"No limit to time in transmat," LaMer mused.

"Theoretically." He gouged a second line, crossing serpentine, over the first.

"What are the mechanics of it?"

"Nothing that can't be programmed. It's more chemical than physical, by the way. The Old Woman postulated something that looks like a third cousin of syn-fab."

"And?"

"And it won't work, according to my Major, whose team's analytical strategy is above reproach, again according to my Major." He started another crossing line on the leg.

"But something like it will?"

He shrugged. "I think something between the Old Woman's theoretical construct and syn-fab will."

"And your Major has a team working on the possible combinations?"

"A whole team of teams, actually."

They sat silently for a time, the Commodore now and then brushing whitish glastic powder from his coverall legs. The design on the rod grew in intricacy and elegance.

"So there's a chance to get somebody away, but away to where?"

The Commodore waved the knife toward the ceiling. "Across the galaxy, past stars charted and uncharted."

"But that's what I mean. Where are they going to end up, and how will they be received without a station?"

"My Major also has a team working on that, though the quite modest design is my own. She has dubbed it, in a flash of uncharacteristic inspiration, the Puzzle Box. The name seems to be sticking."

LaMer took another drink, though the room had begun a slow rotation, and the images on the silent screen appeared off center. "Well?" she said.

The Commodore looked up. "Oh," he said, "just common sense, really. Put a little atmosphere in a box along with a compact, once-only receiving station and a few sensors. Program for the likeliest looking system and send it off."

"Laid in between insulating layer and transmatter?"

"Exactly."

"But what if it drops the transmatter in a place with the right atmosphere and temperature but otherwise inhospitable for any of a thousand reasons?"

The Commodore studied the point of his knife. "We make it a once-only receiving and once-only sending station and layer the box with others, each with its own coordinates. All automatic, you understand. The transmatter won't be received in any but a nominal sense until the sensors have had the time to give the all clear. Of course, the transmatter may be received in the middle of a tribe of one-eyed purple people-eaters before breakfast. You can't program every contingency out. Where would the adventure be?"

LaMer had the drunken sense she was repeating herself. "But how do you decide on the likeliest coordinates?"

The Commodore scratched his head. "Actually, we'll try to avoid the unlikeliest. You know, black holes, stars—"

"Going nova?"

"It's not that exactly, according to the reports I'm getting. At least, not in the classic pattern." He went back to his carving, lost in some private contemplation.

"And then?"

"Oh, past a certain point, we will, theoretically you understand, build in some navigational equipment. Pretty basic. Sort of like, take sightings till a star that falls within certain parameters appears, lock in and go." He put the knife down for a moment and looked at LaMer. "Not infinite, you understand, not even theoretically. Can't bond over a certain point and expect the elements to remain discrete. Whole thing could recombine into a real stew."

He took a drink from the flask LaMer offered, returned it and began to inlay a checkerboard between the lines.

Time passed. "Tell me, what's it like," he said.

"You mean, what's it like to hold the record for time in single transmat?"

"Not exactly." He turned the knife expertly. "What was it like during transmat?"

"You know what it's like. One moment you're here. The next you're there."

"Of course." The Commodore hacked on the end of the leg. He whistled tunelessly.

"That's what you want, then? That's what you're really after? To find out how badly my brains are splattered?"

The Commodore simply whistled and carved.

"I report sensation in transmat, and everybody knows I'm scrambled because there can't be sensation in transmat. They come in here and tell me that it'd be better for everyone if I just tell the truth, and we all know what the truth has to be. I've had a half dozen long, slow winks from well-meaning sons of bitches. So I don't say anything, they don't say anything. But it's there in the report."

The Commodore did not acknowledge her words. The anger in her voice grew as she spoke. "Gunboat Mike needs a crew of transmatters, but the Commodore reads all the reports—or his Major has a team that does—and it's there. Even if we're all going to be dead soon anyway, he can't take the chance of having a crazy blasted from here to there in some half-assed design he's hallucinated. Crazy because a sane person knows that her brains are scrambled if she believes something that can't be true. Crazy because silence isn't enough. Crazy because she won't say it was a passing delusion. Crazy because she won't recant. Crazy because she won't say she *was* crazy."

Still the Commodore whistled and carved.

"So all I have to do to get out of this stinking jail and back to work is say, 'Oh no, I didn't feel a thing. Heavens, I couldn't have. We all know it's *theoretically* impossible. I was out of my head before. Trauma, don't you know? All better now, thank you very much.' Then we all nod and give each other those winks.

"But I can't, Mike. I was there, while it was happening. I can't describe it, maybe, but that doesn't mean it didn't occur. Look, I know what everybody thinks, that my mind came back together just the littlest bit cockeyed. Maybe that's what did happen. But why would a delusion take this form rather than any of a thousand others?"

The Commodore spoke softly without looking up. "Perhaps the basis of the delusion is not neurological. Maybe it's psychological."

"Then it happened the way I reported it, because I know I'm not crazy."

"I know." He looked up. "You're not the only one. There have been other, similar reports. Sensation during prolonged transmat."

She drained the flask. "You're a bastard, Mike."

"Technically, yes," he said. He put the knife away. "Look, I had some orders cut and sent over this way. They should be coming in about now. Welcome aboard, mate."

"Am I to be on one of your Major's teams?"

"No, my crew."

"Thanks, Mike." She handed the empty flask back and he pocketed it. He rose and handed her the leg.

"I thought you'd like a little taper to it."

LaMer examined the design. A large star rose above the checkerboard pattern.

"I'll smooth it up some if I get time later."

"So we'll sail the uncharted seas together, Mike?"

He held her gaze for a long time, then shook his head. "No, mate. We do the sending this time. Production's the barrier. Work out the math for yourself. So many boxes per transmat times so many people...." He shrugged. "Unless the Major's calculations are totally dog shit, we'll have a lot of company. Not that you care much for people."

"A captain and his ship," LaMer said, antagonism returning to her voice.

The Commodore thought to place the reference. "Mate goes before the captain. Think of it that way. Theoretically, I could be the last man on earth."

Some bleak humor surfaced in LaMer's eye. "Theoretically, we could be the last man and woman."

"Aye, we'd make a pretty pair." He turned to go. "By the way, happy birthday."

She shot him a look, but he had already gotten past the broken door and into the corridor. She lay down on the bed and cradled the prosthesis. She ran a fingernail over the intricate pattern. A tension that had held her for a long time began to seep from her body in the form of tiny, hot, and very salty tears. She wiped them away from both her eye and the empty socket with a hard knuckle. She was sitting in the chair, fully dressed and working on the last connection of the harness, when the nurse came in with her orders.

12

Contact, Downside

David sat in his Torino, his stomach churning and sweat drenching his clothing, his eyes on the declining sun reflected in the rearview mirror. The sharp thunder that had, for a time, announced each flaring had diminished to low rumbles. The first flares had come precisely at sundown, but over the previous weeks those boundaries had steadily expanded to include any time from late afternoon till well after dark. Unlike Insiders, residents of the suburbs did not live and work in glass-walled buildings, and most had ignored the First Secretary's call for blackouts. Still, David imagined, everyone had taken to keeping an eye on the horizon around dusk.

A sharp pain, strong enough to make him grip the steering wheel, shot across David's abdomen. When it passed, he lit a cigarette. They had been coming with increasing regularity. He imagined he was getting an ulcer.

Each day the high temperature broke a long-standing record, though by only a degree or two. At night, though, temperatures moderated only nominally. The concrete and asphalt of the suburbs now contained a vast reservoir of energy that the short hours of darkness could not carry away. David and his neighbors had been living in a furnace, until the day before. Then a large cell of moisture-laden low pressure had moved over them, just as the Blue Baby had predicted. Now they boiled.

David pulled on his cigarette only to find it drowned in the sweat of his fingers. He tore his eyes from the mirror and looked out the windshield. The usual sitter and scout horseplay had intensified this evening, despite

or because of the weather, David didn't know. He longed
to stand up by the barrier in the hope of a little breeze,
but he did not wish to invite trouble, and a scout without
sitters could easily be construed as the worst kind of
competition. At least high on the Expressway the flies
weren't as bad. He was about to light another cigarette
when a shadow fell beside the car. David lay his hand on
the seat.

"Old man got it?"

David looked long and hard through his dark lenses,
the pain again tearing at his belly. The boy grinned back.
The pain passed, but not the grin. David wasn't surprised.
People in the suburbs grew up on a diet of hard looks.

"I've got it," he said finally. He rattled the prints in
his hand. "You got your end?"

The boy made a wild grab, and David let the prints
flutter down beside him on the seat. The boy's grin,
almost embarrassed, almost apologetic, widened.

"Just like to look over the production."

"Pay for it first."

"Sure, sure." He looked away. "Some weather, huh?
He doesn't mind the heat, but he hates the humidity."

"You don't have the down, do you?"

The boy, still grinning, shrugged. "He had a little
problem raising it. Let them work something out."

"It's already worked out, Amos Dandy. I trimmed the
down and the percentage because of Ms. Kitty, but I'm
not spending the rest of my life eating protein because
you can't hold up your end." He nodded through the
windshield. "There are a dozen buyers out there with the
cash and the want for this thing. I could auction it off
right now for double the deal I made you."

Two sitters, one large and one small, scuffled in front
of the Torino. The smaller one kicked, but the other, a
girl, knocked the foot aside with one hand, reached in
with the other hand and drug her nails down the boy's
face. Blood welled up from the gouges, and then the
scuffle took them down the line. Two scouts hurried past.

"They pretty rank tonight," Amos Dandy observed.
"Every week's worse than the one before." He returned
his attention to David. "I don't need it. Ms. Kitty knows
them."

"Sure, but not their route numbers. Look, do you want to make this thing work?"

The boy nodded. "Sure he does." David hoped Amos Dandy wasn't trying to have the laugh of him.

"How much you got?"

Amos Dandy went through his pockets. He brought out small rolls of blue bills and tossed them through the window into David's lap. The last, small wad he held up for David to see. "His gas money."

David nodded, and Amos Dandy repocketed it. David unrolled, flattened, and counted the rest. He looked up when he finished.

Amos Dandy grinned. "His uncle didn't get his allotment like he supposed to get."

David folded the money and stuck it in the glove compartment. He lifted the prints from the seat again. This time Amos Dandy saw the revolver that lay beneath them. He gave an appreciative whistle.

"How much for that?" he asked.

"It's not for sale. Besides you still owe me half." He held the prints in both hands and tore the set in two. He handed half to Amos Dandy. "This'll get you started."

Amos Dandy leafed through the prints, then nodded his satisfaction.

"What does he tell them when he calls?"

"Tell them you took over the business. Tell them I've retired."

"Anything else?"

"Talk to McGee about your car. Tell him I told you to. Ask him if you can pay by the week." David started the Torino. The twin exhausts rumbled beneath the floorboards. "Watch out for your sitters, as well as you can." Amos Dandy stepped back and David pulled away. Ms. Kitty sat in Amos Dandy's car. She smiled at him, proud of her front-seat status. He smiled back.

"Hey," Amos Dandy called. "What if they stop coming?"

"Then you can forget the other half." He accelerated down the Expressway.

David drove through Fast Food Alley slowly to baby the antique engine against the heat. The static on the radio only distracted him and he flicked it off. Relief rose like a bubble within him, buoying him up. He savored it

for several languid blocks. As happy as he'd sometimes
been, he'd never been at peace with his life as a scout.
That scouting was a crime had never much bothered him.
Since university and before—growing up where and how
he did—he had broken a number of laws on a more or
less daily basis. Still, his education had shown again and
again that his work carried a historical and cultural
stigma as dark as nearly any. He knew that decent people
of his parents' generation would have passionately
disapproved, and he believed without a trace of cynicism
that his parents had been, at their core, decent. At first,
he had felt himself and his sitters morally superior to
their clients—they did what they did in order to eat. Now,
hunger seemed a distant condition, afflicting a random
selection of people he encountered during his day. He
had, almost, forgotten what the real hunger—days without food or consecutive weeks with far too little—felt
like. Yes, he was relieved, but he wondered if guilt would
trail him, like a car's exhaust, through the remainder of
his life.

He made a smooth turn onto Pine Heights Road.
Mixed, perversely, with his relief, he felt a sentiment he
finally named nostalgia. He had been a young man, just
out of university, when he began his scouting. The boy he
had been was as distant now as hunger. His heart had
been freshly broken, and he had taken up the most
romantic life available. The poet-scout, cruising the skirts
of civilization, had also been a figure loaded with aspects
of revenge. Love was a financial arrangement for his
Insider-clients, but he had been provided with a long
series of ready, if occasional, lovers. David shifted down,
and the ash from his cigarette fell to the threadbare carpet
of the Torino. He looked at the cigarette in his fingers as
he would at a stranger who had spoken familiarly to him.
That was when he had become addicted to nicotine, of
course. He tossed the cigarette out the window. He'd
adopted an image, but it had become more. He had
donned a mask only to find it, a long decade later,
indistinguishable from his face.

He drove on aimlessly through the back streets toward
the far skirts. Scouting cost his writing time and attention, and sometimes he resented that trade profoundly.
The lives of writers he'd met across the barrier, at Inside

speakings that were a part of a regular New City tour, suggested no direction for his own career. He'd meandered too long. Besides, he felt no desire to be in that well-paid and atom-scrambled company. He'd seen other lives absorbed by a romantic addiction to transmatation. He had made a life separate from theirs, and his difference was what, he had come to understand, he valued most.

He found himself idling through the twilit streets, and he accelerated slightly. No amount of relief, nostalgia, or smugness would make a future. He shook his head grimly. It was an old joke, to plan for a day when not even the next hour was certain. It was an irony he was accustomed to living with. Still, it occurred to him to make a clean break with his old life by giving up his teaching job as well. He did not believe that he had ever been a particularly good teacher. Even his best students moved on to other things. Maybe it was time he learned a lesson from them.

He turned a corner at random. Preach, without much apparent effort, nearly always succeeded in a vocation not far removed from teaching. David wondered if some dishonesty ran threadlike through the entire fabric of his life. He felt that if he could somehow know that there was any value to what he did, that he somehow informed his students of life, then he could go on. Instead he felt certain that his students' lives were real, terrible, and the classroom merely a time away from that turbulent weather. None of the students he had taught over the years had accomplished any of their lofty goals. He preferred not to face the likes of Mad Tom, JoyCee, or even Carly again. Yes, he thought, *I'll resign*.

He laughed, despite himself. "Resign" was too grand for a part-time and occasional assistant instructor. He needed only to decline the next class or two he was offered, and he would recede from the thoughts of harried administrators. And if the weather continued to worsen, decisions would be, very soon, a lost luxury.

Sundown was long past, and this one without any pyrotechnics. That had happened before, once for three consecutive nights. David felt another load lift from his shoulders. Such luck gave everyone a little hope. He turned on his headlights. Suburban drivers considered them either optional or, more often, an unnecessary repair and a drain on ancient batteries. He came across the old hospital and accelerated past, afraid of complicating his mood with further memories. He turned in a direction that would take him through the night to his house.

David left his house keys dangling from the lock and lifted his leg to slap at something biting his calf. He had always admired persistence. Another time he might have paused to wonder at the endurance of mosquitoes, but the weather and his long drive had mined all of his curiosity. It was an hour or two before dawn, he figured. The heat had not subsided and the humidity was more oppressive than ever. He found himself missing the dry heat of two days before. He had come to think of it, while it lasted, as desert heat, and though he had never, of course, been in a desert of any kind, he had read of them. He had built an aura around his life in the heat by seeing himself as a character moving across a fictional land-scape, and he had, like the crusty prospector he imagined himself, cursed the weather with considerable vigor and originality. The humidity had robbed him of the energy to play or curse. He slapped again at a bite like two bony fingers pinching his calf. Finally, the old lock surrendered, and he stepped inside.

Felix found the back of his knee with a cold nose. David found the light switch in the dark, then knelt to rub and pet and talk nonsense to the dog. He turned the dog outside. Felix shuffled out onto the lawn, squatted, a dark silhouette in the night, then wandered away. David walked back through the garage into the brightly lit kitchen.

He longed for Ms. Kitty with a physical ache. The loss of her, he imagined, constituted his largest regret. He attempted brutal self-honesty: it wasn't Ms. Kitty he missed. She was just one more in a long line of women who had always been there for him when he needed them. Yes, he acknowledged, that was true. Still, it was she, not just any lover, he missed now. The truth, the *real truth*, he told himself, was that she had been a better friend than sitter. An image of himself growing old alone in the house came to mind. He shook his head, attempted to laugh at the petty melodramas he insisted on imagining for himself, but failed in the swelter of the kitchen. He poured himself a tall gin, extinguished the kitchen light and stumbled to the breakfast nook.

He had to keep a hand on the glass for fear of knocking it over in the dark. He sat for several minutes before his night vision came back enough for him to make out the frame of the window he stared through. When Felix scratched at the door, he let the dog in and topped off his drink in the dark. Felix curled down near his feet. David scratched the bites on his legs, then behind the old dog's ears. He was too tired to think or to sleep. Out the window, heat lightning shimmered like glastic against the blacplastic night. He finished his gin. He decided against trying to work. He filled his glass instead. Felix snored steadily, whimpering once. David decided to check his mail.

He stumbled through the dark house to the study, barking his shin against the coffee table in the living room on the way. The red message block blinked on the screen. He found his desk chair by waving his free hand around, pulled it out, and sat down. He set the drink far to the side, afraid of spilling it into the console, and fumbled for the switch. The screen buzzed to life. It politely asked him to select a function.

He had no desire to wake up some Insider who'd decided at the last minute on a weekend fling, especially when it would require of him a long explanation. He took a drink. Still, he had made the deal with Amos Dandy, and he felt obliged, to Ms. Kitty at least, to keep up his end. He selected "Postal," then "Return Call."

The console began to sort through its options, found it had only one. True thunder rolled someplace a few kilometers distant. Outside, the wind tacked about in a series of gusts. Rain struck the roof, the patterns of sound changing every few seconds in the shifting wind. A face appeared on the screen. David stared at it stupidly. The wind settled its direction and velocity, and the rain pattered down steadily.

"Do I know you?" David asked.

The face studied him. The eyes blinked rapidly, as if the brain behind them was coming out of a dream. David went on guard against their beauty.

"You're David Jones?" The voice was husky, but the woman spoke without the catch of someone just awaking.

"Yes." The face was older, beneath the paint, than it should be. David's customers were, with few exceptions, in their twenties. This woman was twice that age. "I'll have to ask for a reference," he said.

"A reference?" The eyes showed surprise. "I'm sorry. I don't understand."

"Why are you calling?" Lightning flashed beyond the drawn drapes of the study. Several seconds later a sharp crack of thunder followed. The facepaint showed a history longer than the most recent Insider magazine lay-out.

"I'm getting some static on my end," the woman said. "I didn't hear what you said."

"It's the storm. I asked why you were calling."

"A storm? Oh, I see. Certainly. First, thanks for returning my call. It must be very late there."

"More like early." David removed his dark glasses. No one called across time zones to find a sitter. "Maybe I should have waited till tomorrow, or later anyway. I just got the message, you see."

"No, not at all." The tempo of the rain on the roof picked up, and thunder and lightning struck simultaneously.

"What did you say?" David asked. "We're right in the middle of a storm here."

"I said that I'm happy you called, whatever the time. My name is Tella-Dotun."

David resisted the urge to reach for his glasses. "Yes, I know of you."

"Then you understand why I'm calling." She consulted a print. "We're very much interested in producing the manuscript you submitted to us last winter."

David desperately wanted to scratch a particular bite on his calf.

"Is it still available, Mr. Jones? The manuscript?"

David nodded. "Yes," he said. "Yes, it is."

Tella-Dotun waited. When he didn't go on, she said, "Good. I'm sending you a standard contract." She pushed a button on her console. "Please read it at your leisure."

David frantically searched his mind for any response.

Tella-Dotun continued hesitantly. "Am I to understand that you are still interested in having us produce the manuscript? I presume you submitted it for that reason."

David shook himself to life. "Yes. Yes, of course. I'm interested. I'd be very happy to have you produce it."

"Good," Tella-Dotun said with a rising inflection.

"It's just been so long," David explained, "since I submitted it. I'd pretty much forgotten about it."

Tella-Dotun nodded. "It sometimes takes us longer than we'd like. We receive an awful lot of work, and there are only a few of us in this division to do all the reading."

"No, no. I understand. I'm just surprised, is all."

Tella-Dotun nodded, then smiled.

David was in love, if not with the woman, then certainly with her smile. He felt again, for the first time in years, the awkwardness, the sense of being out of place and out of his depth, that had accompanied him his first semester at university. He did not like the feeling.

"Look," he said, "I'm more than happy. I'm ecstatic. This is the best news I've had in a long time. What do you need me to do?"

Thunder rumbled in the distance. The rain kept on.

She spoke through her smile. "First, Mr. Jones—"

"Call me, David."

"Yes, if you wish." The smile dimmed almost imperceptibly. "David, I'd like you to go through the manuscript with an eye to any last changes you might care to make. I think that it is especially important in the light of the recent climatic disturbances."

David's heart sank. "Might that not make the work appear, ah, opportunistic"—he stuttered the word—"if the disturbances, as you call them, pass?"

Tella-Dotun traded the print for an antique pen and passed it from hand to hand. "Yes, perhaps that will be how it works out. In either case, the phenomenon constitutes a significant cultural event."

"You're asking for a rewrite?"

"No. I just think you may wish to bring the manuscript up to date." She placed the pen on her desk at arm's length, picked up a print, and took a breath. "My request has to do with another piece of information I need to share with you. I must ask you to keep this confidential."

David shrugged, mystified, then nodded.

"Have you heard of something called 'Rescue Effort.'"

David shook his head.

"There's quite a bit of rumor about it here."

"We're out of the way of rumor here," David said.

"Very little is known about it, but we have been asked to supply names to a government agency called the Screening Committee. The purpose is, I think, apparent."

"You're kidding?"

"Pardon me?"

"What are you saying?"

"Simply that, David. I must also inform you that we have submitted other names, and that we have no way of assessing the likelihood of your selection."

"I still don't understand."

Tella-Dotun's face briefly showed frustration. She ennunciated carefully. "If you wish us to produce your manuscript, we will forward your name to the Screening Committee for its consideration. It is possible that they will include you in the so-called Rescue Effort if the phenomenon does not"—she lifted a hand as if the right word hovered on the screen before her—"stabilize."

David giggled. "You mean—" he began, then let it drop. He turned away from the screen. Grayish light outlined the drapes. He dismissed the notion that it was all a practical joke. He had first heard of Tella-Dotun during his university days. Older students had spoken of her in reverential tones. The painted butterflies were a hallmark. Smiling hugely, he turned back to her. "I understand."

Her face was sober beneath the paint. "One last thing. There's the probability of a preproduction speaking."

"Where?"

"Here." She smiled at his anxious look.

"Oh my."

Her eyes shifted to something on her screen he could not see. "I have to go. I have another call coming in."

"Okay," David said, again numb.

"Look at the contract. And think about the revisions. We'll talk soon."

"Okay."

"Good-bye, David."

He looked past the butterflies into her eyes. They were positively merry. "Good-bye—"

"Call me Talla," she said with a grin.

"Tella," he repeated stupidly.

The screen went blank. David sat for a while looking at the place where her smile had been. Felix came in, lapped once at the drink by his feet, then placed his head on David's leg. He petted the dog absently, reached down, raised the glass, and took a long drink. He decided against a cigarette. He took another drink. He opened the drapes. The rain had stopped and the new day looked pure, as if the storm had cleansed the world. He touched the tips of two fingers to his cheek. He found that he was crying.

When David's face had disappeared from her screen, Tella-Dotun automatically pressed the "respond" button. A split-second later she jabbed the "delay" button and sat back wearily in her chair. She spent several moments trying to place her first meeting with this new writer in some kind of perspective. He was odd, certainly, but these residents of the suburbs, these blue people, as the bohemian among them called themselves, were odd by definition. She wondered if Mr. Jones was the kind of writer who worked all night. And what had he been talking about at first? Apparently, he had thought she was someone else, or, more accurately, that she wanted something else. She picked up her pen and touched it to "respond."

Jomo's face showed on the screen. He was wearing a robe over his pajama coveralls. "Aha! I caught you."

"So you did."

"You promised you would spend the weekend at home."

"So I did."

"Spend the weekend at home?"

"Promised I would."

"Well, did you get him?"

"What?"

"Did you get him? Jones? The new guy?"

"Yes, Jomo, I 'got' him."

"What's he like? Tell me all about him."

"I don't know. Reception wasn't very good."

"Well, is he young? Old? What?"

"Jomo, he appears to be a standard blue person."

"Hm." Jomo did not hide his disappointment. "How did he take the news he might be sent looking for a new home?"

Tella-Dotun shook her head. "He laughed."

Jomo's eyes widened. "Laughed?"

"Laughed. Giggled. Something."

"Inscrutable people, these skirt-dwellers."

Tella-Dotun found herself laughing. "Have your breakfast, Jomo. I'll see you tomorrow morning."

"Bye, boss."

Tella-Dotun went to the couch, lay down, and kicked off her sandals. Yes, inscrutable, she thought. She wondered if she had, in her exhaustion, started to see things. The moment before she hung up she thought she had seen something in Jones's eyes. She would have sworn he was weeping. She yawned once and fell asleep, her face relaxing into a smile beneath its paint.

13

Housestead

"Leave me alone, whore!" The man took a drunken swipe with a pawlike hand and fell from the barstool onto his knees. "Goddamn little whore! Leave me be!" He reached out for Lu's ankle, and she stepped away. "Sweet Mary's ass!" His voice fell to a mumble. "Can't have a quiet drink without some cigarette kid hitting on you." The man dropped to all fours, then stretched out. He turned his cheek to the grime on the floor and lay down. He began to snore.

Lu looked at Edie. The bar was deserted except for the three of them. The radio on the backbar played static, and silent images mouthed something on the screen in one corner.

"What'd you take in?" Edie asked matter-of-factly.

Lu stepped over the man and sat on the stool he'd vacated. She brought a scattering of change out of her purse. She stacked the coins according to size, then restacked them, pushing every second one across to Edie. When she finished she looked up expectantly.

"Business ain't what it ought to be," Edie said. She closed the open till with a slam. She gathered up the change from the bar and poured it back and forth between her hands. It glistened like water. Lu waited silently.

"What do you want me to say? It ain't working? You want me to say that? Okay, it ain't working. It should be but it ain't."

Edie took a coin from her open palm and pushed it back across the bar. Lu reached a cigarette across to her and palmed the coin in a single fluid motion. Edie dumped the small mound of change on the bar between them, then took her time finding an ashtray and match beneath the bar. She exhaled blue smoke and rubbed her free hand over her hair. "It should be but it ain't," she repeated. She pulled over the stool she kept behind the bar for looking at magazines when there were no customers and sat down. "Hard times is supposed to bring out the drinkers. Always has."

The man on the floor whimpered. Edie stood on the rungs of her stool and craned her neck, then sat back down.

"Supposed to bring out the money. It ain't working."

She stubbed out the cigarette, reached below her, and brought up a bottle. She held it up for Lu's inspection. It was half-full and the design on the label was much more intricate than the usual government logo. Lu held a finger near her open mouth.

"I got nothing," Edie said. "That son of a bitch there ate the last fry in the place."

"Who you, who you calling, who you calling a sommabitch?" The man raised himself on his arms, then rolled over on his back with a thump.

"You! I'm calling you a son of a bitch!"

The man resumed snoring.

"Crazy son of a bitch." Edie got two glasses from the backbar without rising. They clinked together in her hand. After she filled them, the bottle was only a quarter-full.

Edie lifted her glass. "What do we drink to?"

Lu took her glass and shrugged, spilling a little.

"Be careful, honey. You can't get that anymore." She stopped to consider. "Ah hell," she said, "Skoal!"

They clinked glasses and drank. Edie put hers down hard with a ragged exhalation. The liquor was half-gone.

"I got protein!" she said. "Do you want some protein?"

Lu shook her head.

"Nah, me neither. Tasteless, pasty stuff. I don't know how anybody'd be expected to eat that shit." She worked a coin out from the pile before her and pushed it across. Lu set a cigarette down and palmed the coin.

"Jesus, honey, Jesus." Edie lit the cigarette. "What the hell are we going to do?"

Lu met her stare without any expression.

Edie polished off her drink. "Damn straight!"

Lu took a little sip.

Edie's voice was husky. "Where are they? That's what I'd like to know. Just where in hell did they get to?"

Lu shrugged.

Edie refilled her glass, then held the bottle tentatively over Lu's. Lu covered it with her hand.

"What the hell's what I say. What the bleeding hell!"

"It's the heat," she said after she'd composed herself. "It's the heat, and this damn humidity. Sweet Mary, I wish it'd rain. When's the last time it rained?"

Lu spoke in a quiet voice. "A long time."

"Where's the Blue Baby? I can't find the Blue Baby."

Lu shrugged.

"I didn't think she sounded so good. Remember that? Last week I said I didn't think she sounded so good?"

Lu nodded.

"Damn straight." Edie gulped from her glass. "I said that last week." She struggled with a cough until she got her breath back. She stubbed out her cigarette.

"Where the hell are they?" she asked.

On the street outside a car was passing. Edie cocked her head till the sound had diminished to nothing.

Edie held her glass in front of her and studied the contents. "Drink's what'll kill you in this job." She took a sip. "I mean if you drink too much. The old man I took this place over from, he drank with the customers. Pass out, like that son of a bitch there, before closing time." She finished her drink. Lu pushed her glass over.

"You sure?"

Lu nodded.

"It's—hell, what time is it? It must be midnight."

Lu nodded.

Where the hell are they?"

Lu shrugged.

Edie examined her glass. "You get your allotment yet?"

Lu shook her head.

"You put that mailbox up, like she told you?"

Lu nodded.

"You ought to go back down and talk to that lady again. That's what you ought to do."

Lu shrugged.

Edie fell back into her own thoughts. "Hard times, bad weather. It just ain't working."

Lu stood and looked down at the snoring man.

"Don't worry about him, honey. I can handle him by myself. I've done it before."

Lu took a step.

"Hey, before you go." Edie held up two coins. Lu found a cigarette in her purse.

"Last one," she said and handed it over.

Edie put both coins in her hand. "Keep it, honey."

Lu looked at the man again. "Is she sure?"

"Hell, I might just lie down with him." She filled her glass. "Sweet Mary, I wish he had some life left."

Lu stepped around the man.

"Hey!"

Lu turned.

"Don't go putting on the face. If you made your boy a promise, you better keep it. Ain't nothing counts between a woman and a man if they can't keep their promises."

"Okay." At the door Lu turned. Edie sat behind the bar, drink in hand and blue smoke curling up from the cigarette.

It was very late by the time Lu got down the Alley. Except for an occasional bathtub she had never been in water deeper than her ankles, and she wondered if walking in the humidity was like swimming. She worked her way from streetlamp to streetlamp. The dense air carried scents that she could not place. The strangeness made her halt in the dark more than once in the long intervals between working lamps. The hair on the back of her neck bristled, then, with unnamed threats, until her hunger forced her on.

Her visor wouldn't have her back after she'd been late for her shift that day. Her arrangement with Edie seemed sound, but each night fewer and fewer customers showed. Still, she had eaten the same. Each time she'd replenished her supply of cigarettes it'd been a smaller batch. She'd been mystified that her money diminished rather than grew, but Edie had explained it to her. She trusted Edie. Edie always let her have first pick of the scraps that customers left. Now Edie had decided it wouldn't work.

Lu stood in the dark outside the Burger Barn for a

long time, her nostrils flaring at the grease smell carried into the night by the exhaust fans. A single scout and a sitter entertained within the well-lit building. The other franchises' parking lots were nearly empty as well. Even the Insiders were afraid of the new sundowns. At first, Lu had thought that the flares ate Insiders, the way she would a hamburger fresh from the grill. Edie had explained, though, that they, like the blue people, were only hiding.

Lu fingered the single bill among the change in her purse. Though she could read nothing but the numeral on the bill, she understood that it and the glastic coins together meant either a meal or the means to restock her inventory. Food lasted only a short time, and her garden had yet to grow. She stood as near the plate glass wall as she dared. The scout sitting there between his sitter and customer was not Tommy Gunn. She reminded herself to always watch for him, though she hoped the flares had already eaten him.

Behind the Barn was a lidless dumpster. Lu listened for the rustling of rats, as her mother had taught her. Her mother had shown her the puckered skin on her own hand where she'd been bitten. Lu heard nothing. She walked the length of the dumpster with her nose low, sniffing. Her nostrils flared at a strong scent, and she reached into the darkness. The blacplastic bag tore easily under her nails. Her hand came to her face with a scrap of cheeseburger. She chewed the cold lump quickly and swallowed. She burrowed her hand deep into the plastic straws and plates and forks, then raked her spread fingers back toward her. She closed her fist over some fries and squeezed them together into a ball so that she wouldn't lose any. She bit off part of the lump and chewed. She licked her lips to get the cold ketchup smeared there. She thought about rats. She had seen only one in her life, a long time ago. A dog had killed it and was carrying it away at a fast walk. Her mother had told her what it was. Lu didn't think there were any rats left. She thought that the dogs had maybe killed them all. Still, like Tommy Gunn, they were something she was careful about.

She heard the side door of the Burger Barn open and retreated quickly and quietly into the darkness. She'd made only ten meters when the footsteps neared the corner of the building. She crouched down into the night.

She saw the dark silhouette of a man carrying a blacplastic bag turn the corner and disappear into the shadow. She heard the thump of the garbage landing in the dumpster. She waited for the man to reappear from the shadow.

After what seemed a very long time she heard a scratching noise. She nearly bolted, but she saw the flare of the match before she could move. The man held the match under a cigarette, then tossed it away. Each time he inhaled his cheeks shone in a reddish glow. She crinkled her nose at the fragrance of the smoke. He stepped toward her and again she prepared for flight. He stopped, though, halfway from the dumpster. She heard a sharp intake of breath and then the sound of him making water. The odor of his urine made her scuttle back a meter in spite of herself.

The man zipped his fly, snapped the cigarette away, sighed, and disappeared around the corner. After Lu heard the door open and close, she scurried to the glow of the butt in a half-crouch and carried it with her back into the dark. She sat on her haunches and sucked greedily.

Preach lifted one hand off the steering wheel to cover a huge yawn that left him shaking his head against drowsiness. "Lord!" he said aloud. He turned a corner at random and studied the doorways and stoops along the street in the barest beginnings of dawn.

"If I was a betting man," he said, "I'd bet we're in for a little rain." He considered it. "To tell the truth, I am a betting man. What about it? Two souls?"

He shook his head and smiled at his greed. Business was booming. "It's the hard times," he said to the windshield. "It really brings them in." The afternoon before he had umpired the first full-fledged sacrament of baseball since before the Fall. Since his memory of the particulars of the celebration was dim, he'd had to make most calls on his sense of fair play. He let the car coast down a slope while he savored the image of it. "The halt, the lame, the blind," he said, thinking of his communicants struggling through nine hot and humid innings. The Buddhists had won on Mad Tom's homer on errors, the only run of the game. They seemed to enjoy their victory, though, less than the Christians appeared upset by their loss. Carly, who had been left on base three times, was especially disconsolate. He had been making wonderful progress with his stutter, but after the game it was as pronounced as ever.

It occurred, very suddenly, to Preach that his morning rounds might soon prove unnecessary. He enjoyed the quiet drives looking for those in need. He quickly decided he would continue his rounds, regardless. The absence of drunken men and women sheltering where they had passed out constituted a double blessing. Gas was cheap, and the two novices could handle the walk-in trade.

He made a mental note to score more sacramental wine from Mr. Feldon. He revised that. He would mention it to Mad Tom or Carly. Both boys enjoyed jotting things down so much that Preach had taken to working from the lists they compiled. He had such a list in the pocket of his Bermuda shorts now, in fact, although it was almost impossible to get to it through his cassock when sitting. The rain started in a sudden burst. Preach smiled and spoke in the empty interior. "Don't you welch now. Two more souls." He reached for a knob and twisted it. The wipers made a half-hearted attempt to climb the windshield, then surrendered with a short-lived squeal. Three things to tell the boys then, Preach thought. "Mr. McGee and the wipers. Mr. Feldon and the sacramental wine. Two more souls."

Lightning illuminated the sweep of rain. He braked suddenly. Some distance away thunder rolled. Through the spattered windshield he saw a dog jogging down the sidewalk fifty meters ahead. He slowed, hoping it would veer off between the abandoned houses. Preach wanted neither the civic responsibility of destroying it nor the guilt of having let it escape. He narrowed his eyes to watch it.

"It's not a dog after all, you old fool," he said and sped up. "It's a young person caught out in the rain." He rubbed his hands at the opportunity. "The Good Samaritan," he intoned in mock profundity. He rolled down his window and pulled to a gentle stop abreast of the figure.

"Can I give you a lift?"

It was a girl. Rain had flattened her hair to a tight cap and soaked her clothing.

"Can I take you someplace?" Preach called again.

The girl looked up and down the street, then back at Preach. Rain had sprinkled through the window.

"It's Okay. I'm Preach. I like to do people favors."

"What?" Rain ran off her brows and nose.

"Favors. Help. It's what I do."

Lightning flashed and thunder boomed. The girl cringed beneath it. After the noise had rolled away she lifted an arm and pointed up the street. "Home," she said.

"I'll take you there." He opened the passenger door.

She jogged around the car, got in, and slammed the door.

Preach rolled up his window and started the car forward. "This is just what we needed," he said. "It'll take some of the humidity out of the air."

"What?"

"It'll wash things out. The weather will be better after the rain."

"Weather?"

"Yes, you know." Preach made a circular motion with his left hand, indicating outside the window. "Weather."

"Better?"

"Yes, better. You say you live up here?"

"Yes."

"Let me think. Yes, I do know someone on this street. A good friend. Well actually, his parents and I were very close. Still, I see him every so often."

"His is a nice car."

"The Chevy? Good. I like it, too. It's nothing special, but it gets me around. I really prefer my Yammerhammer, but it's strictly a one-person affair. And it's not much good in this weather. Rain, I mean." A wet, dank smell had filled the car. He looked at her and saw nothing memorable except a slim scar lay over her eye. "You'll have to tell me where you live."

"Here," she said suddenly.

Preach braked. "Any one in particular?"

"Here." She had her hand on the door handle.

He got the car stopped. "My friend lives just up the street about a block. Stop in sometime and tell him hello. His name is Davy. It's right up there."

She was already moving around behind the car. Preach rolled down his window and called, "What's your name?"

She turned. "Edie." She walked toward a house.

"Well, good-bye Edie." Preach put the car in gear and drove away. He could not see the girl through the rearview mirror for the rain. He thought about stopping to see Davy, then remembered that Davy, in his line of work, might well not be home yet. He decided to go back to the church. "Three things," he said to the rain outside the windshield.

Lu stood for a minute until the car was lost in the rain. Instead of going to the house she'd told Preach was her home she followed the car. She stopped once at the sight of a single brake light glowing through the rain, then continued up the street.

The force of the rain had subsided by the time she'd made another block. She stood in front of her house for a time, unafraid now that the lightning and thunder had ceased. Rain ran into the spots on the roof where the wind had blown away the asphalt shingling. She wondered if rain soaked through the ceiling and into the rooms. That would explain the large spots of rotten carpet she'd found. She hoped so. She'd thought that dogs had used the house.

She went up the steps and, careful not to bump the precariously mounted mailbox, dragged the heavy door aside. In the dim light, she surveyed the nest she'd made from the blankets that had hung over the windows. She studied the empty packets laid out in a line upon a sill. Beneath the government logo on each there was a picture of a kind of food and some print she could not read. Her mouth watered at the images of corn and squash, beans, peas, and melons.

She walked through the house and opened the screen door. In the backyard, the stalks and vines smiled greenly in the rain. She yawned sleepily, water running into her open mouth. She began the first of the circles she always made before she slept.

On her last pass she walked closer than ever before to her neighbor's house. She was surprised to see him through the blankets that hung on his windows. She backed away a step, but paused since he had not noticed her. "Davy," she said quietly, as if practicing the name. She cocked her head and watched for a few more minutes before moving on. She reentered her house through the screen door and padded through the rooms. Her entire body was caught in a massive shiver, and wet drops sprayed the air around her. She stripped off her wet clothes and wormed her way into her blankets. She snuggled into her nest. She wondered why Davy was crying. She reflected that maybe his friend hadn't told him the weather was going to be better.

14

The Puzzle Box

The Major stopped her pacing long enough to lift her eyes and exclaim, "I wish they'd hurry!"

"Relax, Major, they'll be here when they get here."

The Major's expression suggested to LaMer that her presence had been forgotten. She pushed her chair farther back on its spring.

"You look like you can at least take your own advice," the Major said. LaMer sat behind the main console, both her biological and prosthetic legs up on the work surface.

"Take some of the starch out, Major. You're building for a coronary."

"I was just wondering what was taking them so long. Something must have gone wrong." The Major's tone had changed so dramatically LaMer revised her earlier opinion. Far from forgotten, she was, it seemed, an audience the Major wished to play to.

"Hey, Mike's got them. We're just the last act anyway, and, let's face it, not all that bloody important."

"Your language, LaMer."

"Your sweet backside, Major."

As if on cue, the Major's clean features twisted themselves into a red mask. It crossed LaMer's mind that the Major wished to pick a fight. Though the Major was combative—rank required it—auxiliary control of Home Base was the last place LaMer would have expected to see it displayed. LaMer prepared to get her legs under her. The moment stretched on.

LaMer sighed. "Look, Major, nothing personal. My language is my concern. I take some getting used to. I like it that way. Keeps the toadies at a distance. But what do you say we get along? Mike tells me he needs us both."

"Oh?" The Major's interest was obviously piqued.

"Yeah. I went to him the first day and said, 'Commodore, I respectfully request you transmat your Major back to Moscow,' and he said, 'LaMer, I need you both.'" The Major did not return her grin. After several awkward seconds, she resumed her pacing. LaMer wondered why she bothered.

The Major made three complete circuits before she spoke again. "I suppose it is important for us to maintain a good working relationship. The Commodore would want us to, and it will certainly facilitate our activities here. It would be counterproductive to allow our personal animosities to interfere with an important mission."

LaMer waited for a sign that she wished a response. The Major continued to pace. She did not look at LaMer.

"Look," LaMer said finally, "if you're interested in Mike in that way—"

The Major turned, the color again rising in her face. "My personal interests have nothing to do with it, LaMer."

LaMer shrugged. "Easy, Major. I just thought—"

"I don't care what you thought, you have no right to suggest that I intend a personal relationship—"

"Damn it, Major! Would you let me finish a sentence?"

"—between my commanding officer and myself. Besides, you are totally mistaken!"

The two women stared at each other in silence. "Goodness me," LaMer said finally, "I've found a sore spot."

"Don't start up again, LaMer. I'm warning you."

LaMer lowered her legs and swung forward in the chair. She spoke evenly, her voice carrying only a little heat. "Major, I look at you and I see another office-bound analyst. I've been through that mill"—she gestured to the transmatation booth behind the Major—"more days than not in the last dozen years. I recommend it to you. If you did more of it, you'd know what's worth a warning. Until then, why don't you let me tell you when to get nervous."

"These people are very important. I know the probabilities. Something could very well go wrong."

"What are they going to do? Close down the Rescue Effort if Rover shows up looking like tomato paste?"

LaMer sat back in her chair. "Hell, we're the only game in town."

The Major chewed her lower lip. For LaMer people nearly always fit into a very small number of broad categories. The Major was an authority freak, the kind who fretted over position in the hierarchy. The Commodore's refusal to second her views on LaMer's lack of attention to the ritual of discipline made her anxious. His own haphazard approach made her nervous. The presence of the VIPs downright rattled her.

"Maybe we should have another run-through."

"No, we shouldn't."

"What if I make it an order?"

"I take orders only from the skipper."

"The Commodore never gives orders."

"That's not my fault."

The Major sat next to LaMer. "Then what should we do?"

LaMer shrugged. "Trade war stories?"

"You go first."

LaMer tapped the carved and inlaid prosthesis against the console. "I got this right here."

"I heard."

"Before it was Home Base, of course." She pointed to the ceiling. "Before they started all that construction. And before all the very busy people took an interest. Do you want me to tell you about it?"

"Sure."

"That is, essentially, how it is intended to work, and of course this is all covered in the briefing prints, too. Just request the file if you want further information. Of course, I'm here to answer any questions you might have, as well." Except for the light from the screens arrayed along the wall and the single one from the Commodore's console, the room was dark. "Do you have any questions?" He waited to see who would begin.

"Commodore, this research seems awfully, ah, new. Is it possible that, despite the quantities of funds poured into it, we may not see results, ah, in time?"

"Yes, Governor, it is entirely possible."

There was a chorus of titters from the other screens.

"Touché, Commodore, but could you elaborate?"

"Excuse my flippancy, Governor, but this is not the time for guarantees I simply can't, in good conscience, give. First, the information available to me gives no reliable indication of how much time we have. There is neither a smooth line nor a coherent pattern to the increase in intensity of the phenomenon. There is, as you know, a plethora of speculation, but my reading of the reports is that they are only that—speculation. Most of it doesn't even attempt to build on any theoretical foundation.

"As to whether or not the Puzzle Box will work: yes, it will work. We have analyzed the theory, and we have analyzed our analysis. I am satisfied that it will work, if we have the time to develop it. I'm fully aware that we are in a race against the clock."

"The same holds true for this insulation layer you referred to?"

"Yes, Your Honor. We know how to determine its precise makeup. Each day enables us to discard several of the finite number of possibilities. I feel that we are only days away, at the most, from having the specific structure we're looking for." The Commodore paused. "Ladies and gentlemen, it is entirely possible that we will have it before this meeting concludes. I would certainly be pleased to have the answer routed here this very minute."

"Perhaps we should ask the Commodore how we can be of further assistance to him. Commodore?"

"Thank you, First Secretary, that's very generous. Everything that can be done is being done."

"Couldn't we further enhance production facilities?"

"Thank you, Brigadier. Production is at readiness."

"For both? The insulation and the boxes?"

"Yes sir. The source materials for the insulation are readily available. The boxes are being produced now and the gross navigational and computer components installed. We'll have to wait until we know more to go any further."

"What about an entirely new production facility?"

"I would suggest a good deal more than one, Governor."

"Then perhaps we should direct the First Secretary to authorize them? Tracy?"

"I'll take it as a consensus, then. Do I hear any dissenting opinion?

"Good. Any recommendations for the setting of priorities? Who gets them first, panel?"

"If I might make an observation or two?"

"Go right ahead, Commodore."

"Our report, which you will find filed with the other material, suggests the operative limitation on production facilities for the boxes is design efficiency. Though it is entirely possible to use our analysis of present facilities to design a new, more efficient facility, we don't know, yet, about the final, smaller components. It may be advisable, then, to proceed with only those aspects of the facility that bear directly on the production of the gross box itself, with some open end that will allow for placement of the other components later. We simply can't find the most efficient design for the facilities until we have completed the design on the box."

"That is very disheartening, Commodore. I don't wish to harp on the time factor, but any theoretical breakthrough will be moot if we cannot supply the actual boxes in appropriate quantity."

"Perhaps not entirely moot, Governor, if we have even a few boxes. Time to reach the one million mark, based on immediate initiation of construction of one hundred seventy-three production facilities—that's one of course for every New City—and immediate resolution of all current theoretical delays, is still several years."

"How long, did you say?"

"Thirty to forty months, someplace in there, to achieve point zed one two five of total population, which is set forth, as you might recall, as the goal of Stage Two of the Rescue Effort. The report gives a specific time. I simply don't recall it exactly at the moment."

"Commodore? Do you mind if I ask you a question?"

"No, ma'am, that's why I'm here."

"Well, not that kind of question. What is it you're doing with your hands there?"

"This? I'm rebuilding this circuit, ma'am. If you wish, I'll put it away."

"No, no, not at all. Perhaps we can find someone to do that for you."

"Thank you, ma'am. I find it facilitates my thinking, but I'd be happy to put it away."

"Oh, I certainly don't object. I was just curious."

"Does anyone wish the Commodore to, ah, dispose of his circuit?"

"Ms. First Secretary, I'd like to move on to other items on the agenda."

"Then I'll note it for my minutes, George, that you don't mind if the Commodore rebuilds a circuit?"

"That accurately reflects my stand on the matter, Tracy, and I have no objection to the minutes recording it. Now, if I might proceed?

"Commodore, your people list seventeen separate, potential methodologies pursuant to the addition of the insulation layer immediately prior to transmatation. There are few qualitative recommendations within the file itself. Can you explain to us how you intend to establish research priorities?

"Certainly, Commissioner. The data—"

"—seduced by the tradition. We've been military as long as we know. My father and two uncles were casualties of the Third World wars. My great-grandfather was on the *Potemkin*. Every generation has had its heroes."

"So you logged your routine transmats and went after rank. You don't have to explain anything to me, Major."

"But I want you to understand." She dropped a hand to LaMer's thigh.

LaMer felt cramped from too much sitting and the Major's dramatic mood swing. It occurred to her to take the Major's place pacing auxiliary control, but she dismissed the idea. She minded the pain only nominally. The skin of her abbreviated leg had toughened to the point that only a fraction of the tenderness remained, and she knew that friction against the prosthesis only helped her become accustomed to it. The idea, though, of the Major's keen eyes tracing her limp dissuaded her.

"We simply got off on the wrong foot," the Major was saying. She colored at her gaffe. "I'm sorry, I mean—"

"I know what you mean, Major."

The Major's hand gripped LaMer's thigh. She leaned closer. "Does it hurt terribly?"

LaMer gave her a practiced stare. The hand followed the thigh up a few centimeters.

"Not terribly, Major, and the pain is farther down, where the leg stops." The hand reversed directions. So she'd been wrong about the Major, after all, LaMer thought.

"You certainly run hot and cold, Major." A flush shone across the Major's cheeks, her eyes a feverish abstraction.

"That's what I've been told."

"I'll just bet you have. A half hour ago I'd have sworn you never thought of anything but your job."

The Major slid her hand up the inside of LaMer's thigh.

"I've thought of you," she said.

An intellectual neutrality took over LaMer. She knew it showed plainly in her stare. Some deep part of her was glad it was there to meet the Major's half-lidded gaze.

"And what do we do when Mike walks in with the panel?"

The Major leaned farther out of her chair and slipped both hands around LaMer's waist. "You said it could be a long time. All the discipline, I find myself taking risks sometimes. I don't question it." Her eyelids fluttered as if to dismiss a thought. "You're not afraid of risks?"

"I'm not much afraid of anything."

The Major loosened the collar of her uniform against the flush that had spread to her neck. She put a hand on LaMer's shoulder. LaMer stared at a pink earlobe.

"I'm afraid of us." Her voice was breathless. She stood. LaMer studied the lips falling toward her own. She reached a hand out to meet the warm throat.

She tightened her grip, and the Major's eyes fluttered open in confusion. The muscles of LaMer's wrist and forearm tightened, and the eyes focused suddenly on the pain.

"I see," LaMer said evenly, "that Mike has made a mistake. That's not at all like him." She forced the Major back into her chair with a steady downward pressure before dropping her hand.

The Major filled her lungs with a rush of air. Her face could have been carved from glastic as she mechanically massaged the imprint of LaMer's fingers on her throat. She closed the collar of her uniform and sat back with a shrug.

"I thought perhaps you were interested." Her voice was an even mix of observation and humiliation.

"Another time, another place, maybe. There are some times, though, when I don't wish to be disturbed."

"An old-fashioned girl? Who would have thought?"

"Easy, Major. A minute ago, I was trying to decide whether to make love to you or break your neck. I still have the second option."

The Major gave her an enigmatic smile. "Perhaps you still have the first, as well. I thought that the great LaMer had ice in her veins. That's the rumor, you know."

"You've got some things rolled together that need to be kept separate, Major. This isn't a contest."

"I disagree, LaMer. Everything is a competition of one kind or another. When we recognize that, we come to terms with the real world."

"You and I, Major? We're in competition?"

The Major's look was quick and scornful. "You know that as well as I."

"For what?"

"If you need me to answer that question, you're less of a woman than I took you for, LaMer."

"Even love, Major? A competition, too?"

The Major made a small, sharp motion with her chin, then rolled her head upon her neck, as if to settle it more comfortably. She didn't answer.

"What did Mike see in you, anyway?"

"A top-flight analyst. A superb organizational mind. An efficient team leader. I have many admirable qualities."

"Funny, I'm not overwhelmed."

"If the Rescue Effort succeeds, LaMer, it will be due to those qualities in me and in others. Remember that."

LaMer turned the thought over. It was a more accurate appraisal than she would ever admit. "You didn't answer my question. Do you see love as a competition, Major?"

"Your word for it, LaMer."

"Yes, my bloody word, Major."

"Yes, certainly. Love, too. You know it's true." Her face showed only peace.

"Then I hope the whole damn, muddy ball burns to cosmic ash."

The door behind the Commodore slid shut. "Are we ready?" he asked.

LaMer looked up from the console. "The board's clear, skipper."

The Major stood in the middle of auxiliary control, her hands joined behind her. "The panel, sir?"

"I put them on delay." He strode behind LaMer, looked over her shoulder, then went to stand near the Major.

"Do you think that wise, sir?"

The Commodore shrugged. "I wanted a break. What are the odds that Rover's coming back to us with a bark, Major?"

"Essentially fifty-fifty, Commodore."

He looked behind him. "Light them up, LaMer."

"Aye, aye, skipper."

"Hold that." LaMer pulled her hands away from the console. The Commodore half-raised a hand and gently rubbed two fingers against his thumb. His eyes were on the Major's neck. He looked to LaMer. She stared back.

"Personnel problems, Major?"

"Pardon me, sir?"

"I won't tolerate it. I have neither the time nor the inclination."

"Yes, sir."

"I will relieve anyone whose behavior disturbs the Effort. Is that understood, Major?"

"Yes, Commodore."

He faced the blank screens aligned on the far wall. "Proceed, LaMer."

"Aye, aye."

The screens flicked on simultaneously.

"Sorry for the delay, Ms. First Secretary, ladies, and gentlemen. We are ready to proceed.

"First, let me introduce, for those of you who don't know them, my executive officer, Major Korsikahv." The Major's already rigid back stiffened still more. She executed a downward snap of her chin. "And behind the console is Ms. Jeanne LaMer, whom I'm sure you know, at least by reputation. She is serving as chief of the transmatation team.

"If you look around auxiliary control you will see a normal transmatation center. For those of you who were brought in rather late and have not yet had the time to absorb the file, this until recently served as the center for N.L.A. We selected this procedure so that we could begin our trial runs without having to wait for the construction upstairs to be completed. Later, this will serve as a back-up center, if the need for a second should arise. An ancillary advantage is that we've been able to absorb some part of the old crew here to provide support for the Effort. They are currently undergoing additional training in preparation for a shake-down run to begin in ten days.

"Are there any questions?"

The First Secretary spoke. "I believe we're all eager to see the demonstration, Commodore."

"Yes, certainly. Before we begin, however, I want to say that I believe the request for this demonstration has come too early—"

"We understand your reservations, Commodore."

"Yes, I believe I have made them clear, Senator. I wish only to say that you might prepare yourselves. The Major informs me that her analysis indicates an even chance of success or failure. Failure in transmatation, as you know, can be unpredictable in its nature and is often extremely unpleasant in its manifestation. Since your request was for a demonstration of the Puzzle Box, no life-support equipment was provided to the subject. That, and the length of time in transmat, I'm afraid, combine to make the odds as poor as one in two."

He turned. "LaMer," he said, and she began the procedures that would bring Rover in. Over the years this work had become second nature to her. She felt a clarity and fluidity somewhere just out of consciousness. She heard the Commodore detailing the parameters of the demonstration, as if from some distance. Rover was locked in and forming up in something under a minute.

She sat back to watch the fireworks. Scattered atoms began to recombine low in the booth, a good sign. The booth glowed, too, rather than sparked. Soon the light began to pull in on itself, and, in a matter of moments, had dimmed to show a small, black spaniel.

The Major marched to the booth and opened the door. Rover bounded out and jumped for the Major's hand. She knelt down and rubbed his ears. He licked her face. The Major smiled through swipes of the long, pink tongue.

LaMer shut the system down.

"I am relieved, as I imagine you all are," the Commodore said. "Rover has, over the last—" he looked to LaMer.

"Six hours, nineteen minutes, and thirty-seven seconds."

"—traveled farther into space than any other living

entity. Only the exploratory space machines of the last
century have gone greater distances, Major?"

"Yes, sir. Roll over. Good dog. Sit up. Good dog."

"That the subject recalls tricks taught him previous to
transmatation indicates no neurological disturbance. Keep
in mind, though, how preliminary this work is. Rover
could have easily come back hurt, dead, or not come back
at all."

"I think you're too modest, Commodore."

"Not at all, Senator. That is our best calculation. In
fact, we may find yet, upon a thorough examination, that
the dog has been altered during transmat."

"He appears normal to me, Mike." The dog jumped up
for a bit of protein the Major held in her hand. There was
a chorus of relieved laughter.

"Yes, Tracy, he does." The Commodore smiled.

"Well," the First Secretary began, "the only item
remaining on the agenda is a report on the progress of the
Screening Committee, several members of which are present." She paused as two or three images nodded in
acknowledgment. "Nominations have been solicited from
a wide variety of agencies including professional and
civic organizations. They are coming in at about the rate
we expected, which is to say very rapidly." A bitter
chuckle escaped one of the members of the panel.
"Currently, methods of selection for inclusion have been
discussed. What appears certain is that some method of
assigning numbers in order of departure will be used,
though the numbers within a certain set may be determined by lottery." She paused to look around. Two of the
panel members nodded their agreement. "Immediate family members—spouses and children—will be covered by
the same number. Transmatation of several within the
same box is possible, I understand?"

"Two adults and two children per box is the maximum, if we assign the luggage to a box of its own."

"The idea is that consecutive boxes would be used for
large family groups?" She looked around for confirmation.

She consulted a print. "Every effort will be made to
represent vocations and skills deemed necessary for survival as well as to provide a cross-section of our cultural
achievements. An effort will be made to represent all
cultures, as well. Any questions? Comments? Major?"

"A very rational and laudable system, ma'am."

"Thank you. LaMer?"

"Primitives?"

"Pardon me?"

"Just curious, ma'am. Will representatives from Out There be contacted and assigned numbers?" The Commodore pivoted.

An image leaned farther into his screen. "Yes, Ms. LaMer, we received your report. Quite frankly, we were surprised that so many of your, ah, fraternity, felt so strongly on this point."

"The life forms of which you speak hardly constitute a culture, Ms. LaMer," said another.

"They are, after all, humans." LaMer, unsure whether or not to control her temper, settled on sarcasm.

"Well yes, humans, I suppose," said the first image. "Humanoid, anyway."

"No, they're human," said a third image. "I believe that's been established."

"The fact of the matter," said the first image, "is that no one is entirely sure, as far as I know, whether they indeed exist."

"Isn't the real issue one of protocol?" asked the third image. "Is it within the province of the technical staff to make such a recommendation? Isn't it, rather, a matter for the duly constituted policy-making body?"

The First Secretary spoke. "There is the additional problem of communicating with these people. We have had virtually no success contacting the, ah, rural populations in any of the tetraspheres."

"All very sane and rational," LaMer mocked.

"LaMer!" The Commodore's voice was near a growl. "These are matters for the Screening Committee to consider. Why don't you walk the dog up for his examination?"

"Gladly. I prefer his company." She rose from behind the console and marched across auxiliary control. The prosthesis grated painfully, but she brought her full weight down on it with each step. The Commodore turned away from the blaze in her single eye.

"If there's nothing else—" the First Secretary said.

15

The Running Water

"Hello, the store!"

Two of them sat their horses thirty paces outside a ring of dead and dying trees. Within the trees stood a dilapidated building fronted by an even more dilapidated porch. Beside it was a depression in the ground that had once been the foundation of another building. A little way to one side stood a massive cottonwood and beyond the building they could see the top of a ponderosa pine. Low hills covered with dusty grass rolled away to the horizon in every direction. Two shallow ruts, grass-covered as well, ran from east to west. The two riders and the cottonwood and the ponderosa appeared to be the only living things in the sandy, arid land, and the tiny oasis constituted the only break in the landscape. Cottonwood leaves rattled in the wind.

One of the riders slid off the back of a black stud. Her companion did not take his eyes from the building. "Hell's bells, Fletcher, have a care. We ain't necessarily the only pilgrims in the land."

The black horse snorted and pawed the ground. The wind caught the corners of loose hides on the stud's back, lifting them to expose the bone-white saddle tree beneath. Fletcher looked up with derision.

"Old Joe sees the tracks, does he? Daytime pilgrims leave tracks, Old Joe."

The man kept his practiced eye moving over the door and broken windows in the shadow beneath the porch roof. "We ain't circled. We wouldn't of cut a track coming in behind. Try the Spanish."

Fletcher pulled a big revolver out of the belt that

cinched the twin pennants of cloth she wore to cover what her leggings didn't. Fletcher had split what had originally been a single piece down its length and roughly swallow-tailed the dangling ends. Years of accumulated dirt and grease had given the cloth a dingy black patina. Joe saw through it to the vertical stripes and the field of stars that covered one hip. He had the age to recognize it for what it had been. The wind picked at the fringes of Fletcher's leggings.

"I parley with this," Fletcher said, the final s prolonged in a hiss. She thumbed the hammer back and started for the door.

"Damn!" Joe snapped closed the breech of a single-shot 10-gauge he carried across the pommel of his saddle.

Fletcher trotted within five paces of the building, ducked her shoulders, rolled, and disappeared into thin air.

"Damn!" Joe said again. After a full minute he spotted a strand of reddish hair dancing in the wind. From that he located the curve of Fletcher's shoulder in the shadow. As he watched, she moved again. Fringe fluttered as she rolled through a broken window. He brought the shotgun up to bear.

In a minute Fletcher strolled out, the revolver back in her belt, one hand holding up a tin can.

"Old Joe," she called, "a treat."

"Probably dog food." He spoke more to himself than Fletcher, who did not possess his discriminating tastes. He dismounted, picked up the stud's jaw-rein, and led the horses to beneath the nearest tree. Its bark was gone and the wood bleached white. He tied them, then looked above him into the branches. "Damn the Chinese elm and damn the pilgrims that brought them here," he said. He climbed up on the porch. Fletcher had her knife through the top of the can.

She pried the knife around till she had a hole big enough to bring a sample of the contents out. She held the blade out for him to examine.

"Peas." He took the can and drank. He sloshed the juice around his mouth and swallowed. "They's good," he pronounced and handed the can back.

They sat on the edge of the plank porch, sharing the can. When it was empty, Joe crumpled it in one hand and tossed it into the pale grass. He spat between his moccasins. "At least, we ain't going to thirst out just yet."

"Old Joe worries hisself."

"Me and Jack Wilson got caught in the Sonora once. We near ended. Drank horse blood and rode out double. I got no inclination to travel that road again, is all." He got a pipe out of a pouch on his belt. "What else is in there?"

"Cans and cans." She looked away. "Some bones."

"New ones?"

"Nothing new around here, Old Joe."

"So that's what it's all about. You could of told me."

"And listen to his pissing? His stories's bad enough."

Joe ignored the insult. He struck a match on a plank and cupped his hand to shelter the flame over his pipe. He puffed the bowl to life. "Your turn. Make sure you hobble that stud this time."

"Stud don't need no hobble." She rose.

"I ain't abusing my pony running that rangy son of a bitch down."

Fletcher waved a hand behind her and sauntered to the elm. The wind picked relentlessly at the fringe of her leggings. The thick red braid of her hair swung like a pendulum across the smoke-colored skin of her back. Joe pulled down the brim of his hat against the midday sun and settled his shoulders against a post.

The stud squealed, and he grabbed for his shotgun. The black horse took a wicked swipe at his bay. Joe understood that he had fallen asleep for only a matter of seconds.

"You should of let me cut him down on the Flatwater last year," he called.

Fletcher jerked the jaw-rein, and the black stud left off his pawing. "The day Old Joe gives up his own cajónes," she called, her belly full and her better nature returning.

"I ain't a horse."

"Ain't worth as much, Old Joe means." She led the horses out into the grass, wrapped their reins, loosened their cinches, and sat down to watch them graze.

Joe chuckled, then tried to resume his nap. A fly buzzed around his nose, and neither swatting at it nor ignoring it caused it to lose interest. He sighed and got up.

Fletcher had a horsehair reata around the stud's neck.

The three of them appeared content. Joe walked across the porch, his moccasins making a sighing sound in the sand the wind had piled there. He ducked his head, out of habit rather than necessity, and entered the store.

The interior was dark and smelled of moldy plaster. Three sets of back-to-back shelves, each stocked with shiny tin cans, ran the length of the building. An old cash register sat on a short counter. Along the walls were the dry goods—fan belts and grass ropes hanging on pegs, tins of shoe polish stacked in neat pyramids, a dozen galvanized milk buckets set into each other. Far back in the darkness he saw a raised platform. He walked toward it, his moccasins kicking up faded labels.

There was only a desk and a chair, ledgers and invoices, postage stamps and envelopes, pens and pencils, and bank checks bound in a book. Joe came up another aisle. He stopped now and again to shake a can near his ear. He kept the 10-gauge cradled in the crook of his arm.

He found the bones behind the cash register, some resting in the seat of a chair, the skull and most of the bigger ones on the floor. Coyote scat lay among them. He pushed the toe of a moccasin into some of it, and it disintegrated to powder. He picked up a pistol, found the action gritty and stiff and set it on the counter.

"What was we guarding, night-timer?" he asked the bones. He studied the keys on the register, then brought a fist down on a big button. The drawer popped open with the ring of a little bell. "Not much," he said, and began to go through the contents. He thumbed the green bills, then sorted through the change. He dropped the dimes and a few quarters and halves that looked to be mostly silver into a pouch, then shut the drawer on the rest.

He went down the third aisle. He paused once to study the labels at his feet. He selected a can. The back door, beneath the raised platform, squealed open. Beyond it was a small, screened porch. Old newspapers and soggy rolls of toilet paper lay scattered on the floor. An easy chair, its upholstery rotting off, sat among the rubbish. "What were we looking for, night-timer?" Joe asked. He sat down in the chair and looked out. "Sure," he said after a minute.

He took the hook off the screen door and walked outside. After the mustiness of the store, his nostrils flared with the clean wind. A heavy, iron disk, set into concrete, was near the door. He set the gun and the can down and wrestled it out of its collar. It slid over with a scraping noise that echoed hollowly from below. The cistern was half-full. The wind carried the water smell around the building. His bay mare whinnied and the black stud snorted. He whistled, and, when he heard Fletcher's response, he went back in for buckets and a length of rope.

Fletcher waited with the horses, the stud pawing the ground around the cistern, when he came out. He handed the shotgun to her, then tied a knot around the handle of the first pail and dropped it in. It lay on its side on the water a moment before it began to fill. He lugged it out hand over hand and set it down. The stud quieted suddenly, content to let the mare water first. Joe tied a second bucket to the rope's other end and raised it for the black.

The horses snorted into the bottoms of their second buckets and wandered off to munch grass. Fletcher and Joe drank what they'd left. The concrete collar of the cistern was cool, and they sat on it to smoke.

After a bowl, Joe knocked the ash from his pipe and spoke. "A regular museum."

"Museum?" Fletcher's voice was relaxed.

"Place to go to look at how things used to be."

"Oh."

"Looksee." Joe pointed with the stem of his pipe.

"I been looking." An outhouse stood thirty paces away. An equal distance beyond grew the ponderosa, its base encircled with barbed wire laid out concertina-style.

Joe pried up half the lid of the can he had selected from the store and stared into it. "By god, it's pears. I was hoping for peaches, but I'd forgot about pears. Here."

Fletcher took the pear half off the tip of his blade, placed in her mouth and sucked on it. "Old Joe wants to spend the night?" she asked.

He handed her another pear. He spoke around one of his own. "Been thinking on it." Juice ran down his chin and into his whiskers. "Ain't been nobody through here since Moses built Jerusalem. I doubt me there's a better store of canned goods anywhere in the roundness of the world." He sucked another pear off his knife. "Some's to

match, sure, but none's better." He handed the can to her.
"Even gots a backhouse. How long's it be since you used
a backhouse?"

. "Ain't never used, ain't never using one."

Joe chuckled at his own joke.

Fletcher drank off the juice, then tossed the can into
the grass. She rose. "Let's take a see."

They walked past the outhouse to the ponderosa and
knelt before the circle of barbed wire. Joe handed Fletcher the shotgun. The strands of ancient wire snapped like
dry twigs in his hands. Fletcher brushed the ends away
with the stock of the gun.

Within the circle they found a standing cross and two
upright lengths of dimension lumber, their cross-pieces
on the ground before them. Joe turned one over.

"What says the reading, Old Joe?" Fletcher's eyes
scanned the horizon.

"A boy." He lay down the piece and turned the second
over. "Another one, a little younger. Dead the same winter. Maybe picked up the flues or some such from passing
pilgrims." He looked at the intact cross. "Woman, about
six month later. Must of been the moma, though the
name's different. Died of a broken heart, I guesses. Popa
inside lasted another ten year, by the look of him."

"Moma inside," Fletcher corrected.

Joe'd check the pelvis later, but he had little doubt
that the skeleton had been a woman. And if Fletcher said
so, he was prepared to believe that she had been the
mother of the two boys buried beneath his moccasins.

"Bad business, a mother night-timer this close to the
graves," he said. "What do you think?"

Fletcher continued to scan the horizon. "Bad business," she said, stretching the last consonants, "is what I
thinks." She pointed suddenly. "There."

Joe followed her finger, but experience had taught him
not to expect to see all that Fletcher saw. "What is it?"

"Line of trees. Short day off."

"I expect that be the Running Water, though it must
have a powerful bend in it to be in that direction." He
rubbed a hand through a beard sticky with pear juice.
"Could be a creek leading into it. Maybe the Snake,
even."

"Don't know a name," she said, dismissing it as

unimportant, "but a long run of water to raise up that trees."

Joe thought of riding well into the night to make a cold camp, then sitting awake till first light when he could scout the country. "I's sorely disappointed," he announced. "Least let me use the backhouse once before we ride on."

"We ride on now, she's to ride on with us."

Joe shivered at the chill running up his spine beneath his leathers. "Damn!" he said. "What'd we do now?"

"Been here, ain't we? Opened the water, got her thinking on the river, since she can't lie down with her others."

"Why didn't you see this coming in?"

"Old Joe says she didn't's all."

Joe muttered a curse, then stormed into the backhouse. He leaned the 10-gauge in a corner, dropped his breeches and sat. He should have seen it coming. The previous evening Fletcher'd ridden out from camp alone. She'd been gone several hours, visioning, he'd assumed. At dawn, when she shifted their course a few degrees to the east, he'd said nothing, relying on her superior senses to lead them to the Running Water. She'd led them straight to the store, instead, though there'd been no track that he could see, through a featureless country neither of them knew. The dead woman had apparently been calling to Fletcher for nearly a day.

The one thing about Fletcher that made him jumpy was her predilection for listening to spirits desirous of peace. Joe didn't begrudge them that. Hell, he reflected, his own bones would likely bleach out under the prairie sun. Maybe his spirit, too, would tire of endless wandering. Still, these things were tricky, even for Fletcher, and sooner or later something might go awry. Then they'd have a night-timer who intended to stick to them and, worse, who was peeved about their interference. Joe imagined the malevolent spirit would be the first thing to greet him on the other side, before he could get his nose into the wind, let alone find a friendly face.

He swore and stood. The worst of it was Fletcher maneuvering him into these things. He did himself up and grabbed his gun. If some spooky night-timer wanted to ride along, he decided, it was welcome to do its damnest. He strode out past Fletcher to the bay. "Hell,

I'm for riding on," he said. "Let her come if she's a mind to."

Fletcher stared off toward the trees only she could see. "There's these other things." She pointed again.

Joe stopped and looked. Near the horizon lay what could be, he admitted to himself, dust. "Cattle!" he said.

"Riders, Old Joe," Fletcher corrected.

"Goddamn it!" he shouted. He sorted among the pouches and bags tied to his saddle till he found a brass telescope. He extended it its entire length and looked.

Still he saw only dust, but now he could make out the features of a plume, narrow at one end, widening at the other. Something was kicking it up, all right.

"Cattle!" he said again.

"Riders," she repeated.

"Hell! Let's ride out to meet 'em." He gave the cinch a quick tightening, stuck a foot in a stirrup and climbed up. Dust, as often as not, meant an old friend or two.

"Maybe twenty. Maybe more than you have shells."

"I got plenty of shells. And I'll bet there's more ammunition in that store, if we just look around." His enthusiasm was weakening. There was a lot of dust, and what caused it was moving fast. His friends, Joe reflected, never traveled in bands of twenty. He looked to the west. The sun was dropping quickly, and he didn't relish the idea of traveling in the open through a sundown full of those damned flames. They put him in mind of the fingers of a fist closing around the prairie. He weighed the consequences of riding on or staying put. It was likely that they would run into whatever was moving up there sooner or later anyway. Still, the night-timer deserved a rest.

"Damn," he said softly and slid off the mare. He looked at Fletcher. "Burn or bury?" he asked.

She gestured to the tiny cemetery. "With her kins."

"I'll get a spade, but you do the digging, Fletcher."

While Fletcher made a start on the grave, Joe busied himself with the chores of setting up camp. The wind had settled down to a breeze, and since he saw no sign of a storm in the sky, he decided it was safe to picket the horses beneath the cottonwood. He unsaddled them and threw the bedrolls in the far shade of the tree. He bucketed water from the cistern into a galvanized tub he found

wired to a hook on one side of the store. He pried open
the lids of two more cans and set them of the edge of a
niggardly fire he'd built on the side of the store away
from the plume of dust. He found the big tins of coffee
he'd hoped for on a shelf in the store and set some water
on the fire to boil. He went back inside to search for
ammunition. It was carefully stacked beneath the counter
by the bones. He found plenty of .44s and .50–.30s and
three boxes for the 10-gauge, two double-ought buck, and
one of lead slugs, a much rarer find. He sorted out the
few cartridges that showed bad corrosion. He went to
check on Fletcher's progress.

The sun, a giant, blood-red ball, tiny blue jets flickering
along its lower rim, sat on the horizon. The wind had
died altogether. He shuffled to the ponderosa, suddenly
conscious of the heat.

Fletcher stood up to her thighs in the new grave.
"Don't disturb them others," Joe warned.

She looked up. Rivulets of sweat ran off her chin and
shoulders. "They's peacable," she panted. "Afore I started
I told them they's going to have a family reunion."

Joe squatted down. "Ain't that deep enough, Fletcher?"

"Nearly so, Old Joe. Gets the bones while I finishes."

Joe rubbed his beard.

"Or I'll's get the bones and Old Joe can finishes?"

"No, no, I'll do it." He headed back for the store.

"Don't Old Joe go missing any," she called.

He picked up a water bucket, emptied it and entered
the store. At the counter, he filled and lit his pipe, puffing
heavily till the smoke formed a blue cloud in the darkening
building. He held the pipe and moved his hand in a ritual
circle. He set the pipe on the counter.

He stared at the skull in his hand. Having no one in
particular he wished to send greetings to, he set it in the
bottom of the bucket without saying a word. He gathered
up the long bones and set them on end around the skull.
He swept along the floor with his hands and brushed the
smaller hand and foot bones into little piles which he
gathered up and dropped into the bucket. He set the
pelvis on top, after checking Fletcher's estimation of the
skeleton's sex against his own understanding of anatomy.
He pocketed his cold pipe, picked up the bucket, hooked
his finger through the rib cage and went outside.

Fletcher saw him coming and climbed out of the grave. The shadows had grown long. "My count says we're short a long bone, maybe two," he said and set the rib cage and the bucket down. "Coyotes drug it off, I imagines."

Fletcher shrugged. "I been seeing Old Joe's coffee insides my eyes," she said. "I'll lays her out."

Joe went through the store one more time. The tobacco smoke had driven the odor of decay out. He picked up a hammer and nails and exited the front door. He dropped a handful of coffee into the tin, then picked it out of the fire on the claws of the hammer. This time he walked around the building, pausing only once to drive the grounds to the bottom of the tin with a palmful of cold water from the remaining horse bucket.

Fletcher sat on the mound of dirt she'd thrown up, filling her long pipe. "How close was we?" He set the tin down beside her.

"Takes a looksee." She struck a match on her thumbnail.

The bleached bones were a white outline against the moist, dark sand. As Joe had expected, one leg was missing.

"Damn!" he said.

"Old Joe worries hisself again." Fletcher handed him the pipe. "She don't care. She's whole with her kins now."

Joe inhaled smoke, sat next to Fletcher, and handed the pipe back. They smoked and studied the bones in silence while the shadows lengthened toward night.

Finally Joe rose. He used the hammer and nails to replace the two cross-pieces.

"Old Joe's a carpenter," Fletcher said.

He threw the hammer over the wire into the grass. "Better than playing buzzard, cleaning up the countries we travel through," he said. He sat back down.

"Old Joe got a gift?"

He got a half dollar from a pouch on his belt and tossed it into the grave. It twinkled in the light of the setting sun.

"It was hers anyway," he said.

"That's all she needs."

Fletcher pulled a finger-thick lock of black horse mane out of a pouch and added it to the grave.

"She can travels fast, if she don't like what she sees on the other side," Fletcher explained.

Far off to the west a flame, its base an arc of the horizon, unfolded slowly, rising high into the sky. It obliterated the early stars. Joe wasn't sure if it colored the night red or if the aura he saw was just the impression left by fire on his retinas. He felt a tightness in his chest, as if someone held his heart, and then the flame and the pain were both gone.

"She's home," Fletcher said and rose to fill the grave.

16

The Third World Wars

The next day, a little after the sun had started its descent, they cut the track of the riders. They paused only long enough for Fletcher to study the ground, then loped on through the heat to the Running Water. The horses were lathered and winded by the time they hit the tree line. They traveled the bluff for another kilometer at a walk, cooling the horses, till they found a ravine that led down to the water's edge. They picketed the horses in the shade, after they'd had a drink, and sat down nearby for a smoke.

"Twenty-five, maybe thirty," Fletcher said after they got their pipes going, "traveling fast."

"They knows the country," Joe offered. "They wouldn't of moved out across open ground if they wasn't sure of cutting water again soon."

"Big bend. Maybe half a day, they finds the river again. We'll follow and saves some time."

"When did you start worrying about time?"

Instead of answering, Fletcher rose and went off into the trees to relieve herself. When she returned, Joe spoke.

"Raiding party, moving fast like that. Not rounders, neither. We cut plenty of cattle sign leading to the river, but they's none traveling with that outfit."

Fletcher nodded. "They's still out ahead of us."

"They'll turn back, after they's done made a raid, if I can guess a damn." He spat. "Going to be some destitute damned farmers tonight."

Fletcher nodded again.

* * *

Sundown passed. Fletcher and Joe left the river in the afterglow of two small flares, traveling among a jumble of shadows thrown at the rising moon. Once away from the trees and bluffs they kept an easy pace down the wide and, after the moon had gained some altitude, plainly visible track. Sometime after midnight, a breeze came up out of the east.

"Rain," Joe said.

"Maybe." They rode on.

Near daybreak the breeze picked up. They rested the horses and watched the sun rise behind a heavy overcast. They separated, Fletcher to the north and Joe to the south, and each rode a wide circle. She was sitting on the black stud, waiting for him, when he came back to the track.

He pulled the mare up. "How far?"

"Two kilometers, maybe three."

"Good. Cover?"

Fletcher nodded. "Heavy timber all the ways along."

"If they jumps us, we strikes for it first thing. Lots of blood in the sand before they takes me out them trees."

They spurred their horses into a slow jog along the track. They had traveled only a short distance before Fletcher stood in her stirrups, her nose high in the wind. In a few minutes he could smell the smoke. He held up a hand, and the horses slid to a stop.

They sat atop the heaving animals studying the distance. "You see the river?" Joe asked.

"Not with these clouds."

Joe pulled the mare behind Fletcher's stud. He stood up in the saddle, undid the front of his breeches and relieved himself to the downwind side. Done, he turned the mare in a slow circle around the black stud. He shivered suddenly in the wind that now carried a guarantee of rain. Fletcher's soot-colored skin had gone gooseflesh. She turned in her saddle and undid a roll behind the cantle. She draped a blanket over her, its woolen reds and blues beautiful even though muted by the overcast. Her head poked through a slit, like a turtle coming out of its shell.

"Can't be far," Joe volunteered.

Fletcher tugged her braid out from beneath the blanket. She gazed at the clouds to the east. "No, not far."

She spoke again. "Something else," she said simply.

Joe put the mare into a slow walk and followed his
nose into the wind. Fletcher trailed behind. In fifty paces
Joe picked up what Fletcher had already smelled. In
another fifty, he had recognized it. He turned to face
Fletcher without reining in. "You gots to be old to know
that one."

"Speaks your mind, Old Joe."

"Diesel."

"What's that?"

"Modern damn farmers, they is."

They spurred their horses and loped over the next
series of rises, the odor growing stronger in the wind.
They had covered a mile when they reined back in a wet
draw.

"Right over top," Joe said. Fletcher nodded.

They walked the horses up the rise, topped it and
surveyed the scene below.

A dozen people, half of them small children, milled
around an overturned grain wagon, its tongue still hitched
to the drawbar of a tractor. The tractor's metal skin
showed only a trace of red paint, and its rear wheels were
buried in the boggy bottom up to the axles. The black
stud took two sideways steps at the sight of the behemoth.

"Hello, the bottom!" Joe called. All faces turned immediately to them, and the adults hurried to gather the
children in. Joe held up his hand, the open palm out.

"Let's see how stupid they is," he said to Fletcher.

A woman tugging the hands of two small children
scrambled up the opposite rise. The rest continued to
stare. "Friendlies," Joe called. "Peoples, we means you
no harm."

"Jesus, I hope they's not packing," Joe said in a low
voice to Fletcher. Then he called, "Mind if we rides
down?"

A heavy man caned a step away from the milling
farmers. "Come on down," he called, his words ragged in
the wind.

They held their horses in check while they descended
the slope. Fletcher pulled the stud back a step so that Joe,
his hand still high, led. The horses snorted and danced as
they approached the tractor, and Joe had to drop his hand
to hold the mare. The old man who had called took
another heavy step toward them after they reined in.

"Troubles?" Joe asked.

"Busted fuel line," the man said, his mouth working beneath the bill of his ragged cap. "The Lord's giving us a powerful test. You ain't army are you?"

"Nope," Joe said.

The man shook his head. Skin cancers ran along his jaw line. "You didn't look like it. Are you Samaritans?"

"Just pilgrims," Joe said. The woman and her children had stopped on the top of the rise. She stared down at the parley.

"Thought you might be Samaritans. We've been praying for deliverance."

"Mister—" Joe started.

"Name's Henry. This here's my sister-wife, Lola." He stuck his thumb over his shoulder. An old woman bobbed the long brim of her bonnet to them. Her skin cancers were smaller than Henry's. She hooked a thumb in her suspender strap of her bib overalls, as if daring Joe in some way he did not understand.

"Mr. Henry. I don't knows nothing about them contraptions except the stink."

"Oh," Henry said and looked downcast.

After an awkward silence, Joe asked, "Been run off?"

Henry looked up, grateful for a topic of conversation. "We've been sorely tested. Army came in last night. The Lord showed us a path away from their wickedness, but Donald drove us into a bog." He jerked his thumb over his shoulder. A young man looked at the ground and spat between his bare feet.

"Mr. Henry, I don't means no offense, but you seems less perturbed than others I's met in similar straits."

"The Lord sends them every year about sweet-corn time. We plant extra for them, but they do leave a terrible mess when they go."

"And when's that to be, farmer-man?" Fletcher asked.

"Oh, they're on their way back upriver already, I would say. Wouldn't you, Sister?"

Lola's bonnet bobbed once. The woman on the top of the rise had started back down. The children had resumed their play. Donald was up to his knees in the bog beside the tractor. He held a complicated-looking piece of tubing.

"Ain't you afraid they'll catch you if you stay right here on their track?"

Henry looked confused.

Joe tried again. "What would they do if they caught you out here?"

"Oh," Henry said, "they'd rape the women and kill the men. Wouldn't they, Sister?"

Lola nodded again.

"They done it before," Henry said, confidentially.

"Ain't you scared?" Joe said.

"Why should I be?"

"Why shouldn't you be?"

"Because they always go back upriver."

Joe rubbed his beard. "So they come across open country and then follow the bend back?"

"Sure. They've got to have the river for the stock. Pigs and sheep can't move across open country like a horse."

Joe let go the notion of saying something about the difficulty the tractor was having crossing open country. He'd once, in his own foolishness, taken a good horse into a swamp and, when it'd bogged down, had had to shoot it.

Joe squinched up his face and studied the sky. "Let me get this straight, Mr. Henry. Every year they come and take all your stock and you just run away?"

"Well, they leave the sows and ewes and such for breeding. Otherwise, there wouldn't be anything for next year."

"And you just let them do it?"

Henry gave him a furtive look. "Shall I tell him our secret, Sister?" he called. He finished without waiting for Lola's response. "We fooled them this year. We didn't leave the stock." His eye closed and opened in a slow, huge wink.

Fletcher broke in. "Does Joe hear it?" she hissed.

Joe started. Above the wind he heard a low thunder.

"They's coming, Old Joe."

Joe looked from Henry to Lola to Donald, but they didn't seem to hear. He looked around the circle of playing children and indolent adults. He looked at the wagon behind the stalled tractor.

He heard a long squeal that ended in a grunt.

"You gots your stock in that thing?" he shouted above the growing thunder.

Henry nodded, smiling. "The Lord showed us the way."

"Take a look!" Joe said, and Fletcher spurred the black stud around the boggy bottom and up the opposite rise at a gallop. She stopped the horse with a savage jerk on the jaw-rein that set his haunches on the ground. She turned the horse and spurred him head-long down the slope. The excited children giggled and pointed at the beautiful horse.

"All of them, Old Joe. About half a mile," Fletcher said before she got the stud properly stopped.

"Mr. Henry, you'd best leaves them stock and takes your people up this bottom towards the river. If you makes it, you hides till them's long gone."

"Why," Henry said, still smiling, "it's only the thunder. See." He held out a hand. A gentle rain had begun.

"You smell any smoke in the air the last hour or so?"

"Now that you mention it, I did," he said brightly.

"What's it you thinks burning?"

"Didn't give it a thought, to tell the truth. The Lord shows all the answers he deems we require, though. Maybe he will tell us that as well."

"Well, damn you to hell then. I tells you it's your barns and such that's burning."

"Shouldn't curse like that, mister." His smile was now a cajoling grin.

Joe looked at Fletcher. "We'll be long gone and out in the open before they gets here. We'll circle back around while the killing and raping's going on."

"Old Joe does as he pleases. Fletcher's chose to ride east."

"There's plenty of ways to the Big River, Fletcher."

"This's Fletcher's way."

The rain splotched the dust on her face.

"Goddamn you, too, Fletcher," Joe said finally.

"That does sound like them," Henry said. His lacerated face a study in concentration. "What do you think, Sister?"

But Lola already had much of the stock unloaded. The remaining sheep stepped out of the wagon with a dainty and precise placement of their hooves. The hogs grunted and dropped with squeals. Lola called, her voice loud and raw, for the others to drive them to the river.

Joe and Fletcher sat their horses on the rise, a gentle rain falling into the sea of grass that surrounded them. The horses were easy, now that the smell of the diesel was downwind. Riders topped the next ridge, one by one, reined in to form a skirmish line. In the draw behind Joe and Fletcher, the farmers had their stock moving steadily toward the Running Water. Joe found the boxes of ammunition in a saddlebag and began to fill the empty loops in his bandoliers.

"Puzzle me this, Old Joe," Fletcher said. She ran a leather whang through an eye in the butt of her revolver.

"What's that, Fletcher?"

"Why's they all the same looking?"

"Them farmers? Oh, they's all brothers getting their sisters with little ones. They's in sore need of new blood. Here." He handed her a box. "For that bull pistol."

She dumped the contents into a pouch suspended from her belt. She had the whang over her neck, and the revolver hung at her side. Joe checked the loads in his own pistol and stuck it into his belt. He pulled his saddle gun from its scabbard and levered a shell into the chamber.

"You see any long guns?"

"No," Fletcher said. "Lots of them little macs."

"Good," Joe said. "Not much ammunition around for those and hardly no range." He snapped the breech of the 10-gauge closed and paused. "I gots to tell you, Fletcher, they's an ornery bunch, but given my druthers, I'd rides with them instead of against them. Especially just to gives them farmers time."

"Fletcher rides with no one," she hissed, "except Joe."

He smiled despite himself. A straggling rider topped the ridge and took a position at the end of the line.

"You knows," Joe said, "they's going to get them farmers anyways. We's just adding to the killing's all."

"Fletcher don't gives a good goddamn for them farmers."

Joe loosened his butcher knife in its sheath. "Let's gets the preliminaries over." He raised his open palm.

"Friendlies!" he shouted. "Hello, the ridge!"

A man in the middle of the line, dressed like the

others in green-and-brown camouflage patched with
absurdly bright reds, blues, and yellows, raised his hand.
The wind whipped his words around.

"What's he says?" he asked Fletcher.

"So's they's," she said. "Everybody's friendlies."

He called again. "You boys gots coffee?"

Joe heard, "Coffee?" and a faint trail of Spanish he
could not pick up. Horsemen up and down the line
laughed.

"I guesses they's out." Fletcher said nothing. The
black stud took a single step to one side.

Joe cupped his good ear and caught *viejo*.

"You son of a bitch," Joe said into middle distance.

"Eh?" the man called, leaning forward in his saddle
and cupping his ear. The horsemen roared at the imper-
sonation.

"I says you's a son of a bitch!" Joe shouted.

The man sat back in his saddle and parleyed for a
minute with the rider next to him.

"No *inglés*, then," Joe said to Fletcher. He shouted
again. "I says kiss my sore ass!" He gave the man his
broadest smile, then laughed at his own joke.

The man studied them through binoculars. He pointed and called a long formal-sounding request. The only
word Joe was sure of was the last, *puta*.

"I thinks he wants you for his woman."

"I hears every word he says, Old Joe. Fletcher ain't
deaf, like some's."

Joe shook his head. She was right, he was losing his
hearing. Not thinking about it was one of the comforts he
allowed himself to ease his old age. "Damn," he said,
"coffee in this rain would pleasure me." He looked back
to Fletcher. "I guesses we's almost traded enough insults
with that amateur." He brought the mare's rump around
to the riders. He stood in the stirrups, twisted in the
saddle and pointed to his backside. "Kiss my *culo!*" he
shouted. "You goddamn clown!" He turned the mare
back around.

"They's stopped laughing," he observed. "Something
happened to their humors." The man in the middle was
waving his arms, deploying his riders farther to the left
and right along the rise. "It be time for rock and roll," Joe
said.

Fletcher shot him a fierce grin. "Speaks your fancy speech, Old Joe." She turned her bared teeth back to the riders. Joe felt a giddiness down deep in his belly. The mare tensed between his thighs, and then they were off at a headlong gallop down the slope.

Fletcher cut her circle to the north, Joe around the south. The man in middle quickly regrouped his skirmish line into a defensive perimeter on the very top of the rise. The wind carried the crackle of the tiny machine pistols and the snap of a few handguns. Joe arced a shot into the perimeter, the boom of the 10-gauge drowning out the other weapons. Fletcher used her revolver, then— six evenly spaced shots—and two men dropped beside their horses. Joe broke the shotgun, the empty casing flying over his shoulder, and slipped in another shell.

Joe made it to the bottom, and the mare started up the rise, slipping a little in the wet sand. He flattened out the line of his circle and charged up the hill. When the bullets, at the extreme of their range, pocked the sand around him, he lowered the 10-gauge over his forearm, picked a rider, and pulled the trigger. A splotch of red showed on the chest of his target. He rested the shotgun over his pommel and dropped his weight into the stirrup away from the riders to make himself small. He got the gun reloaded, sighted over the withers of the smooth running mare and fired. At sixty meters the buckshot sprayed a wide path, each ball fast enough to tear flesh, large enough to maim. He veered the mare out away from the perimeter, and she soon carried him to the bottom east of the riders. The black stud ran evenly down the slope from the north. Fletcher's legging was hooked over the horn of her saddle tree, and she was slung low on the other side. She pulled off the last loads in of a fresh cylinder beneath the stud's neck, then regained his back. The horses galloped toward each other. Joe shoved the long barrel of the 10-gauge into the sand between them when they met.

The horses ran on without dropping off their speed, each now closing its circle. Out of range for the moment Fletcher busied herself reloading, sitting tight on the galloping horse. Joe pulled the .30–.30 from the scabbard and brought it to bear on the riders milling atop of the rise. When he heard Fletcher's revolver, he made a cut for the top. Shooting as fast as he could lever in cartridges, he emptied the rifle, then went to his pistol. When the hammer came down on an empty chamber, he dashed to the spot where they'd started. He saw Fletcher coming and felt a surge of relief. They met and reined in the heaving horses.

Fletcher's teeth shone whitely from her dark face. "Good shooting, Old Joe," she said.

Joe rubbed a knuckle in an eye tearing from powder smoke. He took a moment on the dancing horse to catch his breath. "How'd we do?" he panted.

Fletcher studied the far rise. The riders had dismounted. One argued with their leader, gesturing wildly. The wind carried the sound of a pistol discharging, and the man tumbled backward. The leader called the others to him.

"Six, seven. That one makes eight."

Joe spat. "How's them farmers?"

Fletcher studied the draw leading to the Running Water. "Making good time for farmers, but mostly I expect they's ain't going to make it."

Joe started to shove cartridges through the loading gate of the .30—.30. "They's going to charge?" he asked.

"Sure," Fletcher answered.

They busied themselves reloading. Joe had nearly finished with his pistol when Fletcher called, "Here they's coming." He looked up at the advancing line of horsemen, slipped a cartridge in the last chamber, and stuck the gun in his belt.

"Well, let's goes to meet them," he said and took a last deep breath. They charged down the slope, straight at the center of the advancing line, already firing.

Joe stood in the saddle, selecting as targets those horsemen who rose in their own saddles to fire. Fletcher worked the north side of the line with her revolver. The black stud gained on the mare, and Fletcher met the skirmish line first.

Horses reared and squealed, kicked up wet sand, then the dry beneath, till, despite the falling rain, the air filled with dust. Joe reversed the saddle gun and used it to club an oncoming rider from his horse. The stock splintered, and, cursing, he tossed the gun away. A man on foot grabbed the mare's reins, and Joe shot him in the head with the pistol. He spurred the horse in a circle, looking in the dust for another target. Twenty paces to his left he made out the rearing form of the black stud and galloped toward it. The mare breasted a ring of camouflaged men, and he shot the two closest to him. Another leveled a rusty M-10, and Joe shot him before he could fire. He pulled the mare into a tight circle but could not see Fletcher. He spurred her over beside the black stud. He shot two men trying to hold the black horse, stuck the empty gun in his belt, grabbed the stud's trailing jaw-rein, and galloped to the east. He heard very clearly a spurt of fire from an automatic weapon, and he dropped over the side of the mare to ride between the two horses. The 10-gauge still stood barrel first in the sand when he galloped past.

A mile away, when he was sure there was no immediate pursuit, he pulled up, getting the stud and run-out mare under control with some difficulty. He looked back but saw nothing in the rain. He reloaded the pistol. His knife was still in its sheath. He stared to the west for a long time. When the horses began to breathe more evenly he mounted the stud and rode through the rain toward the Running Water.

The cloud cover had passed, and the moon shone through the branches of the trees of the riverbank. Joe tended a miserly fire and studied the shadows around his camp. The horses stood behind him, saddled, sleeping on their feet.

"Goddamn, I drinks my coffee when I pleases," Joe said to himself. In one hand he held a tin that he occasionally sipped from. The other grasped the pistol.

"Speaks to youself, Old Joe!" called a voice. Joe was uncertain of the direction.

"Come on in, Fletcher, whether it be you or just the night-time part that's left." He shivered, as if chilled.

He swung around at a movement behind him, the pistol raised. Fletcher walked in from twenty paces away. He did not see her so much as he marked the change in the shadows the moon threw. She stopped near him.

"Old Joe left something," she said. He put down his coffee to take the shotgun she offered.

"Thanks, Fletcher. I's had this gun a long time." He

studied it for a minute, then nodded to the ground beside him. After she sat, he spoke again. "Well, which is it?"

Fletcher only smiled. "Night times spooks Old Joe."

"Damn you, Fletcher." He reached out and grasped her shoulder with his hand. The flesh was warm. "Welcome back," he said and let the hand drop.

He gave her coffee, and they drank in silence for a time. "What else'd you bring back?" he asked finally.

She brought something up out of the pouch suspended from her belt and balanced it on her flat hand to show him. It stretched from fingertips to wrist, a little narrower than Fletcher's hand. One end was tapered nearly to a point, and the other was thick and lumpish. The moon colored it gray.

"I sees that sorry bastard called his last name."

"On eithers side, and in eithers language." Without further ado, Fletcher tossed the tongue into the flames.

17

In the Garden

The speaker fell momentarily silent just as David set his empty wineglass on the table. The glass made an unexpected, audible click against the real wood, and several people at nearby tables swung their heads around. David did his best to ignore them, leaned back, and tried to relax. The man behind the podium started to say another pome.

For a time after the Fall, when he was small and the world of adults around him tense with fear, David had suffered with nightmares. His mother had given him a mantra, promising him that repeating it would keep the bad dreams away. Night after night she had sat with him at bedtime to help him learn and use it. Now he could hear her voice, again, inside his head, chanting. He attenuated his breathing to match the voice's rhythm. In a few moments he felt less anxious and less drunk. The scrabbled feeling in his stomach and head he'd had since he'd been received that afternoon remained with him, however.

Tella was looking at him. The marvelous blue-and-yellow butterflies stretched their wings across eyes that showed concern. He straightened in his chiar, and they both turned back to the speaker, whose gestures, late in his performance, had become intensely dramatic. David tried hard to listen, though he'd heard all he cared to.

Jomo placed his elbows on the table and cupped his chin in his palms. He sighed at each swing of the speaker's arm, the flutter of his fingers, and gasped when the speaker presented his profile to the audience and paused. David gave up trying to listen and looked around the

darkened room. Scattered at these tables, he thought, sit
members of the Screening Committee.

The man behind the podium held his silence, and
the whole room burst into applause, none more enthusi-
astic than Jomo's. In the midst of it he turned to David
and spoke. His lips were painted a shade of green that
David remembered from one of Ms. Kitty's fashion
magazines.

"Pardon?" David said.

"He takes such risks!" Jomo's voice fell off as he
spoke, as if in a swoon. David felt his supper churn
dangerously in his belly.

Still, he nodded in agreement, a sort of professional
courtesy, he told himself. Jomo turned back to the podium.
David found himself writing a review in his head, one he
would attempt, if the circumstances were different, to
have produced. *Shallow* and *facile* came to mind, and he
could almost hear the keyboard clatter of ... *delivery
remains merely theatrical ... a compensation for a lack of
substance ... a niggling drivel.* When Jomo looked back at
him, curiosity on his face, David brought his hands
together. He added a slow clapping to the general bedlam.

A tall woman crossed the stage to the podium and
leaned forward into the microphone. In the last crackle of
applause she began to thank a long list of people. David's
stomach wrenched at the mention of his name. His imagi-
nary review forgotten, he concentrated very hard, again,
on the mantra. The muffled sounds of chairs pushed
back on thick carpet filtered through to his consciousness, and he knew the evening's formalities were, finally
and mercifully, at an end. He mumbled, "Pardon me," in
Tella's general direction and rose hurriedly. Twice someone in the milling crowd stopped him, took his hand, and
made a polite remark. He smiled through his nausea and
nodded his thanks. He moved in a near-panic through the
double doors of the ballroom. He hesitated in the long
corridor outside, spotted the washroom door very near
him, and hurried through it. He charged into the first stall
with no more than a prayer that it was unoccupied and
dropped to his knees. The hydroplast protecting the seat
was slick in his sweating hands.

When he'd emptied his belly, he stood, went to one
of the rows of basins, and rinsed his mouth. The door

opened, and then Tella stood in the mirror beside him. He tried to make a joke. "There should be a lock on the door." He smiled weakly into the mirror.

She did not smile back. "I feel responsible. I should never have made you eat. It's just that it often makes people feel better after they've transmatted."

He shook his head. "It's not your fault. I'm just not any good at this sort of thing. I used to think I would be, but I'm not." He cupped his hands in cold water and leaned over to wash his face. Drops plopped back into the basin. "I'm sorry if I disappointed you."

She began a gesture, then let it go. She lay her hand on his shoulder, instead, as if fearful of response. "You did very well."

David patted his face with a towel. "Not nearly so well as what's-his-name."

Tella shrugged. "Mostly form and not much substance."

He held the crumpled towel in one hand and examined his face in the mirror. "Do you think the Screening Committee will recognize that, Tella?"

She started. "We don't even know if they were here."

"But they will see it, later, if they weren't?"

"More likely the staff than the Committee itself, at least for now. There are an awful lot of nominees, David."

"What if they don't like what they see?"

"I think we have to trust in their ability to distinguish between artifice and art." Tella paused before finishing. "Perhaps the work of the Screening Committee won't even be necessary."

"Then I go back to my life in the suburbs."

"You can have whatever life you choose, David."

David shuddered. He felt himself a coward. At the moment, he wished, more than anything, to be honest with Tella, but the beauty of her eyes had made mush of his brain and, he feared, his integrity.

He faced her. "Sometimes," he said deliberately, "I'm sorry you even nominated me. The possibility of it all, the uncertainty of it..." he trailed off and looked back into the mirror. He tried again. "The suspense is killing me."

She laughed softly with recognition.

"Maybe it would be easier to stay and face what comes."

Tella reached over and straightened the blue ribbon around his neck. "You shouldn't talk like that. You need to have hope." She patted the ends of the ribbon flat against his collarbone. "Let's get some air," she said.

She took David by the arm and led him out into the corridor, then down its length toward another set of doors. Through the clear panes he could see a roof garden awash in light. He discovered her hand in his. The brown of it made his skin appear very pale. The blue-and-yellow fingernails, exquisitely manicured, glowed. His own were ragged, he noted. "It is very odd to touch you."

She chuckled. "I've looked forward to meeting you too. In person, I mean. It's hard to know someone, really, from a screen." She stopped at the doors and turned to him. "I thought you'd be taller." The butterflies sparkled.

David relaxed. By degrees, he became aware that he was gazing into Tella's eyes. Self-conscious, then, he looked away. Outside chairs, tables, and love seats glistened in the light. He rapped his knuckles against the pane, desperate to find something to talk about. "Is it real?"

"Oh, it's glass. This place is loaded with antiques."

He nodded beyond. "I meant that."

"Yes, that too. Moonlight's not so beautiful, I suppose, as backlighting, but I prefer it."

Tella pushed through the doors. David followed several steps across the roof before either of them spoke again. "It makes that much difference—artifice and art?" he asked.

Now Tella smiled and reached for his hand. "All the difference in the universe. But do you really consider the moon art?"

"I guess I meant—" In another step he tried again. "Before—I was afraid the light was coming from Out There."

"Oh no," Tella said, surprised. "With the city lights and all, we see just a flicker."

"Sometimes, where I live, it's very bright."

"Yes. That's what the media says."

They reached the waist-high barrier that ran along the perimeter of the roof. Tella turned to David and smiled. The summer breeze, cooler at that height, ran over their skin and through their hair. They stood comfortably, her hands resting upon his shoulders, until David was seized by vertigo. It was as if Tella's dark eyes were water that he saw from a high place. He leaned forward. She dropped her hands and presented her profile to him. "Look," she said, "you can see the Old City."

At the far end of the mall David could see a small open arc. Tall against the night sky, the silhouettes of the skyscrapers darkened the horizon.

"Can you name them?" he asked.

Tella shook her head. "Isn't it terrible? I've lived here my whole life and I can't tell you which is which."

David gazed until his eyes tired and the shadows became indistinguishable from the night. "Does anybody live there?"

"A few crackpots and misfits, I'm told. Very few."

"I wonder why," David said, almost to himself.

Tella turned to him. "What a strange question!"

He persisted. "Tell me."

Tella thought before beginning. "I suppose that, no matter how tolerant a society is, there are people who, finally, just don't fit in, who can't make it. Maybe it's better to live there than an old-time institution. I don't know. They're still to be pitied. Why do you care?"

"You forget where I live." He was sorry for the tension in his voice. He looked to the west. "Wondering why people live where they do is a hobby of mine," he said more mildly.

"Why do you live there, David?"

"It's good for my work."

"Don't cut the monkey with me." Something a little shrill in Tella's voice, coupled with the strange phrasing made David turn quickly to her. Her patient, steadfast gaze made him doubt that she had, in fact, spoken.

"I really want to know," she said in the voice he was used to.

David wondered, not for the first time, what the butterflies hid. He wondered how long he would have to know Tella before he could dare to ask. He leaned over the protective wall. "Look, there are people down there."

Tella did not look. "Of course. What did you expect?"

"I'm not used to seeing many people. I'm not used to heights, either."

They were quiet a while, David looking into the mall below, Tella at the distant, virtually deserted buildings.

"Is it true you'd never transmatted before tonight?" Tella asked. "That's what Jomo said."

David lifted his gaze. "Not entirely. I had to transmat when I attended university, but I did it only once in and, when I graduated, once out. I was a scholarship student, and there wasn't any money for trips home. My parents thought it better that I spend my time studying, anyway."

"Oh," Tella said.

"My roommates, though, and some other friends I met through them, were transmat fanatics. I hung around with that crowd. They were very cliquish. Sometimes I think the only reason they tolerated me was that what they did scared me to death. They loved to tease me."

"Have you kept in touch with them?"

David shook his head. "Some. I did for a while, anyway, as long as I could. They're mostly gone now—dead or institutionalized." He paused, then corrected himself. "Hospitalized, I mean."

"I'm sorry."

David thought about how to explain it. "They seemed... unconcerned by the dangers. They were certainly aware of them. And I really don't believe that there was any kind of death wish at work. It's just that they wished to...live intensely, I suppose."

"Yes," Tella said absently. "I've known people like that. It's as if they require risks."

He nodded. After a minute Tella looked at her watch. The numerals glowed brightly, even in the moonlight. "We need to get you downstairs," she said.

They had walked part of the way back across the garden when the doors burst open and Jomo rushed toward them. He was breathless. "Oh, there you are. You need to get down to the booth right away. It's almost time for the pickup."

Tella responded for them. "We're coming."

Jomo held the door for them and chattered away meaninglessly as they entered the corridor. He fell in step behind them, talking to their backs. "I just want to tell you how much I enjoyed your work. Tella's been raving about you, of course, and I hoped I'd be able to meet you, at least on the screen. In person is so much nicer, of course." The elevator arrived and they stepped in. Jomo talked as they descended. "It's just the most wonderful thing, to be here this evening when so much that is wonderful is going on. It's history. Really, it is history." The elevator slowed to a stop, and the door opened. The lobby was empty except for the Law who, leaning against one wall, watched them cross to the transmat booth. Jomo piled one inanity upon another, his voice rising and falling in step with them. "You take such risks!" he said to David.

David hesitated before the booth. He turned to Tella.

She smiled. "Get in there! Or all they'll pick up will be empty air."

"Thanks for everything," David said. "I'll talk to you in a few weeks." He took the hand she offered. It was soft and warm and dry. He wished to hold onto her forever, but Jomo swept the hand away and replaced it with his own.

"Such risks!" he said again, and David backed into the booth. The glastic door swished closed before him.

In the booth everything was very quiet. David heard his breathing, his heartbeat. He listened to the mantra again, this time in his own voice. Through the door he saw the Law straighten himself and, evidently satisfied with something, walk away. The read-out above his head showed thirty seconds before the Port Authority picked him up. He gave Tella a little wave. She smiled back. Jomo busily chattered into Tella's ear. Tella kept her smile focused on David. The read-out clicked down.

Tella said something.

"What?" David said and jumped at the sound of his own voice within the insulated space.

He watched closely as she mouthed the words.

"Yes," he said more quietly, "the revisions." He gave his head an exaggerated nod. He placed his hand upon the door, his fingers spread. Tella placed hers over it. His body tingled, and he knew the pickup had begun. The last that he saw outside the booth were Tella's dark eyes within their butterflies. The last that Tella saw in the booth was a slender column of sparkling light.

PART III

18

The End of the World Comes
to the Suburbs

A gust of wind, its arms full of dust, scurried up the
deserted street. It twisted past faded and peeling houses,
rain gutters dangling like hanged men, then ran through
the tall grass. It rattled the late-summer foliage of the
trees. Oaks, maples, dogwoods, and seedless cotton-
woods shifted their stark shadows as it passed, stilled
again slowly as if waving good-bye to the dust devils
skittering away. Only when the shadows of the trees
crossed the faces of the houses did their vacant expressions change.

Inside one of them, its yard clean of debris, all its
doors hanging straight on their hinges, in a darkened
room silent except for a low hum, David sat in a high-
backed, thickly padded chair. Intent on the screen before
him where, fixed like night stars, green characters glowed
and dimmed with a weak pulse, he took no notice of the
wind that passed beyond the wall. His hands spanned a
keyboard, and, occasionally, the little finger of the right
moved far to the side and depressed a button. When that
happened, the lines of characters started a stiff-legged
march up the screen, much like small children climbing
stairs. Infrequently, David's other fingers stiffened, arched,
and jabbed at the keys, and the symmetry on the screen
disintegrated. Fragments of sentences, marks of punctua-
tion, letters, and numerals darted about, circled, grew,
and shrunk in a mad free-for-all before skidding back
into place on the black screen, piling again into a
whole. The hands, then, resumed their position, the
room recaptured its stillness, and the finger resumed
its tiny counterpoint.

183

Felix came to sit beside David's chair. Except for his gray muzzle, he formed no more than a shadow in the darkened room. Had David paused, he might have thought about the functions of the dog's neo-cortex in the same way a Christian monk six centuries before might have lifted his weakened eyes from his gold-leaf and careful transcription to consider the souls of animals. Did a dog, even one so ancient as this, think beyond *fetch* and *ball* and *food*? What did the dreams of dogs teach them? What did a dog make of *thunder* or *birth*? How did this dog recollect his seasons, understand the phases of the sun? Now, David only patted Felix's head absently. Felix lay down to wait.

In the upper right-hand corner of the screen a pale red rectangle appeared. After a time it began to flash. David paid no more attention to it than he had the wind. He perceived only the world presented by some second, interior set of senses, the images of that world palpable to those senses only at the end of a long journey through the maze of his own neo-cortex, articulated only after much bargaining between his soul and his native, his only, language.

Much later, after the last line of green characters staggered off the top of the screen, David found himself staring at the red message box. He shook his head to clear it, found the "respond" button on the keyboard and pressed it. The screen read "Please Wait," the second word in letters twice as large as the first. He was rubbing his eyes when he heard Tella-Dotun's voice.

"Hello, David."

"Hello, Tella." He moved his fingers away and shut his eyelids hard, fluttered them open. "Long time, no see."

"You look tired."

"I've been working on the revisions. What time is it?"

Her gaze moved up over her screen. "Almost midnight. Eleven your time." She met his eyes again. "Sorry about asking you to wait, but it's really very busy here."

"That's all right. Sorry about not getting back to you sooner." David could only stare. After weeks of trying he had still not determined what it was that made Tella-Dotun the most beautiful woman he'd ever seen.

She laced her fingers before her. "David, I'll have to

make this brief. There are several things I need to talk to you about, and I have several more calls to make. Since you mentioned them, how are the revisions coming?"

"Done, just now. Unless you want something more after you see these." Perhaps it was the line of her neck, or the precision with which she moved her head.

"Good. I'm glad. I'm sure they'll be fine."

No, he was in love with something in the hypnotic depths of her dark eyes. Falling into her gaze panicked him, and he'd found that, awash in confusion, he said and did things, without thinking, to make her avert it.

"There won't be time for any more changes," he said.

She looked down at the fountain pen that had appeared in her folded hands. "No, the risk is too great. We'll go with what you've done. And we've decided against galleys as well, by the way. I hope you understand." When she lifted her head her face rose as if out of water.

David shrugged.

"Good. And we've made payment."

"Payment?"

"I suppose it's odd, but we do have a contractual obligation."

Maybe it was her hands, the tapering length of the fingers, the perfect, blue-and-yellow nails, the unblemished and unlined pigmentation of the backs. "I'd forgotten. Under the circumstances..."

"It might not make much sense, but it's important to keep to the procedures as much as possible. I'm afraid that they're what's keeping us sane."

They were both silent. Then, David looked up, startled. "It just occurred to me that I've written my last."

Tella gave him a small smile. "Everything we hear from the Rescue Effort people is very positive."

"Do you really think it'll come off?"

She nodded slowly. "Yes David, I believe it will happen. I have to have faith in something."

"Have you heard about an orientation date?"

She looked away. "No, but we think they've started with them. The rumors are flying pretty thick here."

"What do the rumors say, Tella?" He hoped he did not sound as desperate as he felt.

She blinked once, a long slow descent of her eyelids followed by a quick fluttering. "There are some problems

with the technology. That was to be expected. We've been
told to expect numbers and dates, all the specifics, any
day now. We're proceeding on the assumption that it will
work."

"But I'll see you for the orientation, if it happens?"

"Yes David, I'll be there when you're received."

It was her smile, the perfect teeth and the flawless
skin. Again, he tried to imagine her without the butterflies. "You better be. This time I'll probably faint."

"Don't worry, David. We'll take care of you. Just remember to send the revisions."

"Okay."

"See you soon, David."

"See you, Tella."

The screen went blank. David leaned back in his chair,
lolled his head on the rest. The cramped muscles of his
shoulders, neck, the small of his back began to unknit.
Felix sat up with a sharp little bark.

"Hey, Felix," David said, reaching for him. He worked
his fingers into the loose coat, moved a hand up to
scratch behind one ear, then the other. "Just a moment,
boy."

With his other hand he rummaged through an open
drawer for his cigarettes. He lit a bookmatch one-handed,
watched its reflection blaze, then settle into a tiny flame
in the blank screen. He found an ashtray. "Felix," he said
after his first drag, "I don't think there's a whole hell of a
lot more I can do about it. What d'ya think, boy?"

The dog met his gaze, made another little bark.

"All right, all right." David stubbed the cigarette out,
punched up Tella-Dotun's route and ID numbers, hit the
"send" button. A vertabra in his neck clicked against its
neighbor as he stretched his hands toward the ceiling. He
got to his feet and made his way through the living room
to the kitchen, Felix trailing behind. For the first time in
weeks he felt hungry.

David gazed into the almost bare kitchen cupboard,
lost in thought. Felix placed a cold nose on the back of
his thigh just below the fringed hem of his cutoffs. "All
right, Felix, all right." He pulled a blacplastic bag out of
the cupboard and filled Felix's bowl. The old dog crunched
steadily, bits of compressed green protein occasionally

dropping from his mouth to the linoleum with a click.
David popped a handful of nuggets into his mouth and
returned the bag to the cupboard. He gazed through the
window above the sink to the west as he waited for tap
water to run cold on his hand. He could see the backs of
three houses, all of them abandoned, and, in the gaps
between them segments of the horizon. There, every few
seconds, a finger of fire would beckon. Above, an effect
like sheet lightning colored the moonless sky bluer than
day.

The protein turned to paste in his mouth. Gagging, he
filled a glass, the water still tepid, and washed it down.
He filled Felix's water dish and set it before him. "Would
you like to go swimming, old dog?" he asked. "You used
to like to go swimming." The dog, still chewing, raised
his eyes. David smiled, bent down, and ran both hands
down Felix's neck. He patted the dog once more, straightened, and turned to stare again out the window. Felix
returned his attention to his dish, an echo of the word the
man had used resonating in his brain.

Out of the corner of his eye David noticed movement.
Next door his neighbor lugged an ancient Rainbird sprinkler and its car-wheel base into her backyard garden. She
set it down, straightened, walked out of the frame of the
window. David watched the sprinkler sputter, spit, then
spiral water down onto the twisted and sunburnt plants.
The girl walked back into David's line of vision, paused,
arms akimbo, at the corner of the garden to examine the
sprinkler. She stood within the swirl of water for a
minute, then walked away two paces to sit on a rotting,
redwood picnic table.

"Felix, ball." The dog clicked away. David hurried to
the refrigerator, pulled the door open and various-sized
glastic bottles out. He mixed drinks beside the sink,
glancing occasionally through the window. Felix, an orange ball in his mouth, clicked back in to stand patiently
behind him, then followed as David made his way clumsily, a drink in each hand, out the back door.

David stood a moment on the concrete patio to accus-
tom himself to the heat. Beside him a couple of folded
lawn chairs leaned against the house, the nylon webbing
of each faded and frayed, the ends dancing in the breeze
like tattered pennants. The girl watched him through the

pale night as he set the drinks atop a burnt-out gas grill.
He started to raise a hand to wave to her. In the west a
thick finger of fire began to uncurl slowly into the sky.
Instinctively, David turned to it. A house blocked his
view of the base of the flame. The building pulsed for a
moment, its windows standing out white against the
shadowed wall. David slapped his hand over his eyes
and, in the moment before he could wrench his body
away from the fire, saw clearly the veins and bones of his
hand.

When he could no longer feel searing heat against his
back, he opened his eyes, then slowly removed his hand.
His eyes rolled as if in sockets lined with grit, and he
blinked until moisture started to come. He found himself
in a fetal crouch, and, when he straightened, the burnt
skin of his legs and arms crackled with stiffness. He
heard Felix's whimper, but he could not see the dog in
the sudden darkness. He felt along the wall until he
found the open door to the garage. "Come on out, boy,"
he called. "It's done for now. Come on." His voice shook.
The dog came through the door to meet him. David knelt
beside him and Felix licked his face. David ran his hands
over the dog. His vision was coming back. Felix appeared
to be all right.

David looked next door. He heard the swooshing of
the sprinkler and spotted the white of the girl's T-shirt.
"Are you okay?" he yelled, too loud.

Her voice carried across the dark. "She guesses so."

"Can you find your way over?"

"Yeah, she thinks so. Sure." The white T-shirt wafted
closer. She slipped once in the wet garden and cursed. He
found the drinks and gulped down half of one. The ice
had melted, and the gin was warm as tea. He finished it.

"Here, take this," he said. She took the glass from him
with both hands, her fingertips dry, and drank it down.
The glass came back into his still outstretched hand.
"Come on," he said, "I'll fix you another."

Even the little light from the breakfast nook hurt
David's eyes. He turned to the girl as she came in. One
cheek burned red under her tan, and a tear coursed
through a film of dust. "Sit down," he said, "I'll get some
towels." He made his way through the house to the
washroom, turned the tap on and tossed towels into the

tub. He draped one over his neck and carried the others,
dripping, back to the kitchen. He handed several to the
girl and fixed her another drink. He risked a look out the
window. Glowing cinders floated on the breeze. He ran
Felix more water. He sat down across from the girl at the
table.

"Can you see all right?"

She removed the towel from her face. "Better now."
She stared into her glass between quick gulps. David
looked at her. She was small boned and dirty up to the
roots of her dishwater-blond hair. Acne ran across her
cheekbones and her hairline. A slim scar lay across one
eye. When she looked up he saw that her eyes were green,
the iris of the scarred one rimmed in red.

"That was a bad one."

"He wants to talk about it?" She stared so intensely
that he had the sensation of falling into the bloodshot
eye.

"What do you want to talk about?"

Her expression became a burlesque of cunning. "They
could talk about what he has in his cupboards."

"All I've got is protein. Tell you what, I'll take you out
for a hamburger in a minute. Let's just see if this has
settled down for the night."

"Where's the protein?"

David rose and gathered the blacplastic bag, the gin,
and the tonic. She pulled the bag from his hand and
shoveled green nuggets into her mouth. He fixed drinks,
left the gin out of hers. When she drank, tonic water ran
down her chin.

"I was on my way over with a neighborly drink when
it flashed." She stared at him, still chewing. He tried
again. "Felix and I were going to play a little game of
fetch." Her animal gaze did not change.

"Just keep him out of her garden," she said around a
mouthful of protein. She looked for the dog, her expression fearful. Felix lay quietly in the corner by his bowls.

"Felix won't hurt you." David slowly chewed a single
nugget. "Look, do you need something? Is there anything
I can do?"

She did not pause in her chewing while a series of
contradictory expressions—confusion, anger, fear, then

certainty—flashed through her green eyes. She swallowed. "She'll take the money,"

"Money?" He felt stupid.

"She does what you want. For the money." Her fist moved more protein to her mouth.

David did not remember ever seeing her before she moved in. Still, he did not know every sitter in the suburbs. "I didn't mean—" He cast about for a way of finishing his sentence. Finally, he blurted out, "Where are your parents? Your mother?"

"Her mother was a see-through glastic whore."

"Was?" Her open mouth was half-full of green paste. Her crooked teeth showed yellow. "Is she dead?" he asked.

She shrugged and began to chew again.

A sour odor rose above the mineral smell of the protein. "What's your name, anyway?"

The girl considered. "Lu," she said finally.

"My name's—"

"Davy. His name is Davy."

David felt unperturbed that she should know his name, even in a form he could not recall, at the moment, anyone using since he was a child. He decided he was too tired to care. "Look Lu, that shit isn't any good for you, no matter what the media says. Let's go get a hamburger."

Lu shoved one last handful of protein into her already stuffed mouth.

Felix followed across the room, his tail wagging.

"No, you stay here." David closed the kitchen door almost on the dog's nose.

Felix listened to the garage door run up along its overhead tracks and the car start, then pull out into the drive. Only when he could no longer hear the sound of the engine down the street did he start a slow, padding circuit of the house. He returned to the kitchen with its dim light, walked around his blanket once, and curled down to sleep. He saw the orange-chew-soft arcing above him in the over-blue and he was running, running, watching to see where it met the water-brown. The orange-soft bobbed out there, and he leapt once and then ran again except now in the heavy-water-brown toward the bobbing-bright, all the time Davy's voice behind him.

*   *   *

David held his left hand open to the wind his speed made. Locusts circled the working streetlamps. They met a car and, in a moment of sudden gladness, he honked his horn. The car's driver honked back. Even the static buzz of the radio failed to dampen his mood. David knew almost nothing about radio, but he imagined that it had, like any technology, glitches. The Blue Baby would come back, despite the weeks of her absence. He smiled. Tella would like what he'd done.

"He has the money, doesn't he?"

His spirits dropped. Lu's face was obscured by shadows. The dashlights showed only her legs, the knees pitted and scarred. "Yeah, I suppose I do." He pulled a roll of blue bills out of a pocket. He rested an elbow against the wheel and peeled off a couple. He tossed the rest to her. She began to stack them on her lap. Her fingers shook with excitement. He twisted the radio knob, and the white noise ended with a click. David knew, with a certainty he could not explain, that something terrible and irrevocable had happened, not to the machinery of radio, but to the Blue Baby herself.

Lu, her voice timid, interrupted his thoughts. "If he has the money, why doesn't he move Inside?"

David pulled up to a stop sign and started to turn. The Torino stalled. He turned the key and the engine cranked twice, then caught. Far to the left were the lighted signs of the Alley: Burger King, Arby's, Taco Bell, Pizza Hut. The Torino idled in a rough lope. He hoped for an answer to Lu's question, as if the truth might arrest the despair growing within him. None of the reasons that flitted through his mind adequately explained his choice. He had a kind of independence that he knew existed for only a very few Inside. He had gambled that he would find an Inside audience interested in a life that would seem, to them, exotic. Perhaps that risk had suddenly paid off, though, even more suddenly, it didn't matter. He wondered if the young man he had been had thought about his life in the cold, analytical terms of a career choice. He wondered if he had thought about his life at all.

"Why doesn't he go?" Lu asked.

"Do you know the real name of this street?"

"Pine Heights Road," she said, proud as a student who knew the correct answer when called upon.

"Anything strike you as strange about that?"

"What?"

"No damn pine," he said, "no damn heights."

"Oh," she said.

A car with a single headlight drove past. It honked, and David honked back. He turned the Torino and headed down the Alley. He supposed he had stayed in the suburbs because the suburbs were his home.

"May she help him?" The tiny girl behind the counter, no more than ten, wore as a dress a uniform meant as a smock. David returned her smile and looked up at the lighted menu, though he knew it by heart. "Yes, please. Two quarter-pounders with cheese, two large fries, two chocolate shakes." His mouth began to water. This is one reason to stay, he thought—the food.

"She's sorry, sir, there's no cheese tonight."

He shook his head. "No problem."

"To stay or to go, sir?"

He glanced around the deserted dining area. The windows to the west were covered with sheets of warped plywood. "I'm with her." He nodded to Lu waiting at a table.

"To stay, then." Her smile vanished before she moved away to start his order. David was not surprised by the change. The children who worked the fast-food counters came, most often, from intact families. They were hired for the social graces learned by members of such units. David wondered what she had been told about sitters. He didn't want to know what her parent had said about scouts.

Feldon waved as he passed behind the grill and fryers. David waved back. He read the graffiti spray-painted on the walls, the molded-plastic furniture, even the windows. Almost every graduating class of the last twenty years was represented by two numerals. A mop stood in a pail in one darkened corner. The door was stopped open with a cinder block. He smelled their food cooking.

The girl said something to him. He handed her the bills he'd kept. "The change is for you."

"Thank him, but no tipping allowed." The old register wheezed. David guessed it was the only one in the line that worked. The girl counted glastic coins into his palm without any clumsiness over the amounts. She gathered up his order and placed it on a tray. She slid it across the scarred aluminum counter. "Enjoy his meal, sir." She turned and began to scrape the grill. David took his time getting plastic straws and paper napkins from their dispensers. When he turned away he left a neat pile of change on the counter.

Lu ate with a single-mindedness that saddened David. Finishing the revisions had made him act as if he lived in the world his parents had told stories about. He'd started over to Lu with drinks as though he'd slipped back to a time before the end of the world was in sight, to before the Fall even, when, the stories suggested, neighborliness was a way of life. Chewing his own food slowly, he recalled an image of his father towering above him, wearing an apron with graffiti on it. Hamburgers and slabs of unground meat sizzled on a grill, and people filled the backyard with shouts and laughter. Brightly colored plasdiscs sailed through the air. He could almost remember the smell of beer.

After the Fall no one laughed much. David's mind fixed on the image of his mother's face, the pronounced lines of worry, the exhausted eyes on an invisible point somewhere beyond his seeing. David fought to hold the portrait. While his parents' neighbors had left in droves for the New City, where, they had heard, a new order was being built, or Out There, where, it was said, one could grow his own food, they and a few like-thinkers fought to stabilize their community. David remembered those late night confabs in their house. He'd sit quietly at the edge of the dome of light cast by the kerosene lantern. He remembered clearly the night Preach had returned from the New City with their first accurate information about the new technologies. He recalled another time when the talk was of his mother's plan to reestablish electrical service. That must have been years later, David thought. Later still, they argued governmental autonomy, cottage industries, bartering goods and services. His parents had gotten him the university scholarship, although they'd had deep misgivings, not so much about his leaving the suburbs as his going Inside. By then they had begun to view the New Cities with vague suspicion. By the time he had finished school, both were dead.

David thought their deaths for the best. The suburbs

had evolved in ways that would have horrified them. A
nagging thing from the time of his grief surfaced. Preach
had talked to him at length as each death occurred,
despite the cost of the long-distance calls. He had, again
and again, informed David that his parents' most fervid
wish was that he complete his education, but in all that
talk Preach had only partially explained the causes of
death. Now David wondered if his mother and father had
died from the recognition of the world that was coming.
Had they realized that their idealism would prove insuffi-
cient for it? Their hopes for an honorable life had gone,
like their son, renegade.

Lu finished her fries and looked up. David pushed the
remains of his across the table and looked out the window. Much of what his parents would have abhorred was
finished now. Since the sun had gone haywire, few Insiders ventured out. Amos Dandy had told him what they
said—they didn't have time. David was bewildered by
how hard they were working in the face of doom. It
occurred to him that he had worked just as hard. The
exhausted face he saw reflected in the plate glass window
could have been his mother's.

"His is a nice car." Lu spread her fingers across the
dash.

"It needs a tune-up."

"Her boy had an Omega."

"What happened? Couldn't find parts?"

"No, he took it. He went Out There." She nodded past
the blocks of houses to where the blue lightning flared.

"When was that?"

"Oh, like a long time."

He slowed the Torino, pulled into the driveway, and
cut the engine. "I'm sorry, Lu."

She shrugged. "No big deal." She still stared to the
west. In a moment she said, "What's he want it be?"

David considered it, then said, "What about a movie?"

David stared at the ceiling, hands beneath his head.
The sheets clung to his skin.

Lu sat at the foot of the bed in a half-lotus, her elbows
on her knees, her chin cupped in her palms. Her hair was

still damp at the neck from her shower. He could count the vertebrae of her spine. Credits rolled up the screen.

"Why the casters call it film?" she asked without taking her eyes from the screen.

David roused himself, looked past her. "Oh, film was what they used to record on, a kind of plastic. Like in cameras." He rolled onto his side, cupped his chin in his hand, and looked at her profile. The set of her eyes told him he'd gone too far too fast. "A camera was used to take photographs—stills—first. Then they found a way of moving the film in the camera so that it made movies." He nodded toward the screen, where the last of the credits was just disappearing. "That movie was first recorded on film."

"She's sorry she asked." Lu stared at the blank screen.

He lay again on his back. After a while he asked, "Do you want to stay the night?"

"Whatever he wants."

"No, whatever you want. You decide."

She looked at him with the same transparent cunning he'd seen earlier. "Why is the sun doing that?"

"You watch the media?"

"Sometimes. They just guessing. They don't know."

"No, and neither do I. Nobody does." He thought for a moment. "And they can't stop it."

She dropped her gaze. She clenched her fist until her knuckles gleamed white. "What's going to happen?"

David rubbed a hand over his eyes. He'd listened, like everyone, to the media's hired experts, watched the docu-specials, hour after hour of them. He knew what all the technical talk came down to. "Maybe just a big bang, and it'll be over."

Lu cried quietly. David sat up and tried to put an arm over her shoulders. She shook him off, looked into his eyes, then clamped her hands to the sides of his head. He was startled by how tightly she held him. Her face was very close to his. She sobbed, "And maybe what?"

He felt her fierce breath on his face. "As gradual as it's been so far..." He could think of no other word. Not sure she'd understand he said, "Firestorms."

She dropped her hands and stopped crying very suddenly. "Oh," she said, "maybe she likes that better." Bewildered, he pulled her into the cradle of his arm. He stared at the ceiling. After a while he asked, "Would you like to see another movie?"

"She doesn't understand a lot of from the other one."

David said nothing.

Lu raised herself. "Her boy isn't coming back," she said, wonder in her voice.

David shook his head, slowly, from side to side.

19

Home Base

The entries of the book climbed up the screen with the maddening monotony of water dripping on a rock. LaMer shook herself out of a near-doze. She saw nothing in the room's soft red and slowly pulsing light worthy of a swift kick. Even the joke in the name, widespread among the Rescue Effort staff as a long series of glitches slowed the completion of main control to a snail's pace, failed to better her humor. She called up elapsed time and read 10:22:23. She depressed a key, and the Commodore's face appeared on one side of the screen.

He did not look up from what he was doing. "Your exception's already logged, mate."

"Fuck the log."

"Then what is it?"

"I thought you'd like to know we've set a new record."

"Setting records isn't what worries me. What worries me is shoddy elements." He held up a transistor board for her to see. "She's on her way back, then?"

"Yes."

"Any sign of trouble?"

"No."

"Steady as she goes."

"Aye, aye, skipper."

His eyes went back to the board. "Keep in touch."

The book again filled the screen. "Piss-ant son of a navy bitch," LaMer said to it. She wished the Major was there to harrass, especially since the Major had now traveled farther than any living thing, including LaMer.

She straightened in her chair, reached out and split the screen. She hammered a series of commands into the keyboard, following the machine's logic through a maze of files to the ones she wanted. The half-screen before her showed a double column of names in letters so tiny she had to squint to read them. She depressed a button and the list was replaced by another, and then another. List after list showed on the screen, each speedily replacing its predecessor. She stared at the scurrying names, holding at bay the thought that each represented a living human being.

She lifted her finger, and the half-screen came to rest on a single list. She asked the machine for a series of totals, then a sum of the series. She whistled at the number. Warming to the mathematical exercise, relaxing with the simple work, she compared current and pre-Fall populations of civilized Earth.

Every school child was taught the human cost of the Fall and the Third World wars. Starvation, disease, and slaughter, organized and random, though, lost much of their horror when reduced to a history lesson. She asked for a ratio of the first sum—the total number of nominees to the Screening Committee—to the current population. She scratched her head at the number, then checked the calculations. They appeared sound. She shifted uncomfortably in her chair and stretched her prosthetic leg out. Even if all current nominees were transmatted, something only the most optimistic hoped for, well over ninety-nine and ninety-nine hundredths percent of the inhabitants of the planet would be left. Their deaths would be as terrible, perhaps, as any ever recorded in the history books. *And when it's over,* LaMer thought, *history will cease to exist.*

LaMer whistled again. Perversely, the magnitude of the tragedy constituted, for her, a personal affront. She attempted to calculate the number of people she had come into contact with as a child, a university student, an adult moving down the malls and through the buildings of the New Cities she'd lived in and visited. She gave it up as a meaningless statistic. Instead, she thought of specific days from each of those periods. She wished to approximate the total number of people she had known by name, but only a few faces came, as if reluctantly, before her mind's eye. It did no good to prod herself to remember further. She grinned at the thought that she still had the fingers to count the people she'd been close to.

The screen broke into quadrants one of which showed the Commodore's face. "What are you doing down there?"

"Probabilities. What are you doing up there?"

"Possibilities. Everything proceeding normally with our volunteer's return voyage?"

LaMer got a time and a progress report on the screen's fourth quadrant. "Sure enough," she reported. "You've got just under nine hours to chill the champagne."

"Okay." The Commodore looked apparently done with business but with no intention of signing off.

"Do you want me to mention that you could have gotten that information on your own?" LaMer asked.

"Not necessary, mate."

"Did you want to see if I was still awake."

"No, I figured you were still awake." He grew more uncomfortable with each second. His face twisted into an expression resembling resolve. "Still mad at me, mate?"

LaMer looked at him for a long second. "Mike, you're the one person I can't stay mad at forever."

"The only one?"

She thought about it. "More or less."

"Good enough for me. I'll send someone down in a couple hours to relieve you."

"Thank you, Mike."

"Thanks, mate."

LaMer sat without moving for a long time, shadows of the faces of the living and the dead playing on the screen before her. Some part of her heart gladly greeted each. She gave each face a careful scrutiny, savored memories, forgave mistakes. She turned the faces over in her mind, as if they were precious gems whose facets she wished to examine. She found herself saying good-bye again and again.

In a while LaMer came out of her reverie. She asked the console to calculate the odds that any one of five names would appear on the list of nominees to the Rescue Effort. She compared that fraction to the ratio of nominees to the current population. Their values were remarkably similar.

She went back to the lists of nominees and gave the console a specific name to locate. It gave her six with the same spelling. She requested addresses for each. The machine gave her what she asked for. "I'll be damned," she said to the empty center. She phrased her next command.

"I'm here to relieve you." The voice came from behind.

"Hello, little sister." LaMer swung her chair around. "You're welcome to it. That's different, isn't it?" she asked, indicating her facepaint. "I like it."

"Thanks." The young woman blushed beneath the cause of the compliment and hurried into the chair LaMer had vacated.

"Scrub that for me, will you, little sister?"

"Yes, ma'am."

"Anything happens, you call me first."

"Count on it. Do you want a call before reentry?"

"Five minutes. I'm going to eat and drink for a couple slow hours, then sleep as long as you let me."

"Yes, ma'am."

Frieda watched LaMer leave, a warmth growing in her. Guilt was a luxury she did not make time for, at least not around LaMer. What they did at Home Base was too important.

After the door had closed she looked to the screen. She wondered vaguely why LaMer had called up the file for a somebody with a suburban address. She shook the thought off, erased the command, and began the half-lidded vigil that would allow her to read the book through the night.

LaMer's dream had the convincing feel of actuality about it. Even while it was happening, some part of her mind attempted to make sense of its chaotic flow. It was an argument, she realized, and she felt herself drowning in a sea of talk. Her own voice, as well as the other, sickened her. She longed to end this niggling talk, talk, talk. She needed freedom to move, to run. She was no longer a little girl, nor had she become the woman she now was. Neither of those incarnations cried in such breathless, sobbing spasms. She was caught on a turn somewhere, listening to the talk, talk, the endless talk.

She rolled out of her rack into a sitting position. The click of the glastic leg against the floor brought her into a present she did not immediately recognize. She stared at the alien prosthesis with vision inexplicably monocular. She reached up and adjusted her eye patch, the need to make some physical movement paramount, while every second brought her closer to understanding. She did not pause to consider which featureless cabin she sat in or which of dozens of klaxons she now heard. She punched a button on the screen beside her bed.

She could not find a name for the face on the screen. "What is it?" she asked.

"She pulled the rip cord." The young woman's voice was matter-of-fact; the eyes showed panic. "She's stalled out there someplace. And she's early."

"I'll be right there." LaMer considered what else might be expected of her. "Alert the Commodore."

"Yes, ma'am. Do you want a medical team?"

"Have them stand by, but outside. We don't need the clutter."

"Yes, ma'am." The image disappeared. The Major was coming in, and the Major was in deep trouble.

LaMer strode into auxiliary control, despite the bite of the prosthesis. The absolute barrenness of the transmatation booth, the slow slide of red light off its sheer sides, gave her a fleeting impression of frost.

"What do you know, little sister?"

"Nothing that makes sense." The reply was crisp. "The distress signal measures three light-minutes away, but she shouldn't be that close yet."

"Where is she?"

Both women turned to look at the Commodore.

"Do you want me to tell you the obvious, Mike?"

"It won't hurt my feelings, if that's worries you."

"Someplace within three light-minutes, and, we've got to hope, closing."

The Commodore walked to the console. "What's that mean?" His voice was soft.

"It means one of the Puzzle Boxes received her out there. And the transmat was abbreviated. Only the program could do that."

"Let me have it." He slipped into Frieda's chair. "I feel better if I have my hands on something," he explained.

"Yes, sir. Should I cut the klaxon?"

"Doesn't bother me. LaMer?"

"Turn it up, as far as I'm concerned."

"Why would a box receive her? This is Operation Snakeskin, right! The Commodore lifted his tired eyes to LaMer.

LaMer nodded. The idea was a test run of the Puzzle Boxes, each sloughing off in turn like a snake losing old skins. "Unless we both lost three days in the schedule."

The Commodore shook his head. "Then there's no reason for her to form up out there."

"She left with life-support equipment, Mike. Tell me what that was about."

The Commodore was busy running through the program. "Say again, LaMer."

"We sent her out into the great unknown in a life-support suit. I figured it was just the Major's timidity in matters of practice rather than theory."

"I didn't authorize a suit, mate." He gave her a heavy-lidded look.

"She was wearing one when she left, Mike."

He swore under his breath. He attacked the keyboard with a different rhythm. He no longer simply scanned the program but commanded the machine to do specific things.

"Ma'am, I don't understand," Frieda began uncertainly. "Why should she be received?"

"I'm getting a line now," the Commodore announced. "She's on her way."

"Because that's the way our Major wanted it, little sister." LaMer turned to the Commodore. "Right, Mike?"

He nodded, his eyes still on the screen. "Yes, here it is. She programmed in a stop as well as a compensating reduction in distance. The time's still wrong," he observed.

"You didn't have anything to do with it, did you, Mike? Accelerate the trial runs, that sort of thing?"

He kept working. "I'm getting some of the monitor feeds trailing in behind the distress call. She had it set so that she controlled the duration of the event. She must have hung up there for ten minutes, maybe longer." He studied the screen. "She doesn't look good."

"Okay, she had to punch a button to send herself home, but why the delay?"

"One: she was enjoying the view. Two: some kind of

glitch she had to deal with to enable the transmat. Three: she had trouble punching the button. Take your pick."

LaMer continued to regard him closely. "That still doesn't explain why she reprogrammed in the first place."

Frieda studied the screen over the Commodore's shoulder. When she spoke, her voice was thoughtful. "Physical trauma started with the reception in the last Puzzle Box."

"Number three, then." LaMer looked around. "Put it all up there, Mike. I want to see this for myself."

The screens around auxiliary control lit up one by one, each bearing different information.

"You still didn't answer my question, Mike."

"What question's that, mate?"

"Did you order her to take a peek at the universe?"

"I don't order anybody to do anything. You know that."

"Why the life support?"

"Precautionary, I imagine. In case of a bad seal. Not much atmosphere in one of those boxes, either. Remember, she wanted a look around." The Commodore shrugged with a massive shift of his shoulders. The motion took a wrong turn and became a shudder. "The Major was a great one for back-ups." He slumped in the chair.

"Jesus, Mike!"

"'Was?'" Frieda repeated.

The Commodore pointed to a screen. "Burn victim."

Only when the transmatation booth began to glow with reception did anyone speak.

"Lock the door, little sister," LaMer said. "The medical team is not to be allowed in till I give the order."

"Yes, ma'am." Frieda leaned over the Commodore's shoulder to move a toggle switch. The Commodore stared at the screen, oblivious to LaMer's words, Frieda's movement, or the growing fire in the booth.

Frieda wondered what the Commodore had meant. Whatever it was, LaMer had recognized it immediately. The Major was forming up in the transmat booth, the silver of the life-support suit already visible in the golden fire. Frieda looked to a screen for the medical read-outs. She didn't understand all the data, but she recognized brain activity. In fact, the Major's brain seemed to be working terribly hard. Frieda thought that was consistent with having had the first long-distance view of the solar

system in history, not to mention an emergency fifty
million kilometers from the nearest help. The Major was
injured, certainly, but her brain, which was, Frieda reflected,
her essence, did not appear damaged in the least.

The atomic fire in the booth subsided, and the door to
the booth opened. The Major stood, wobbled just a little,
and stepped out with deliberation. The Major took a
second step. The suit and the silvered bubble of her mask
reflected the red light of auxiliary control. Frieda gasped
at something she did not immediately recognize. The suit
absorbed and darkened with the light. The brightness of
the silver had dampened with red. The Major took yet
another step. In the moment she collapsed, Frieda
understood.

The three of them knelt around the spasming body.
The artificial and natural skins had recombined to form a
porous membrane connected to the brain by millions of
traumatized nerve endings. A thin keening came from
beneath the visor. A guttural noise sounded in counterpoint. Frieda was gagging.

LaMer shot her a look. "Breathe through your mouth."

The Commodore lay his hands upon the visor. "At
least, this remained intact," he mumbled.

"The helmet held it away far enough," LaMer whispered,
"but the lining around the sides and back will have
recombined as well."

The Commodore spoke more loudly, then, and very
distinctly. "Major, it's Mike. I believe you can hear me."

The keening became a quick series of short snufflings.

"What you're feeling is the result of extensive recom-
bination. There is exposure of the nerves to an unnatural
tissue. Your brain will make some adjustments to that in
a few moments." He wiped the back of his hand across
his mouth. Frieda had begun to pant.

"Major, I'm going to remove the visor. Your eyes may
be painfully sensitive to the light. When I tell you to, I
want you to close them."

He looked at LaMer and jerked his head toward Frieda.

LaMer took Frieda's arm and whispered, "Go away."

Frieda resisted the pull on her arm, her eyes fixed on
the tinted visor. She shook her head. "No," she panted.

"There may be no eyes to close," LaMer whispered.

"No," Frieda repeated.

LaMer let go of Frieda's arm and put her hands on the visor opposite the Commodore's. She nodded once. The Major's body continued to spasm between them.

The Commodore spoke. "Major, I want you to close your eyes now. I want you to keep them closed until I order you to open them. Do you understand?"

Again the keening became a snuffling noise.

"Ready, mate?"

LaMer nodded.

"One, two, three."

They separated the silvered, glastic visor from its seal with a smooth upward movement of their hands.

Frieda saw that the Major's eyes were, indeed, gone. Whether they lay whole beneath the greasy cover of mottled skin and flesh, or whether their tissue was simply one of the ingredients to this new and terrible face, she could not guess. The nose remained only as a bridge of proud flesh and a tag of exposed cartilidge bent to the side. The lipless mouth had been narrowed to a tiny, perfectly round hole. Frieda felt an odd calm descend upon her.

The Commodore locked his gaze on LaMer. He spoke evenly. "Keep them closed, Major. We need time to acclimate you." The body between them spasmed, one long, undulating motion from head to foot after another. The keening became more ragged. "We're going to give you something, Major, to make you rest," the Commodore said, his eyes still meeting LaMer's. She sighed, reached into the top of her boot and fished out a razor-thin blade. She held the tip of the haft between two fingers and passed the point of the light blade under her own jaw.

The Commodore shook his head, then motioned with a backward snap of it to the locked door. He spoke into the mass of tissue that had been the Major's face. "You may experience some additional discomfort for a moment, Major. We have to adjust your life-support equipment before we can give you the medication. Keep your eyes closed."

The Commodore rested his hand on the Major's new skin near her collarbone. He kneaded lightly with his fingers. The keening picked up its rhythm and grew hoarse. He found what he was searching for and gave it a sharp twist. The Major's breathing sharpened to a high, thin whistle.

"The trachea tube was knocked out of kilter, Major. You're breathing on your own now." The Commodore looked to LaMer. "We're going to be moving you up on a stretcher. We're giving you something for the pain now." He reached out and touched her shoulder. "You're going to sleep now, Major. I'll talk to you soon."

LaMer placed the blade between her teeth and bit down hard. She gathered the woman's shoulders together and lifted. She placed a hand on the back of the helmet and pressed the new and terrible face hard into her breast. The whistling subsided abruptly. LaMer rocked back and forth. She looked to Frieda. "Get the medical monitors on a screen where I can see it," she said quietly.

They knelt there together while the seconds ticked away. After something less that a minute, the spasms increased in ferocity, and LaMer struggled to hold her. The Commodore threw his arms around the two women and clamped his hand behind LaMer's against the helmet. In forty-five seconds, the savage convulsions trailed off.

The Commodore relaxed his hold. "You can open your eyes now, Major," he said.

Three minutes later, when the tracery on the screen had lost its peaks and valleys, when every line showed flat, he dropped his arms from the women. He sat back with a groan.

LaMer shuddered and lay the dead woman down. She put the stiletto back in her boot and clamped her eyes on the Commodore. "She'll see us both in hell."

The Commodore simply nodded, reached over to the dead woman's throat, and reopened the valve. Compressed oxygen escaped with a hiss. He looked at Frieda. "If they ask, you don't have any idea who locked the door. It was a mistake, but nothing could have been done anyway. We were very busy doing what we could. Do you understand?"

Frieda bobbed her head once. When she spoke her voice was breathless. "Yes, sir."

"On my signal, unlock the door and call them in."

"Yes, sir." Her voice stronger. She took several backward steps toward the console before she could tear her eyes from the scene on the floor.

The Commodore rose, turned, and started for the door.
"Mike?" LaMer called.

He stopped but did not turn around.

"How do I know you didn't suggest this stop to her?"

The Commodore faced her. "If I wanted her to stop,
would I be stupid enough to program it within our own
solar system? With all that's going on here?"

"Was the Major that stupid, Mike?"

He studied the corpse. "Yes mate, though she shouldn't
have been." He looked at LaMer. "Why would I do it?
Why?"

LaMer struggled erect and moved, nearly dragging the
prosthesis, past him to the console. She punched some
keys, found an apparently superfluous feed from the still
suspended Puzzle Box, and called it up on an overhead
screen. "No reason, Mike. Unless you wanted a look at a
dying sun."

It hung on the screen above them, absurdly tiny at that
distance, red with twin auras of blue and white. LaMer
ordered magnification, and the image of the sun leapt
huge. As they watched an arc of the perimeter within the
auras collapsed in on itself. A giant flame rose from the
crater it'd left, extended beyond the limits of the screen.

The Commodore still stood above the Major's corpse,
his eyes on the screen, his face a study in awe. "There
would be that." He looked down, then turned away. "I'll
remove the altered program, and we'll go with the back-
up. It'll take fifteen minutes."

"Aye, aye," she said, her voice tired.

Next to the image of the sun the screen still read the
flat traceries from the Major's life-support monitors. The
Commodore came to the console, pushed a button, and
the sun disappeared. He hit others, each with great
deliberation.

The duty roster appeared. "You're next up, chief."

"Aye, aye," LaMer said again, her eyes on her name
listed beneath the Major's.

"I take it you'll not be wanting life support."

LaMer stared at the Major, then at the intricately
carved glastic rod beside her boot toe. "I'll just be taking
the leg. Nothing else in that booth. Agreed?"

"That's the way I planned it."

"And no sight-seeing, Mike."

"Out and back. A new record." He looked to Frieda and nodded. When she hesitated, he asked, "What is it, tech?"

"It's just that, with the trauma coming immediately after reception, she never saw it. The sun, I mean."

"No, she couldn't have," the Commodore said matter-of-factly.

Frieda flipped the toggle switch and walked briskly over to the door. LaMer began to get out of her clothing. She had the zipper of her coveralls half-way down when her thighs abruptly shuddered and threatened to give way beneath her. Her hand went reflexively to rest over her heart. The cloth there was wet with the Major's saliva, greasy with drying blood.

20

A History of Humankind to Date

David stood in the open garage door, drinking a Pepsi, taking in the view. Two dozen or so junkers dotted the wide asphalt apron that had once served the now abandoned K-Mart. McGee was bent over the fender of one of them, only his hips and legs visible. Beyond, David could see the back of the Burger Barn. Feldon came around the corner of the building with a blacplastic bag of garbage in each hand. He tossed them on the heap that overflowed a lidless dumpster. David waved, but Feldon didn't look his way. David drained the last from his glastic bottle, burnt skin crinkling as he arched his neck. He looked to the sun. His glasses mixed a green tint into its colors. The core, two-thirds now of the sun, half again as big as the last time David had dared look, pulsed dark red. Concentric rims of orange, yellow, ivory, and white led to the perimeter. There, the blue curls of fire reached out into space in a slow ballet. David looked down to the asphalt. Bright spots swam before his eyes. He could feel the stiff sunburn on his cheeks. He wondered whether he'd just damaged his retinas.

McGee, filing the resistor end of a spark plug, walked past him into the dark interior of the garage. David turned and followed, dropping his empty into the antique crate by the machine as he passed. McGee's head and shoulders disappeared under the hood of David's Torino.

"I picked the best three I had." His voice was muffled. "I cleaned them up. They should run you a year."

"You think we got a year, McGee?"

McGee brought his head out, stared at David, then beyond, out the garage door, to where light glanced off the asphalt. He shook his head from side to side. His face broadened in a grin. "Not a chance in hell." He stuck his head back under the hood. "What do you college boys figure?"

"All I know is what I see on the media."

McGee worked a minute, the ratchet of his wrench the only sound. "But what do you figure?" he asked the Torino's engine.

David shrugged, turned half-away from McGee's back. "Nobody knows, from what they say."

"They ever lie to you before?"

"Probably. Sure. But I think they're pretty straight about this. If they knew, anybody who'd care to turn on a screen would know. If they're going to lie to us, they'd tell us they had it figured out, invent some science that we couldn't understand. But what would the point be?"

"Keep all the folks Inside stroking?"

"Maybe. But the Insiders I know have written it all off, and they're still stroking. And so are you, McGee."

McGee pulled his head out, shot a quick grin, went back under.

"What do you figure?" David asked.

"What I figure is this," McGee said after a moment, "the way it's acting we're going to burn up pretty damn soon. Or, maybe, it'll take a turn and freeze us out. If we can stand the temperatures, which maybe we can if we pay attention to when we go out, the ecosystem's still going to start shaking like a bitch in heat. The energy drain for the food systems Inside'll be too much. All those efficiency spaces are going to demand lots of energy for cooling or heating or both, depending on what the climate does. Mass transit'll have to be shut down." He grunted as he set a plug. "Hell, what I figure is we got anything from ten seconds to a couple of months before that thing either sucks us in for fuel, sputters out of gas, or blows our atoms out into the universe. It'd be good if it happens faster than our brains can register, is what I figure."

David smiled. "Well, that's a load off my mind."

McGee looked up. "What I can't figure is why they haven't announced the Rescue Effort yet. Anybody with two millimeters of sense knows that they're going to try something." David didn't answer. McGee shrugged and went back to work.

David wandered over to the open door. He had his usual heat-induced headache, and McGee's mention of the Rescue Effort, about which the media constantly speculated, had started his stomach in a series of queasy somersaults.

Across the asphalt, a pack of fifteen or twenty dogs had gathered around Feldon's dumpster. They were dragging garbage bags down from the heap and tearing them open.

David hurried back to the Torino, leaned into the passenger's side window, flipped open the glove box, pulled out his revolver and a box of shells. McGee saw what he was doing and stopped his work. "Get your gun," David said. "We're going to do someone a favor." He marched across the dark garage and through the door into the light.

"Do someone a what did you say?" McGee asked his back.

David quickly checked the load in the gun as he walked, then kept his eyes on the dogs, none of which had yet noticed him. He stuck the gun in his belt, dumped the contents of the box into his right palm, then pocketed the shells. He flipped the box away. He was within twenty meters when the first dog looked up. It bared its fangs and growled deep in its throat. David stopped, lifted the revolver and shot it in the head.

At the sound of the gun the heads of the remaining animals snapped around. When David shot the second animal, the pack began to move away from the garbage and out onto the asphalt. He shot a third as they moved in an unpanicked trot toward the far corner of the Burger Barn. David heard the solid crack of McGee's rifle behind him, and another dog went down with a quick bark. The pack broke into a run and started to disappear around the corner of the building. A shotgun boomed, and the leaders reappeared and, now at a dead run, moved out across the open asphalt toward the deserted K-Mart a hundred meters away. David took his time and shot two more dogs. Three, bunched up at the rear of the pack, went down in a furry, yelping ball when the shotgun again sounded. The remaining animals had lined out in their run. McGee

fired three times more, twice making spaces in the string
of running dogs. David took his time, chose to use the
last round in the cylinder on a long-tailed, short-haired
dog toward the front of the line. It was big, muscular, the
best physical specimen in range. Its back legs went out
from under it, and it rolled over twice, got to its front feet,
and, yelping and whining, began to spin after its tail.

The rest were gone, into or around the K-Mart, David
wasn't sure. Feldon came around the corner of the Barn,
stopped a few meters from the three dogs he'd shot at
close range. One was still on its feet, bleeding from the
flank and barking. Feldon shifted his shotgun to his left
hand, drew a short automatic from beneath his apron, and
shot it. It died with a yelp. David walked carefully among
the dead dogs, punching out spent cartridges and reloading
as he went, his eyes on the dog he'd wounded. He walked
to where it spun, snapping at the hole in its hip, kicked it
in its side, and, when the dog straightened out, shot it in
the head. He transferred the revolver to his left hand. His
right trembled, and he felt that he might vomit.

They sat on the asphalt in the shade of the Burger
Barn's eave, eating hamburgers. Fifty meters away flies
buzzed around the dead dogs piled in the back of McGee's
pickup. No one had mentioned taking the ears for the
bounty. McGee finished his hamburger, pulled the bill of
his cap down, and leaned back against the wall. David
popped his last bite in his mouth, chewed, swallowed. He
glanced at Feldon. "Where do you get this stuff?"

"The same place I get these." Feldon held out a
cigarette. David looked around, then shook his head at
his own irrelevant anxieties. He hadn't seen any sign of
the Law in a month. He lit the cigarette on Feldon's
match, inhaled smoke into his lungs, coughed once.

"And where's that?"

"Oh, the syndicate works it all out. Reps from the
chains take a couple trucks Out There. There's a place."

Feldon studied him through blue cigarette smoke,
then glanced at the pulsing sun. "Want to know all about
it?"

David nodded.

"I take my turn like everyone else. There's a road. It's
pretty broken up. You follow it left, then right, and then

left again to the river. It takes the better part of a day, maybe a hundred fifty, two hundred kilometers. Down under the trees in the river valley there's a place called the Yarz. You settle on a price, pay them, they separate out what you want, cut their throats and skin and gut them. We pick up the carasses, cover them up with blacplastic and head like hell for home before the meat spoils. We grind it up to hamburger. The syndicate's got this big freezer out on thirty-five near the fuel tanks. You've seen it."

David shook his head.

"Concrete block building? No windows?"

David nodded. "Must really be something to see."

Feldon didn't require much prompting. "Man, there ain't nothing like it in the real world." He stared off toward the dead dogs. "Real Old Westy, you know. Like old movies and stuff. They climb up on those horses and ride in among the animals like it was the most natural thing in the world. The butchers and skinners are red from blood, grinning like they were watching themselves on the media. Hell, they'll be butchering an animal, and they'll just reach in, pull out the heart and take a bite, like an Insider eating a peach for dessert." He turned his face to David. "That's what they live on, you know. Organs, the tongue. They eat the insides right out of animal. Some of the reps, once they've seen that, they won't go out again. They think they're zombies or ghosties or something."

"What do you think?"

"Oh, they're alive, like you and me. Just different is all."

"Where do they get the animals?"

"That I don't know for sure, but I think they just grow wild Out There. These Rounders, that's what they call themselves, they'll go out on a gather, what they call it. I think what happens is they find a herd of animals and chase them down to the Yarz. Then they just keep them there until somebody comes for them."

David considered what Feldon had said. The language sounded vaguely familiar from his university courses in period media. "What do they do with the money?" he asked.

Feldon grinned. "Maybe they use it to buy stuff off

each other. I don't know. I think they'd sell you meat for
bumper jacks if that's what you had."

"What about the rest of the stuff, the milk stuff?"

"It comes in in wagons, an old truck once in a while.
Same kind of deal. You haggle for a while, then give them
what you expected anyway. I heard once it comes from
goats, the cheese and stuff. Tobacco comes from the same
people." He smiled. "You can get more than you imagine
Out There. Hell, I've seen marijuana. Tried it once. Made
me nervous. Besides, I didn't want to get addicted.

"You see," he continued, "they got these little stores
down in the Yarz, and people will throw up tents made
out of blacplastic or skins or whatever. You just go in and
see what they have to offer. It looks to me like the whole
place used to be a town. Lots of foundations sticking out
of the ground, that sort of thing. You can tell."

"Is that what happened to all the people who went
Out There? They became Rounders or raised goats?"

"No," Feldon shook his head. "At least I don't think so.
We brought a guy back in with us once." He paused to
study the sky. "Been years since I've seen him now.
Anyway, we found him on the way back. He was almost
dead, but you could tell he'd been a big strong man, and
he was smart, too. He'd left the skirts a month before with
a big group, a dozen or so. They'd been shot at by
villagers, run down by the Rounders when a couple of
them tried to steal some meat. The rest of them were
dead, the guy said, at least the ones he knew about,
which were all but one or two. Hell, they were starving."

He shook his head again, then continued. "No, those
Rounders are wild, all right. Those are the people who
never came in, them and their children."

McGee sputtered out of his nap suddenly. He raised
his arms to stretch. He looked at the two of them, then
addressed David. "Say, you still got that little sitter at
your place?"

"She sort of moves between her house and mine. I
don't think she was ever much of a sitter, though."

McGee stood and stretched again. He looked out of
the shadow toward his pickup where it sat in the fierce
light. "Whatever," he said. "Well, let's dump that load
out in the skirts before they start to bloat up in the heat."
He walked off toward the pickup.

Feldon watched him walk away, then looked up. He held his gaze on the sun. With one hand he tossed his apron aside, reached into a pocket. His hand came out with a box of cigarettes. "Take it, I'm grateful for the..." He trailed off, looking for the right word. Finally, he said again, "I'm grateful."

Lu waited in the shadow of the front of the house with Felix. David pulled into the drive, got out to open the garage door. Instead of running to greet him as David expected, Felix sat patiently beside Lu. Lu absently petted him and stared at David. "How're you two doing?" he asked. Lu did not answer, nor did her expression change. David ran the car in. He came back through the house with drinks.

He sat down on the step beside her. Lu took the glass he offered. After a swallow she said, "She thought he wasn't coming back."

"It took longer than I expected. There were dogs."

"Oh." Lu stroked Felix and sipped her drink.

"Does Davy want to sit in back?" she asked in a while.

"It's too dangerous now. We've got some shelter here."

"Okay."

Another minute ticked by. "Look," he said, "I have to check my mail. I'll be right back."

"Okay."

David entered the house and made another drink. A red rectangle flashed on the screen in the study. He took a deep breath and punched the "respond" button. The screen read "Please Wait." Fuck it, he thought, and got one of Feldon's cigarettes from his pocket. The screen brightened. Tella-Dotun sat there, her back rigid and her shoulders squared.

"I hoped you would call earlier." The yellow-and-blue facepaint failed to cover the puffy skin under her eyes.

David sipped his drink and took a hit from his cigarette. "I needed a party."

Her jaw dropped slightly. She regained her composure. "This is stupid, very stupid. If we're being monitored, you'll be without a code. I imagine your status with the Screening Committee would change as well."

"Now, Tella, are you going to tell me the Government's

wasting its time monitoring me? Or that you never flirted with the wild side?"

Tella's eyes brightened, though her face remained stern. "No, I won't tell you that. But you are of particular interest to the Government now, and there could always be a random monitor. I suggest you try to grow up."

"No time like the present." He raised his glass to her.

"You know yours is not the only project I have."

He stubbed out the cigarette and moved the ashtray away from the screen without taking his eyes from hers.

She glanced down at a print. "The book is fine, David. I've shown it around. Everyone agrees it's a masterpiece."

"Tough time to make that judgment, don't you think?"

"Maybe a better time than any other." David found himself falling into those very tired eyes. She continued. "That's what I do, after all, make that sort of judgment."

"Will it be out in time?"

"The holographs are running around the clock. We don't do much with format. It'll only take a couple days, maybe less, depending on what speed the print shop can make. Later we can make a longer run, if there's time. We'll send copies to Home Base as part of your allotment. I understand they'll be automatically sent with you."

David studied her. "What does that mean?"

"They've assigned you a number," she said simply.

David waited, not at all sure he wished to know it.

Tella shifted through some prints. She lifted one off the keyboard. It was very white in her brown hands, and it fluttered slightly. "Do you want to write this down?"

He shook his head. "Tell me something first. Why me?"

Tella sighed, lowered the print. "We nominated you, the Screening Committee gave you a number." She shifted a fountain pen from hand to hand. "Why do you find it so impossible to believe? You represent a cultural constituency. It's a small constituency, but one that, I think, deserves to have its story told." The pen was gone, and her hands wrestled the cap off a glastic prescription bottle. She popped a tablet into her mouth, washed it down with something from a large, ornate mug. "Now, do you want your number or not?"

David considered asking Tella to whom she thought

he'd be telling any story, but his mouth proved too dry for speech. He nodded instead.

Tella kept her eyes on the print. "Okay, it's 1 0 0 9 2." She looked up, waited for his reaction.

David showed none for a full thirty seconds. He felt something, then, welling up in him, a giddiness. He laughed. He thought he should control himself, and that thought struck him as hilarious. He laughed harder, huge, slow chortles that came from deep within. He threw himself back in his chair, bounced forward, threw himself back again. He laughed and laughed.

Finally, with a long sigh, he sobered. He wiped a tear from beneath his eye. Tella wore her stern expression, and it was only the exhaustion in her eyes that stopped another outburst. "I'm sorry," David said as meekly as he could:

Tella closed her eyes, rubbed them delicately with the tips of two fingers, stared again at David. "What is so goddamn funny?"

He refrained from reminding her of the Government Monitor. "Sorry, Tella, I was only thinking: ten thousand and some odd. So much for the creator of a masterpiece."

"Look," she said, unappeased, "a lot of people, I among them, worked very hard to get a number this low for you. I mean, David, there are physicists, chemists, social scientists, other artists, technicians, food supply specialists, energy people; representatives of every culture, Moscovites, Liverpudlians, Athenians, Cantonese, Delhians, Buenos Airians, Logosians." She sputtered to a stop, started again. "David, where do you think you'd be if the politicians and the military hadn't opted out?"

"A captain and his ship."

"What?"

"Oh, it's something I found among my father's papers once, on an old-fashioned carbon. He used it in reference to the presidency in the old order, his sense of bravado."

"That's the old order, David. These people made a very brave decision."

"Yes, I'm sure. Look, what about the Rounders, the primitives, from Out There? Are any of them going?"

"No. Of course not. There is no contact with them." Tella was plainly startled. "Some people claim that they're only legend, anyway. Why in the world do you ask?"

"Oh, nothing. Well, you said 'every culture.'"

"What's Out There, if anything, is hardly a culture."

David shrugged. "Perhaps only slightly less civilized than the suburbs. It's just a matter of degree."

"I hardly think so." David did not persist. Tella looked again to her prints. "There are just two more items. One, your orientation date's been set. It's in three days."

David stiffened. "Okay."

"Two, it's local. Evidently, there are enough selectees there. Rather than transmat all of you to Home Base, the orientation team will transmat there. That's what I gather, anyway."

A moment passed. "Then I won't see you again."

"It's highly unlikely."

David leaned forward in his chair and placed a fingertip on the screen. "I'm sorry for that."

Tella placed a finger against the image of his. He felt a small electrical charge.

"Friday, noon. The Holiday Inn."

David thought he might cry, wished he could. He desperately searched through his mind for something to make her stay a while. He thought he saw a tear smudging the yellow paint beneath her eye.

"Good-bye, David, and thank you."

Before he could respond, she had hung up. He stared at the blank screen.

After a while, he stood, walked through the house and out the front door. He sat down beside Lu. Felix was coming back in the blue twilight, the orange ball in his mouth. Lu said, "He was gone a long time."

"I have to put some things in order." He took the ball from Felix and threw it across the street. Felix trotted after it, too old to really run now. He picked it up and came back even more slowly. David threw the ball again.

"I have to go Inside soon." When Lu said nothing, he added, "I'd like you to stay here, to take care of Felix."

"Will he come back?" Her green eyes shone dully in the twilight.

"Yes, I will come back." He hestitated. "And I have to make another trip."

"Can she come?"

He draped an arm over her shoulders, pulled her

close. She resisted only for a moment. "No," he said, "someone must take care of Felix."

The dog, perhaps hearing his name, lay down at their feet, the ball trapped between his front paws. Soon they could hear his light snoring. They watched the moon come up over the abandoned houses across the street. It rose gently, full, scarred, and cement gray.

"She heard Davy before. Laughing."

"Yes. He thinks he may be going insane."

21

Those Who Never Came In

David placed his lip over the rim of the coffee mug and let the moist steam rise into his face. His eyes burned, the muscles of his face felt atrophied, and his body ached. Even two hours before dawn it was already too hot, he knew, for coffee. Still, he took a sip and shuddered gratefully. The read-out on the screen flicked ahead another minute. He sat back in his chair and took a deeper drink. Sweat began to run from beneath his arms. Felix padded in, yawned widely and lay down beside him. David pulled the cleaned and oiled revolver out of the loose waistband of his jeans and lay it on the desk to one side. He sipped more coffee.

When the cup was half-empty, he leaned forward and typed in a message. He addressed it with routing coordinates and signed it with his ID number. Another minute ticked by. The screen read "Accepted." He had access to the data banks he needed.

He typed

FIND: Anthropology: Current: Interior:
Continental Northwest Tetrasphere.

The screen dimmed as the little machine worked hard, then reported "OK."
David typed

FIND: Out There/Primitives/Rounders

and the screen again dimmed. This time when it came back on full it read "Not Found."

David sat back again and ran a hand across the whiskers under his chin. He leaned forward and typed

FIND: Out There/Primitves

and the screen read, almost immediately, "OK." David ordered

SELECT: Most Current

and when he again received an "OK" he typed

REPORT: References In Common

and sat back to watch a series of bibliographic entries appear on the screen. He leaned forward one more time to ask for a print, then went to the kitchen for more coffee. When he returned the printer was silent. He tore off the list and began to request the references one at a time.

By dawn he'd found out very little that he hadn't already learned from Feldon. The government had always believed the primitives were more than a legend and had tried to find out about them. Reconnaissnace aircraft had taken stills of small acreages under cultivation. Through the grainy texture, David could make out the rough squares of buildings. Ministry of State anthropologists, bilingual and unarmed, had been sent out several times. None of the long-range expeditions had returned; the shorter sorties had discovered almost nothing. Military patrols had scouted the populated areas, but the villagers had fled as soon as they had sighted the Land Rovers. The commanders-in-the-field had not wished to confirm the villagers' apparent fears by chasing after them. Examination of articles in the homes suggested that the inhabitants were Hispanic émigrés from the time of the Third World wars, which supported the general theoretical consensus.

The most recent and ambitious attempt by the government had been a military plan to set up a series of stations, one after another, deeper and deeper Out There. Only one such station had been established, and it'd been abandoned after the first flares of the sun had been detected.

Among the files, David found the abstract of a media investigation. Media agents had infiltrated the suburban fast-food chains, operating on the inescapable deduction that the meat and lactic products they served came from Out There. The investigators' penetration had been, David thought, remarkably shallow, but suburbanites were traditionally mistrustful of Insiders, and Insiders found it nearly impossible to pass themselves off as suburbanites. In any event, they had found out virtually nothing that could be verified. They theorized, however, the existence of small, nomadic bands that provided meat, which they harvested at will from the herds of ruminants that dominated, as the reconnaissance aircraft had clearly shown, Out There. The cheese and milk, they further hypothesized, were bartered for or looted from the villagers and delivered to the various suburbs through an elaborate black market. The results of the investigation were so speculative that the planned media presentation had never been produced. The abstract concluded that there was no reason to believe that either the members of the Ministerial expeditions or the millions of suburbanites who had fled Out There immediately after the Fall had been "absorbed," though it was hoped that that was the case.

The speculations of the investigators coincided with what Feldon had told David. The only real deviation between the two versions was that the real black market was much less sophisticated than the one the investigators had suggested. That, however, was a matter only of degree, not substance. David sighed and shut the console off. The last still, showing abandoned vehicles against a majestic backdrop of mountains on the skirts of Old Denver, faded through sepia into black.

David thought of Lu as he drove. He imagined her awaking, rising, feeding Felix, finding his note by the bag of protein. It occurred to him, very abruptly, that she might not be able to read it. He braked suddenly, but just as quickly shook off any notion of turning back.

The potholed road was no better than Feldon had said. At first it differed from a street only in that there were no buildings along it. Before the morning was half-over, though, it had deteriorated considerably. David followed stretches where there was neither concrete nor asphalt, only two parallel ruts in the dirt. He kept a careful eye on the gauges of the Torino. It ran a little hot, but the needle of the gas gauge dropped with a slowness he found reassuring.

The openness was what David was most unprepared for. By noon he was well into an area dominated by tall hills. Long grass, pale green and dusty yellow, dotted by patches of wilting wildflowers, stretched as far as he could see. Giant, rusting machines listed in the shade of scattered clumps of trees. Mountains of lumber that had been barns and houses rotted back to earth. He slowed the Torino again and again to observe the fauna. Once he came to a complete stop not more than fifty meters from actual cattle. They were much bigger than he would have thought and apparently not much afraid of him or his car. He gazed at them in open-mouthed awe, like a schoolboy among sitters awaiting the Saturday night el. Their curiosity awakened, the cattle began to approach in a lumbering gait. David reasoned that he was safe in the car, but when they came close enough for him to see strings of spittle hanging from their cud-chewing mouths he made a quick decision to not test his theory.

Later he thought he saw, in silhouette on a far hill, dogs running along a ridge. The distance was so great and the impression so fleeting, though, he wondered if it had been his imagination. He drove on and on, finding Feldon's vague directions easy to follow. Even at its roughest, the road showed ruts and, often, tire treads. The others he crossed had been cracked with sprouting grass or covered with drifting sand. Through the early afternoon, his thirst growing, he traveled toward the river. Once a pool of water, vapors rising in the heat, appeared on the road a half-kilometer before him. He sped on several minutes, less careful of holes and ledges in the road, before he realized the water was only an illusion. Later he made out, in the distance, a line of dark green against the light grass. He prayed it was the lusher growth of river-fed vegetation, not another trick.

His thirst plagued him. His sweat had stopped, as if some part of his mind had instructed his body to conserve liquids. The line of green gained definition. He became more and more convinced of its reality. Soon he was driving toward a vision his mind gave him of his arrival at the river. In it he saw that the green line was formed by tall trees. He saw the car passing through them. He saw the sandy bank of the river. He saw himself leaving the car, walking across the narrow beach, kneeling, cupping water to his mouth with his hand. In a few moments, the vision had changed so that he dropped to his knees, fell prostrate on the sand to drink with his face in the water. He imagined the color of it to be, first, blue, then a cool green. In two more kilometers he saw himself swimming in ice water clear as crystal.

When he could make out individual trees in the line he accelerated, despite the Torino's rising temperature gauge. Trees flashed by now, taking individual form again only when he slowed to a stop. He shut the engine off, jumped out, and trotted through the last trees toward the white-hot sky beyond. He was scratched, bleeding, and panting in a moment. He pushed aside a low branch, forced his way between two last trees. His foot came down on thin air.

He grabbed for the branch and swung out, his body twisting in a sudden breeze. He kicked wildly in an attempt to find his footing, but that only increased the torque of his grip on the branch. The pressure on his wrists stopped him, and he hung in the air. A hundred meters below and two hundred meters farther on, the river, brown and serpentine, flowed. David swallowed once, his throat rough and dry, then swung his feet back toward the base of the tree. He tested his footing carefully before letting go of the branch. He heaved a sigh of relief, then sat down to study the view, his thirst forgotten.

At first it was as if nothing moved below him but the muscular current of the river, but soon he began to see and hear birds. It seemed every square meter of sky held one or more of them. He watched a large, white-headed bird drop, as if shot, toward the river. It struck the brown water, then rose and soared away, a silvery fish dangling from its talons. It flew straight up river. David watched until it was only a dark point, like a period. Something rustled like the wind sighing. Automatically David looked along the ridge to the sound. A deer stood among the trees, its antlers forked like their branches but covered in velvet as soft as the eye that studied David. The breeze shifted, and the deer, in the flicker of an eye, was gone. David rose and walked, slowly, back to the Torino.

The shadows ran long to the east by the time he found any sign of the Yarz. Two children, alerted by the sound of his engine, waited when he came around a long curve. They stood fearless and, except for a few rags and scraps of old stiff leather, naked. One held a ball in her hands. Spotting the car, they disappeared into the trees almost as neatly as the deer. Within a kilometer he came upon the first foundations, concrete barriers less than a meter high, the edges rounded and the sides scarred by the weather. He stopped the Torino farther down, at the first skin tent. He checked to see that the tail of his loose shirt covered the pistol butt, then pulled the keys from the ignition.

"Hello," he called timidly. When no one answered he approached nearer. He knelt beside the opening that served as a door and called again. Again there was no response. Carefully, he moved the flap that hung there and looked in.

After driving in a burning sun all day the interior of the tent proved very dark, and he saw nothing until his eyes adjusted. Then he made out a few dented and dull pots and pans near a ring of stones in the middle of the tent. Around these he saw the humped shadows that he finally understood were piled skins. As he stared the colors became clearer to him—ebony black, brilliant reddish brown, silky white. Several poles, coming together at the top of the tent, formed the framework on which the walls rested, and from these hung more skins, a fragment of a mirror and a rifle on a leather sling. Only the rifle appeared well cared for. The gray ashes of the fire looked cold, but he dared not enter to confirm his impression.

David pulled his head out and looked both up and down the road. He went back to the car and locked the doors. He began to walk, butterflies flitting in his empty belly.

Soon he could hear the distant voices of people shouting back and forth. After a few more paces he stopped. Ahead the road was bordered on one side by a cluster of tents and on the other high pens constructed of split logs. In the pens cattle, like those he'd seen on the road, milled, and far down the road he saw two horsemen moving away at a gallop. The sight of the horses, far more beautiful than all his reading and viewing had led him to believe possible, stunned him. A knot of small children ran through the dust the horses had kicked up. They paid David no mind as he watched their play. They took turns so that one of their number was always chasing the others. Their giggles and squeals filled the air. A sudden recollection of playing the same game caused him to remove his hand from the butt of the revolver.

"That's better, stranger. And keep it away."

Despite the startling closeness of the voice David turned slowly, careful to do as it instructed. An old man, taller by a head than David, stood only a couple of meters away. David tried to control his breathing. "You scared me," he said, his open hands before him.

The old man laughed. The laugh turned into a cough, and the old man was shaken by it. When it was finished, the old man pulled himself erect and peered down his nose at David. He looked him over, from the top of his head to his toes and back. He said, "I doubt that takes much doing."

David gathered himself and studied the old man in return, if not as thoroughly, then just as slowly. He was dressed in what even David could see were several different leathers, some of them fringed, some with the animal's fur still showing. His feet and ankles were wrapped in leather, and thongs ran around and around to keep it all in place. Atop his head he wore a stiff, thick hat, the brim shadowing his face. He held the barrel of a well-oiled shotgun, the butt resting between his feet. Full bandoliers crossed his chest. In his belt he carried a long, sheathed knife, and over his shoulder was slung a large bag, stuffed tight. "It might not take much," David said, "and you're plenty."

The old man laughed again, this time more quietly. "I's been listening to you coming for half the day. I thought maybe you gots lost up on top."

David shook his head. "No, not lost. Just slow."

"It's best to takes things that way, I figures."

David nodded.

The old man cocked his head toward the sun. "Angry, ain't it?"

David nodded again.

The old man hoisted his gun. "Well, comes along

then," he said and turned. David followed him back off the road and up the slope into a stand of trees. They wound through the timber on a worn path for several minutes, neither of them speaking. Several times David cast an anxious glance back over his shoulder. Once he hooked a toe under a tree root and nearly tripped, and once the old man let a sapling slap back when he wasn't looking. It caught him in the eye, and the eye began to tear immediately and profusely. His throat was gritty by the time they reached a clearing. The old man stepped to one side. He spoke as if he hadn't just negotiated a difficult hike up a steep slope. "Goes on in and cools yourself," he said, "I'll gets some spring water."

A cabin made of logs, its roof possessing almost no pitch, squatted in the clearing. Glassless windows were cut into the wall facing him, and a plank door fit snugly against its jamb. The eave of the roof was studded with horned and antlered skulls. A stone chimney reached over the roof on one side, and a wisp of smoke rose from it. Behind and off to the side stood a corral built of the same kind of logs, though smaller in diameter, as the house. In it two horses, a black one and a brown one, stood nose-to-tail in the shade of a large cottonwood tree. Their eyes were closed and their lower lips hung slack. Behind all rose the wooded hill. David walked to the corral and leaned against the top pole.

"Pilgrims and ponies," the old man said from behind him. David turned. "The first can't gets enough of the second, and the second don't wants no commerce with the first. Goes on in where it's cool. No percentage in standing in an angry sun. There'll be time for petting ponies later, if you got the yen, though that black one might just takes a hand for his troubles. In the meantimes, *mi casa, tu casa.*" The old man walked to the door of the cabin, the shotgun in one hand now, balanced by a tin pail of sloshing water in the other. He ducked and entered. David followed.

The old man had told the truth. The interior of the cabin was wonderfully cool after the heat of late afternoon. In the sudden darkness David could see only what fell in line with the light from the windows. To his left two chairs were pushed near a plank table. To his right, a line of horns studded the wall above a raised platform covered with skins.

"Sits down, pilgrim, at the table, and I'll dips up some water. Didn't even brings a water can with, did you?"

David shook his head, then did as he was told. From his seat he could see farther into the dark corners. In one place a few logs of the wall were gone, and someone had burrowed into the hill behind the cabin. There he could make out dark lumps hanging from pegs driven into the earthen sides. Strange scents, thick, spicy, and almost overwhelmingly sweet, came to his nostrils.

"Them's what's left of my winter meats." The old man placed a tin can, its gleam gone and specks of rust showing around the rim, in front of David. The can was full of clear water. The old man sat opposite with a can of his own. "Drink up," he said.

David obeyed. The water possessed a flavor, which surprised David. He found it pleasant, though, almost like the mint garnishes he'd sampled Inside.

"Best water along the Big River," the old man said. "Underground seep's back there in the hill, and I makes up a little cistern of rock to hold it. Just for drinking, you understands. Them others drinks the river water mostly. Knowings I do the shit and shinola you peoples drop in, I don'ts even let my ponies guzzles there. South of civilization, anyways."

They drank again. The old man sighed and wiped his mouth with the back of his hand. "They still taking fish out?"

"Sure," David said. "It's either that or beans or synthesized nuggets."

"Dead meat," the old man said. "Dead before they ever pulls it out of the water. White and lifeless. Just about right for Insiders, I figures." He held out his hand. "Name's Joe. Least, that's what I'm called in this locality. Some says Old Joe, but I prefers the other."

David took the hand and shook it. "David Jones."

"Likes in the locker?" Joe guffawed. "Well, maybe I can remembers that then." Joe moved his hand to rest on the haft of his knife. His voice went suddenly cold. "Before we goes further, stranger, what's it you comes for?"

"I came here to see if what I heard was true."

"Is it?" Joe's eyes fixed in a level stare on David's.

"I expected more, uh, excitement."

"Well stranger, the night, she ain't even properly commenced. Savvy?"

David felt the color drain from his face. He decided against a try for the pistol.

Joe laughed loud. "That's right, stranger, leaves your hogleg be." The laugh settled to a chuckle. "So you hears about us from a meat-runner, did you? They's the only ones thinks anything out this way's exciting. We do tries to keep them entertained. Good for business, don't you knows?"

David nodded. "Who else comes out this way?"

"Oh pilgrims, pilgrim," Joe said dryly.

"And what happens to these pilgrims?"

"Now that is a funny thing. Most times they comes looking for us, and when they sees us they don't much likes us, and they goes looking somewheres else. Except there ain't no place else to looks except where they comes from."

"Nowhere?"

"Nowhere, stranger. Why, I's traveled up and down this river, I horse-tailed many another. I been to the giant Rockies, and I gones to the swamps deep south. I been up on the spine of this continent, and I been in her belly, and I seen me some sights, but there's noplace else but here. And where you was first light."

"So what happens to the pilgrims?"

Joe smiled. "Breathe deep, stranger. Nothing happens to him here who don't gets to messing with things he shouldn't. There's always a few who thinks he can ride that horse or that that woman should be his. Ain't that kind, is you?"

David shook his head.

"Good," Joe said before continuing. "Mostly they takes that single look at us and says to themselves, 'Hell hoss, this ain't what I signed up for. These people, they's not living right. They's dirty and bloody, and they's not refined.' Most oftentimes, then, they goes out to make friends among the farmers."

"What happens then?"

Joe stretched back in his chair. "Inquisitive pilgrim, ain't you?" David didn't respond. He went on. "Well, farmers is funny people. They gets up regular times, I means early, and goes to bed regular times, I means late. And in-between times, they's working like I wouldn't works my horse. And do you know what they's working at, pilgrim?"

David shook his head.

Joe gave him a withering look, then exploded at the success of his trap. "They's farmers! They farm! They grows food." When his mirth settled, he went on. "Now along comes some slick Insider, looking for the way to better living. Now he's already passed on the blood, so he thinks that maybe a nice vegetable garden'll be the thing. So he polishes up the one or two Spanishes he knows and walks out into the hills."

David waited for a moment. "Then what?" he asked.

Joe shrugged. "Oh, I never said farmers couldn't be counted on for a meal or two in dire straits, but they's got no inclination to feeds an ignoramus food theys been raising up to brings the childrens through the winter. After a night's sleep, pilgrim's generally asked polite to moves on. Asides, farmers don't live where they do 'cause they's overly fonds of strangers. They prizes their privacy."

"What happens to them then?"

"Well stranger, they's given up their vehicles by that time—whole line of them starts not twenty miles off from here—because they can't gets them through or because they can't carries enough go-juice, either way. They's been turned out by farmers who know how stubborn goats and gardens is in giving up a ton of food per person eachest and everyest year, and they begins to wander back in, knowing that they can lives off the land."

"And then?"

"You writing a book?"

"In a way."

"Well, Book, even if they's lucky enough to be moving when something's ripe, they can't tells a chokecherry from sumac. If they don't poisons themselves, they's more than likely gets the runs, which's bad withouts a steady supply of good water or a diet that's looking up. They passed on blood once, and even if the farmers didn't disarms them, by the time they comes back around to it they's too weak and ignorant to knocks anything down. What would you do about then, stranger?"

David shrugged. "Fish?"

Joe nodded. "A true Insider, eating that pale stuff. Problem's the same, though. It take a certain talent to pulls them out of the water, which is where they wishes to stay, with your bare hands, even if you can finds the right water. No, then you'd probably gets sick to death."

"And then?"

Joe stared, incredulous. "Sick to death, Book! You dies!"

"Oh."

Joe stared, his good humor apparently gone. David tried not to squirm. Only a little light came through the windows now. The cans before them on the table stood empty. David could feel the springwater heavy in his belly. Finally, with one fluid motion, Joe sat up straight, the long knife in his hand, the polished blade gleaming in the last, indirect rays of the sun. David moved his hands to grip the edge of the table.

"You ever eats ham, Book? Off a real wild pig?"

David shook his head. "No." He swallowed.

Joe smiled. "Well, it's suppertime, Book."

22

The Burial of the Dead

The flames of the fire danced up into the pale night. They were repeated on the face of the river a few meters below the steep bank. Far to the west, over a sheltering knoll, other flames licked at the sky. David took another long drink from the can he'd carried with him from Joe's cabin. The salt of the meat lined his mouth, and, though it made him thirsty, he was glad not to have lost the taste. A horse tied a little way off whinnied and was answered by another farther downriver. The faces around the fire were intent upon the flames. Alvarez spoke.

"*Amigos, amigas*, this thing we see in the sky is nothing but the natural heating of the sun. In ages past the world slept under a blanket of ice, as is still the case, I have heard, far to the north and high upon the mountains. Only when the ice melted away as the sun became strong did the monsters with skins of snakes retreat into the shadows of time. Only then did the earth, our mother, bring forth her favorite children. Only when the sun, our father, became *masculino* did we rise upon our back legs and take *dominio* over our mother's lesser children. This is as I recollect the story given to me by my father who was taught it far to the south in the school of the sisters." Alvarez shrugged. "Is it not natural then? If such strength was good before, is not the more strength better? I say this: The growing of the sun's heat means many good things, for the father's power is also that of the children." Alvarez sat down in the circle.

Except for the crackle and sparks of the fire, all remained quiet and still for several minutes. Each face reflected flame, one profile dark, the other, except for the deep shadow under the brow, brightly lit. Even there, the light of the eye shone. Then a tall thin man dressed in a ragged black coat rose from the circle and strode to the fire. He waited as Joe rose to add a large log to the fire. After Joe returned to his place beside David, he whispered, loud enough to be heard by several people, "Holds on tight to your pants, Book. This man here be called Damnation, and there's plenty reason." Several seated nearby snickered.

Damnation began, his voice deep and far carrying. "I have heard," he rumbled, "all that has been said tonight by my friends and neighbors. I have often broken bread with all here"—his eyes rested on David for a moment but he did not change his expression nor the cadence of his speech—"and I aver that I share Jaweh's love for you all." He paused so that the weight of his love for humankind could be thoroughly felt by all in the circle. "But," he continued, "I have heard things that have made my heart sore with grief, for these things have been blasphemies in the ears of Jaweh, and blasphemies bring with them the brimstone fires of hell." He lifted one arm and pointed a long, gnarled finger to the flames in the west. "Yes, brothers and sisters, that is what burns brightly on the horizon, those flames that consume the earth and march toward us, bringing with them eternal pain for the wicked, the nonbeliever, and the infidel among us."

David's elbow was jostled. Joe offered him a pipe, its bowl glowing. "Care for a little red willow, Book?" he whispered hoarsely. David inhaled and fought back a cough. His eyes went dry and his nose numb.

Damnation slowly pivoted, the finger pointing at the faces of the circle in turn. "Yes, blasphemies," he said. "My brother Alvarez speaks to us of the sun's growing strength, but it is not the strength of the sun we seek. Are we no more than the ancient, heathen Egyptian? The Aztec who offered their god, the sun, the sacrifice of human blood upon a slab of rock? Perhaps a virgin to appease the anger of the sun? Is that what you would have us do when the sun begins to bake us within our very skins?"

David tried to give the pipe back to Joe, but he whispered, "No, pass it rounds." David offered it to the woman on his right. She took it, her wide smile flickering in the firelight.

Damnation joined his hands behind his back, dropped his head and paced before the fire. He stopped suddenly and looked up. "No, it is much, much too late for that already. Spilling blood will availeth us naught, for soon blood will boil in the brains of the unfaithful, brains will boil in the skull, and the eye that looks upon evil without flinching will burst in the rapturous fever of the purification."

David felt the jostle again. The pipe, a coal deep in the bowl, had completed the circle impossibly fast. He smoked a moment, then passed it on.

Damnation stood very close to the fire, his hands held almost in it. "No, we seek the strength not of the pagan sun but of Jaweh. There cometh the fire of purification, brothers and sisters, of Jaweh's holy cleansing." He reached out to them suddenly. "And some say 'this is a natural thing that we need not fear.' I say to you, woe to the man or woman who cannot recognize the hand Jaweh moving forth from Heaven to punish. Woe to those whose faith is so little, for if Jaweh governeth the sparrows in the trees and numbereth the hairs on your head, can you believe He blinks at the changing sun? Believe that He sees not and be damned, brothers and sisters. Believe in the cleansing fire and be saved!" Damnation dropped his head in a bow.

The silence held for a moment, then Joe began a slow clapping. One by one the others joined in. The tempo quickened until the circle nearly thundered. Damnation looked up, a smile on his lips and the fire gone from his eye. He nodded all around the circle, placed his hands in front of him as if in prayer and bowed again. Now added to the roar of applause were hoots and whistles and shouts of "Bravo!" Damnation bowed once more, danced a few steps, bowed again, and sat down.

Joe poked his elbow into David's ribs. "Didn't I's say he's something? Didn't I!"

David nodded, his applause as vigorous as anyone's.

Joe nudged him again. "I'll bets you that part about the Aztecs got your hairs standing on single foots. And whats 'bout that part with the busting eye? Yes, I's say, that about the busting eye was gooder even than the cleaning and putrefying." Joe stuck the stem of the pipe between his teeth. "Author!" he yelled from around it, "Author!"

The fire had burned down to a miniature of its former self. Only rarely did anyone rise to feed it, and then with just a small stick or two. The circle had been lost as some people had left, and others now lounging, their full lengths stretched at odd angles to the fire on the river bank. David still sat, his legs folded beneath him, scanning the stars high in the night sky. For some time he had been listening to a distant drum, the tempo slow and deliberate, and behind it a melancholy choir of voices. He studied a particular spot in the night sky, intrigued by something in the formation of a half dozen stars.

"Getting ready for a long ride, Book?"

Joe lay on his back, the brim of his hat pushed down over his eyes.

"Why do you ask?"

Joe made a snuffling noise and rolled over on his side. David studied the stars again. With sudden clarity he saw what it was he looked at. "Pegasus?" he asked.

Joe mumbled. "Don't knows no Greek, leastwise no more I's don't."

"But it's a horse?"

Joe answered with a ragged snore. The constellation dissolved. David still saw the stars, but he could no longer discern a form. Joe snored away. David's resolution disappeared with the vision of the horse. As far as he knew Pegasus wasn't even a constellation, or, if it was, whether it was visible in the northern tetraspheres. He was no longer sure even that Joe had spoken.

The drum and the voices became louder, as if they were bearing down directly on the fire. David was staring at Joe when he opened a single eye. "Funeral," he said. "They'll comes through in a few minutes so we can pays our respects."

"Oh." David sat straighter.

Joe began a snore, caught it in the middle, sputtered unintelligibly, and climbed into a sitting position. He shook his head to clear it. "Little Gibson boy. Out swimming and the current tooks him. They's taking him up to the hills where his spirit can rests easy aways from water."

"Uh."

"Drowned ones usually prefers the dry ground up high someplace. Mostly folks goes to join the stars. Pretty sight to watch them goes. They burns on a pyre, and they rises with the sparks. Real pretty on a windy night."

"I thought maybe I was hearing things."

Joe gave him a long appraising look. "You may be seeing some things before this night's over."

The drums and the dirge moved in from out of the dark. Most of the others began to rise from their beds upon the bank. David thought he saw a shadow pass before the fire.

Joe addressed a spot in the dark. "Speaks up, Fletcher," he said. "Tells what's on your mind."

David remained very quiet, stilled by the presence he could not define. Perhaps he heard breathing close by. Then two eyes appeared, as if suddenly opened, the whites very clear and rimmed in red, in the spot Joe had spoken to.

"I's been listening to this goings-on all night. Ain't nobody takings things serious."

Joe did not look into the eyes. "Oh, they's taking it serious, except for the show people, of course. Alvarez was trying hard. So was whosits—the paranoiac."

The voice fairly hissed. "Old Joe, you tells me you believes it's an Insider plot. A conspiracy?" The voice ran long and wet on the last word.

Joe shook his head side to side in the rhythm of the approaching drums. "No, I's tells you nothing of the kind. I tells you, though, that on pure aesthetics, I likes the burn theory."

The woman began to take form in David's eyes. He could make out the lines of her jaw and shoulder, could see white teeth and the red of her mouth when she spoke.

"They's burning the old cities and the smoke's coloring the sun?" She turned sharply. "It's so?" she hissed.

David sat mesmerized. Her hair was pulled back very tight over her skull, and she was the color of dark smoke. It looked to be her own skin and not clothing. He wondered if it was body paint.

Joe sat with his hands in his lap. "Fletcher, appears

you already knows Book. Book, this here's Fletcher. She's little use for civilizations."

The eyes did not blink. "I don't knows him nor cares to, but I knows he knows if they's burning the cities down."

Joe kept his eyes on his hands, "Answer her, Book."

David found his tongue. "They're not burning the old cities. I haven't seen, but I truly believe they're not."

"Old Joe, you says you likes that theory."

"On aesthetics alone. Explains the change in the look of the sun as well as the flames on the horizon. The old cities offer them nothing, at least nothing they can perceive. I did not say that I accepted the theory."

Fletcher hissed, "Speaks your fancy speech to me, Old Joe? Is that what come of hanging around a Book?"

Joe spoke quietly. "What's gots you heated up, Fletcher? Why's you wound so tight tonight?"

Fletcher straightened and stared down at Joe. "I's been to the tops of the hills. I's been visioning."

"And what sees you in your visions, Fletcher?"

Her eyes rolled wildy in their sockets, and her head rolled crazily upon her neck. With great effort Fletcher stilled the motion, her profile now to David against the fire. He saw highlights of red in the hair that hung in a thick braid down the smoke-colored back. A sheen of spittle shone on her chin. Her mouth work stiffly, as if her jaw had been fused. The lips pulled back from white teeth.

"Old Joe, I sees the earth rising to joins the stars, and there ain't no one left to leads a fancy funeral." With that she whipped her spine and head into a line that her arm extended. The funeral procession stood two meters away, as if she'd produced it with a snap of her fingers.

The dread David had felt all the time Fletcher had spoken evaporated and a sense of innocent wonder rained down to fill its place. Before him stood a bull, immense in shadow but with firelight sparkling off its spread of horns. On the other side of the fire a horse tossed its long mane and cantered in place. Beyond stood the drummer and the chorus of singers. Between the bull and the horse and quite near the fire stood a pale, naked boy of perhaps ten years. Before him he held a leather sack by its open mouth. Some of the people from around the fire roused

themselves to approach, one at a time. Each dropped a
trinket into the sack; some spoke to the boy. Others sat
quietly and stared.

When it was Joe's turn, he took a shotgun shell from a
bandolier. He used a small knife from his pouch to cut
away one end. He poured the shot onto the ground and
held the half-empty casing before the boy's face. A smile
appeared among the boy's gray features. "Pour the powder in a line, then strike a spark to it," Joe said. He
crimped the open end of the shell and dropped it into the
sack.

David felt the beat of the drum in his blood. He knelt
before the boy, then realized he had nothing to give.

"Gives him a page of your book, Book," Joe said softly.

David pulled his ancient notebook from his hip pocket. He opened it, tore out a blue-ink–covered yellowed
sheet at random, lay it on his flat palm and offered it to
the boy.

The boy's smile widened. He picked the page off
David's palm and held it to the fire, turned it over and
dropped it, fluttering, into the sack. The boy brought his
empty hand down on David's palm with a cold, stinging
slap.

The dirge rose in volume. The singers fell in behind
the bull, the horse, and the boy. They took a single
dancing step. A gust of hot wind caught the fire and
stretched the flames to one side. The singing fell off. The
drumbeat faltered, then stopped. Two men, one holding
the horns of a bull, the other a mask with long hair
trailing from it, stood in the line. A shadow of confusion
passed over the boy's eyes, and then Fletcher knelt before
him.

Several people started forward, but Fletcher hissed and
swept a hand around her. Those who had advanced now
retreated. "I's yet to gives him my present," Fletcher said
to the circle. After one last, menacing look to them she
turned to the boy. He gazed into her eyes, his gray face
slack. Gently, Fletcher placed a hand behind the boy's
head and one upon his back. Tenderly, she drew him
close, turning his face to her as she did so. She placed
her open mouth upon his and closed her eyes. The boy's
eyelids fluttered, then closed. After a long moment his

hand came to rest on Fletcher's neck beneath the trailing braid.

She pulled back, and the boy opened his eyes and smiled. The drum began again. The bull and horse made themselves whole, and the procession started out into the dark. A shadow passed before the flames of the fire and was gone.

The sun rose quietly over the edge of the world, sending long shadows out across the river and the road that Joe and David walked. David stopped and turned to Joe, as if prepared to speak. Instead, he only shrugged.

"Maybe you dreamed it all," Joe said.

"No, the page is missing. I know what was on it."

"Maybe some sneak stole it during the night."

"Sure." They resumed their walk.

They arrived at the Torino. David unlocked and opened the door, then leaned against a fender. Joe placed the butt of the shotgun between his feet and rested his weight against the barrel.

"You're an educated man. You didn't grow up out here."

"Boston. Government anthropologist." Joe paused. "I was educated here, though." He considered something. "You raised here, maybe you end up like Fletcher."

David nodded. "I thought so. Why?"

Joe tugged at his beard, twisted his chin to one side and arched an eyebrow. "Long story. Mostly, we had to sink or swim. I'm still swimming."

"You sorry?"

Joe shook his head. "Just that it's ending too soon." He motioned with his head behind him to the rising sun. "Course, I should of been dead a thousand times before now."

Birds, early risers, squawked, hooted, and peeped in the trees. The curent made a scraping noise against the sand of the bank. Down at the Yarz a cow bawled.

"You never did have a chance to play with the ponies."

David persisted. "Maybe it was the red willow?"

Joe shrugged. "Didn't hurt. Not everyone sees it, not even some last night. You notice how not everybody saw?"

David nodded.

"It takes a predisposition to see it. Some people goes through long lives and never stumble over a miracle. Others expect one for breakfast and see it in the rising sun." He shook his head. "Course, that's a miracle I wants not to dwell on overlong." He looked into David's eyes.

Joe went on. "Something's died, and no one gives it attention, it stinks. Stink's from rot. Rot's just another way of burning. Fast or slow don't make no difference."

David studied the old man.

"You know, you could wait for it here."

"No, I've got—there's somebody waiting for me."

He got into the car and started the engine. He turned the Torino around and waved. Joe ran over and stuck his head in the window.

"Hey," he said, "you ever get that book written, file it with the Ministry of State. Tell 'em it's my report." He hooted. "They's most probably not expecting it."

He patted the young man's shoulder and backed away from the car. David saw him in the rearview mirror, standing in the middle of the broken road, until he followed a curve around some trees.

It was late afternoon again, and he was perhaps twenty kilometers from the skirts when he found her. First, he took her to be a bundle discarded on the shoulder of the road. He pulled over and stopped. He was close enough then to recognize a human form. He got out of the Torino and approached. She sat with her head down and covered with a blanket against the sun. He watched for breathing. He saw none. He knelt. "Hello," he said. He touched the blanketed shoulder and felt no life. As gently as he could, he reached into the blanket and pulled the face up by the hair on the back of her head. When the head's center of gravity shifted, he cupped the back of it in his hand. Through the blisters and the deep, crusted-over lacerations he saw that she was no more than sixteen. He was examining an ear that appeared to have been gnawed when the eyes fluttered open, a blister on one lid breaking. David jumped at the movement but kept her head in the cradle of his hand. The liquid from the blister trickled away down her temple like a tear or sweat. Her eyes moved randomly until they fixed on his face. In a cracked whisper she asked, "Blue Baby?"

Her eyes rolled back up into her skull and she took three panting breaths. Her chest convulsed and she vomited a thin stream of water. David lay her down and turned her head to clear her mouth. The last of the vomit was tinged with red. She made a rattling sound deep in her chest. He tried to shade her with the shadow of his body. He found no pulse, but he sat with her for an hour, looking without luck for a sign of the trail she'd made across the open country.

Finally, using the lug wrench as a pick and a hubcap as a shovel, he dug a shallow grave in the light of the flaring sun. Almost as an afterthought he placed his earring in her hand. He wrapped the blanket tightly around her and lay her in the grave. He covered her and left the hubcap as a marker.

He drove into the skirts. Lu was there when he arrived, asleep in his bed.

23

Deus Ex Machina

David turned left, powered down the Alley, hit fourth, settled back, and relaxed. It was good to be up and on the move early in the morning. The overcast to the east flickered yellow and red. He tried not to think about all that the colors had come to mean for him.

It wasn't any use. David was sure he knew everything he needed to know about transmatation. Two of his university roommates had majored in physics with specializations in transmatation technology, and another had paid for his tuition working as an inter-City commerce courier. Through them he met others with the same interest. Transmatation was the most spectacular of the technologies that promised a new age, a phoenix civilization rising from the ashes of the pre-Fall, pre–Third World wars world. The brightest, most adventuresome students were caught up in it with the fervor of revolutionaries. David had never really trusted their anachronistic romanticism, and he'd certainly never wanted to be disassembled into elemental bits till he was a chain kilometers long traveling at the speed of light. To travel and see the world was all his roommates had dreamed of. Nights at school, David dreamed of home.

And, for a while after they'd all graduated, they sometimes called him to show off some new scar they wore like a badge—a ragged hairline or a creased skull from premature transmatation, separated cartilage or skin damage from sunspot interference, a missing toe from incomplete reception. They insisted on using the screen, despite the extra cost, so that David could be suitably impressed. They'd haul up their skirts, drop their trou-

sers or place a calloused four-toed foot a half-meter from
his nose. Sunspot interference. The horror stories about
so-and-so, one colleague or another, who looked perfectly
fine on reception, except she couldn't hear, or couldn't
think beyond some primary-level spelling or addition. Or
the transmatter could remember pages of the most difficult text university had ever presented him, maybe the
entirety of Frost's pomes, replete with archaic rural rhythms
and accents, but not his own name. Or maybe the crani-
um was as empty as a child's rattle, and she'd stand for
thirty seconds in the transmatation booth before collapsing.

Oh, these transmatters saw themselves as modern
buccaneers. They would talk to him for hours of the latest
technical advances, how it was getting so safe that soon
even little children would be transmatted, although they
never said why little children should be. Then the stories
started to catch up with them, and one by one his friends
became episodes in the legend. Finally, the calls stopped
coming, the fear too powerful to hide, too great to share.
For his part, David had systematically avoided the media
reports of transmatter trauma and death. Yes, David knew
all he needed to know about transmatation—he knew the
odds.

He pulled the Torino around the curl that led off the
Alley and onto the Kennedy Expressway. Below him was
the cemetery, beyond it the Government Complex with its
Consolidated School, Public Hospital, and Cop Shop.
The car climbed smoothly, and happiness about McGee's
work chased away, briefly, David's anxiety. At the top he
slowed, then stopped the car, its bumper almost touching
the barrier. He got out, stretched, grabbed his bag from
the backseat and lugged it to the meter. He dropped coins
into the slot until the small screen read "36 hours." The
view of Inside caught his eye. He placed both palms
against the meter-high pressed plastic curb and leaned
forward.

Only enough of the Expressway remained opposite to
provide a platform and twin rails for the el which now
made its way toward him. Where the road had been,
glastic-sided buildings gleamed, despite the overcast. To
the south the channeled river ran yellow, and on its near
bank he could see white adobe walls, the red-and-green
tiled roofs of expensive, modular efficiency spaces. David's

gaze followed the river out past the fishery till it disappeared into the haze of the horizon. He looked into his upturned palms and fought the urge to bury his face in them.

He grabbed his bag and walked Inside, nodding to the Monitor screen as he passed. He walked across the platform as the el glided to a halt. He stepped through the automatic doors onto the deep carpet of the cell floor. As far as he could see in either direction the el was deserted. The media gave the local news over the screen at one end of the cell, and the screen opposite illustrated a long list of prohibited activities with animated cartoons. The media caster made no mention of the sun. David marveled at the quiet of the cell, its sparkling cleanness. General media interrupted with an update of the day's top story. The Rescue Effort had been announced that morning.

David's heart rate jumped, and he reached a sweaty hand into his bag for a cigarette. Out of the corner of his eye he noticed the Law making her way through the cells toward his. He promised himself to keep in mind how it was Inside. He brought his hand out empty. The Law entered, nodded, and made her way into the next cell. David stared out the small window opposite him, watching the green tops of trees and gleaming sides of buildings fly past. Then he saw it. Written in a small, neat hand, despite the spray paint, on the otherwise unblemished wall of the cell were the words The End is Near.

David walked down the mall toward the Holiday Inn. His bag made him self-conscious. He concentrated on the screen at the corner, which alternated the time, the temperature, and the names of the walks intersecting there. At nine o'clock, an hour before the normal workday began, the mall was already filled with people dressed in business coveralls. David paused to stare through the glastic walls of the trout-pond-on-the-mall. The endlessly recycling water bubbled and boiled, but the fish lay indolently at the bottom of the huge tank. It was famous the world over as a stopping place during the migration of certain species of ducks, and it had been widely copied by other New Cities. David had seen the media reports of the beautiful, multicolored birds, though he'd never been Inside during the right season to see them in person.

He picked up his bag and walked the last block. He pushed through the revolving door into the lobby and stopped, taken aback by the opulence of the hotel. The carpet beneath his sandals was thick. The whole of the wide, deep lobby was tastefully lit. Thickly upholstered chairs and lounges were scattered about. David recognized the canvases of several well-known artists. The desk was fifteen meters long and apparently of real wood.

"I'll take that for you, sir." David let the bag go into the hand of the bellhop and followed him toward the desk. Without his bag and with his eye on the small man's neatly creased red-and-green uniform, David felt suddenly shabby. The worn denim that felt so soft, the embroidered cotton shirt that seemed so showy in the suburbs, now bound and chafed.

The clerk looked up smiling. He touched the tip of his little finger to the end of a painted eyebrow.

"You have a reservation for me, I think." David handed over his Card.

The clerk inserted it into a slot and glanced at a tiny screen. "Oh yes, sir! Of course!" He turned to the hop. "Meshaak, take Mr. Jones's luggage to suite ten o one. I'll escort Mr. Jones there myself directly." He touched the eyebrow again. "We're pleased to have you, sir. My name is Willow. If there's anything you need just ask for me."

"There is one thing." David caught Meshaak's attention and awkwardly retrieved a small package from his bag. Meshaak smiled tolerantly, then hoisted the bag and, after a quick nod from David, left for ten o one.

"I need to send this," David said and handed it to Willow. He was embarrassed by the clumsy wrapping job.

Willow examined the address. "Parcel post?"

"No, first-class. I want it to get there today."

"Yes, sir. I'll put it in the pouch myself." Willow hurriedly recopied the address on a brown envelope, dropped the package in and sealed it. "Now sir, the Red Cross Orientation will be conducted in the King Room, just down that corridor there, sir." He handed David his Card and leaned over the desk to whisper conspiratorily. "We just heard it on the media this morning. It *is* the Rescue Effort, isn't it, Mr. Jones?" Willow's eyes begged. David nodded. Willow whisked through an invisible gate in the desk. "Oh, I knew it! I dreamed it last night, in

fact. Mr. Jones, I'd like to congratulate you." He extended
a green hand.

David shook it.

David capped the bottle of tequila, tossed off his shot,
and rose to answer the door. He took a deep breath,
gathered himself together, and opened it. He got only a
quick glimpse of the big man's face as he shambled past
him into the room. The man stopped, dropped a black
bag on the coffee table next to the bottle, and turned.
"Hey," he said.

"Hello," David said and shook the hand he offered.

The man consulted a slip of paper. "Jones?"

David nodded.

"Name's Mike." Again they shook. David felt like a
child taking the paw of a good-humored bear.

"Call me David. You're with the Rescue Effort, right?"

"Hell man, I am the Rescue Effort. Do you mind?" He
indicated the bottle.

"Help yourself."

Mike pulled the cork with his teeth and spat it out. It
bounced twice on the table. He took a long pull, then set
the bottle down hard. "Oh-h," he said, "that's the good
stuff." His eyes took a moment to focus. "Yeah, I'm here
for your medical." He opened the black bag and pulled
out a stethoscope. It appeared terribly fragile in his
grip.

"No one said anything about a medical."

Mike studied the stethoscope as if it were an artifact
from an alien culture. Finally, he gingerly placed the ends
in his ears. "Nobody goes without a medical. Policy." He
examined the silver disk that hung upon his chest.

"Are you a doctor?" David asked, very suddenly nervous.

"I can't hear you. I've got these thingamajigs in my
ears." He held the disk to his own wrist. "Seems to be in
working order," he mumbled. "Hike up your shirt."

The disk was, like every other one David could remember, ice. Mike listened to him in several places front
and back, sighed, and removed the stethoscope.

"Congratulations," he said. "You're alive."

David's anxiety dropped by half. "Good to know."

Mike dropped the stethoscope onto the table and

pulled out a slim flashlight. He got a thumb on David's right eyelid and yanked it up.

"Ouch!"

"Hold still. Look up. Look down. Left. Right. Now the other."

David did his best not to duck at the sight of the thumb descending to his left eye.

"What'd you say before? I didn't hear you?"

"I asked if you were a doctor."

"Look around. You know the drill." Mike paused to study the eye, then shut off the light. He set the flashlight beside the bag. "Mind if I have another?" he asked.

"Not at all."

Mike again upended the bottle. Air gurgled and bubbled up through the tequila. He slammed the bottle down and shuddered. "Man that's good!" He addressed David. "I don't drink much anymore, but I've been busting my hump on the job, like a dog, you know. Then, I just finish up a piece of work, and my friend—I've got this friend, see—and my friend says, 'Let's take a little trip,' and I say, 'Gee, all right.' Turns out she's got a friend—another friend, one she hasn't seen in a long time—and I'm supposed to do another piece of work while she has this reunion, see?"

"I guess."

Mike pulled a complicated-looking electronic gadget out of the bag. He stared at it. "Yeah, I'm a doctor. Well, I've got the degree, see, but you know the damned service."

David shook his head.

Mike didn't take his eyes from the gadget. "Well, first I'm a doctor. Psychiatrist, anyway, but you've got be a doctor first, you know, to be that. Then I'm this, then that, now I'm a doctor again." He very deliberately flipped a switch. Nothing happened. He grimaced and selected another. There was whirring noise and several zeros appeared on a little screen. "It's just the damned service." He looked to David. "I'll need a little blood."

"What for?"

"Usual."

"What's the usual?"

"Drugs."

"Really?"

"Here, I'll show you." He pulled a pointed instrument

the shape and length of a writer out of the bag and jabbed
at his finger. "Ouch is right!" he said and grimaced. He
massaged the finger until he had a drop of blood balanced there. He rummaged in the bag with his free hand
till he found a tiny envelope. He tore the top off with his
teeth, extracted a piece of filmy material, and wiped it
over the blood. He fed the material into a port in the
machine, then hit a switch. The machine whirred again,
and he studied the numerals on the display. "Hell," he
said. "Way out of whack. It shows intake well above what
I drank." He tossed the gadget back into the bag.

He threw the rest of the paraphernalia into the bag
after it and snapped it shut. He gestured toward the
bottle. "Mind if I have one for the road?"

"Not at all."

"You sure?"

"I've got another."

"Okay."

Compared to the first two drinks, this one was a mere
nip. Mike brought the bottle down and looked at David
through a cocked eye. "Jones, right?"

David nodded.

"I told my friend it was probably a mistake. How
many Joneses are there?"

"Got me."

"Well, I can tell you." Mike thought a minute. "No, I
can't. I forgot. But I looked it up. There's a bunch of
Joneses in world." He stuck out his hand. "Hey," he said,
"got more of these to do. Good luck, buddy."

They shook hands a third time. "Thanks," David said.

"¿Qué pasa, hombre?" David let the knob slip from
his hand and stared at the woman standing there, legs
spread, filling the door. "I thought it must be you."

"Bullshit. You thought I was dead."

"Sometimes," he admitted.

David brushed LaMer's extended hand away, grabbed
her in a bear hug, and lifted her from the floor. He set her
down and gazed at her. Beneath her pompadour, the
hairline showed a network of tiny scars. A red eyepatch
of iridescent material covered her left eye. The right eye
was sky blue, and a single, slim stripe of the same color
ran down her forehead and nose, over her chin, down

into the open collar of her loose blouse. He stepped back to look at her. A carved, glastic rod exited the pantleg where her right foot should have been.

"You look great, roomie, what's left of you," he said and picked her up again. The ribs under his spread fingers, her breasts against his chest felt real enough. "God, it's great to find someone, something," he said into her ear. He sighed and put her down, stepped back. Her arms fell slowly from around his neck.

David and LaMer stood smiling. Then, she feinted with her left and punched him hard on the shoulder with her right. He stumbled back out of the doorway. LaMer strode past him, looking around as she did. "About time you invited me in. Where the fuck were you raised, the frigging suburbs? You don't have the manners Allah gave a pig." She walked around the sitting room, with only a negligible limp, and then into the bedroom, shouting insults, from the tone of her banter, in, from what David could make out, three languages other than English. David stood by the door, stupidly grinning. LaMer came back to the bedroom door, leaned a shoulder against the frame, placed a hand on one jutting hip.

"It's good to see you, trash."

David walked over to stand close to her. The muscles in his cheeks ached from smiling. "You're here," he said, "for the orientation."

LaMer reached slowly out to him, caught David's earlobe between her thumb and forefinger and began to massage it. "Now why did everyone in school say you were so stupid?" And then, "My confrere will explain it all to the three technical types and the child prodigy downstairs, as well as their assorted bloody dependents." She let her hand slip to the back of David's neck. "Me, I've done my bloody part, and I'm in bloody need of a frigging break." She brought his head to her and kissed him. Her tongue made a slow electric curl down toward the root of his soul. "Baby," she said, "I *am* your orientation."

"Bloody damn!" LaMer exhaled. "This is too good to be legal." She handed the bottle over to David.

"It's not." He took the bottle and pulled on it, sank deeper into the pillows propped behind him. "I got it from a guy who got it Out There from some primitive store.''

''No shit?'' LaMer settled closer against David. ''Well, I've had tequila before, sometimes I'd like to forget. Always synthesized, you know.'' She rubbed the inside of his thigh absently. ''You know, I told them they were making a bloody fucking big mistake not sending a couple primitives.'' David watched LaMer's profile. It and her voice became somber. ''Most of the transmatters thought so.''

''Why do you say that, that primitives ought to go?''

''For the tequila.''

''No, seriously.''

''I'm not sure. It's hard to explain.'' She took the bottle out of his hand and tipped it up. She swallowed twice, held the bottle in her lap. ''Your average person is a little too goddamn perfect. It's like they gave up something for that perfection, though, traded something. I don't know what it is, but it's like they all were received at the end of transmatation without something they started with. Like a foot''—she nodded in the direction of her own missing foot—''but something in the spirit.'' She looked down, embarrassed. ''I guess that's your specialty, though.''

''What'd they say? When you told them?''

She shrugged. ''Policy's not made by technicians. Further-fucking-more you don't kidnap people.''

''They weren't sympathetic to the idea at all?''

''Furthest thing from it. It scared them to death.''

''Scared them?''

LaMer considered before responding. ''People who've planned and perpetuated a perfect society, as they see it, are nervous about other people, people who survive outside that society. It's all balled up in their minds. They'd never admit it, never say it outright, but to them everyone who's not Inside is a Third World Warrior. Or some people, deep down, blame the primitives for the Third World wars, the Fall, everything that went with them. And, if not that, then at least they failed to do their part in building the new order.''

''That was a long time ago. That's all over. The Fall wasn't something people Out There caused. It was something that happened to them. The wars have been over since before I can really remember. I don't see any armies massing in the skirts to attack the New Cities, anyway."

"Well, people need someone to blame. For the wars, for the Fall, and for why their perfect lives leave them so dissatisfied."

"That's crazy."

"That's my point. You're thinking rationally about other people thinking rationally. That's just not the way it really works. You know that. One of the damnest and most dangerous things is when people start to believe they're rational."

The quiet was interrupted only by the hum of the air-conditioning. The bottle passed back and forth. David thought about what he'd been taught in school. The worldwide, spontaneous revolution had quickly degenerated into widely separated, independent armies roaming a wasteland, battling each other into extinction. At least, that was the theory and the hope expressed by his teachers. The lessons had painted the revolutionaries, David suddenly realized, as both monsters and clowns.

LaMer's speech was slurred. "Want to see my leg walk itself?"

"What?" David giggled. "Sure."

"You always believed anything, you, you—yuppie."

"That's an extinct bird, like a dodo." David thought very hard. "You mean guppy."

"Do I?"

David took another pull. It took a moment for him to find his voice again. "Boy, this will, like my grandfather said, put lead in your pencil."

"Your grandfather? You remember him?" She took the bottle back.

"I remember him saying that. That's about all."

"What's it mean?"

"I don't know for sure. He said it just once."

LaMer shook her head. David took the bottle from her. After a while, LaMer asked, "Lead in your what? Why would you want lead in it?"

David choked on the tequila, started to cough. Some of the liquor came up through his nose, burning. LaMer pulled him away from the pillows and began to pound his back. "Goddamn it, stop!" he shouted. "I'm all right." He cleared his throat. "It's like, you know, a pencil?" He had

to concentrate very hard to find words. "About so long?"
He held his hands twenty centimeters apart.

"Yeah, yeah. Like to write on paper with."

David found himself nodding furiously. He stopped.
"Well, the lead's what makes it write." LaMer's single eye
stared. "Finish this," he said, handing her the bottle.

Eerie early morning light filtered through the window.
LaMer drained the bottle, tossed it circling into the air,
caught it by the neck, and, in one smooth motion, threw
it across the room into a small wastebasket.

"There's still no lead in a pencil. What makes it write
is goddamn ink. Or grease, I forget which."

"It doesn't matter anymore," he said and placed a
hand between her thighs. He leaned over to kiss that one,
pale blue, wide-open eye.

"I can explain the technical end of it to you, but you
don't want to hear it and I don't really want to repeat it."
LaMer waved the waiter away and looked down at her
fish.

David swallowed his last mouthful of soy toast. "But I
know as well as anybody you stop on the mall that
sunspots cause big problems, and if what's going on up
there isn't a lot like sunspots, except a thousand times as
big, I'll eat your peg leg."

"Taste better than this." She put her fork down. She
touched a napkin to her mouth and leaned back. "That's
what I'm trying to explain. We've insulated the chain,
that's the breakthrough. Here's what will happen: the
sensor will let us pick you up wherever you are, whenever
your number comes up. We'll bring you through Home
Base. As you're going through we'll add the insulating
layer and tack on your three hundred kilos of baggage and
survival gear, put the whole sparkling mess into the
Puzzle Box. Then we shoot you out into the great beyond.
Think about yourself as a bunch of peas in a peashooter.
You only have to worry about solar activity while you're
still in the solar system, and the insulation will hold,
theoretically, that long. You won't be worrying about
anything during transmat, anyway."

The waiter filled both cups with coffee, left a bill in a
glastic tray on the table, and departed silently.

"I've never gone long distance before."

"This is long, long distance. Nobody's gone this far."

"I've only transmatted four times in my life," David persisted. "And one time it made me so sick I vomited in the washroom of a hotel even classier than this one." The memory called Tella's face up before his mind's eye. He shook his head to clear his vision.

"Will I feel, know anything?" he asked finally.

"Nothing. Not much, anyway. The usual numbness when we lock on, of course. A thrilling sensation when we start to pick you up. That should be nice, with the power we're using—ought to be orgasmic. Then nothing during transmat. More or less."

"What do you mean, 'more or less'?"

LaMer tapped her spoon on the rim of her cup, then absently and expertly twirled it in her fingers like a miniature baton. "I've been doing this as long as anybody—the pioneers are pretty much gone now, what with this accident and that—and on particularly long transmats—stacked up due to receiver malfunction, that sort of thing—I've felt—well, not really *felt*." She paused to organize her thoughts. "When I lost my leg, I was up there nearly an hour in real time. In situations like that, you just keep circling till they latch on to you. When they brought me in, I knew that time had passed. I shouldn't have known that, you see. Some of the medical staff thought I was crazy, but similar experiences have been recorded."

"And you felt, or almost felt something?"

"I hope everything was satisfactory?" David jumped and LaMer's spoon tumbled from her hand. Cat-quick, she caught it centimeters from the carpet. Willow smiled above them, green hands folded in front of his flat stomach. David concentrated on slowing his heart.

"Except for the bloody help," LaMer said.

"Oh," Willow gasped. He was pleased even by an insult from LaMer, a reminder of the legendary status of transmatters. David recalled how the restaurant chatter had quieted abruptly when they had entered.

Willow stared dreamily into LaMer's eye. "Ms. LaMer, the next session is just about to begin. Do you require anything further?"

"Mr. Jones and I will not be attending the session with the others." LaMer impressed her Card upon the check. "Mr. Jones's status is such that he requires individual orientation. And yes," she said, handing the check to Willow with two fingers, as if it was unclean, "we require a bottle of champagne be sent to Mr. Jones's suite."

Willow glowed brighter. "Of course, of course. Right away! Immediately!"

He scooped up the empty tray and scurried off.

LaMer turned to David. "Silly little peckers, aren't they?"

All heads swiveled as they rose to leave.

LaMer sat on the bed struggling with a tall boot. David set the ice bucket with the champagne on the nightstand and straddled her leg to tug the boot off for her. He held it for a moment, surprised by the feel. "Real leather?"

LaMer nodded. "So's this," she said, fingering her vest. "Cost a fortune." She started to work on the prosthesis's fasteners. "Had to go to bloody Havanna for them, the end of the earth as far as I'm concerned." She shot David a tired smile, lifted off the leg and dropped it across the boot. She slumped forward. "End of the frigging earth," she repeated, shaking her head.

David sat on the bed behind her, began to work at the bunched muscles in her shoulders. She sighed.

"Tell me about the feeling."

"Maybe I'm too old for this business." LaMer turned to kiss him. "Maybe I am going a little happy in the head. I don't know." She reached for the champagne bottle. "Lately I've, I guess, experienced the transmatation. Some of the sisters and brothers have told me the same. I'm aware, in a way. I mean, there's awareness but it's not really me who's aware." The champagne cork flew across the room. She drank from the bottle. "Terrible shit." She gave it to David and went on. "There's a sort of sensory input, but the senses aren't discrete, so there's no vision, per se, or hearing, but a single reception of all the senses, an integrated processor for them all." Her voice had gone dreamy. David leaned on an elbow, watching and listening. "But the consciousness that's aware doesn't feel like me. It's more diffused than that." She turned to him abruptly. "That's all, except that the phenomenon becomes more pronounced with time in the particular transmat and the transmatter becomes more aware with experience. Do you understand what I'm saying?"

"I think so," David said slowly. "That a career of intermittent transmats on a global scale can only suggest the consciousness that might evolve."

"And?"

"And rather than transmatting for real time periods of milliseconds my atoms'll be buzzing around the cosmos for decades. Or centuries."

"Or millenia."

In the light of a single guttering candle David knelt on the floor beside the bed, holding LaMer's knee in his hands like an icon. He bowed his head to kiss the smooth stump below it. The hair on his neck, wet from their shower, was cool. LaMer had combed it back from his forehead, and he was conscious of the absence of a forelock. The paint she had applied to his face and body crinkled his skin as it dried. LaMer lay on her back, left leg dangling off the bed. She inhaled deeply the smoke of one of David's cigarettes. She cupped a red breast in a blue hand, flicked a white nipple with a maroon nail.

David ran his tongue along the inside of LaMer's thigh. He nuzzled into her pubic hair. He turned his face to say, "Tell me about the Puzzle Box again."

LaMer moved her hips up, caught David's head with her thighs. She pulled again on the cigarette, smoothed his hair with her free hand. "Ah, the real quantum prize-winning breakthrough. Just like a Chinese puzzle box. A box within a box within a box within a box. Each box a transmatation booth, both receiving and sending. Each booth equipped with sensors and guidance systems. If there's a place to run to, the Puzzle Box'll find it. Can't turn 'em out fast enough. Working around the clock, still can't manufacture enough." She locked her fingers in his slick hair, pressed him to her. "Still finite, though. The Puzzle Box. You'll run out finally. Finally. If the sensors don't find anything, you'll finally run out. The last glass booth will receive you. A couple cubic meters of air. Hang there in space. You in it. The others dangling around you. Finally."

24

Trial by Fire

David sat in his cell, feeling, he imagined, much like a condemned prisoner who'd finished his confession to the priest. He stared at the media screen, not seeing it. His right hand was under his shirt. He held the sensor LaMer had given him. "When I want you, I can find you," she'd said, dropping the chain over his head. The facepaint pulled at his skin. LaMer would be at Home Base two thousand kilometers away before the el got him back to the suburbs, was probably already there. She would die there when the world met its end. His heart ached beneath the sensor. If he saw anything on the media screen above him it was only a single blue eye. The el started the climb to its terminus.

David felt the power of the automatic braking system before he understood the quake had begun. The rapid deceleration threw him against the front of the cell. He sat on the floor, touched his head where the nerves tingled. His fingers came away smeared with paint and blood. He had a second to stare stupidly at the cushioned wall, looking for what had cut him, before the el began a slow lateral drop in a series of teeth-rattling shimmies. David clung to the bench as the track creaked and buckled. When all was still again, he was stretched along the steep angle of the floor. The doors of the cell, one above and one below him, popped open. His bag, one corner red with blood, slipped out the open door below, hit the roof of an efficiency space complex fifty meters below and burst. David began to pull himself up and out the door above.

He knelt, panting, on the smooth side of the listing el.

When he looked down its length he saw other passengers beginning to make their way down the slope of the tracks toward the lavender clouds of sunrise. The Law, standing erect, blew his whistle and signaled the passengers with his hands. When the first aftershock came, he jiggled off the edge of the cell and disappeared below the level of the buckled tracks. The platform was fifty meters above David. He began to crawl.

The skin of the el was polished smooth, and David's palms were wet with sweat. Every few meters, he gathered his legs beneath him, took a deep breath, and leaped across the open door of another cell. Once, a tremor began as he jumped. He came down flat on his stomach. The el twisted and shuddered, and he slid back toward the open door, his nails squealing against the cell's surface. They broke. The tremor ceased.

The nose of the el jutted four meters from the platform. The twisted, narrow tracks between glinted in the rising sun. David kicked off his sandals and rubbed the soles of his feet against his jeans to dry them. He retreated down the last cell to its open door, rose and ran up the incline, leaped into space. He hit the platform with a bone-crunching thud. Only when he had pulled himself over the curb, back into the suburbs, did he rest.

The Torino was gone. At first he thought that the quake had somehow shaken it off the Expressway. Then he realized he had stayed too long with LaMer, and the Law, steadfast in the pulsing sun, had towed it when the meter ran down. He started at a jog down the Expressway.

He reached the bottom without any further aftershocks. Without pausing, he turned to cut across the cemetery toward the Cop Shop. A deep fissure made its jagged way among the stones. He tried to keep his eyes from its depths as he ran, but he saw the exposed caskets and blanket-wrapped corpses anyway. Halfway across, sweat stinging his eyes and lungs bursting, he gave up. He stood, hands on his knees, while his empty stomach heaved and heaved again. When he could finally straighten he realized he stood upon a grave. The stone, old, dark, and large, was familiar. He got his bearings and began to walk.

An only child, the only surviving relative, he had been left to mark his parents' graves after their deaths. A

boy who would later make his name with words, he
could see even then how little their power was in the face
of death. Finally, he had had only their names chiseled
into their common white stone. Those names stared back
at him now, and he dropped to his knees, then prostrate
before them. The long, untended grass was cool in the
growing heat of day. A small tremor vibrated the earth
beneath him. He did not wish to go on. He slept.

He awoke with a start. He found himself curled upon
the graves, living grass clutched in one hand. He lay still
in the high, hot sun. The sounds of dogs, not near or far
away, made him look up. A pack milled, tails wagging,
between him and the Expressway. He stood slowly, the
grass in his hand tearing from its roots as he rose. As he
watched, a mastiff scratched his way out of the fissure,
dragging something David could not identify. It made its
way, snarling, through the snapping pack. A breeze came
up behind him. When it reached the dogs, their noses
went into the air. David looked once at the white stone
before he began to run again.

He ran and ran, jumping the fissure when it crossed
his path, never looking back. Ahead the Torino was
parked in front of the Cop Shop. He fought the feeling
that the dogs' breath was hot on his legs, that he could
hear them snap, the click of their teeth. The Torino came
closer and closer. He ran and ran. He jumped the fissure
again and again. He came out of the cemetery, out into
the street. He was across it, tugging the keys from his
jeans pocket. He had a hand on the door. It was unlocked
and he jumped in across the bucket seats. He twisted
back and slammed the door.

He looked through the rear window. The dogs had just
reached the opposite side of the street. He heard gunshots
and saw the dogs start to go down. In the windshield he
saw the Law, this one dressed in khaki coveralls, wobbling in an open window. Every few seconds the rifle she
held bucked in her grip. David punched open the glove
box, pulled out his revolver, stepped out of the car and
aimed at a retreating dog. He saw its yellow head over the
vane of the barrel. He followed the head, fighting to
steady his breath. He let his arm drop. He looked down.
In his left hand he found a ball of grass.

The Law had rested her rifle on the windowsill and

now stared at David. He pushed his gun into his belt,
began to separate the blades of grass, smooth them in his
palm. He folded them in half, then in half again, gently,
and pushed the bundle into his shirt pocket. He walked
around the car, pulled the keys from the door, opened it.
He looked up. "How are the streets into the skirts?"

The Law raised the rifle a few centimeters off the sill.
"The streets?" she said. "What do you care about the
streets? The Law takes care of the streets."

"Yes, I know. Of course. But I want to get home."

"Drive safely. Obey all traffic laws."

A sheen of sweat glistened on the Law's face. Her eyes
worked independently. David started to slide into his
car.

"Oh, you can't take that car."

David spoke carefully. "I want to go home."

"But you can't. The fine isn't paid. That car is
impounded. When the fine's paid, the registered owner
can pick it up." The Law had shouldered the rifle. "That's
the law."

David turned half around and pointed above them to
the broken el a kilometer away. "Look, I was on that thing
when the quake began. My Card's in my bag. It's still
Inside."

She was petulant. "The law," she whined.

David felt that in a moment they'd both be in tears.
"Look, I want to go home for the end. To the house I was
born in. Can you understand that? You understand that."

"Don't raise your voice! I'm the Law, and you must
respect the Law!" She had begun to cry.

David wished to walk to her, to reach up to her in her
window, and embrace her. "Listen—" he began quietly.

The Law cut him off. "No!" she screamed and tightened
her grip on the rifle.

David shot her in the forehead. The Law stood for a
long time, the center of the wound red, its perimeter
already purpling, then crumpled down out the window.
The rifle clattered on the sidewalk. David got into his
car and drove off toward home.

David left the car in the drive. Leaves crunched under
his feet as he walked to the door. He stopped to look
around. He could see no damage from the quake, but

something tugged at his mind. Then he saw, understood, *the leaves*. The generations of decorative, imported trees swayed orange and red and amber in the hot wind. Leaves fluttered on branches, spiraled down into the street and onto the overgrown, garbage-strewn lawns. As he watched, the trees began to lose their forms. The sun was waxing. The weight of the gun dangling in his hand brought him out of his reverie. He went inside.

Lu looked up when he entered the kitchen. Her face was dirty and tear-streaked. A media caster's voice carried from the large screen in the bedroom. He put the gun on the counter, walked to Lu and pulled her head against his belly.

"She didn't think Davy was coming."

Felix whined from his bed in the breakfast nook. The old dog sat, wobbling on his front legs, his eyes clouded.

"He's been like that from yesterday. He can't eat. He can't sleep. His back legs don't work."

David sat down and petted the dog. Felix collapsed, lay on his side, his back legs twisted beneath him, panting. David picked him up, carried him toward the back door. "Bring the gun," he said to Lu as he passed her.

David stood in the rising heat staring into a glare that hid the houses beyond. Lu came up behind him, touched his elbow. "Her garden." David followed, lost Lu in the light, bumped into the redwood picnic table, found the garden. He lay Felix down among the wilted and bent half-grown stalks of corn. He turned and took the revolver from Lu. He raised the gun, lowered it. He faced Lu again. Felix whined in the heat. Lu took the gun from David. His face centimeters from hers, he watched her steady it. Her scarred eye did not flinch when the gun went off.

David patted the last of the earth down with the flat of the spade, then stared at what he could make out of the dog's grave. Lu tugged at him. "Davy has to come in. He'll burn up out here. Look what happens." David shifted his gaze to the hand she extended. It was his, though he was not conscious of any connection to it. She moved it closer to his face. The paint was pocked with blisters. She pulled him toward the house. In the light he could not see her ahead of him. When he heard the door open, he thought to drop the spade he'd been dragging.

He stood in the kitchen. Lu made her way through the house pulling shades and curtains. She came back, took him again by the hand. "It's best in the bedroom."

On the big screen, a panel of theologians droned on. David sat on the floor, his back against the foot of the bed, Lu curled beside him. He brought the grass out of his pocket. It had been cured in the heat, like farmers' hay. Make hay while the sun shines, hay while the sun shines, while the sun shines, he chanted. He separated the blades and lay them in a neat row on the carpet. He began to braid them into a chain.

The media caster came back on to recap the top stories. Solar activity dramatically increasing. More quakes expected. Death count in the tens of millions. The Rescue Effort had been disrupted at number 439. The end was thought to be very near.

The local media came on, giving the time. It would soon be evening; some relief from the heat might be expected then, though speculation was that quake activity would rise in inverse proportion. The caster repeated the list of precautions. David braided the ends of the chain together. Full bathtubs, underground shelter, battery power....

"What's that?" Lu pointed to the screen. David pulled the last end of the last blade tight, dropped the tiny garland of grass into his pocket. A small red rectangle pulsed in the upper right-hand corner of the screen.

"There's a message," he said.

"Is he going to get it?"

David struggled to his feet, ambled out the door and through rooms bright despite heavy drapes. The study, on the east side of the house, was darkening now. He pressed the "respond" button.

The screen fluttered. A standard logo came on alerting David of audiovisual technical difficulties and asking him to stand by. In a moment the logo disappeared and a green message came clicking on. Complete it read

Global communication network in shambles. Attempts to reestablish order abandoned at 3:30 PDT. Screening Committee's priority system abandoned with #439. Be ready. I have the controls. LaMer.

David lurched forward in his chair, spread his fingers across the keyboard and typed

How soon?

The response began to appear

Not very goddamn—

The screen flashed from its customary black to white. Black characters marched across the screen:

GOVERNMENT MONITOR: Use of profanity either in visual, audio, or symbolic communications strictly prohibited by the Law.

David's heart quit beating. Another message came through:

Security code 218. Clearance 1AA.

The Monitor responded

Code and level irrelevant.

The last message stared out from the screen like the vacant sockets of a skull. Panic rose in David's belly. He reached for the keys, ready to beg.

LaMer responded

Irrelevant?

There was another long pause. Then

Legally.

LaMer let the word hang there for a full thirty seconds, then typed

I wish to proceed. File and sign your report.

This time the response was immediate.

Proceed.

The screen went black.

LaMer typed, the characters showing green

45 minutes, hour maximum.

David punched the "hold" button, jumped from his chair and ran to the bedroom. Lu sat where he'd left her, curled before the screen, which read "Please Wait." She looked to David, then pointed to the screen. "What does it say?"

David grabbed her by the extended wrist and pulled her to her feet. "It says we're getting out of here." He ran, sometimes dragging her when she stumbled, through the house and sat down before the console. He typed out

Dependent.

LaMer responded without hesitation

Congratulations and best wishes. Keep her close. Program follows.

He looked up to Lu standing beside him. "Marry Davy?"

She stared at the screen. "Okay."

The program appeared. "What's your full name?"

"Louisa Mae Carlton," she said, emphasizing each syllable.

He typed it in. "ID number?"

"N/A." He looked up. "She never got one."

He typed in "N/A" and held his breath.

The program gave the next question. David exhaled. "Date of birth?" he asked.

"Does it matter?"

"No, no, just give it to me." He was not at all sure that it was irrelevant as that.

"Fifteen October twenty ought six." David entered it, shook his head. Lu was a month shy of fifteen. He typed in "wife" and turned to her.

"Next of kin? Family?"

She shook her head.

He typed in "None."
Another message clicked on.

OK. Half hour. Good-bye and good luck.
Love, LaMer.

David stood and kissed Lu. He held her tight and
waited for the numbness that meant LaMer had them. He
closed his eyes and saw a field of velvet blue, and in that
field stars shone blue and white and red and yellow.
Constellations formed and swirled, kaleidoscopic, around
him, dispersed. Meteors flew by like diving, flaming birds.
All was breathless and at peace.

David loosened his embrace. Something caught his
eye. The screen was again white.

GOVERNMENT MONITOR: No record of marriage posted.
Dependent wife disallowed.

Lu pulled away. David watched her retreat from the
screen, one hand reaching out to it, a finger pointing. She
looked to him. "It says they have the laugh of her?"

"Lu—" He held out his hands. He found, suddenly, he
could not lie. He nodded.

She said "No, no, no, no," again and again, each
syllable growing in volume until she screamed. He took a
step toward her and she backed into the rows of books
opposite the console. She slid down the packed shelves,
sat, stared at the screen, still pointing. The scream suddenly died. She began to rock and moan.

"Forget it. Just let it go." She did not respond. "Just let
it go," he repeated. "Here." He cut the power to the
console. The screen went black. "See, it's all gone." Still
she rocked. He grabbed a heavy book from the shelves
and threw it into the screen. Sparks jumped and leads
hissed. "See?" He walked to her. "See, it's all gone, all
over." He knelt beside her, kissed her, and then kissed her
again. Finally, her lips shuddered alive, locked onto his.

He pulled away. "Come on, there's still a chance."

David pulled the Torino to a screeching stop at the
end of a long line of cars. In an entire life in the suburbs
he had never seen so many vehicles gathered in one

place. He waited for the traffic to clear. He looked down at the instrument panel. The red needle of the temperature gauge lay flat, pointing to the right. He looked up. He could make out the church steeple and the cross atop it, a far shadow in the glare. He looked to Lu. "Let's run," he said.

The asphalt sucked at and burned his bare feet, the air seared his lungs. The sweat that dripped into his eyes was colored with facepaint. The revolver dragged at his arm.

They were very near when Lu called, "Davy! Wait!" She veered off across a yellow lawn toward a bed of flowers dying in the shade of a church eave. He started to follow.

He was caught, an insect in amber, one hand reaching out, balanced on the toes of one foot, his lungs half-full of superheated air, but the heat was gone, the pain of his blistered feet. A little electrical charge danced on his skin and he felt himself receding. His eyes stayed caught on Lu where she bowed over the flowers, snapping them one by one from their brittle stems. She stood and turned back to him. He wanted only to say good-bye, to kiss her once more. No, that was not enough, he realized. He knew he wanted to stay. His brain fought to get his body back.

25

An Act of Piracy

Edie paused on the duckboards behind the bar long enough to swat at a fly and miss. "They've gone light-speed!" somebody yelled. Edie waved a hand through the cigarette smoke hanging in the room.

"It's the damned heat," the woman at the end of the bar said. "The hotter it gets, the faster they go!"

"Hey, bring me another one of those!"

"God, this tastes like piss!"

Edie pushed the tap open on the last keg of beer on the planet, hoarded for decades in the walk-in cooler for a special occasion. Warm beer frothed in the glass, the head rolled over the rim. Edie slapped the glass down on the bar.

"On the house." She stopped to light a cigarette.

"What they saying now?" someone yelled.

"Who?"

"Them guys!"

"What guys?"

"Them. On the screen, for chrissakes!"

"Doom and gloom. Gloom and doom."

"I didn't ask their names, goddamn it! What are they talking about?"

"Turn the sound up. I ain't nobody's hearing aid!"

Edie pumped the keg up, ran another glass.

"Keep 'em coming, honey."

"Don't 'honey' me, you old sot!" she called back.

"Here's to you, honey!"

Edie drew another, then another. The third she sipped herself.

"Okay, you win."

"Double or nothing, we don't last another hour."

"I'll take that. Hey, can I get another glass of that piss?"

Edie slammed a glass down, paused and smiled. It never failed. Hard times packed them in.

The horses, lathered and heaving, galloped over the knoll and jumped for the river. The heat of the yellow water forced them out before the spray had evaporated, and they whirled and gained the top of the knoll in three strides. They disappeared over the bank, the bay whinnying shrilly, the black stud screaming.

"Damn, I hates to see something like that."

Fletcher squinted against pipe smoke at the old man. "When Old Joe sees anything like this before?"

Steam rose from the river, and behind them they could see gray smoke billowing up from burning prairie grasses.

Joe took the pipe, inhaled, and considered. "I's been around, Fletcher," he said finally. "Just you remembers that. Why, once, down south it was, I's chased down a volcano, boiling lava a-snapping at my pony's hooves the whole time." He handed the pipe back.

Fletcher again regarded him narrowly. "Why's it you never stories that before?"

Joe shrugged. "Heat's put me in mind of it."

Sweat rolled from Fletcher's shoulders, and the old man's leathers were soaked through. "It's hot enough."

"Yes, but leastways the humidity's down." Joe rocked back and forth in laughter, hacking on the forward motion, roaring backward.

Fletcher gave him a tolerant smile, understanding only that it was one of her friend's jokes from before she knew him, a time before she was even born.

Joe settled down enough to take the pipe, but good humor caught him every time he put the stem to his lips. The horses thundered by again, leapt down the bank twenty meters away. This time the bay somersaulted as her front legs broke down under her. She struggled up and tottered there, a fractured foreleg dangling. The stud stopped before he got to the water, galloped back, and circled her. Finally, he stopped to nuzzle along the mare's neck.

"Let me sees your bull pistol, Fletcher."

She placed the butt of it in his outstretched hand. "*Por favor, amigo.*"

His hand closed on the pistol. He nodded once, got to his feet, and struggled to the horses. When he came within two meters, the stallion, heat-mad and protective, took an evil swipe at him with a front hoof. Joe shot him, and he went down, shivered, and died. Joe draped an arm over the bay's neck, patted her while he studied a heat- and pain-crazed eye. "*La diferencia entre los caballos y los humanos,*" he explained. He moved away a step and shot her below the ear. She fell without a tremor. Joe held the gun in both hands and looked it over. He shook his head, then heaved it by the barrel into the roiling river.

He shambled back through the yellow light to Fletcher. Her back was straight, her features rigid and tears ran with the sweat.

"Best horse I ever had."

"Take the pipe, Joe. It's full again."

McGee honked the horn again. Rusty came around the corner of her shack, wiping her brow with a greasy rag. She came to the window.

"What'll it be, mister?"

"Fill 'er up," McGee siad. He watched her walk to the back of the pickup in the side mirror, pulling down the frayed hem of her abbreviated coveralls to cover an exposed cheek as she went. She put the nozzle in the tank.

"Windows?"

McGee nodded.

She got her short stepladder, climbed up and began to wipe away the dust and bugs. McGee watched without blinking, his mouth agape. Sweat ran out of his hair from beneath his cap, dripped onto the damp collar of his T-shirt. She went to the other side. When Rusty stretched the length of her body against the windshield to rub away a particularly recalcitrant bug, he gasped.

"Check under the hood, mister?"

McGee swallowed hard. "Please, it's knocking a little."

Rusty nodded judiciously. "Could be the timing. Start her up."

McGee did as he was told, then climbed out of the cab and followed Rusty and her stepladder around front. "I'll show you," he said, but she had already popped the

catch on the hood and raised it. The huge engine idled in
a lope. Rusty grabbed the accelerator linkage and revved
it a bit into a smooth, deep-throated purr. McGee stood
behind her.

"Sounds all right to me, but it could be the timing."

"Sometimes it loses power."

"That sounds like the timing, all right. I can put a
light on it, if you want."

She climbed back down. McGee held something flat
and folded out to her.

"For you."

"What's this?" She eyed the offering suspiciously.

"Coveralls. Take a look."

Rusty took the coveralls by two fingers of each hand
and shook them out.

"They may be a little big."

"That's all right." She looked them over. "The ones I
got are a little small."

"You can put your name right here," McGee explained.

She nodded. "Why?"

"It's a favor," he said, as if he'd rehearsed it.

Rusty draped the coveralls over her arm. "I'll get the
light. More often than not it's the timing."

Tella-Dotun locked the door, then went through the
outer office into her own. She locked that door as well,
then stood considering things. "Oh," she said softly and
went to her console.

"You're still here."

"Tella, what can I do? There must be something!"
Jomo's unpainted face was tear-stained and twisted gro-
tesquely in fear and grief.

She shrugged. "We've done everything we can do."

"No one?"

Tella shook her head slowly. "None of our nominees,
Jomo. You know that."

"But *somebody* must, or what's the use?" he pleaded.

"Perhaps there is no use."

"Tell me what to do?"

"I can't, Jomo."

The young man wept unashamedly. "I wouldn't mind,"
he sobbed, "if my life had been for something."

"It was. Believe me, Jomo, it was. You just don't understand, but I believe your life meant something."

Jomo's crying subsided. "Do you really think so?"

"Yes," Tella lied.

"Stay with me, Tella," Jomo pleaded.

"No. I have something yet to do."

"Please?"

She rose. "No, Jomo. Good-bye, Jomo." She put a finger to the screen.

"No, Tella! Stay with me!"

"Good-bye," she said again and walked away from the screen toward the washroom. She heard Jomo call her name again and again until she shut the door.

Inside the washroom all was quiet. The tub of water looked cool and inviting. Tella began to undress.

She was sorry for Jomo. She had had a wonderful life, she reflected. For decades she had labored to braid a new culture from the strands of all those that had gone before. She thought it possible that, from her pinnacle in time, she had been able to exert more influence than anyone who'd gone before. Jomo would never have such a grand opportunity. He would die young and all that he could have been would be wasted.

Tella carefully folded and stacked her clothing. Such self-serving consolations tasted like ashes on her tongue. In the light of the aborted Rescue Effort, her most significant contribution might well have been the tiny comfort in the lie she'd told Jomo. She paused before the mirror, found her brushes, and began to touch up her paint. That would have to do, she thought grimly.

She put her brush down and stepped toward the door. She could tell Jomo something about faces. If he understood about a person's face, what it really was, how private one needed to keep it, and how best to present it to the world, then he might know how to accept death. She halted. He could never understand, and she knew she could not explain now what she had never spoken of before. She picked the brush up again and traced a careful, blue line.

Tella made sure the package was on edge of the tub, then lowered herself into the fragrant water. She relaxed for a full five minutes, the faces of the great and near great she'd known passing in review. She wondered if they had understood the significance of their work as she had understood. She decided not. She lifted away the tissue of the package and took out David's gift. It was ancient and it was beautiful, and she wondered if David understood all that he had given her. She studied the brass and the ivory inlays, then clumsily hooked the blade open. It was a man's thing. Worse, she thought, it was a rich man's thing from a time when rich meant white. She steadied the blade and pushed the corner of it deep between the bones of her forearm. The flesh opened easily, and she moved the wrist into the water. A flower of blood blossomed there, and she watched it pulse and grow. No, she was sure he had not understood. She ran her thumb over the ivory. Her heart beat furiously, and in it she heard the majestic trumpeting of long-extinct elephants.

Through the window of the Motel–12 they could see the air had turned golden. Ms. Kitty rose and closed the drapes against the glare. She lay back down in the curl of Amos Dandy's arm.

"He'll take care of it," Amos Dandy said with the little confidence he could muster. "She shouldn't worry."

"Oh, I know he will," Ms. Kitty said and raised herself to give him a smile. "He shouldn't worry."

After a time he spoke. "He wishes one thing."

"What's that?" Ms. Kitty asked.

"There was something else to watch on the screen."

LaMer punched a series of keys, then read the screen. "Goddamn him!" She searched through her mind for an alternative. Finding none, she fed in another command. She lifted her hands from the keyboard, and her hold on a single form two thousand kilometers distant was lost. "Goddamn you, too, David," she said, more quietly. She sat back, her body slack. In a moment, she again attacked the keyboard. The Commodore's face showed on her screen.

"Can you believe this? We're going to asphyxiate unless we open the ports to the outside. If we open the ports, the temperature's going to take a five to ten degree jump, just like that." He snapped his fingers.

"Goddamn you, Mike! What do you think you're doing?"

He looked from one empty hand to the other. "You mean the override?" he asked them. "Well mate, that's the book."

LaMer hissed, "I don't give a flying fuck about the book. I already got a Government Monitor who doesn't know when to lie down and die. Now I've got you, too."

"Well, maybe you should take your own advice. It's over. We're officially out of commission."

"Maybe I'm not ready to quit yet."

"You've got no choice, mate."

"Yes, I do! And I could use a little help!"

"I can't do anything about the Monitor."

"Yes, but you make the operational decisions. You can take the override off and let me get at what I want."

"It's set up that way, LaMer. We go in order or we don't go at all." His face showed almost no life. "We got 439 of them out of here. Isn't that enough?"

"Not for me, it isn't! I want something else. I want it for me, Mike! It's personal!"

LaMer heard a loud tearing through the screen. It was followed by a pop and a wash of brilliant light. She fought to keep herself out a reflexive crouch.

The light and noise subsided, and she could again see the Commodore's face. He was looking past the screen around main control. His face showed little, if any, concern.

"Shit, LaMer," he said calmly, "we just blew a whole bank. I'll bet every circuit in the works just fused."

"Am I still operational down here?" He continued to survey the damage around him. "Mike!" she called.

"You people moved away from the walls into the center of the room," LaMer heard him say. "You! Help him. He's hurt. Drag those away, Okay?"

LaMer spoke quietly. "If you're not going to help me, Mike, at least get out of my way."

Mike returned his attention to her, studied her face on the screen, then his empty hands. He wondered how few LaMers there had been since the beginning of time. No one else he'd ever known had done what she'd done, time after time, and survived, her sanity, if not her body, intact. Hell, he thought, she just gets saner and stronger. He leaned forward and readied his fingers. After all, she was just doing the job he'd signed her on for. "I'll take the override out," he said.

LaMer reached quickly to terminate the communication.
"Hey!"
She looked up at Mike.
"Aren't you going to thank me?"
She gave him a half-wave that might have been a
salute. "See you in hell, skipper."
After LaMer's image had gone from the screen, the
Commodore typed in a command to terminate the override, sighed in relief when it took. He decided against
opening the ports, since to do so would flood Home Base
with oxygen, and oxygen would only feed the fires that
burned all through the facility. He monitored LaMer's
program. Something caught his eye.
"Well, what about that?" he asked himself.
He punched a couple of buttons, thought about calling
down to auxiliary control, then dismissed the idea. "We'll
just see what we can do."
The book rolled by with infuriating slowness. He sat
back. "Let's just think this through," he said amid the
noise and confusion of main control. He brought one
giant hand up and slowly scratched his temple. He leaned
forward suddenly and called up a specific component.
The high-lighted entry on the screen pulsed. "Sure enough,"
he said. "Just common sense." He punched a button and,
when nothing happened, he slapped the side of the
printer beside him. It whirred into action. He ripped off a
sheet, rose and walked through the hissing and popping
of shorting circuitry. A young woman sat in the corner by
the door of main control. She stared through the thin
smoke at an invisible point a meter before her face, crying
quietly.
He knelt beside her and took her shoulder in one
hand. Her collarbone was delicate and hard beneath her
flesh.
"Ah—" He realized he couldn't remember the tech's
name. He recalled LaMer speaking to her. "Little sister,"
he said finally, "I want you to go down the hall and into
the stores. Find this element. Take it to auxiliary control."
She took the print dumbly, made no move to rise.
"I'd do it myself, but I should monitor the program.
We might lose a half dozen elements before she's through."
Still the woman made no move.
"It's for LaMer."

Her eyes brightened, and she began to get her feet beneath her. The Commodore helped her stand, then opened the door for her. "Take the stairs. Come right back, in case I find something else."

"Aye, aye," the tech said weakly. The Commodore watched her legs steady under her and her pace quicken, despite the lack of oxygen, as she moved down the corridor. "Tell her to hurry," he called.

He went back behind the console. He surveyed main control, decided he could do nothing for any of them. The transmat program rolled again on the screen. He took a wild guess, found the element he looked for was in working condition. He took another shot. He was always happier, he realized, when he had something to do with his hands.

Air rushed into his lungs, and David collapsed to his knees, the hand without the pistol breaking his fall. He panted, struggled to rise. Lu got a hand under his arm and lifted. In the other she had a bouquet of wilted marigolds. David got to his feet, took a deep breath, nodded, and they ran down the walk. They turned, and he stumbled twice going up the steps into the building. They burst through the doors.

Inside the noise was deafening. Hundreds of people lay and sat scattered about on the floor and in the pews. David looked through the crowd. He had a quick glimpse of Carly, dressed in a black cassock, bandaging a small girl's blistered arm. He pushed his way down the aisle, dragging Lu by the wrist. Directly before them Preach broke off a conversation with an elderly woman and turned.

A smile broke across his weary face. "Davy! It's certainly good to see you, no matter what the circumstances." He gripped both of David's shoulders. "And who's this?"

"My financé," David said. "Marry us, Preach? Please?"

Preach gripped David harder. "Marry you, you say?" He tightened his grip even more. "Why yes, of course I will, Davy. It will give me great pleasure. This is perfect! Yes, yes. Before we do anything else."

He took Lu by the arm and led them, through the intense red and blue and green and yellow light streaming through the stained glass, toward the front of the church. They had to step over and around those sitting in the aisle. The limbs of some were roughly splinted and bandaged. In the din of hundreds of conversations, David could hear someone keening.

Preach chattered under the backdrop of noise. "No, no," he was saying. "I guess I don't know your family. But Davy's, that's another matter. I baptized him right there in that font. Oh heavens yes. Why, Davy's parents and I worked together on many a cause. Excuse us, please. Trying to get things back to normal, you understand. But of course you're too young to remember normal, aren't you, dear? It was the good fight we fought, though. I think the Lord's fight. Pardon us, please. They died trying to make things better, within just a few months of each other. The days I spoke over their graves were two of the saddest I ever lived. Truly wonderful people. Pardon. Oh, Lord bless me for a fool, though, I did know some Carltons, your grandparents, I imagine. Sorry to say I did not know them well."

They had reached the chancel. Preach turned and, his hands on their shoulders, positioned each of them. "Now, it'll just be a moment." Preach stepped to the side and busied himself at the keyboard of an ancient console. Soft music filled the church. The din quieted.

Preach placed himself between Lu and David, facing them from the step above. He leaned to them and said, "My children, the ceremony must be brief. There are many gathered here who need my help." He straightened, raised his arms, and addressed the refugees.

"Friends, a great thing is about to happen. Great because the simple affirmation of marriage is always an occasion for joy among us, and great because it happens today amid pain and suffering and uncertainty. We are blessed to witness it." He drew his attention closer. "Lu, do you take Davy to be your husband?" She stared at him wide-eyed. "Say you do."

"She does."

"Davy, do you take Lu to be your wife?"

"I do."

Preach leaned and stage-whispered, "Do you happen to have such a thing as a ring about you?"

David pulled the circle of braided grass from his pocket and placed it carefully on Lu's finger. It held.

Preach stared, dumbfounded, then threw his head back and roared, "In the sight of God and this congregation, I pronounce you wife and husband. You may kiss the bride."

David clutched at the old man's shirt. "Preach, we need to register this right away."

"Davy, such legal technicalities at a time like this? Kiss your bride, son."

"Please Preach, it's very important to us."

Preach looked deep into his eyes. "Why of course. If that's what you wish." He led them to the console, punched a few buttons, slapped it sharply on the side when it did not respond. The white-screened government program came up. Preach turned to them, suddenly bright. "Now Davy, you enter the information while I set up the equipment."

"Equipment?"

"Of course. What would a wedding be without stills?"

Preach pulled, first, a black box, then a collapsed tripod from beneath the console. A hymn played. David entered the information.

Preach was looking over his shoulder now. "Fine," he said as David filled in the last blank. "Now, just let me put in my ID number and code." He moved David gently to one side, hit a few keys. The screen read "Accepted and Recorded." Preach plugged the end of a coaxial cable into a jack in the console, jabbed pale fingers at the keyboard. He led them away from the console. "Now, you two just stand here...."

Preach looked into the viewfinder, adjusted the box to center David and Lu there. She is awfully young to be married, he thought. Two young people, one painted and streaked, barefoot, a big gun in his hand, the other a child. The world was all too ridiculous, too sad. Oh, but what times he'd seen. There, in the viewfinder, the couple held their kiss, seemed to pulse, then glow. Preach pressed the shutter, looked up, and found them gone. He turned to his congregation. No one made a sound, and he could see nothing in the fiery light. Mad Tom approached, then, with a chalice containing the last dregs of communion wine. Preach took it from him and drained it. The wine was hot as blood. He lifted his eyes to heaven, and, in a loud voice, proclaimed, "Our God, we praise You for the miracle You have shown us." He raised the empty chalice in both hands. "Glory be to God!"

LaMer's hands were poised above the keyboard. Her eyes scanned the screen, looking for trouble in the program. She was alone, deep in Home Base, standing in the jerry-rigged auxiliary control. Above her head, twenty stories of glass and metal alloy melted down. Ancillary systems lining the walls hissed and shorted. For a millisecond something flashed in the booth before her, then was gone. She punched in a code and, in doing so, added the last bit of power at her command to the program. The screen told her that David and his new wife were chains of atoms strung out along a trajectory that would take them out of the solar system. She thought of those atoms, each a little sun circled by the planets of its electrons. She thought of the stars David would soon race among, each a sun, perhaps circled by planets, planets perhaps capable of supporting reconstituted human beings. She thought of her own sun, now consuming the planet that had circled it for millenia past counting. "Let it go. I've seen it all," she said aloud. Suddenly she was intensely happy. She looked up with one blue eye that could see beyond the melting concrete, through the hell of fire and pain she knew held sway above, to where heaven lay. She extended both middle fingers to God. "Fucked you again, you diseased old whore." She was still laughing when the earth boiled to gas.

ABOUT THE AUTHOR

J. V. Brummels is Poet-in-Residence at Wayne State College in northern Nebraska, where he teaches English and writing. He has published more than 100 poems in such journals as *Prairie Schooner, The Iowa Review, Quarterly West,* and *The Hollins Critic,* and in 1982 Abattoir Press brought out *614 Pearl,* a collection of his poetry. His fiction credits include sales to *Rolling Stone* and *Isaac Asimov's Science Fiction Magazine;* **Deus Ex Machina** is his first novel.

SPECTRA SPECIAL EDITIONS

Bantam Spectra Special Editions spotlight some of Spectra's finest authors in their top form. Authors found on this list all have received high critical praise and many have won some of science fiction and fantasy's highest honors. Don't miss them!

☐ **Out on Blue Six** (27763-4 • $4.50/ $5.50 in Canada) by Ian McDonald. On the run in a society where the state determines one's position in life, Metheny Ard takes charge of her fate, turning from model citizen to active rebel.

☐ **The Nexus** (27345-2 • $4.50/ $5.50 in Canada) by Mike McQuay. The tale of an autistic girl who can literally work miracles and the reporter who brings her story to the world.

☐ **Phases of Gravity** (27764-2 • $4.50/ $5.50 in Canada) by Dan Simmons. An ex-astronaut goes on a personal odyssey to centers of power all over the earth in search of an elusive—but powerful—fate he senses awaiting him.

Buy **Out on Blue Six, The Nexus** and **Phases of Gravity** wherever Bantam Spectra books are sold, or use this page for ordering:

- -